THE SIL

Matty Matthews has been .. .. .guil before. Stationed there with a small group of soldiers during WWII, it was here that Matty fell in love with Rosanna. It was a sweet, short-lived affair until the soldiers unexpectedly got orders to pull out. Matty never got to say goodbye. Now he's back in Sicily, drawn to the mountain town after all these years. But the citizens of Forza d'Aguil are easy to offend, and when Matty inadvertently crosses Pino, the *mafioso* sabotages his leaving. Trapped in Forza d'Aguil, hemmed in on all sides by the oppression of the town and its silent citizens, he's stuck in the middle of Mafia country with no way out. He has only the help of the innkeeper Vinciguerra, a man he can't understand, and the passion of the sweet Sophia. Or is she part of the sinister web, too?

THE RETURN OF MARVIN PALAVER

Marvin Palaver dies at the worst possible moment in life, just when he is coming out even with his nemesis, fellow scrap seller Sidney Minsk. He is so close. The contract is signed and Sydney has just bought back his own scrap, the deal of a lifetime. Marve knows happiness supreme. But as the tears of joy make his eyes swim, there comes a bump in his chest, and he is dead before he hits the floor. But death doesn't stop Marvin. His masterful *schwindel* must be complete. So Marve finagles his way back to the material plane for a bit of artful ghosting. Sidney has hidden the contract away, confident that he's the only one who knows about it. All Marve needs to do is get him to reveal it—he should live so long!

PETER RABE BIBLIOGRAPHY

From Here to Maternity
(1955)
Stop This Man! (1955)
Benny Muscles In (1955)
A Shroud for Jesso (1955)
A House in Naples (1956)
Kill the Boss Goodbye (1956)
Dig My Grave Deep (1956)*
The Out is Death (1957)*
Agreement to Kill (1957)
It's My Funeral (1957)*
Journey Into Terror (1957)
Mission for Vengeance (1958)
Blood on the Desert (1958)
The Cut of the Whip (1958)*
Bring Me Another Corpse
(1959)*
Time Enough to Die (1959)*
Anatomy of a Killer (1960)
My Lovely Executioner (1960)
Murder Me for Nickels (1960)
The Box (1962)
His Neighbor's Wife (1962)
Girl in a Big Brass Bed
(1965)**

The Spy Who Was
Three Feet Tall (1966)**
Code Name Gadget (1967)**
Tobruk (1967)
War of the Dons (1972)
Black Mafia (1974)
The Silent Wall (2011)
The Return of Marvin Palaver
(2011)

As by "Marco Malaponte"
New Man in the House
(1963)
Her High-School Lover (1963)

As by "J. T. MacCargo"
Mannix #2:
A Fine Day for Dying (1975)
Mannix #4: Round Trip to
Nowhere (1975)

*Daniel Port series
**Manny deWitt series

THE SILENT WALL

HARD CASE REDHEAD

THE RETURN OF MARVIN PALAVER

BY PETER RABE
Introduction By Rick Ollerman

STARK HOUSE

Stark House Press • Eureka California

THE SILENT WALL / THE RETURN OF MARVIN PALAVER

Published by Stark House Press
2200 O Street
Eureka, CA 95501
griffinskye3@sbcglobal.net
www.starkhousepress.com

ISBN: 1-933586-32-x
ISBN-13: 978-1-933586-32-8

Cover photo and design by Mark Shepard, SHEPGRAPHICS.COM
Proofreading by Rick Ollerman

The publisher wishes to thank Rick Ollerman for all his help on this project.

First Stark House Press Edition: January 2011
0 9 8 7 6 5 4 3 2 1

The Differential Peter Rabe; an appreciation

By Rick Ollerman

Peter Rabe is often thought of as a lean, unsentimental writer. That description is a simple one, however, and belies not only the complexity of his work but the range of emotions he manages to impart to the reader. His sentences are often stark and at the same time rich with subtext; idiosyncratic, yet so deftly written their intent remains clear. It's this unique style that not only makes his writing accessible, but rewards repeated readings with an ever expanding sense of the stories themselves, of the quality of the writing behind them. Familiarity breeds appreciation, as it were.

When he died of lung cancer in 1990, he left behind a body of work that is often considered the product of one of the best and most influential writers of the paperback originals era. Indeed, as Harlan Ellison said, "In the most golden of the Golden Days of exquisite hardboiled suspense writing, not one of us considered the Best could wait for the next new Rabe. Peter Rabe was an entire genre unto himself. Paying attention to him was, and is, a banquet."

He gave us anti-heroes as realized as any in fiction. He gave us mobsters with mental illnesses, burnt out political leg men, terminal losers with bad judgment and matching ambition. He gave us spies betrayed by countries, women, and most importantly, their own friends. In *Anatomy of a Killer*, he gave us a hit-man driven to quit after he inadvertently touches the arm of one of his victims with his foot. Just a small kick to nudge the lifeless limb aside and this merest of contacts sets up an internal struggle for the killer's sanity. Even when we don't understand them, when we *can't* understand them, Rabe's people are real and we know them because he makes us feel them.

A good writer manages to push these buttons in our minds, he makes us care what he's writing about, and who he's writing about. What can be even more important to some is *how* he pushes those buttons, the manner of his accomplishment. Few writers ever achieve the ability to write beautiful or stylish prose without getting in the way of their stories, and Rabe was a master. His novels fit squarely into their respective genres, yet the quality of their writing binds them all as something unique.

Take this scene from *Murder Me for Nickels*, a wonderful novel about Jack

St. Louis, a fixer for the rackets (and a precursor to Rabe's own Daniel Port character). There's a stunning fight scene that plays out in a warehouse full of records (the old-fashioned music playing kind), where St. Louis is outnumbered three to one and escapes upward to the tops of the big shelving units. Beating one man but then brought down at gun point by another, he surprises the gunman and ends up with the pistol, using it to hold off their boss:

I have never shot anyone, and I don't think shooting's easy. It isn't like throwing a stone, or a punch, or anything like it. You press the trigger, and the thing is out of hand. It's out of your hand; something else does your hating, and you either fear the damage you'll do or you know ahead of time that you'll be left as before; same hate, same rage, just a bullet gone. And someone dead whom you did not even touch.

Benotti rushed me. While I stood around he made his rush. He cracked me across the side of the face and before the pain even came I felt like going to pieces. I had held back too long. I rocked across the aisle, hit a rack, and cracked open. The ball inside, is what I'm talking about. Then I was almost done and so was Benotti. My reach is better and I had the pistol.

I pistol whipped him, and I hit and hit, not a watermelon, or a sack, but always Benotti.

He was just short of raw meat when I left him and was done.

The earlier fighting in the scene is perhaps more memorable for playing out on top of and among the towering racks of records, but the climactic portion above hints at the underlying complexity in most of Rabe's writing. You can read it as a straight through tough guy passage, but the point is that even though St. Louis ended up with the gun, it didn't end the fight. He isn't a killer, and he hesitates, and his opponent does not, being so enraged he actually disregards the gun. Or he convinces himself that St. Louis won't shoot. Maybe he just hopes the bullet will miss. Rabe never tells us any of that, he just paints the picture.

We know about St. Louis through his own thoughts, and we learn more about Benotti through his actions. At the end, we get another glimpse of a previously lighthearted Jack as we see how he ends the fight. It's a tough, hard-boiled scene yet while fulfilling its function in the plot the characters take on additional layers; the fight is not the only thing that happens in that fight scene.

Over the course of his career, Rabe wrote crime novels, mobster novels, spy novels, novels of political intrigue, media tie-ins and even sleaze. In this he wasn't so different from other working professional writers of his time. While some books are clearly more successful than others, all of his stories showcase the same inimitable sensibility. Each of his books maintain their own internal consistency. Once Rabe establishes the laws of his universe, he never breaks them. There is no *deus ex machina*, no outrageous coincidence, nothing external to the story that suddenly appears to save the hero or tie up a loose end. He plays fair with his readers while at the same time managing in book after book to surprise, even when a particular outcome appears inevitable. The magic isn't in where you're going, it's in how he takes you there.

Rabe consistently zags where other writers will zig. He'll give us A, but he'll follow it not with B or C, but instead offers Q or H or P. This is one of the hallmarks of a Rabe story and when read for the first time, an initial bit of head scratching may give way to the sudden right-ness, the clear and pitch perfect point of what you've just read. This is what makes Rabe, as Ellison said, a "genre unto himself."

His first novel, *Stop This Man!*, was the closest thing he wrote to a gimmick novel. A lifelong crook steals a load of radioactive gold from a college laboratory, and it proves eventually fatal to those who come in contact with it. Not only does he use this device, it's also his only book where boy-meets-girl, boy-falls-for-girl, girl-falls-for-boy, and an unbreakable bond of true love is formed in less than five minutes.

Halfway through the book, though, something happens. As necessary as he may have felt the radioactive gold bit to have been, however desirable the requisite lightning-fast love affair was to a genre book of the time, he pushed it all aside midstream and let it become something different. The result is a bit schizophrenic but Rabe discovered himself somewhere in those early pages and didn't wait to begin a new book before exploring that emerging talent.

This dichotomy is entirely gone in his second book. The writing to accepted tropes has utterly vanished and he gives us the hard-boiled and noirish *Benny Muscles In*. In *Benny*, Rabe introduces us to a two-bit loser of a hood, an uneducated but ambitious bottom feeder, amoral and willing to do whatever it takes to move up in his world. Indeed, it's his willingness to actually be big that he feels entitles respect from those around him. It doesn't work that way any better for Benny than it does in real life. You want to get somewhere, you've got to earn it. (Or read it in another type of literature.)

What's remarkable in *Benny* is that Rabe can tell the story in a starkly unsentimental fashion and yet make a thoroughly unlikeable, even repulsive, character compellingly sympathetic at the same time. It's difficult not to go back and forth about Benny, first despising him and then rooting for him, throughout the book. The character of Benny is so well written and so well understood that an empathy is struck with the reader, and even though he is a completely reprehensible fellow, as long as he stays in his own dark underworld we find ourselves willing to go along with it for a while. But then his cockeyed scheme to advance in the organization spirals out of control as he hooks his kidnap victim on dope in order to keep her going along. He'll not only ruin the life of someone else to get what he wants, but it turns out that the life belongs to someone he actually cares for. Benny's simply not capable of being anything other than Benny. Is this a story of redemption? Of happy ending? Not with Rabe behind the typewriter. The book may lack sentiment but at the same time it is imbued with sympathy, and Rabe's ability to push and pull the reader through these contrasts is compelling. We may feel the positive emotion but we may not know quite where to assign it.

Rabe makes you feel that you understand Benny, that god help you, you've come to know him. You're never comfortable with the guy and you hope your path never crosses one like his, but he's a fascinating study, a fearless depiction of a wider set of boundaries that most writers never allow themselves. Rabe would do this even better with another mobster, only this one is already at the top of the criminal food chain, in the book *Kill the Boss Good-by*. Rather than claw his way to the top, the character Fell has to show that he can still cut it, still hold off the competition, even though at the beginning of the book he's suffered a mental breakdown that his doctor fears may be permanent.

Despite occasional similarities in theme, Rabe never wrote the same book twice. This is another distinction, one which holds true for any era but especially that one. He didn't follow the same formula book after book, he didn't use the same plot over and over again. Perhaps he may have been more commercially successful if he had, but it was the courage to write what he felt that allowed him to be as good as he really was.

As it is, we have books as different as *The Box*, an evocatively moody piece about a man, a crooked lawyer as it turns out, placed in a crate and shipped around the world as punishment for his own ruthless ambition. There is something Hemingway-esque in the atmosphere and deep sense of place Rabe gives us, and is as unusual a crime novel as you're likely to find. From nothing, with no money, no friends, no knowledge of what's going on around him, he makes an uncanny attempt at taking over the local action. You're never sure if this is something he can actually do, or if he's off in his head for even trying.

During his career, Rabe wrote two series, one featuring a political fixer working for a corrupt ward boss, and the other about a troubleshooting corporate lawyer named Manny DeWitt. The first book in the Daniel Port series, *Dig My Grave Deep*, shows how Port gets himself, he thinks, out of the rackets once and for all, something no one does and lives. The following books take on an almost "Fugitive" like quality, with Port moving from place to place, helping people who need help, sometimes less than willingly, and at other times to preserve the uneasy truce he's forged with the mob.

The three DeWitt books stand apart because they are the exception to the rule of not writing to formula. Good guy lawyer Manny DeWitt travels the world doing odd jobs for his employer, wealthy industrialist Hans Lobbe. The books are quirky to a fault, filled with a humor that is not entirely successful. In *Code Name Gadget*, for instance, a policeman is describing an automobile accident to DeWitt. After hearing the car "was fairly smashed," DeWitt says, "Blue?," meaning to ask about the car itself. The policeman interrupts with, "Blew? Nothing blew. Driver safe and sound and unconscious behind the wheel. Cracked a rib or so, by the looks of it."

Bits like this are more distracting than funny and they crop up throughout, especially in the second entry, *The Spy Who Was Three Feet Tall*. While consistent within the series, they are by no means 'typical' Rabe. In an interview, he himself said they "fall short" from his point of view, and that the stories were "arched," with a "prettified" and "very self-conscious humor." The series improves as it goes along and although a certain style is very much in evidence, the books never quite satisfy in the same way as Rabe's other books. It is interesting to note, though, that even here Rabe doesn't cheat or shortcut the reader. The plots are still complex and at times unconventional, but the books read as though Rabe had an inside joke going in his mind, one that didn't translate cleanly to the typewritten page.

In addition to *Stop This Man!*, he wrote a few other novels with the straight-ahead Gold Medal feel, such as *Journey Into Terror* and *Agreement to Kill*. Two of his best books are the spy thriller *Blood on the Desert* and the hit-man novel *Anatomy of a Killer*. In *Desert*, Wheeler is a spy being recruited by an Englishman, Major Pitt, in an attempt to find out why three normally feuding African chieftains have suddenly stopped fighting. What's more, the Americans had offered them arms and were rebuffed. Clearly something is in the offing and Pitt asks Wheeler to find out what it is:

"Find out what?"
"What it means, for heaven's sake!"
"No," Wheeler had said. He was at his calmest when the other man showed exasperation. "I'll find out for you what they're doing, Major. You figure out what it means." And then he had smiled again. It covered the importance of what he had said.
He's aping that Fairchild friend of his, Major Pitt had thought. Thank God he isn't as unprincipled yet, only aimless.

This passage hints at the depths Rabe takes us in what is really a routine scene which serves from a plot perspective merely to get Wheeler onto an airplane. Pitt doesn't simply order Wheeler into action, expecting a smart salute and a snappy "Yessir." Wheeler has to agree to undertake the mission his own way, and even while he calms himself he frustrates the other, and he smiles to underscore his seriousness. Pitt ultimately lets him get away with it because he has no other choice, and because he can excuse it to himself by labeling his agent as "aimless."

The scene could have been presented in rapid fire, short sentence tough guy speak, with the result being that Wheeler still would have left for West Africa. Read only the dialog from the same text:

"Find out what?"
"What it means, for heaven's sake!"
"No[.] I'll find out for you what they're doing, Major. You figure out what it means."

By using the slightest of digressions, by lightly going over some of the same ground, Rabe gives us the push and pull, the back and forth, the subtle conflict, in what is really just an ordinary interchange between a superior officer and his man. We can read the same passage for the plot aspect of it (Wheeler gets on airplane) or we can read it for the richness of texture and personality that Rabe surely saw in his own mind.

It's precisely for this reason that Rabe's works are so enjoyable to re-read. Not because doing so is necessary to understanding the real meaning of the book or what Rabe was actually trying to say, but because it is such a pleasure to discover just how rich and how deep his words can present as a story in your mind. Re-reading leads to greater appreciation, a more rewarding experience, not, as odd as it may seem, to a greater understanding of the plot. Really, the plot itself is clear enough the first time.

Here's another example of an "ordinary" scene, this one from *The Box*, where Quinn, the man rescued from the crate, has just been attacked after sneaking into the docks after dark:

"I don't get this," said Quinn, "how a smart man like Remal will pull such a primitive stunt. He gets me beaten up right there where he doesn't want me to look around, and then when I wake up he's standing over me with a lantern."
"Why do more?" said Turk and shrugged. "He just wanted you beaten. If you should want to know about Remal and his business, you can always find out. He did not try to hide things from you, but he tried to tell you what happens if you interfere with him."

"He'll have to do better than that," said Quinn.
"He can," and Turk laughed. "However, at first, he is polite."

Again, the sense of depth here is unusual for an event so commonplace in crime fiction, a man getting beaten up by thugs. The depth, the real conflict in the book, comes from how neither principal is capable of understanding why the other man does what they do, despite the fact that they're in the same line of "work." Against this powerful subtext, the cadence of the sentences, the tone of the dialog, and even the quirky attribution ("said Turk and shrugged," "and Turk laughed") shows how uniquely Rabe renders the routine and ordinary. As a reader you become extraordinarily involved. The last sentence is note for note perfect in tone and message.

Between 1955 and 1962, Rabe wrote 19 of his 30 novels, beginning with *Stop This Man!* and ending with *The Box*, all but two of them for Gold Medal. This includes his only hardcover issue, the riveting *Anatomy of a Killer* (Abelard-Schuman) and the last Daniel Port book, *Cut of the Whip* (half of an Ace Double).

His pace slowed markedly after that, and it was here that he suffered some severe health issues. He said he wrote for the money and to meet the demands of a quick market. He wrote one book for Beacon under his own name, *His Neighbor's Wife*, and two more under the pseudonym "Marco Malaponte." One of these, *Her High School Lover*, was mostly a typical "sleaze" novel. The second, though, *New Man in the House*, isn't really sleaze at all. It is interesting in that it is a Rabe book through and through, only instead of a crime oriented plot it reads like a Machiavellian Lolita-esque story. It's a coming of age book with a theme of corruption, with an especial emphasis on the sexual kind.

Rabe went back to Gold Medal with the three DeWitt books, and then published a novelization of the movie "Tobruk" for Bantam. The last two of his original novels published in his lifetime were *War of the Dons* and *Black Mafia*, again for Gold Medal. *War of the Dons* shows Rabe hadn't lost a step in the seventies, and the book is the suspenseful story of an attempted mob takeover by an ambitious trio of brothers. Two novelizations of scripts from the "Mannix" television series appeared under the name of "J.T. MacCargo" in 1975 which, as is typical of many such "house name" books, read very little in the usual style of the actual author. Accounting for Rabe's first actual book, a non-fiction, humorous account of the birth of his first son (*From Here to Maternity*, Vanguard, 1955), we have the entire oeuvre of Peter Rabe.

Until now, fully two decades after his death.

In a late 1998 interview with George Tuttle, Rabe says that he had still been writing, only not for publication. Shortly before his death, he sent two unpublished manuscripts to author Ed Gorman, who tried to place them with various publishers but without success. These books are *The Silent Wall* and *The Return of Marvin Palaver.*

Marvin Palaver is a short, 18,000 word novella told in a very humorous and informal style. It is a continuous conversation between Marvin and the reader as the old hustler goes through the motions of conning the man who forced him out of business. It's unlike anything Rabe has written before, with a tightly plotted scheme at the core of this slightly supernatural thriller. In Marvin we're not quite sure if we have a true scoundrel or just a dabbler, an actual bad guy or someone who's just been pushed too far. In either case, there's nothing Marve won't do to complete his revenge on his nemesis, the weasely Sidney Minsk.

In contrast, *The Silent Wall* could hardly be more different. Both are told in the first person but *Silent Wall* is as dark and heavy as *Palaver* is light, almost breezy. The atmosphere is similar to that of Rabe's *A House in Naples*, only the main character is not a bad guy trying to reform himself (a character situation Rabe used a number of times). In *Silent Wall* we have Matty Matheson, a good guy, or perhaps just an average guy with his share of faults, including a bit of a short temper, who finds himself ensnared in a physical and psychological trap that he just cannot escape.

Where *Palaver* takes us on a wild, keep-up-if-you-can kind of ride with the machinations of its highly motivated narrator, *Silent Wall* is a masterpiece of foreshadowing and constantly ratcheting tension. Once Matheson makes his way to the town of Forza d'Aguil, the locals allow him to do just about anything he'd like, except leave. Matty is trapped in a town-sized pressure cooker and the reasons for it, as well as the connections to his past, are revealed to us only gradually throughout the book. It is perhaps his most densely written novel.

It's difficult to know what to make of Rabe's assertion that because he wrote so fast he could "jump the line" and "get very sloppy." With the complexity of his plots and elaborate style of his writing, Rabe appears the antithesis of a careless writer. While he occasionally used the same words in sentences too close together, he didn't do it often. Sometimes his protagonists stray a bit far from holding the reader's sympathy, which may not have always been his intention, but he usually brings them back. Both of his last works, *The Silent Wall* and *The Return of Marvin Palaver*, show such a deft touch with layering his plots that there's never any sense of winging it or improvisation. Rabe is a writer who seems to know exactly where he wants to take you, and how he wants to do it.

In the Tuttle interview, Rabe also mentions writing short stories, only two of which are known by his estate to exist. One of these is titled "Hard

Case Redhead" and it is a dark thing, as brutal and noirish a story as Rabe ever wrote. During the getaway after a heist, two thieves kidnap a surprised witness and hold her while the heat dies down. What follows is a picture of distrust and strain, a short, accelerating spiral of desperation. It is rich with close atmosphere and psychological suspense as the younger hood fails to measure up to the veteran ex-con. Rabe throws us a twist at the end reminiscent of an early Hitchcock film.

The other story is "A Matter of Balance," a perfectly titled depiction of two soldiers, one emotionally charged and prideful, the other cool to the point of detachment. The conflict between the two, only one of whom really understands what it is about, ends with a wonderfully moral and thematically ambiguous ending, indeed, a perfect "balance." A very different story from "Redhead," yet like the differences in his novels, it is still unmistakably a Rabe work.

One gets the feeling from the Tuttle interview that Rabe was somehow dissatisfied with his writing career, which is unfortunate. Whether it was because greater commercial success did not come his way, or that his own opinion of his books was lower than that of his fans', no one can easily say. A writer is, after all, sometimes his own biggest fan and at other times his own harshest critic. Rabe certainly appears to have placed himself in the latter group. Surprising to him or not, his classics include *Kill the Boss Goodby, The Box, Anatomy of a Killer, Murder Me For Nickels, Dig My Grave Deep*, and on and on.

Widespread popular success seems to come mostly to books that entertain a lot but challenge just a little. They can satisfy a reader's search for more of something they've seen before, just maybe in a little different way. Rabe was a unique writer, and his books are hugely entertaining but they pave their own way in regards to style. It's difficult for a reader to get what they think they're looking for when seeing something new for the first time. Rabe can be challenging yet at the same time, he doesn't require it of the reader. It's this mix that has brought him back into print and will hopefully keep him there for many, many years to come.

Rabe himself may have been surprised to see his works re-emerge in his own later years, but those who have read his books should never be. Now, with the addition to the published canon of *The Silent Wall* and *The Return of Marvin Palaver*, long-time fans and new readers alike have the chance to dip back into that same, classic storytelling vein that helped define not only the genre at the height of the paperback era, but influence major authors and legions of readers for years to come. It's been far too long for "new" Peter Rabe to appear. If only there were more.

LITTLETON, NH
APRIL 2010

THE SILENT WALL

By Peter Rabe

Prologue

Hitch was with this great, high-heeled monster of a woman and the only reason I was along, I spoke Italian and Hitch did not. It turned out that the woman was not Italian at all, she was Sicilian, and her glue-voiced accent was so heavy that I understood almost as little as Hitch. Not that it mattered.

But Hitch claimed that a little conversation with a whore ahead of time was a very nice thing, that it made them feel like a lady soon to be seduced, and what lady, he would say, does not love such a feeling.

We sat in the café with a big, noisy square to one side, no trees, no umbrellas, just the sun beating down which made the big woman sweat profusely and without any effort.

"Is she getting excited?" said Hitch. "Ask her."

I didn't bother because what whore gets excited at ten in the morning and Hitch knew that very well.

He and I had shipped out on the same tanker for about five years, always about the same run to and from the Near East through the Mediterranean, but we had never put in at Messina before. This stop was for repairs.

Hitch, who was second man to the engineer, had tried to explain the little defect to me but I had not been very much interested. I'm the radio man and I'm not even very much interested in the radio.

It is true that for a while there had been a great fascination in having a gadget which I knew inside and out and with this gadget I could talk to ghosts from everywhere, voice ghosts, bleep ghosts, click ghosts from almost everywhere and sometimes I would not know where that was.

That had been a while back though. By this time, by the time we were laid up in Messina, being radio man was a job and no more and the best thing about it for me was simply the place where I worked: I sit at my bank of instruments, there is always a light on where I sit, day or night, because my radio room is just a little thing right aft the bridge. I sit there with coffee at elbow, book out in front of me (this is where I study languages), and then, several times on my watch, I get up and step out. Now there is always a great switch in everything. The wind always blows. I am high up over the ship which looks improbably flat and low on the water, just a sliver really in all that water. It is raining perhaps and the water is metal grey, pitted and solid. Or the sun shines and the water is molten bright, slithery and full of motions and whatever I see is never enough. In a while I go back inside. This inside and this outside, I don't think I could bear one without the other. I must have both—

"Matheson," I keep hearing. "Hey, Matheson," and then I came around again to see Hitch there at the table with his high-heeled monster of a woman who at this point looked a little bit anxious.

"Come on, Matty," said Hitch. "You're supposed to be of some help. What's she want? Ask her."

I don't have to ask her. She was sitting there with an empty glass and afraid that Hitch wants to jump into bed with her at ten in the morning. So I called the waiter and ordered her another Benedictine. A woman like that has always at least one affectation and with this one it was Benedictine, sweet as marshmallow and thick as glue, at ten in the morning. I ordered myself another bottle of Cyclope.

"Hey," said Hitch, "I didn't say nothing about you having another one."

"It's only wine."

"We got three days. You don't have to lump it all into one forenoon."

Very suddenly I felt fairly annoyed with Hitch and his talk and his woman. I said nothing and sipped from my glass.

Cyclope is a beautiful light wine with a fresh, green color in the glass and a flavor which is always cool. They grow this wine in the black ash on the slopes of Aetna and I drank this wine because I remembered it from a long time ago.

But it did not taste the same. Which is, perhaps, just as well. This wine is always new.

"What's she saying, Matty?"

I nodded at her and asked her to say it again.

"*Anque lei?*" she said and something else, very vulgar, something I wouldn't attempt to translate for fear of losing the imagery. It only sounds right in Sicilian. That language lives so close to the ground and so close to the things that live under a stone, it can say things which no other language can grasp.

"What?" said Hitch. "What, what, what?" sounding greedy.

"She wants to know if we're both going to screw her."

"What?" said Hitch as if he had been goosed. "At the same time?"

"Either way."

"Oh boy!" said Hitch and sounded like a little boy admiring a Christmas tree. But he was looking at her, all the white skin bulging out of a black dress, all the spit curls which she wore like a trademark around her potato-type face. He was really licking her all over now, with his eyes.

"Ask her something for me, Matty. Ask her if she knows...."

"Ask her yourself."

"What kind of attitude all of a sudden?"

"Or show her."

"You some kind of a prude all of a sudden or something?"

"Why don't you shut up, Hitch, why don't you," and I ordered another bottle of Cyclope.

He didn't say anything. Hitch, my friend, has a certain respect for my moods. But not the woman. She said something about two for the price of one and a half, even though I was twice the size of the other one. She wiped sweat with nonchalance.

By now I was sweating too. Sun and wine taken together will do that to me and to sit like that can be pleasant. Hitch, of course, was not sweating. He never does. He was all this time winding himself up for the great battle with this great woman and her versatilities.

"Ask her if anything extra costs extra," he said.

Now the Cyclope tasted like muck. I had wanted to remember a taste and a touch and some sounds even, to remember them safely while not sitting alone, that's why I had gone along to sit with a woman who meant nothing to me one way or the other, and with Hitch who knew nothing that mattered one way or the other.

It had not worked. It had often worked, but not there in Messina which was close to the other place where I had been for a short, interrupted time. Hitch made me feel as if I were he, buying those things cheaply so that the loss would not matter. And the woman made me feel like a waster of everything because that was what she had done with herself. I blamed her and him and the wine too. It did not work. I felt rotten.

"Listen, Matty. I asked you a polite question about extras...."

He shut up when he saw me get up. I hadn't even finished my bottle. He was a buddy now who didn't ask any questions but I did not want a buddy around or anyone else. When Hitch said, "Goddamn it, here comes Chapman."

I could understand his tone of voice. Chapman was the chief in the engine room and who wants to sit and drink with the chief when the plans are so much more exotic.

"You too!" Chapman yelled when he saw me leave the table.

I sat down again. Sometimes right after I feel very rotten a great nothing feeling comes over me and I just as soon sit down to one side and watch something else, something which has nothing to do with me. Such as Hitch and his woman, and Chapman now.

I watched him come up the street which seems to lead straight into Calabria. You cannot see the water at the end of the street but only the other side of the Straits of Messina, the tall shore which is the brown bottom of the Italian boot.

Chapman came up to the table and said, "If you see any of the others, tell 'em too." Chapman always had this backward approach. Next came the beginning of his sentence. "We'll be laid up at least for a week."

I said, "Goddamn it," but did not care to make clear to myself what I had meant. I clapped my hands and when the waiter looked my way I pointed at my warm bottle.

"What's that?" said Chapman and sat down at the table without being asked. "What are you ordering there?"

"I'm ordering the fillibrating solenish which you need in order to replace the broken solenicking fillibush in your engine room, Chapman, so that we can all get out of here this very same afternoon."

Chapman was as small as Hitch. It struck me that everybody in the engine room must be small and shrunken because how else get around all those crazy pipes and pistons down there. Also, Chapman had no sense of humor. He just nodded his old head when I was done talking and I watched the dry skin swing back and forth under his jaw.

"That stuff in the bottle," he said. "What is it?"

"An extremely light wine."

"Hah!" said Hitch.

"Something local?" Chapman wanted to know.

"Yes," I said. "It's good for all day."

"How come you find out these things so quick?" Chapman wanted to know next.

He is constantly asking questions like that. He was constantly improving his mind with those goddamn personal questions.

"He's been here before," said Hitch. "That's how he knows how to get a cheap drunk by the local methods."

"When was that?" Chapman, of course.

"The war," Hitch said for me.

"Really?" said Chapman. "You been fighting all over Sicily?" For a man with constant and automatic questions he did not know very much.

"We left Africa," I told him. I leaned back, glass in hand, and felt like somebody's memoirs. This made everything very safe. "We left Africa and hung off the coast South of here for ten days while the Navy shelled Taormina. When we landed all we had to do was walk in. The Germans had left exactly ten days before."

"I'll be damned," said Chapman.

"That's what we felt like."

It was such a melodramatic thing to say, I hated myself almost as much as I hated Chapman and his questions.

"What I mean is," Chapman said next, "we got at least a week here, waiting for the engine part. What's interesting in Sicily?"

"Syracuse is full of ruins," I told him.

"Stilll?"

"Not from the war, Chapman. From the time of the Greeks."

"Mention something else."

"Get a map, Chapman."

He paid easy attention to the way I was getting irritable.

"But you been here, Matt. Where?"

And then I told him for no good reason except for the reason of a very great pleasure. "Forza d'Aguil," I said.

"What?" said Chapman. "What's that again?"

"It means Fart on the Hill," I said and felt like spitting.

Then I got up very fast, making the chair jump behind me. I left without saying another word. Almost out of earshot I could hear the big woman say in Italian, "That's Mafia country— And women are cattle there—"

Nobody at the table could have understood her because she had not said it in English. I walked away and wished I had not heard her at all.

I wished that she had not known the place, that only I knew that place, which is the only way of keeping a secret. I would have liked that the black, unfinished thing which I had left in Forza d'Aguil had also remained a secret from me.

And I wished that she had not said, "Women are cattle there—" because that was not true at all. That was never the way it had been with me in Forza d'Aguil. I really wanted to believe that.

I have moments of truth sometimes, knowing that there is only one thing to do and nothing else. I had one week now of nothing except to sit in Messina. I wounded myself over and over, thinking why I had let grey sand of disuse drift over something in Forza d'Aguil, something which had really been beautiful. Or perhaps I had made a romantic flower of memories grow in the grey sand though there was really nothing at all in Forza d'Aguil, or ever had been.

I had one week and could settle everything in less than a day. I went and rented a Vespa. Then I stopped by the ship to change into a heavier shirt and to take my peajacket along. Once the sun would be down it would get chilly. Then I took the highway out of Messina, going South, and later turned West, going inland. Soon it did turn much colder, and dark.

Chapter 1

Five major civilizations have lived and then died in Sicily. They came with their best and then died there. The island has kept nothing but the ruins and has produced nothing but the Mafia. Forza d'Aguil was both. Forza d'Aguil means the strength of Aguil but nobody remembers who he might have been. He built a town on top of a rock, a town so old that you can call it ageless. Aguil's strength—and this is still true today—was simply the rock made taller by frightful walls.

They are frightful to see because all this looks like a shut face, a balled fist. On the other side of the wall are compressed, no-air houses and dark, gutlike streets. And all this is way up in the sky, so high that you can see the Mediterranean. But the sea is no part of this town. You can only see it. The town is all stone with thin air overhead.

The first time I had gone there was because I had been sent. Right after the landing I was stationed on top of the rock. It was a fine place for a radio post and I was with a signal corps team. I and the rest of the crew were billeted up there and why else would anyone go to Forza d'Aguil. We used to wonder about the natives.

I geared the Vespa down into second and swung into the cutoff which then wound itself up the flank of the rock. After a weekend pass I used to come back this way in a jeep.

I used to hate that ride.

Now the weird view caught me again. From the road I could see the bare land below, like dry wrinkled skin, and then, when I was higher, I could catch a far flash of sea.

When you could see the water all day from the rock then it was good up there because the air would be bright with sun and the sky very high. But it was a bad day when there was only the late flash of sea in the evening when the sun glinted away after all the daytime hours behind a low sheet of clouds. When all the best landscape is in the sky, when that is the real sight of the day, then a grey day can be like ruination.

I pulled the Vespa to one side of the road, balanced the machine between my legs, and buttoned my peajacket higher. The town was right above me now, a big thrust of stone wall which seemed to be leaning away from the sky. I looked at the shut face and listened to the high nightwind building up and thought, it's time. I'm almost there and what in hell am I doing here.

I tried to light a cigarette inside my hands but the wind was too tricky now and Italian matches are too short for my fingers. I burned myself twice, threw the last match away and then the cigarette.

Of course I knew damn well why I had come this far. I would never have come if the ship had not been laid up for repairs in Messina but then the decision to come and look at the rock had been mine. It was now just a matter of saying, yes, I'll look, or no, I'm through. I stood and let the wind pluck at me and I made excuses about not deciding. Now the sun was down and immediately, fast like the clap of the hand, it became dark. I could not see the lights in Forza d'Aguil, only the wall.

Yes, or no? It was late to drive back to Messina. I thought about it and was a coward to make the thing casual. It is only natural, being this close, to go up and at least to have something to eat. It's only natural, I was explaining to myself, since I have all this time to come by and have a look. See how things turned out. See how things have turned out—for her. Though, most likely, she would not be in the town anymore. Most of the young ones leave after a while.

I blew on my hands and then I started the Vespa. I fiddled around in the dark till I found the switch for the light and that took a while because several little buttons were all on the same unit and I blew the horn a few times before finding the light. It was an awkward, wrong sound in the nightwind and I hoped no one had heard it.

So I went up for a look to see what had happened to her.

I did not think once about how she might have changed, but I did think a few times that no one up there would recognize me after all this time. This seemed important.

I remembered all of the town and the hush of it as soon as I came to the gate. It was the only entrance to Forza d'Aguil and looked as if it had been this way forever: the arch was gone. The two solid legs of the gate were hefted together from ragged squares pried out of the living rock. Where the two columns ended they had shaggy heads of long grass.

Past the gate came a sharp rise and then I was in the first *piazza*. It existed only to give you a choice of four streets. Over the mouth of each street hung a lamp which swayed from an iron antler attached to a wall. The square was empty. There were closed shops, closed with shutters, and there were little apartments over the shops, also shuttered. The plague might have hit this town, though it hadn't. After dark you close the shutters.

The square was paved with little white tiles. This was new. I remembered cobblestones. I saw nothing else, just the four lamps hanging blinkless over four black mouths, and all the sharp lines of the tiles running off in perspectives. Nobody walked in this wind.

The street I took would lead me to the second square, higher up. I passed two more lamps and many more shutters. I was alone in this gut which rose slightly and interrupted itself now and then with sets of shallow steps. A Vespa could make it, a bicycle, or a slow walk. Or there was enough room for two donkey carts to pass each other.

The second square, which was really the center of town, had a tree in the middle. The tree was still there. Everybody took good care of this tree, did not touch it too hard or lean things against it. Here, in this square, were a few lights. The hotel showed two lit windows and a donkey was tied up in front. Opposite was the light from the *osteria*. There was no donkey in front of the eating place but a hand cart and four Vespas. This looked very prosperous. I looped around the square and parked near the tree in the middle. I saw one black-shawled woman cross the square, bent because of the wind, and from the other direction a cat came leaping along. Then the square was empty again, except for the wind.

I thought to myself, nobody knows me here and I don't know this place either. I know it no better than having once seen a picture.

Next to the *osteria* was the open store. This store had always been open, always lit with that single bulb of clear glass so that the filament showed and bit into your sight. I walked into the store and the smells were the same and so were the sights. There was now an electric cooler behind the counter but the rest was the same. Salamis soft as cheese, salamis hard as rock. There were slabs of stockfish leaning against the wall with their little tags threaded through the bone-dry meat saying that this piece of fish had been cured in Norway. And one wall was nothing but drawers, brown, old drawers full of dozens of different pastas.

Mostly you smelled the spice. Rosemary lay in brittle bundles to one side of the counter and oregano, rubbed and crumbled, lay heaped in an open sack. The olive oil gave no odor though the three black barrels holding three different grades of oil smelled like wet wood or greased boots or a combination.

The old woman behind the counter and the old woman on my side of the counter stopped talking and looked. They looked because that's what the eyes are for and that's all. I did not know them and they did not know me. The one on my side of the counter had a smell of wax and the one on the other side of the counter was closing a coffee tin and smelled brown and burnt.

I bought a stick of bread, a wedge of cheese, and a length of sausage. She wrapped everything into the same sheet of brown paper and when I had paid I walked out.

It would by far be the easiest, was my thought, if no one remembered me. Those two hadn't remembered me and buying my things in the store had been a pleasure. Suddenly I felt cold.

It was going to be one hell of a miserable ride back to Messina at night and I better eat first. And if I don't walk into the *osteria* now, then I never will—

I walked in and it was warm. There was a pot of rice and beans cooking on the stove in the back which gave a sweetish, boiling meat kind of odor. The table which served as a counter was still there. It had a new type of espresso machine on the top, ugly like a jukebox, but the rest I remembered like always. High walls, bulb hanging down from the ceiling, garlic ropes hanging down from nails. Pink Pope Leo still blessed from the cardboard portrait (the nail went through the second crown of his mitra), a pope revered when the old *patrone* had been a child. I sat down at one of the small, wooden tables and put my brown paper bundle on top.

Blank stares from the other tables. I sat and did not look up for a while. I felt stiff and tired and fingered around my peajacket, opening it up. Somebody slid a plate and a knife in front of me and stood waiting. It took me a while but then I looked up.

How old they get, I thought, though I recognized the *patrone*. He looked like his own grandfather. He stood there tired of waiting and resigned to waiting which makes for the most unfriendly expressions of all. It is how I recognized the *patrone*. I told him I wanted a black cup of coffee, *lungo*, which means a tall glassful instead of the one-swallow cup.

He nodded and walked back to his machine on the table. He had not recognized me. I now started to eat the stuff I had bought and no longer felt tired. I felt free now to look around.

They stared the way they always do. Nobody stares like a Sicilian. It is not an animal stare, in fact, animals do not stare at all but simply look. These eyes, turned on me, are a shut, one-way affair. They do not want you to see into them, they only want to suck everything out of you. This act is not hostile. It is no more hostile than the leech who hangs onto your skin.

I looked away from them and it was like a rest. I chewed food and rested and watched the couple a few tables away.

They did not talk. They just sat, bent inside their clothes, looking past each other. She was shawled and dressed in the eternal black of the death-watching they do. There is always someone dead in these very large families and when the one year of mourning is up someone else will have died. He wore heavy corduroy, brown like his face. Her face was white. They were both old, or just worn, I don't know. It is hard to tell age with these people once they are past the mid twenties. This comes from hard work and it comes from not caring for many things which go with being young. And this comes from that airless life behind high, permanent walls which are built into these people. Strength, turned in on itself, causes this old age which is not really earned.

I knew the old couple. The first time I had been in Forza d'Aguil they had often sat together at that same table—

"How would you like," said Jack very often, "to have a piece of *that?*" We looked at the couple from our table. He wore brown corduroy and had a brown face which, in a curious way, told you exactly how he would look when he would be over sixty. You couldn't say the same in her case.

She looked lovely young to us and juicy ripe and we would talk at length about this inconceivable business of her lover sitting there with her for hours and hours in stultified silence, looking past her, fingering his glass of red wine. Sometimes he sighed at her and she smiled. When they were gone we would talk at great length about how this girl would be in the sack. No girl could be as good in the sack as we thought this one would be in the sack. All this talk and this sitting around with Jack or with Bundik or anyone of the crew was not simple G.I. talk about sex but a much more desperate thing. We were the conquerors of Sicily and, if you please, had no women.

In general this had to do with the fact that Forza d'Aguil was not a town conquered in combat. This changes the whole native attitude towards the victor. Forza d'Aguil had not been liberated, it had been intruded upon. I know what it feels like to be a victor because later, when the Strength of Aguil was far and faint I was there when we marched into Rome. The victor laughs, catches flowers in midair, kisses right and left, drinks anything, and of course screws. If not that, he might have a real affair. In Forza d'Aguil we did not feel like victors.

It seemed as if only the wind talked to us up on that rock. And the stone. Stone came to mean silence. The stone houses talked silence. They were not open to us, they told us nothing. The wall which contained the town like a monstrous rib made a silence. This cage of rib constricted the life and the breath of everything living inside, all motion slowed down, limb motion, heart motion, and the free motion of eyes. The Natives stared. You do not stare at a victor.

Now, about the women, they were not really different from the prevalent Mediterranean type who has dark, heavy eyes, heavy hair, heavy breasts, who are a pleasure to see when they walk with all the strength of their self-possession and with that grace which comes from knowing what they are built for and what they can do.

Of course they could have had their breasts on their shoulderblades and we would have had just as much appetite. It's part of the victor stance and then, as I said, we weren't getting any. I have described how things felt up there. Also, the resistance went further. There was a blonde kid by the name of Colony in the team who thought himself irresistible and needed proof of this quality time and again. The whores in Messina did not fill the bill and he had to start messing with one of the girls on the rock. She was not married but she was engaged. They were all engaged if they were not married. I don't know if Colony ever got into the girl because very soon he disappeared. Four days later the warrant officer who headed up our team found a note in his room describing where Colony might be found. It was an address in Messina. There was an OP in Messina and our warrant officer radioed them the message so that everything was taken care of from there.

They found Colony in the basement of an empty house. He was alive. I heard two or three different versions of what they found there but Colony was alive. He was naked, bound hand and foot, and suffering from all the things that afflict the body after four days without food and drink and proper rest. He hadn't been able to get any rest whatsoever. Strapped into his groin and packed entirely around his genitals was a large lump of rotten liver. This is bad enough in itself but then there had also been these large rats which run all over Messina. They had not hurt Colony in any physical sense, so went the report, though what else might have happened to Colony or what changes night have occurred inside him, none of that was officially mentioned.

It had been a Mafia act. I had not known until then that its eye had been that close to us.

Colony was sent somewhere else and was never replaced. That left seven of us until we were pulled out. In the meantime we tried as often as possible to make it down to Messina, to escape.

Chapter 2

The *osteria* closed around one at night and at that time I started my shift at the shack at five o'clock in the morning. I had spent two days in Messina, slept into the late afternoon, and then headed back to the rock after dark. There was no rush because I wasn't on till five in the morning but then, one third into the hinterland, I became hungry. We never raced back to that place but I did this time because I wanted to make it in time to get some of that heavy soup at the *osteria*.

I swiveled the jeep up the rock, bounced through the gate, snaked up the gut which led to the center piazza. Yes, the light was still on in the place, shining through the two panes of glass in the door and this made me feel unaccountably happy. I bucked the jeep to a stop and ran the rest of the distance with that habitual stoop you soon learned up there because of the wind.

The narrow room inside was warm and steamy. I felt very good.

Benson was there and a Pole whose name I forgot. I think we called him Poochy or something because it reminded at once of his name and also a small, shaggy dog. Poochy looked that way.

"Hey, Matt," he called from the table. "Hey, come on over here and wait till you see...."

"Never mind," Benson told him. Benson had a very sour face and long, bony hands which never held still. I sat down and looked at Benson who looked at me as if I had the plague. He always looked that way. "He knows already."

"You do?" said Poochy.

I think I said, "Huh—"

"The way he comes running in," said Benson, "with that eagerness and that disgusting grin of expectation."

"I'm hungry," I said and looked to the back.

The *patrone* was near his pot and when I caught his eye I waved at him and showed him with ladling motions what I wanted from him out of that pot.

"Weekend pass in Messina," said Benson, "and he comes home hungry."

"I meant food," I told him.

"How did you know already," asked Poochy, "if you just come in from Messina?"

"I don't know any more now than when I left. We pulling out or something?"

When Benson is truly disgusted he cracks the lumpy joints of his fingers. He did this now.

"No," he said. "And it's nothing. It's nothing to a puling humper of a man who wastes his precious essence on hairy hookers in that dirty Messina town."

"Stop cracking your knuckles, will you please?"

"Yeah," said Poochy, "will you please?"

Benson cracked once more and looked at the ceiling. "Yes. Vile goings on and rampaging while we spend the time esthetically."

"Esthetically?" said Poochy.

"That's what you call it when you just look," Benson told him.

"It means you're horny," I explained further.

It was the usual talk and only the vocabulary might differ, depending with whom you were conversing.

"You're wrong," said Benson. "This is not the usual talk between trips to Messina. We," and he raised a finger, "have a new one in town."

"Where the hell is my soup."

"Are you listening, Mathew Matheson?"

"You look. I want to eat. Where is she?" It was an afterthought.

"Aha!" said Benson. It was always this kind of turn in a conversation which made him almost happy.

"You don't get it," said Poochy. "This one, you know, maybe this one you do more than look."

"I smell liver," I said. It was an expression we sometimes used, ever since Colony had left us.

"On account," said Poochy, "she's also an out-of-towner."

"Oh?" I said. Poochy might be right and it would make a difference.

"And she works tables right here in this dump!"

"Precisely," Benson mumbled, "why we are here."

My soup came.

"When does she shave?" I asked my tablemates because it was the *patrone* who brought me the plate of soup and I thought my remark was therefore funny.

They didn't think it was funny. They looked at the *patrone* whose mustache swung forth and around like the horns of a ram and whose jowls were bristling with stubbles. I looked at my soup and smelled it. It was pasta and peas but this time there were also chunks of pepperone inside.

"Man," I said. "Look what I came back to."

"You disgust me, Matheson." Benson of course.

"We don't mean him," said Poochy who sometimes talks more stupid than need be. He had the fastest sending finger in the crew but he never received very well. He wasn't now.

"While I eat this—"

"That's not the word," said Benson. "While you ravage those little peas and all, yes?" and he cocked his head at me.

"While I do this go ahead and tell me about Scheherazade."

"Who?" Poochy wanted to know.

"How's your soup, Matty?" Benson could be warm and charming to you, if it cut somebody else.

"Good."

Poochy said, "Are you crapping me, Benson? Because I don't like it, you crapping me, you know that, Benson?"

"Pardon?" and Benson leaned towards him now.

"Encora, per favore," I called to the *patrone*. I was finished with the first plate and folded my arms on the table, listening to this hassle my buddies enacted here. Maybe Benson knew it was really a routine but I'm sure Poochy did not.

He said, "I'm not even interested in your Babylonian hoor no more, so just forget I asked, asked anything at all and aside, it's got nothing to do with the new one. She's no hoor."

"How do you know?" said Benson. "She denies it?"

"Don't crap me, Benson."

"How do you know?"

"She's too young. That's what."

Poochy surprised both of us. He really surprised us with that argument and for a moment we didn't know what to say. Poochy liked that silence. It made him bold.

"And besides," he said, "she is very beautiful."

"Your argument defeats me," said Benson. "I am trapped by your logic and your fund of vast, past experience in these matters."

"Is he still trying to crap me, Matty?" and Poochy looked at me in the manner which had earned him his name. Next, he might just lick my hand.

"He gets mean when he wants something," I told him. "Because he can never get what he wants. Benson is tragic that way, aren't you, Benson?"

"You sound better when you eat, you know that, hoghead?"

I felt more like talking to Poochy.

"So tell me," I said. "Here is this new, young, beautiful—what else is she, Poochy?"

"Girl," said Poochy. "She's a girl."

Benson cracked his knuckles.

"And she does not shave," he said. He thought a moment, really caught up in the thought of this girl and then he was obviously getting sick of his own spleenish ways because he said very seriously, "She's esthetic."

"And built. I mean it," said Poochy.

I was getting a picture which was not very consistent and besides I had to subtract for steamy imagination.

I said, "Do we worship her or do we...."

She came out of the kitchen and I turned my head as Benson dropped his large hands beneath the table. Poochy said something softly in Polish as she moved to an empty table in the corner and began to clear dishes. The *patrone* looked once in our direction and went through the swinging door to the back.

Benson kicked me under the table. "See any esthetics like that in Messina, Matty?"

I ignored him and the three of us watched her as though it were the most natural thing in the world. She didn't need to be beautiful to be arousing but she was, even in that place.

She was taller than the other women of Forza d'Aguil and carried little of the constant weight of that place. Her skin was smooth but with small lines around the eyes that made her pretty rather than old. They were large eyes, bright and olive-colored, a shade deeper and brighter than seemed natural in that light.

The girl was beautiful with a beauty not dependent on her youth. She was that, too, but it was not in the way. Benson said something else but I didn't hear it as we watched her do her work, following her from table to counter and back again.

The steam was rising from our chairs. I suddenly felt very conspicuous in the room. She was leaning over a table now, wiping it with a cloth, her face toward us but angled down so that her hair fell across those magnificent eyes. I was hoping they would be closed, that they would not see three soldiers with their minds working as they were, directly across from her.

She finished her cleaning and stood, turning away before she tossed her hair back into place with a shrug of one shoulder. I still wanted to see her eyes and as she turned back I knew each of us were looked at in turn. Those eyes were open. Poochy had said that she was not from Forza d'Aguil. She left and I picked up my spoon.

"Hey," said Poochy. "Call her back, Matty. Talk to her."

"About what?"

"You talk Italian. Say something to her."

"Let me eat."

"Matty, come on."

"He will," said Benson. "After we're gone."

"If I talk to her, Benson, it might not be esthetic. Better stick to looking."

He craned his neck around and looked at her where she was wiping a table. When he caught her eye he waved at her to come over.

"Order me some wine," he said to me.

"You can say *vino*, for chrissakes."

"Your Italian is so much more musical, Matheson. Say it like you're ordering a love potion. For me," he added.

She stood by the table and looked at us one after the other.

"My friend would like some wine," I said. "He is too shy to ask you himself."

"First," she said, "ask your shy one to take his hand off my leg."

You couldn't tell by Benson's face what he might be doing. As usual his expression only conveyed that something very unpleasant was going on.

"Or I will hit him with something," said the girl.

"Benson—"

"Alright, alright," he said and folded his hands on the table.

"I apologize for him," I said to the girl. "He has admired you from a distance and the closer you came the more lonesome he felt."

"It's nothing," she said. "What wine does he want?"

"The Country wine. From the jug without the water."

It was not an insult but the way you ordered here.

When she was gone I looked at Poochy and smiled.

"Well, how was it?"

"What?"

"I talked to her. You asked me."

"Oh," he said. "Yeah. I like her voice."

It was true, she had a lovely voice. It moved through various tones when she spoke and in back of it lay that slight hoarseness of many Italian women.

"And what did you like, Tiger Benson? Was it esthetic?"

"Your musical conversation with her. Did you make a date, you fink?"

I said go frig yourself and started eating again but now the girl was back. She had filled a slim bottle from the barrel in back and had also brought three glasses. She put them down, one by one, while I watched her hand. It was small and mobile. Not a work hand, I thought. Then I looked at her arm.

"Stop nibbling at her with your eyeballs," said Benson from across the table. He had both his hands on the table and acted righteous as hell.

I felt a little stung by his remark and gave him an unfriendly look. And at that point the girl threw her head back and burst out laughing.

None of us knew what this was all about and I felt a little uneasy. Her timing had been just a little too uncanny.

"You understand English?" I asked her.

She stopped laughing and wiped the wine bottle with one end of her apron. Her smile was highly amused.

"I don't understand English," she said. "I understand the way you looked at me and the way he sounded when he saw how you felt about looking at me. You are very funny, you two." She laughed again and poured the wine.

"I have a dirty feeling," said Benson to Poochy, "that those two know each other, God damn it."

And in a way he was right. I did not and could not know the shut people who lived on this rock but the girl was different. She had shown how she felt right away and in that way she had let us know her. I picked up my glass and nodded at her.

"*Piaceri,*" I said which is not a toast you make with a glass of wine but it simply means I am glad to know you.

"*Anche mio,*" she said and you don't hear that very much either unless someone is actually pleased. Then she left.

We had a little silence at our table. Finally Poochy said, "Boy—"

Benson sighed and then he folded his arms.

"Well now," he said. "Let us review this maneuver step by step. Item: I offer to share, guilessly, a simple esthetic pleasure with a farting boor. Elevate him a little, if I do say so myself. Item: The farting boor, in affected gratitude, offers to lend a hand, talented hand I might add, with the rapprochement. Item: The next thing...."

"With the what?" said Poochy.

"It means to make a pass."

"Oh, yeah," said Poochy and nodded.

"Where was I?"

"All wrong," I said. "You were all wrong."

"You are a disgusting fink, Mathew, and deep down in your noodle and pea-packed bowels you know goddamn well you just made that broad as good as if you had made that broad. Whereas *you* were supposed to *lead* her to *us.*"

"Listen," I said. "How do you figure for me to make up in two minutes flat what you ruined by copping a feel off her leg, huh? Answer that!"

"Copping a feel helps."

"Forget it," and I drank wine too fast so that it scratched in the throat.

"You didn't cooperate with my assistance," said Benson. By this time his irritation was genuine, and so was mine. Benson cracked a knuckle and said, "First you cop a feel, which causes startlement or embarrassment or maybe both. Second—and this is where you were supposed to come in—you become supportive and reassuring. This immediately establishes...."

"Bullshit. She wasn't embarrassed and she wasn't startled."

"That's right," said Poochy.

"Another rat fink?"

"Forget it," I said. "She had the worst reaction of all. She thought it was ridiculous."

"*Fermato por favore, fermato!*" said the *patrone* to everyone which was alright with me because it interrupted this nonsense here at the table. The rest we did in silence, the foot shuffling, pants hitching, the heavy buttoning of jackets once you were standing up, and then we carefully doped out how many coins to leave, plus the few lira. In American, that only comes to a few pennies. Benson didn't leave any.

At the door I turned around and in the back stood the girl, looking at us. I waved at her and said, *ciao,* and she smiled immediately, making the strange little hand flutter which also means *ciao* when you don't want to yell over a distance. Then Poochy and Benson and I went out into the square.

"Chow," said Benson and I could imagine the look on his face. "Most ridiculous greeting I ever heard. Call her mashed potatoes, pigs's knuckles or something and be done with it."

But the attempt at a joke was too late and he knew it. I didn't answer and we went across the square to the hotel where we had been billeted and didn't say another word.

The little rift might have told me that something more might have happened to me than the usual bickering that goes on with Benson. But I had only seen the girl for that very short time—

Chapter 3

Her name was Rosanna. Somehow everyone in the team knew her name by next morning when I want on shift.

I had slept my few hours and then one of the team, acting the orderly in rotation, would wake us up in time. The rules were pretty flexible and I had arranged for a call as late as four thirty. It wasn't far to the radio shack, just steep. I was still bundling myself going down the narrow stairs of this house which rented rooms like a hotel, past the restaurant door (someone was baking bread on the inside), and then out and across the square. Just a thin light at this time of the morning giving the stone houses a color of dry grey which did not look at all heavy. Then you go up the second street which very soon becomes nothing but steps. It's much darker here in the gut than out on the square, the houses lean heavily here and leave just a pale strip of sky overhead, shaped like a crack in glass. Then comes a sharp jog where only one man can pass at a time. The step there is a black monster of living stone, twice as high as all the others and very imperfectly hewn. (We called it the Sobering Stairwell. Almost all of us, at one time or another, had barked shins there and then clattered down a few yards, trying to make that turn drunk.) Right after that turn the street widens and the steps become almost palatial in width. They lead to the big, windy terrace which surrounds the church.

I don't know how old that church is. Since it commands the best view from the town, there must have been something up there for a very long time. Some parts of the wall are Sarazen. Where the yellow plaster had cracked away you can see the sharp little rock chinks they used for packing a wall together. One corner (where you turn towards the cemetery) is made of the monstrous, square blocks which the Normans used. But most of the church showed only the thick, yellow plaster and the baroque pleasure curves where a severe religion had turned around and put many tinsel lights and a great deal of pretty festivities into its ritual.

The church is always open but it is often quite empty.

I went fast around the entire terrace, to the back, where you cross into the cemetery. It is not very large, big oyster sky overhead, and at the other end comes the last finger of rock pointing nowhere.

We had cut the steps into this one, straight and sharp, not too many, and then came the rock plateau where we had our metal shack. There was just the shack, the thousand foot drop and the sky.

The vast, cold view ripped at me and then I went inside. It's adequate.

Two walls of instruments, a cot and a table, and in one corner a partition
with the chemical toilet. Whoever used it last on the swing shift got that
detail—

"I haven't seen her but Benson last night, when he hit the sack, he said
he'd go back for more."

"More of what?"

"Looking. What else in this monastery."

"But she's new here. Maybe...."

"Her mother lives here and she's probably just back from her back-
breaking labors in Messina, for a rest."

"Hey Matty, you seen her?"

I grunted something and we changed shifts.

"*Osteria* tonight? Battle of the *Osteria* tonight! Fighting for seats—"

The talk didn't bother me but I wasn't interested in it. Off and on I
thought of Rosanna. I liked thinking of Rosanna. I thought of how to meet
her again. I was not going to go the obvious route, hang around there in
the *osteria*, because that way around was going to be so routinized, stan-
darized, and shut tight, why waste my time. I looked for her in the streets,
in the daytime, but never saw her. When I did see her again I literally
bumped into her.

We had ten hour shifts by then (because of Colony missing) and I was
going fast around the church corner at the end of my shift, three PM.
That's still siesta time, close to the end of it, when you are getting ready to
go back to work. I made the turn fast, crashed into someone, and we
bounced apart.

"Rosanna—"

"You—"

"Are you hurt, honey?"

She had a shawl over her head, held tight with one arm across her middle. With her free hand she was cupping one breast, stroking it. She looked
very angry. Then she exhaled deeply and looked very cool.

"Honey?" she said.

I had said everything in Italian, except for that automatic word, so I told
her what it meant in Italian. She pressed her lips together, which could
mean anything, and then she started to giggle. The word makes no sense
in Italian the way it does in English. She laughed and said that to her the
word means something much more sticky than sweet.

"That's alright too," I said. "It suits me fine too."

Then the joke was over, we felt suddenly serious now but did not know
what to do with it. We each took a step towards each other but looked out
over the balustrade of the terrace where only sky showed.

"I've been looking for you, Rosanna."

"*Anque io.*"

"Why me?" fishing for some marvelous compliment.

"Because you are the only one who never came back."

* * *

Then, I did not think the remark prophetic. On the church terrace with the wind whipping us, it was only deflating. I laughed, and she laughed, and next she settled her scarf to show that she had to be going.

"I did not want to see you at the *osteria*, Rosanna. You understand? It's no good there."

"I know."

"But I want to see you."

"I wanted to see you too. Don't ask why. I don't know."

"I know. Something with the eyes. Something went back and forth between us."

"Words," she said and shrugged. But she smiled at me in a way that made her look as if she wished she knew the right words but then again, perhaps they weren't necessary.

"I have to go now. I want to visit my father's grave but I must get back soon."

"I'll wait for you."

She nodded and went down the steps into the cemetery which looked like a forest of stones. She wound back and forth and then up the slant of the cemetery and found a grave which looked exactly the same to me as all the others. There she knelt down for a while and probably prayed. She did not stay very long.

"I'm sorry about, uh, him," I said.

"*Meno male,*" she said and her off-handed shrug meant the same thing as the expression. "I did not know him very well."

"Oh—he was gone?"

"I was gone. They were very poor so they sent me to live with relatives in Catania. A big, ugly town." She stopped at the wide steps which led back into the innards of Forza d'Aguil. "And this is a small, ugly town. A cage. *Meno male.* Now he died and I am back to take care of my old mother."

"How nice—" like an idiot.

She looked at me and gave a short, strong laugh. We went down the steps.

"She is an old woman and we sleep in the same bed. Ha! I sleep in bed with an old woman. She yells at me and I yell at her and that is not *nice.*"

She drew up her shoulders under the scarf, like the start of a shudder.

"*Cara mia,*" she said, very low now. "To think I might die in this town. I am already dying in this town."

"Yes," I said. "It needs no explaining. I feel it too."

She nodded at me and then went ahead to snake her way through the Sobering Stairwell. I caught up with her.

"I want to see you tonight, Rosanna, after you're done."

She didn't answer until the next turn in the street.

"What is your name?"

"Matty."

"Yes, Matty."

* * *

We touched in the dark, a place at the big wall itself. She opened her scarf like wings and I stepped into them. We talked with touch only, we knew everything, and what we did not know was not important. We made love that first night.

It was a problem. Outdoors was too cold and there was no indoors for us. There are quick, outdoor ways, of course, such as kneeling, or leaning against a wall, but we wanted more. After much wandering through the streets, after moaning and laughing and cursing about our frustrating walk we ended up on the other side of the gate and there, up the incline which came dawn to the road, was a small shed for goats.

"Come on," I said. "With the animals."

"Ah—I should have thought of it. And it fits."

All the goats were in the low, single stall and along the stall ran a crib full of hay. It smelled of hay, of goat, and it was warm.

"Into the...."

"I know, I know," she said.

We made for the crib and I got butted just lightly on the way.

"Wait now," I said. "I make a bed."

I made the bed. I took my coat off first. I took her shawl.

I opened her dress while she held still, I could feel her slow breathing with my hands. When she was naked I undressed and then we went into the crib.

I knew her in the dark. I knew her as well as if I had been with her in all other nights, places and moments—

I lay on her and reached for her mouth and when I found it her lips were pressed hard together.

"Rosanna—"

She turned her head away and then she burst out with a giggle.

"The goat," she managed. "The goat is nibbling me."

* * *

After a while we managed it. We had to stop laughing, we had to figure a stratagem, and finally I got out of the crib and put on my boots. The next step needed boots because I had to walk through the goat-part of the hut, fling open the rickety door, and chase out those goats. Being naked except for his boots makes a man cautious and it took me longer than need be to get rid of the goats. They did not want to leave where the hay was. Behind me I could hear Rosanna laughing in all manner of ways, from a squeek to a guffaw which soon became breathless. She could see my silhouette. When I finally slammed shut the door I was in a fine state of rage and Rosanna, when I got back into the crib, in a state of total exhaustion. But in a while it got better. We talked less and less and made love more and more and came together strong and willing for each other which left us together and happy.

"I am cold, Matty," she said in a while.

"That's because the goats are gone."

"Hah," she said. "I have my *capricorno*."

"I know you, *cara*. You want all of them."

"*Disgraziado!*" she hissed. Then she bit my ear and pushed me away.

We got up and picked little leaves and haystalks off each other and would have stayed with that novel diversion much longer except that it was really getting cold now. We dressed and tapped our way to the door, wondering to each other where the goats might have gone.

They were all there. They stood silently in a group close to the door of the shed, looking. They did not say a word but there was a yellow puritanical glare in their eyes. And then, still without a word, they made their dainty footed way back into the shed, nodding their heads with an air of self-involvement, disdaining to notice us. We went back into town.

I was to leave Rosanna by the alley of her mother's house (it ran off the second square) and when we stopped something changed.

"*Ecco*," she said and held on to my lapels hard, head down and rubbing her forehead against me. "*Pazzeria*," she mumbled into my coat. Then she bit into one of my buttons while her hands were still clamped into my coat.

"What is it? Hey, look at me, Rosanna."

She took a deep breath and then she looked at me.

"I am such a fool, you know, Matty. Such a fool. Now I want more and I want more for a long time, but I want it from you. *Ma—*" which can mean either disdain or a try for indifference. "I want it from you, and you are leaving."

We talked a while but it was no good. The funtime thing had already changed, had become deeper.

This shadow, to which she pointed first, never left us again. We often felt this threat of separation. (Price of the victor: he loses.)

I have often thought later that it was precisely this threat of losing each other which made us strong lovers, which carved deeply into us what we felt as love.

✱ ✱ ✱

We saw each other often and in many places. We got very good at it. There was a place on top of the wall where you could not be seen from the church or the radio hut. In the middle of the nine foot wide wall some square blocks of stone were missing. Once the base of a catapult had rested there but now it was just a square trough. When the afternoons were hot we went there for a while. We made love or we sat there and talked, rock clad on all sides except for the high metal of the glaring sky. After a while we stopped.

"Even the blankets don't help much," said Rosanna. "You are too big and heavy on me."

"What we could do...."

"No. In bed I do anything, but not here."

The real reason why we quit the square hole an top of the wall was because it felt too much like a tomb, lying there.

For a while I arranged to owe time on my shift and then I arranged to make it up on the afternoon shift. The arrangement to get the shack all alone at that time was of course also financial.

We had the bunk and sidled up way over together so that we could lie there and look out at the sky, big afternoon sky full of blue light and white cloud light and yellow light from the sun.

"I see it all the time," she said, "while you have to look at the pillow."

"I don't care," I said. "I don't care about the sky when I'm making love to you."

She held still and held me very close. Even though she was less than half my size, *size* had nothing to do with the way she could hold on to me.

"I was lying, to tease," she said. "When you make love to me I can really see nothing at all and cannot care about anything else."

But at this point of knowing each other there was not too much talk anymore. This was partly because we did not need it, but also because we felt some slight nudge of fear—

The wind just mumbled that afternoon and there the arythmic crackle from the radio bank. And the gas stove hissed. The flame was blue and the porcelain mesh cherry. Rosanna covered herself with her shawl.

"I hear," she said, "that you are moving out."

She often spoke without any transition.

"What's that?"

"Look," and she held up one bare arm. "Look where you made a mark."

"Hey, listen. Who told you? General Montgomery?"

"There will be new landings soon, further up on the mainland. Where the world continues."

"Who told you, General von Keitl?" And if she was going to go on with that I would next say, who told you, General Patton? When I get terribly anxious I also become very stupid.

But she said nothing else. She sat up and took her scarf. She stood up and wrapped it around her hips, below the nip of her waist, and tied it there. She stood with arms crossed, each hand holding a breast with much tenderness. Her tight wrap showed the lovely curve of her belly and thighs.

"Rosanna."

"*Si.*"

"I love you like never before. I don't think I have loved before."

"I believe you, *caro.*"

She stood and I sat and we did not touch.

"Not having loved before," I went on, "made this so big and, for me, so much easier."

She looked away from the window and down at me.

"You are wrong, Matty. That makes it harder. I love you for that too."

We did not lie down again but got dressed and left.

* * *

What happened next came with painful speed, or perhaps it was a blessing.

I found our warrant officer and before I got my mouth open he said, "Where in hell have you been?"

After that I did not have to ask a thing because he went right on.

"Get ready. I don't know exactly when but it's any time now. Something big up north."

I swallowed air dry as soot from a furnace.

"We leave in two groups. You're in the first, Matheson."

"Look, if it's all the same, sir, I'd like...."

"The first! You're not good enough at equipment assembly to take the gear out with the second group." And then he gave me a few orders which I now forget.

I ran to the *osteria* but she was not there yet. I ran back and did chores as ordered. I ran back to the *osteria* and she had four tables to handle while I stood by the door, waiting, sweating, until she came over, wiping her hands on her apron.

She kept wiping and wiping while we looked at each other and saw our faces freeze over, without a word. We did not have to say a word. I finally moved and took her by the arm out to the square.

A small splash of light from the late sun still made one end of the square yellow. The rest seemed blue. Siesta was over and anonymous women with baskets walked in the square, and small, stony men leading donkeys. Once a Vespa backfired and then a donkey screeched.

"Rosanna, it's soon. I don't know when but it's soon."

Her face never changed. I was close to tears seeing her like this but she showed nothing.

"I must go inside."

"Rosanna, I want you out of this dead town, alive with me. We must arrange this. Not this moment, I know too little, but we must, Rosanna."

"I had the best of you, Matty. *Grazie tante.*"

"For God's sake, woman. I am going to pieces! Your face is like the walls—"

"I will cry later, Matty."

"Listen, you idiot, at two o'clock when you get off, I'll be here."

"*Un bacho, caro. La ultima volta.*"

"No!"

"*Un bacho e non de pui?*"

I gave her the hastiest kiss ever, full of fear, greed, and defeat.

We would meet at two in the morning at the mouth of that street, when the *osteria* closed. At two o'clock, it turned out, I was to leave in the lead jeep with the first group of our detachment. Therefore, I had to see her before.

From eleven o'clock on, when I started checking, Rosanna was no longer in the *osteria*.

"Her mother needed her," said the *patrone.* "They had to go for the priest." The look he gave me could only have come from that place.

Between then and two AM I never found her. A man named Angelo had seen her on the upper corso, a kid by the name of Pepino had seen her with the priest at the church.

At two AM our two jeeps were idling to warm up for the trip. We had two jeeps, the second one with a trailer. We sat in the jeeps, bundled up, shivering.

"0205, Matt." Poochy sat next to me.

I sat in front of the hotel, watching the mouth of the alley. Three late people came out of the *osteria* and then the lights went out there. One was an old man, the other two were a couple.

"0210, Matty, for chrissakes."

So we started up and I made the slow swing around the tree and the square and I slowed at the mouth of the alley.

She was not there.

With a frantic feeling it struck me that I did not even know her last name!

Then the footsteps. The silent young man in brown corduroys and the round girl with the moon colored face walked by. They did not speak, they just walked into the alley.

He does not speak and perhaps rarely touches her but she knows at least this, that he is there by her side and does not leave her.

Chapter 4

And here they still were, the old man bent inside his corduroys, and the old woman with a face the color of moon. I am not saying that this was good. I don't know. But they at least had not been interrupted before finding out.

Of course there were reasons. There had been Anzio and finally Rome. I had not known her last name and that posed a problem, but I had been all over the world since then, so why not Sicily?

Not having loved before, that makes love harder, Rosanna had said. I had thought about it off and on, quite often, before I understood what it meant. I had not loved before because when you start a love and then it grows big, inside it somewhere there sits a fright. That's why I had not loved before Rosanna—and that's why I had not come back. It had taken a lousy accident in the engine room before I had come back.

I watched the old couple leave and kept sitting there with my guilt. To hell with it. It was much too late and all done anyway.

There were three young men at the further table, long shawls around their necks and with their jackets hanging over their shoulders. It seems like a class symbol down here, the poorest wearing their coats like a Napoleonic mantle. Now that the old couple was gone they had a clear view.

First they stare at the shoes. Shoes are status symbols, like cars in America. And then the eyes slide slowly up. In this way they sniffed me all over, their mouths childishly open, the eyes sliding, never a full look, just that drooling stare with no end so that everything stays as meaningless as in the beginning.

I clapped my hands for a coffee and when it had hissed out of the machine the *patrone* did not bring it but one of the three men brought it over. He put the cup down on my table and then he kept standing there, staring.

This is nothing unusual. You come up for a closer look.

I got irritated and waved my hand at him. He stepped away immediately, but, I noticed, as though he thought he had been interfering with my view of his friends. In a moment he came to my table and sat. That too happens.

"*Ciao,*" he said, very familiarly. "You're a sailor?"

I said, "Yes."

"From Messina? I've been to Messina several times."

"I'm glad."

The unusual thing was that he had started to talk, because that is not part of the habit. Next, he broke himself off a piece of my bread.

He had reddish hair which was as coarse and as dry as a pig's.

He had a muscular face and a muscular neck. His fingers were as short as if one joint each was missing. For the rest he had the short, cramped build which puts me in mind of some chronic malnutrition. I reached over and took the bread out of his hand.

"The next time you want some of my bread, ask me. Then I'll give you some."

He had a mouthful and stared at me. The mouth, of course, was open. I could see what was happening to the bread. Suddenly he swallowed and then he laughed. He turned around to his friends and said something quick and slurred in Sicilian which I did not get. Then his friends answered and they laughed too. After that he turned back to me.

"How come you're here," he asked. "A sailor."

"I'm laid up a few days in Messina so I'm taking a ride through the country side."

"Oh yes," he said. "On the Vespa. You got a nice Vespa."

There was nothing to answer, so I didn't. And how in hell had he known I had come in a Vespa? He couldn't see it from here, in the dark square, he could not hear it from here, because of the wind. And I hadn't gunned the motor once.

He grinned into my face, raised his hand, snapped his finger.

His two friends came over and one carried a half liter of wine. The one with the pig hair took the bottle, yanked the cork out and waited. The other two sat down and one of them gave me a clean glass. The bottle, I noticed, was a fresh one. Then my host poured me first.

"*Benedicide,*" he said with a bow and then none of them drank until I did.

This word he had used is a Sicilian expression and it means something like "wishing that you would bless me." You say this when passing a padre. If you say it to anyone else then the word is an insult.

But I was a foreigner who spoke only broken Italian—

I drank some wine. It was red, *corriente,* and very good.

A blast of air hit the back of my neck and then the door banged shut. The heart of town, I thought, like the other time—

A number of people walked in, rubbing their hands, scraping chairs, saying this and that, which—in Sicilian—sometimes sounds like gurgling. One of them was a policeman, *the* policeman perhaps, wearing grey. They have a great number of police uniforms and I don't know one from the other. Sometimes you forget that this is now a democracy.

This policeman was unusual because he was six feet tall. He had a thin face, a hooked nose, and his long teeth seemed to hook too. I could tell because he was smiling. He slapped one of my table mates on the back and went to the rear to get his espresso.

He'll be over next, I thought, to find out who I am, how long I was staying, and where I would go next. This is not just a brief question and answer thing but involves lengthy paper work which they pile up for no reason at all except that they have been doing it for such a long time. But when he got his cup of coffee he turned away from the room and chatted with the *patrone*.

Again I got the cold blast of air in the back of my neck and at the same time two of my table mates jumped out of their chairs. One, in fact, left. The man who now came to the table nodded at me, rubbed his hands, and sat down. He asked the pig-haired one something or other and the answer was yes.

The question turned out to be a request for some of the wine on the table because now he got a glass and then some of the wine. He sniffed it, smiled, and took a few little sips.

This man reminded me of a shy mouse, with hands like a mouse, soft and awkward. He had a big shock of black hair and a small crumpled face. I thought I might know him, but then he did not recognize me.

I sat at the table and felt like a lump. Cheese gone, bread gone, and the sausage too salty. If I wanted anything at all out of this visit besides the discomfort and boredom of something resembling a deathwatch, then talk to the man. I took out my cigarettes and offered them around.

"How big is this town?" I said. "I couldn't tell in the dark."

"This is Forza d'Aguil," said the pig-haired one. I had not been looking at him and wanted to talk to the older man who looked like a mouse.

"It's not very large," he said. "So small, we will have to die out to be able to live here."

If he had been a big man the remark might have come out sullen, but he was a small man, and it sounded sad. Then, because of the strangeness of his answer, I remembered him. He ran the hotel across the square where we had been billeted. I remembered how he could puzzle with double meanings, how he could pull at your insides with his small resignations, and his room. The window sill was piled high with books because he never opened the window or the shutters outside. The permanent lamplight spread colored gloom through the glass facets of the shade and threw a bright yellow circle of light where the lamp stood on the table.

Vinciguerra was his name. I remember it because it is such a big name for such a small man. The winner of war.

"Are you visiting long?" he asked me.

"No. Nothing like it. I'm just coming through."

"I only ask," he said, "because I run the hotel."

"I'm just coming through," I repeated. "I've got to leave tonight."

"Ah, just exploring then," and he looked sad. "Exploring in the dark."

"Something like that. Would you like a cup of coffee?"

"Yes, thank you."

"The fact is," I told him, "I don't know anybody here. But I ran into some-one in Messina—I'm laid up in Messina for a few days—and he is from Forza d'Aguil originally and suggested I might take a look at the place."

"Yes," he said and leaned back. Vinciguerra could say yes in the most meaningless way. "Someone from here in Messina," he said. "That is pos-sible." The policeman came and put Vinciguerra's coffee in front of him. "Sometimes we move out instead of dying out." The policeman went back to the espresso machine and Vinciguerra coughed a small cough into his hand. "We are everywhere."

I looked at him and how crumpled he looked in the face—like newspa-per crumpled up—Christ, how everybody gets old here, with an intensity as if age were the true glory of life. And that's my clue, I'm going to cut out of here.

All the uselessness of a revisit hit me then, a thing dry and impartial like a walk through a museum, something sick and hopeless like embalming a corpse— Get out, get out now. I felt terribly anxious.

"Of course," said Vinciguerra, "daytime is not as cold as it is now. And you might like the view."

"You may be right. But I have to get back."

He shrugged while I picked up my cigarettes, and he thanked me while I paid for the wine and the coffee.

I had almost forgotten the redhaired one but he got up too now and left without a word. I got the blast of cold air in the back of my neck again and then the door slammed shut.

"Who was he?" I asked Vinciguerra.

"I think," Vinciguerra folded his hands, "you offended Pino."

"Sure." I buttoned up my peajacket. "He sits at my table uninvited, he eats my bread uninvited and therefore I offended him."

Vinciguerra ignored it. He watched his little mousehands go gently up and down with his breathing where they lay on his stomach. "Did Pino, by chance, bring the bottle of wine to the table?"

"Yes."

"Then you offended him by paying just now for what was meant as a gift."

I gaped for a moment.

"Then why in hell didn't he open his mouth and tell me about it?"

"That's not the custom," said Vinciguerra.

He looked at me this time—he mostly talked with his head sadly down—and I got the feeling that Vinciguerra felt sorry. Not about my being too stupid to know all the customs, but how strange to see, I read in his face, that you are not resigned to all the customs there are.

I said, "Tough luck," in English and then I walked out.

I stood in the empty square for a moment, empty of people, and now empty of ghosts. It was good that I had come back and had learned that there is an end to things, and it was good that I was leaving. Rosanna the ghost was gone out of me now, though my mistake with Rosanna was real. I would continue to bear that.

I slapped myself because it was cold and also because the jar would bring me back to the present. I got on the Vespa and kicked the starter and the thing wouldn't go.

I found what the trouble was in a while even though I'm not a mechanic. I stayed in town that night. I felt this was bad luck all around, even though I'm not superstitious.

Chapter 5

When I walked back into the *osteria* and told Vinciguerra that I wanted a room he got up immediately and nodded his head.

"Of course, *signore*. A wise afterthought."

"Nothing of the kind. I'm out of gas."

We walked across the square, leaning into the wind, but before we got to the hotel Vinciguerra stopped.

"I can show you where the pump is," he said, "if you really must...."

"I've been there. The pump is locked and the house is dark and then the cop came by, because of my pounding. He said the owner was out of town, till about ten in the morning."

"Yes, that's happened before," said Vinciguerra. He sounded gloomy.

"So that's that."

"Perhaps someone who owns a Vespa or Lambretta will sell you a can of gas."

"The cop thought of that too. He took me to three houses but nobody had a can of gas. No. One of them did. There was one cupful in the can."

"*Dunque,*" said Vinciguerra. "At least you will sleep well tonight. It is quiet here," and he held the door for me to walk into the downstairs of the hotel. "The wind dies," he said like an afterthought, "about one hour from now. Always."

Fixed and certain like a custom, I thought. Always.

I let him lead the way even though I remembered the layout very well. First there was the tiny hall which seemed all filled with the very steep staircase. There is one door, with glass panel, to the left. It leads to the restaurant. In contrast to the *osteria* you cannot bring your own food there but you can order different things. The shut door to the right leads to Vinciguerra's room.

On the first landing stands a pot out of which a small tree is rising. The tree is brown paper maché for the stem, green crepe paper for all the leaves. From there a corridor runs right and left, full of little doors to the rooms which are like cells in a row. One of these doors led to the toilet.

"I will call the girl," said Vinciguerra and he left me standing there by the tree while he went to the top floor.

The top floor, I remembered, had a corridor going to one side only and one of the rooms was a closet really, without window and a ceiling which had a sharp slant. This was for the maid. She had been a hag then and I could imagine how worn she would look now. But when Vinciguerra came back with the maid she turned out to be somebody new, someone young, and the other one was probably dead by now. I stood there and felt I was spanning two ages, and none too welcome in either of them.

"*Con riscaldamento,*" I told Vinciguerra. I felt cold and wanted a room with stove.

Vinciguerra looked at me for the second time since I had seen him, then he just nodded and passed. Next came the maid, then I.

Her hair was very thick, not entirely black. But it shone and would be fine to the touch. It stood up on one side where she must have been sleeping on it. She hardly opened her eyes which would be black, I imagined, and they would be round. But as I have said, she seemed almost fully asleep, like some animal of hibernation which makes a minimum move because it is forced to do so. This sleep-relaxed face looked younger than she could possibly be because she seemed fully grown. She wore a big flannel robe, a man's flannel robe which was like a sack on her, so I could see nothing of her figure. But she had that walk. A child doesn't walk like that.

She took linens from a closet, blankets and a towel. This she sleepwalked to a room where Vinciguerra snapped on the light.

"Where's the stove? *Il riscaldamento?*" I asked. "I just asked you for one."

He turned away and said, "Later." Then he left.

I sat down on the chair in the room and watched the girl make the bed. There was nothing else to look at. Just the girl, the bed, the window—shuttered, of course. The wind whistled badly between shutters and windowpane.

I said, "Goddamn that wind," and she looked up from the bed and said, "*Cosa?*"

The English, or my voice, must have startled her because her eyes were really open now, big and black. Her mouth held unusually still.

"The wind," I told her. "Maybe I'll open the shutter and it won't whistle so."

"Oh no," she said. "Leave them shut." It was another custom. "It will stop in an hour or so," she went on. "It always does." Then she turned around again to finish making the bed.

She had a fine, round rump. It was all I could see, what with the robe she was wearing, but it was just a passing thought, with no intention of staying.

When she left I closed the door after her and found that there was no lock. I was too discouraged to get suspicious about that, got undressed and put my money and papers under the pillow. I turned off the light and was just pulling the covers up when the light went on again.

I had no idea who she was but she made clear without any delay why she had come. She closed the door and unbuttoned the front of her dress. Two enormous breasts flung themselves out and down all of their own volition. She kept unbuttoning. Her being here did not make any sense to me and I didn't want her.

"Go away," I said. "I want to sleep."

"Why?" she said. "What happened?"

"Nothing happened! Out, please!"

"Oh!" she said and raised two heavy eyebrows. "But then, perhaps I can help you," and started to shake the dress off her shoulders.

"No! I need sleep, that's all. I know about these things."

"You mean it?"

"Yes. Out!"

She frowned and then she snorted though her nose. *"Poverino,"* she said, with disgust and pity about equally mixed.

She stuffed herself back into the dress, buttoned up, and left without another word.

"Turn off the light!"

She didn't even close the door.

I was now properly mad and decided to smoke for a while when Vinciguerra came in.

"I don't want you either, I want my stove," I told him. I was still cold as well as angry and suspicious though I could not account for the last of these.

But then it turned out very simple.

"Obviously," said Vinciguerra, "there has been a misunderstanding," and then he explained it.

You walk into a hotel and ask for a room *con riscaldamento,* that means you want heat in your place. But in Sicily, depending upon the hotel, the phrase also means that you want a woman sent up to you.

I didn't laugh, I didn't thank him, I just said okay and would he please turn off the light.

After he had gone I lay there in bed wide awake, way past the time when the wind had stopped. It was very quiet now and black as pitch in the room because of the shutters. I also heard no sounds through the walls. Perhaps, besides myself there was only the maid in the hotel and Vinciguerra. And why had Vinciguerra assumed that a passing stranger would know enough of the local vernacular to understand that double talk about a stove in a hotel room? Perhaps he mistook my request for a stove because there were no stoves in his hotel and so, naturally, I must have meant the other. But then, why would he assume I would know that there are no stoves in his rooms? Unless he had recognized me! But if he had recognized me why hadn't he said, *"Ola, Yanchi,* you are the G.I. who ran the radio shack over the cemetery."

I was woolgathering and that put me to sleep.

* * *

I had breakfast in the restaurant in the morning, a big glass of sweet *café latte*, a long bun to dip into the coffee, and a marvelous rat cheese called *fontina*. After that, still feeling empty, I had black espresso and a dish of blue figs. The young maid was waiting tables.

At first I did not recognize her because now the heavy housecoat was gone and she no longer looked sleepy. She looked wide awake. Same mouth, same eyes, all wide awake. Her hair didn't stand up on one side anymore but was combed down all around (except for an open forehead) so that it gave a live bounce when she walked. She was quite young but had that well-jointed walk I had noticed before, using all of her body. She had a fine, ready looking body. She carried her head well, face composed. I mean by composed that there was a still expression. It just seemed to rest there, but it might well go into any direction. I had to imagine all this (she stayed composed) but a laugh, fright, sullenness, curiosity, any of those would have looked right on her face.

"Woke up, finally, huh?"

At first she just looked, and then, "Oh yes. I always do." Then she laughed and I was right. The laugh looked wonderful on her.

"Sorry you had to get up," I said.

The smile dropped out of sight as if it had never been. Now something showed between sullen and anger. But that went very quickly. She put down a knife for my cheese and a napkin under it.

"What was that just now?" I asked.

"*Mu*—" she said.

As I said, that is the verbal equivalent of a shrug in Sicilian, and when this girl did it she dismissed everything within sight.

"You don't like Vinciguerra," I guessed.

Her face stayed indifferent when she said, "He didn't have to get me out of bed to fix a room. There was a room all ready."

"For me?"

"Why you? Just ready."

"So why did he get you out of bed?"

"He always does, when he can. It's his way."

Then she left the table and went back into the kitchen.

I ate my breakfast and after that smoked a cigarette and looked at the long room with the three windows looking out at the square. Then I started to think.

I thought about Pino, the kid with the hair like a pig, and I thought about Vinciguerra, the quiet hotel keeper who was a little bit sad. I even thought about the policeman and how helpful he had been.

And he had never asked me to register my arrival. But that made sense. They give you twenty four hours and I had been in Forza d'Aguil less than twelve.

But now the second item. I had stayed in a hotel all night and nobody had asked for my passport.

It was plausible that Vinciguerra would look at my passport this morning, when I checked out. Vinciguerra read books in the main and ran the hotel on the side.

And the queer thing which the maid had mentioned, that a room had been ready while Vinciguerra had woken her up to fix me the other room. Though I couldn't make any intrigue out of that because nothing had happened to me in that room without a lock. Plausibly, her own explanation was the one that applied, some private thing in the night between the hotelkeep and his little maid.

That left the matter of Pino. I had offended him and his answer had been a stupid schoolboy trick. On one hand I could have sworn there was enough gas in the Vespa to take me from Messina to Forza d'Aguil and back. But then, perhaps not. When I had checked the Vespa the night before there had been no gasoline smell around the machine, which meant the tank had not been drained on the ground. Though that did not really mean the tank had not been drained. The tank spigot on the Vespa is easily accessible and you can hold a small can under it and in turn empty the small can into a larger one until the tank had run dry. A few drops spilled would leave no trace of an odor with the kind of wind that had been blowing across the square.

But that didn't explain enough, as I came to think of it—

The girl brought me my espresso and the figs at this point.

I smiled at her and she gave me a little nod for an answer, no more.

"What's your name?" I asked her.

"Sophia."

"Nice name. Where were you born, Sophia, here?"

"No. I'm from Rome," she said with a touch of pride. This is customary with Romans.

"What a place to come to, after Rome."

She just shrugged.

"What I meant was," I said, "have you been here long enough to know everybody in town?"

"Oh yes. The town isn't large."

"Yes. Well, I was looking for an acquaintance last night. I don't mean an acquaintance, I mean a friend in Messina told me to look this man up, if I came to Forza d'Aguil."

I bent down and sniffed at my figs while she stood by the table, waiting.

I looked up and said, "And I forgot his name."

"*Dunque,*" she said and sighed at the ceiling, "then you can't very well look him up."

When she looked down again I could tell by her face that she thought this had all ended up very funny. Suddenly we both burst out laughing.

If this were not Forza d'Aguil, I thought, I could like this little one very much.

Then I said, "I don't know how many gas pumps there are here but this man runs a gas pump."

"Oh that one. There is just one gas pump and Salone has it."

"Of course! Salone was the name!"

"Just two turns down the street, that one," and she waved her arm just past my face. Then she straightened up again. "I think your espresso is cold."

I was beginning to wonder whether I was talking to her because I had a topic or because I liked talking to her. The way she had waved her arm had been impulsive and very graceful, and when she worried about my coffee getting cold she had not sounded like a waitress. Unaccountably, both these things made me feel happy.

I nodded, cleared my throat, and got back to the topic.

"Well, then. I'll try again today."

"What?" She cocked her head like a child.

"I'll try again today. I missed him last night but he should be back today."

"Back from where?"

"He was out of town."

"You have the wrong name," she said. "Salone was here last night, playing taro. Then he left the game and went home to sleep. His wife came to get him."

"Is that so," I said and slowly tore a fig open, from the stem to the fat belly. "Perhaps I have the right name but the wrong town."

"Yes," she said. "You could have the wrong town."

Then I started to eat and she left.

Of course there had been something wrong with thinking of Pino playing little schoolboy tricks. Pino and his shattered honor. These Sicilians take themselves very seriously and to drain the gas would simply not have been enough. It fit much better now to find out that he had gone into some detail to pay me back for an insult. The point of his action was as stupid as ever, but his method was not.

One more question and that might round it out fine. I pushed my plate away and clapped for the girl to come back. While she gathered things up I said, "You know this Pino? I met this Pino last night."

"There are many Pinos in this town. A common name."

"Oh," I said and watched the bare inside of her arm while she brushed off the table cloth. "Do they all have reddish hair?"

"Three of the Pinos have reddish hair."

"His reddish hair is coarse like on a pig."

She looked at me and then she suddenly laughed out loud again, except this time with much more amusement.

"Oh yes! Ha, I never thought of his hair in that way, oh yes, I know him."

"You know him."

"Yes."

And then I said without a change, "Is he *mafioso*?"

"Oh sure," she said.

Well. She wasn't half as excited about her answer as I had been about my question. She kept brushing the table and said, "So are four of the other Pinos."

Then she left, not because she was trying to avoid the topic but because I wasn't asking any more stupid questions.

Nevertheless, what I knew now explained why there had not been any gas for me in the whole town. This was Mafia in the dry heartland where it had been born. It commanded, and all fell in step, even more so than its spawn in the big cities Stateside. And who took me around, just for show, after telling me that the man with the gas was out of town? The Law, the hook-toothed cop with the smile. I sat at the table and disliked the cop more than the punk with hair like a red pig.

And all this elaborate conniving just to annoy me? To delay me!

It had to be that. An insulted Sicilian who is also a *mafioso* would do infinitely more than harass his enemy by draining his gas tank and then prevent him from filling it up again. Especially when his enemy was cooped up in the walls of a fortress like this.

I left a tip on the table for Sophia and walked out of the room. I went across to Vinciguerra's door where I knocked because I wanted to pay my bill. I was in a fairly foul mood by then and could only think of leaving this town.

Vinciguerra wasn't there, or at least he didn't answer my knock. This delay I had not expected and for a moment I stood around by his door not knowing what to do. The restaurant door opened in back of me and Sophia stuck her head out.

"He's asleep," she said. "He sleeps a few hours in the morning because he is awake most of the night. It is when he reads."

I felt impatient with that quiet mouse behind the closed door, sleeping his few hours.

"How much was my room, Sophia?"

She told me it was five hundred lire which I gave her with my good bye message for Vinciguerra. "Tell him good bye."

I would have liked to have said more to Sophia but I felt suddenly very awkward with her. She stood there in the dim hall and looked up at me with eyes that seemed all black and very still. But there was really nothing to say to her and I kept my sudden feeling for her on the inside. Sentimentalists always think they are missing something, including when there is nothing to miss. So I quickly nodded at her, smiled, and left through the front door.

Chapter 6

If that Pino pig was planning anything for me it would have to be now. I stepped out into the square where the sun was shining with a hard, still light. My Vespa was still parked near the tree and also a donkey who was looking down at the ground where his halter rope was lying. A woman walked by with a bundle of greens on her head but she didn't look at me. Maybe she didn't know how to turn her head with the bundle on top.

I stood a moment and breathed the dry, sunny air and looked at the houses which all had a certain heaviness in all the light. I found it difficult to feel the weight of last night and all the threats of my nighttime speculations. I looked up at the sky and saw how deep and clear it was. I remembered how deep and clear it had always been, and that's all I'm going to remember about this place, *basta*.

I unlocked the steering column of the Vespa, checked the air in the tires, and then I pushed the machine across the square. When I came to the mouth of the first street leading down I hopped on the saddle and coasted down. It was a cushiony silent ride and best of all I was heading out of town. The street was dank, too narrow for sunshine, but the odor in the air was spicy and sweet. The smell comes from a bush they cut on the hillsides and then the bakers use it in their ovens and all the good smell goes up in smoke.

I kept rolling downhill, through a few turns, over a few shallow steps, and I rolled all the way to the pump. The gas pump was locked, with a padlock on the releasing lever. But the shutters of the house were open and Salone should therefore be home. I knocked, and he came out, chewing bread.

"I'd like to buy some gasoline."

"One moment," he said and went back inside.

And if Pino had more in mind, this would certainly be his last chance. I could see the town gate from where I stood— And perhaps Pino would now jump out of the house, knife in hand, knife in each hand—ridiculous. But the tension did not leave and my right shoulder started to ache. I felt like hitting somebody—

Salone came out of the house, adjusting his black hat on his head. He had it down good and square by the time he got to the pump. He unlocked the pump and started working the manual lever. Down by the gate, on the other side of the square with white tiles, I could hear someone hooting and clucking. Next I could see the herd of goats and then the boy who was driving them. Salone pumped gas.

"Had a good trip yesterday?" I asked him.

"Yes. It was sudden but there was no strain."

"Except for somebody wanting to buy gas."

"That's true," he said and listened for the liquid to come up inside the tank.

"Nice, to be able to take off like that."

"*Mbu—*" he said. He had added the b-sound which adds a to-hell-with-you note to the expression.

I thought to hell with you too, old man, and how I hate stupid school-boy tricks like this one somebody had told Salone to play. And I'll forget you the moment I drive away—

He closed the tank, hung up the hose, and I paid him. I started the motor and thought that this was a sweet sound indeed.

And then I shot down the tiled square to the gate, going fairly fast and with a second gear noise all the way. Pino was too late or Pino had not really cared that much. At any rate, there was nothing he could do now. It really was only a bottle of wine.

Once through the square I had to slow sharply because of the dip going down to the gate. Everything here looked sunshine bare too. Then through the gate and the highway was also empty. I threw a quick glance up the incline to one side of the road where the old goat stable was. It did not seem to have changed. I did not look at it closely.

Going fast down the highway now I did not entirely feel like a fool about my vague fears in that town because Mafia means fear and suspicion and the Sicilians, after all, had not only invented it but had kept it alive. So I rolled away from Forza d'Aguil, down the first grade, through the first curve, and then into the shadow side of the grade. I was happy to be on my way. I knew no more of Rosanna but I was out of that place.

The goats were ahead of me in the next curve and when the boy heard me he started to yell at the goats and to run around waving his stick. The goats milled and bucked and pressed into each other. Then they disappeared in the turn.

I caught up with them sooner than I had expected because the goats and the kid were still right behind the turn.

U.S. fighter pilots stationed in Europe, I suddenly remembered, were forbidden to ride on a scooter. It's a court martial offense on account of the danger. I remembered this suddenly and then I found out for myself.

I don't know what happened to the Vespa that instant. I was alone, flying through the air. Next, there were goats.

The most idiotic animal in a crisis is the goat. From a sense of superiority which comes with the horns, the goat rarely runs away but will stand stock still. Or maybe the boy's yelling confused them or they were following his superior example. He simply screamed and jumped up and down. Now the goats jumped up and down, and I was underneath. There were kicks, butts, and a strong smell of goat. Once a two-pronged hoof kicked a charley horse into my calf and then I got slapped in the face by an udder. It was one of the most stunning experiences I have ever had.

When I got up I saw most of the goats cascading up and down the rock face to the left of the road. I saw two goats butting each other, and one lay on the pavement with a broken leg. None of the animals were making any noise anymore, except for the quick, scrambling ratatat of their hoofs on the rock. But the kid was screaming. He was holding his stick at one end, jumping and screaming, trying to pull it free. I got up, feeling lousy and saw what had happened with the stick.

It had a steel point. This point was dug into the front tire of the Vespa which lay on its side by the retaining wall of the road.

"Stop screaming," I said.

I walked slowly because I hurt all over.

"Stop your goddamn screaming!" I yelled into his ear because otherwise he would not hear me.

He finally stopped. He also got the stick out at that moment, and the tire made an obscene sound and went limp.

I didn't get angry because I was preoccupied with my body aches and felt helpless in the face of idiot goats, idiot kids, idiot me. I decided to change the tire.

The kid just stood by and watched.

I had a spare on the rack in the back, but I couldn't find any tools. There are very few places to hide things on a Vespa. I looked at all of them, but there were no tools.

"Signore," said the boy. "You owe me for the goat."

I sat down on the retaining wall and wiped my face. I found there was something sore there, on my face, and blood came off on my hand. There was a pounding behind my eyes and it was difficult to distinguish his words.

"What was that you said?"

"You owe me for the goat."

I sighed and looked away. Two men were coming up the rise, pushing their bicycles. They walked slowly and it was now very quiet.

"Little man," I said, "get the hell out of my sight."

"You owe me for the goat."

"I'll tear your ears off in a minute, little man, and then I'll owe you for that too." I just wanted quiet and I just wanted tools.

He didn't even step back.

The two men disappeared but unless they were goats too they would show in a short while, coming around the next bend.

"I'll call the police," said the boy, "and you'll have more to pay than if you pay me now."

He was making me mad. Here was this little monster giving me black-mail. I got off the wall and walked towards him feeling big like a bear in my jacket and that's how I was going to give it to him, just slap his ears two or three times, like bear cuffs, even though my hands felt raw.

Then he crouched at me, held up the steel tip of that stick, and his little face turned into a most inhuman mask of emotionless intent. He was just as soon going to run me through.

"Pay me for that goat," he said, hard as hard.

They were going to love him in the Mafia, once he'd get to be fifteen.

I took another step, keeping my knees bent and feeling alive on my feet, which was to ask him to lunge at me. And the little bastard did.

I'm sure he was quicker than I and I felt handicapped by thinking of him as a child, but there was so clearly no hesitation in the way he charged, point low at my abdomen, that I got angry very suddenly, which—in my case—is a help.

First though, he fooled me very well. I swiveled aside and grabbed for the stick that way, but the whole thing was a feint on his part and the tip came up in a swift arc and he just cut me under the jaw.

After that he even stepped back for room and more stick work, but as I mentioned, I was mad and that's good for me.

He didn't finish the upswing with the stick because I grabbed the thing going past my face, and didn't bother to yank. That way, the stick inter-ruption just stopped him from moving, close enough now for a kick in the rear.

He let go of the stick, made his turn, and that's when I let fly. I had never kicked a child before and don't expect I'll ever do it again. I got him in his skinny rear and he just flew.

The two men with the bicycles stood a little ways down the road. They might have been standing there to catch their breath, to rest, to absorb the panorama. Then my archenemy who had skidded into the wall, threw a stone at me. I'd had it.

I caught him by his dirty leg, threw him belly down over the wall, wedged him good, held his neck, and whaled his backside with the stick I was holding until I felt satisfied and fairly tired.

I let go then and he hung on the wall for a while and if he would like to jump off there, straight into the panorama, that was alright with me too. I looked at the stick in my hand and then I threw it over the wall where it disappeared and made a late clatter below.

"Who are you?" said one of the men.

They stood there with the bicycles, just as quietly as the bicycles, and I could hardly tell one of them from the other. They had the stone-still eyes and the deprived kind of monkey face which I have seen in people who are constantly hungry.

I didn't bother to answer them and limped back to my Vespa.

That worm of a monster I had been fighting was over by the goat with the broken leg, kicking the animal so that it might get up.

"We don't like to see that," said one of the men, "somebody beating our children."

I said "Screw yourself," and picked up the Vespa. Something twitched in my back from the pain.

"Maybe you didn't hear," said the other one, and they were closer now. "We raise our children the way we like to raise our children and we don't like...."

"Look, John Dewey, he went after me with that lance."

"We know. We saw you trying to kill his goats."

"*Minquia*," I said, which is something unmentionable in Sicilian.

The goat was up and the kid kept kicking it so that the goat would limp where the master wanted it to limp. The goat was making no sound but his child-fuehrer was cursing the foulest there was.

Then I said, "How in hell do you know what happened."

"We saw everything."

"How?" And now I was back to last night again, black night with black touch of wind on me, something howling through an empty square, whistling through a shutter because it will not be kept out, this wind is the touch of suspicion and—like wind—cannot be touched back, can't be grasped, and there is so little to see in the black vagueness, that there is so much more to fear. "Do you know Pino?" I asked, knowing they would not answer.

I walked back to Forza d'Aguil pushing the Vespa ahead of me and with the stares of the two Sicilians riding my back. Except for the flat, the scooter rolled easily enough, but the grade was so steep and I felt so sore from the fall I had taken and from the stomping by the goats while I had been down, the walk back took me close to an hour, with rests. Every time I stopped, the two men behind me stopped. They always kept behind and they always looked at me, and if I had walked straight up the side of the cliff, they too would have walked straight up the side of the cliff.

I had ugly and depressing thoughts and most of the time I was fighting for breath.

By now I was so convinced of Pino's part in all this that I kept looking for him. I never saw him but he was everywhere. He was behind the stares that kept pushing me up the road, behind the corner of every street, and he had put the hawkers on the square, to look innocent.

I stopped in front of the hotel and Vinciguerra came out. He watched me hike the Vespa up on its stand and looked across at the two men on the bicycles. They stood by the tree in the square, watching. When I turned back to Vinciguerra, he was shaking his head at the flat front tire, but said nothing.

"Where's the repair place in this town?" I asked him.

"I'll get a boy to fetch the machine," he said. "You look bad."

"No thank you," I said. "No more boys."

He shrugged and then he came down the steps.

"I'll take you," he said. "It's a few minutes from here, but the way is complicated."

Then he offered to push the machine for me and I let him. I felt beat and preoccupied but the preoccupation was vague. What to think about, what was there to grasp—

Vinciguerra, a small man, was sweating. I put my hands out for the handlebars but he closed his eyes and just shook his head. Rather a strange gesture. We walked in silence while I pushed on the saddle. I heard his breathing and he must have heard mine. In a weak way I began to love Vinciguerra. He had been the only one in this town to show me any human consideration whatsoever and one unkind word from him now and I would have felt shaken. I felt weak and depressed and my head still ached but worst of all there were again the suspicions. No, that is too specific since I did not know what to suspect. The feeling, plain and simple, was dread.

Like Forza d'Aguil, where dread built the wall, squeezed the houses together, twisted the streets—

The repair place was in a dark alley. There were Vespas inside the shop and a lot of bicycles. There were also cartwheels leaning, long spoked and wooden. The carts have not changed in design for several centuries except that they now have rubber strips from old tires nailed to the circumference of the wheel.

The shop was like a deep cave and the man there was dirty and old. But he had white hair, pure white hair, and a soft old voice when he talked. I felt relieved to have found someone else whom I would not have to suspect.

Vinciguerra did the talking for me. The tire would be repaired in something less than an hour.

I walked back with Vinciguerra to sit in his restaurant, in the hotel. I asked for a small pot of camomile tea which is a gold colored, harmless brew made of flowers. Vinciguerra went to the kitchen to order it for me.

In a while the girl Sophia came out. She stopped halfway to my table and looked at me. She raised her hands in front of her and held one in the other. For one brief moment it looked like a gesture of supplication, or a gesture of wishing for something. Then she let go again and came to the table.

"You," she said. "You look bad. Is it bad?"

"I have fallen amongst goats," I said but she looked at me with a frown because my Italian phrasing must have made no sense at all. I cleared my throat and said, "And now I'll have tea."

"Tea?"

"Yes, *camomila.*"

"But look here," she said, "you need something for that scrape down your nose, and the cut under the chin."

"Please, please," I said and felt an entirely foreign smile on my face. It was to guide me and guard me because even more so than with Vinciguerra a while ago I was again melting inside, loving her look and the wish in her look. I actually wanted more of Forza d'Aguil in me, the cold strength of it.

She went back to the kitchen and I smoked a cigarette. My hands were filthy and swollen on the inside where I had scraped. When Sophia came with the tea I was calm. My thinking was pointed again. I thought of my actions with the boy through a great distance. Then I thought of my escort back to this place.

"Have you seen Pino?" I asked her.

"Pino? Ah, the one with the hair. No."

She put the cup and the pot down and the steam that arose from the flat snout smelled like meadows. Then she went to the bureau where the oil and the vinegar bottles stood, the parmesan jars, salt and pepper, oregano dish, and the sugar. She came back with the sugar.

"But I heard," she said, "that he left on his Vespa. Last night. One spoon?"

"Please."

"*Prego.* His mother sells greens and she told me this morning when I bought the greens for the kitchen."

"Thank you, Sophia."

The bright sun from the windows that looked on the square shone on her bare arms and made a line of light along a smooth curve, through the almost invisible down on her skin. Her hands were folded on her belly and moved slowly with her breathing. Sophia did not breathe with her chest, but, like babies and animals, with her belly.

"I would like to bring you...."

"No," and I shook my head without looking up at her. When I did not say anything else she left.

Chapter 7

After the tea I looked at my watch and thought, alright, I give the old man with the wheels another twenty minutes. At this point Vinciguerra walked in.

"Please," he said, "I would like you to come to my room." He walked out to the tiny hall and across to his room. There he left the door open.

I watched him go there and wondered if his room still looked the same as it had all those years ago. It seemed an unnecessary thought and certainly most unimportant in view of my experiences here since arrival but I thought it anyway, got up, and went across. On the way I thought more important thoughts, such as, yes, the goats had been an accident, and yes, Pino, after all, is out of town. Nothing there. Except, this was Forza d'Aguil around me and a lot of it now inside me too. I shrugged and walked into his room.

There seemed to be no change at all. The shutters were closed and the sill of the window was piled high with books. On the round table stood the lamp which gave a dim, glassy light through the top of red and blue pieces of cut crystal and it gave a round lake of yellow light which lay on the table. I stepped from the cool daytime light into Vinciguerra's dark yellow evening where he sat, looking patient, next to the table.

"First of all," he said, "I will wash your hands."

"What did you say?" I shut the door and came closer.

"You are injured," he said. "Please let me help you."

He got up from the upholstered chair and his hands waved small begging gestures. When I went to the chair his little mouse hands touched each other as if in great peace, waiting.

There were more things on the table, besides the lamp. There were cotton fluffs, very white bandages, and little bottles of things standing in line like a whole row of helpful dwarves waiting for wishes. Right in front of me was a porcelain bowl full of warm water. I could smell the warmth.

"Perhaps you should first take off your jacket. It needs dusting and you might be more comfortable."

In this room and with his soft little voice Vinciguerra could have charmed snakes or mesmerized rabbits. He could have convinced me that he was not acting from kindness at all but from harsh, selfish need, such as, please, allow me a pleasure I have found, I find it so rarely, which is to wash hands and heal wounds.

I thought goddamn it this place is getting me. I should simply have said yes to Sophia to do a neat, quick bandaging job. But now I could not say no to Vinciguerra. It would have been like taunting a dying man, like stealing his bed, for example, and telling him that his death would only release him into discomfort.

I took off my peajacket, let him wash my hands, and make soft daubs and little annointings.

He was incredibly gentle. I sat there and felt that I suddenly knew why he had this room. It was not in Forza d'Aguil at all. It's a soft hole of shadow inside the hard light in the square, inside the stone of this town, but it's not Forza d'Aguil. And if I lived here for any length of time I would visit here often, I might even build—

I cut that thinking out right then and there and in a matter of minutes my machine would be fixed. Good bye crazy indoor thoughts. The pounding in my head seemed to slow.

"There," he said. He stepped back and sighed and his hands were holding each other again.

"You did a beautiful job, Vinciguerra. Really. Thank you."

I had a bandaid under my chin and light bandages on my hands, all soft inside with creams. I felt clean and cared for.

"How did you know my name?" he said.

I had to sit still for a moment, nothing more. He must have thought I was trying to remember who had told me his name because he himself had in fact never mentioned it. But I sat like that to let the suspicion die down first, this thing that had jumped on my back as soon as he had asked the question. Why again? Just because in his room I had forgotten where I really was, just because I knew his name from a time which was dead and unmentioned, just because of my thin little nerves in my heavy body.

"Your maid told me," I said. "And her name, I think, is Sophia."

"Of course," he said. He took the bowl of water away. "Yes. Her name is Sophia."

"I'd like to go now. I think the old man is done with the tire."

Vinciguerra looked at a clock which ticked in the shadow somewhere.

"Give him another fifteen minutes or so. I know how he works." He took the small bottles and things and put them into a wooden cabinet which hung on the wall. The little door had deep carving on it, faintly painted, gold and blue. It looked very old.

"I can offer you some cognac. A glass may help you, please?"

I told him yes, I'd have a glass, because without further sentimentalizing I now wanted to know why he kept me here. Let him talk and I'll get my bearings. I'll forget about the dear little mouse hands touching me with their attentions, I'll forget the room like a nest and my own maudlin sentiments. In a way it would be like losing a friend, saying yes to Vinciguerra's tactical cognac but it was best to get used to that.

"You remember Pino?" I said when he came with the glass and the bottle. "The one at my table in the *osteria* that night."

"You mean last night. Yes."

It had really seemed like more than last night. I watched him pour.

"Yes, that one. Is he around?"

"I don't know. I don't think so. He did not have coffee at the *osteria* this morning."

He gave me the glass of brandy. It was a heavily cut glass, the size for wine. The rim had a gold line painted around it.

"Where's yours?" I said.

"I don't drink. But I would enjoy watching you enjoy it."

I will now think he is a poisoner. Mathew Matheson, you are going nuts. I drank from the glass.

"Sometimes I would like to go to New York," said Vinciguerra.

"You're nuts!" I was that surprised.

"I have read about the magnificent library there."

The cognac was French, and very dry. It had that taste which reminds me of dust.

Then I said, "You mean leave here, your home town, your friends, and your—uh, nice room?"

He looked at his little hands and then at the room.

"What you say doesn't make too much sense in my case," he said, "though it's true that I would rather not leave." He put his head to one side and when he looked at me he gave a most hesitant smile, a pure sight of shyness. "What I would really like—you understand I am talking a fantasy now—I would like to be able to stay here in the room and dream of the library and know it in full detail."

"Oh," I said.

"That would be almost ideal, don't you see?"

I nodded, not knowing what else to do.

"Of course a dream of books is in a sense twice removed, since it is a fantasy about fantasies, and on the other hand I quite frequently like nothing better than to talk to somebody real. To sit across from each other and talk. A quite different touch is involved." His fingertips played with each other.

"There is," I said.

"Oh yes. Even this," and he waved his hand, "the little we allow ourselves to say to each other, even this I have not had in years."

"Since when?"

"No matter. So then the next best thing might be a dream about a conversation. However, such a fantasy is so close to reality—one of the conversants being actually present—that the lack of reality is that much more painful."

I drank, I nodded, I followed everything he said.

"So I remove things further, you see, and dream of reading. And then a bit further, about reading a book that is not even here." He shrugged. "And so on." Then he got up.

He had me again. I could not feel familiar with him but something reached out from him and silently spun me into a web.

"Perhaps we best go now," he said. He had been standing there, waiting.

"And now another hundred years," I said, "before you find the next conversation?"

"It does feel like that, yes."

We went outside and it felt like good bye, a dream of good bye. I shook my head.

There were now just two bicycles in the square and beyond these the men. There were the two who had followed me back into town after the accident and when they saw me they stopped talking. The others stopped talking too.

Now their stares were not the way I have described them before. They were not like a tongue licking you or a hand snatching, but these stares were full of something which jumped at you. There was dislike. It could be hate.

"Am I glad to be getting out of here," I said to Vinciguerra. "You have no idea." It felt dangerous to think of Rosanna.

"But I do."

I saw that he had been looking across the square, at the men.

We turned up the alley which was the street of the repair man, and a woman passing and two girls passing had also the look in their eyes which had jumped at me from across the square. I put my hands in my pocket and felt like a fool and then I hunched my shoulders, and felt like a coward. We walked into the repairman's cave and there was my Vespa lying on its side and the wheel wasn't there anymore.

"He is slow," said Vinciguerra.

I then saw the old man in the gloom, huddled over the wheel. He was just stuffing the tube back into the tire. He apologized.

He is slow and I am nervous and never in my life have I felt quite this way, a rheumy old man with slow hands throwing me into a tizzy. Vinciguerra and I stepped outside again and waited in the alley.

"You are not well?" said Vinciguerra.

"I got the Mafia chills," I said.

"You get used to them," said Vinciguerra.

So I paced back and forth and said nothing else. The old man with the white shock of hair like a lamp in that cave, he was crawling across to the Vespa and putting the wheel in place.

"That Pino is a mafioso, isn't he?"

"Many people here are."

"Are you?"

"If I were I would lie to you and if I am not I might say the same thing and you end up still not knowing anything."

"That's true." I checked the old man inside and saw him working to get the wheel back on the axle. "That's true and it must be a very, very lovely way to live."

"You have no idea," he said, "what kind of way it is."

I ran back into the shop and the old man was still struggling there. Back on the street, Vinciguerra was lighting a cigarette.

"You didn't say anything," he said when I came back. "After my remark."

"I know you like conversation," I said, "but I'm nervous. Would you ask the old man about that wheel? I don't speak Sicilian."

Vinciguerra shrugged and went to the door and talked and the old man talked.

"He says it won't be but a minute. He doesn't understand it but it will be just a minute, he thinks."

"That's double talk even in Italian," I said and then I lit a cigarette too.

In the shop the old man was standing straddle-legged over the Vespa on the ground, as if he had just fought her down, pinned her to the floor, and would next do something terrible to her.

"Alright," I said, "alright, alright, alright."

He looked up and seemed to be panting from effort, wishing to understand what I wanted.

"Come on, move over and let me," and I nodded at the old man to step aside.

There was a stream of fast words at me while Vinciguerra came and while the old man wouldn't move over for me to get at the wheel.

"He says—" Vinciguerra started, but I cut him short.

"Tell him to move over," I said. "I'll do it myself."

"He knows how to do the job," said Vinciguerra. "If you give him time he'll put the wheel back on and you won't be offending him by doing...."

"You think I give a good goddamn who else gets offended around here just because I'm trying to get out?"

I was loud and irritated and I moved in front of the old man. He was talking rapidly most of this time.

"Like this whole lousy town's been sitting up here on the rock like some spider, just waiting for somebody to walk in and get caught," (I was working the wheel on the axle all this time) "and when that doesn't come off spider-quick, they all call it a blow to their honor and I should apologize!"

I was working myself into a sweat and into a rage because it was sticking and then I had the wheel down on the axle, though not all the way. I straightened up for a moment and took a deep breath.

"He says—" Vinciguerra started and I cut him off again,

"I know. He's offended. And tomorrow, crack of dawn, we'll have it out with bicycle chains at 2 paces."

"He got it down that far himself," said Vinciguerra.

"Hurray." I kicked at the wheel to make it spin.

"He's worried of hurting the axle if he...."

"Just a minute. Just hold it," I said and looked down at the wheel spinning. I made a sound.

I stopped the wheel and then hefted my weight on top of the wheel, making it slip all the way over the axle, the way it should be seated. Then I kicked it again. It turned so far and then wouldn't spin. The old man was explaining something.

"What's he say?"

"He's been saying the same thing for some time. When you had your fall," said Vinciguerra, "you must have bent the axle."

I kicked at the wheel again but it jammed, because the axle was bent.

I straightened up very slowly, I don't know why slowly, perhaps because I had no idea what to do next, or I did know what next but was afraid. I stood up slowly and found the old man standing close enough to grab and yanked him my way so that the suddenness of the jerk snapped his head back. I saw that but didn't care.

"Say that again about the axle," I said into his face. "Say that again, old spider."

"When you had the accident," he started, his Italian understandable enough, but then I snapped him up closer again, with a sharp pull on his arm. I held him still like that and felt both mean and afraid.

"Vinciguerra," I said. "Come around where I can see you."

Vinciguerra stepped closer, his eyes worried, his face small and upset.

"You pushed that Vespa before," I said to him. "Was the wheel jammed?"

"I didn't notice."

"Louder, Vinciguerra, so Old Bones here can hear you."

"The wheel wasn't jammed then," said Vinciguerra. "You are right. The axle was not bent before."

I let go of the old man with a small push. I pushed him away so that he and I faced each other now, and while I felt as if I were swelling up more and more, the old man looked as if he were shrinking, drying out, as if on the point of collapse, termites inside, and one tap, one small tap now, and the whole thing collapses into a dry heap of dust.

"Who bent that axle? Who hammered that axle out of line right here in your shop?"

He said something but I didn't care what it was and Vinciguerra didn't bother to translate it for me. I put my hand out slowly, the left hand. I'm right handed and so held him with my left, to be more punishing with the free one.

"Who?" I hauled back slowly, very slowly, and could hear the crack on his jaw already, or the jaw cracking, and enjoying the grunt of breath I'd push out with that blow, and how angry I felt.

"Who?" I suddenly screamed at him and felt myself tremble.

"What good will it do you?" said Vinciguerra.

He said this so quietly, with so much resignation, there was so much of it that, like a silent poison in the air, it was all around me and inside me. Yes, what good would it do, what was there to beating an old man, after beating a small boy. I'm now going a little bit out of my mind, boy beater, grandfather beater, afraid of empty doorways but a bull and a lion when beating small children and bent cripples. Suddenly I wanted to sleep.

I let go of the old man with the weakness all the way up and down my arm and in my hand and the old man actually sunk down on the ground, like a bundle of clothes sinking together.

"I'll give you another drink," said Vinciguerra.

"Listen," I said. "I've got to get out of here. You know that?"

"Yes."

"I'm not often afraid, Vinciguerra, but I'm afraid now. Look at him," and I waved at the collapsed bundle on the ground, at the old man there. "Look. I'm afraid of him."

I think Vinciguerra knew it. He only nodded.

Then I stepped away and took a deep breath. I stood by the open door for a while and breathed the cold air from the alley where the sun never went. I lit a cigarette, inhaled, let it go again.

"Alright," I said. "I know what next," and turned around. The old man hadn't moved and Vinciguerra stood there as before. There is a point of resignation which can look almost serene. Vinciguerra, I thought, was closest to that.

"Look," I said to him, "not that it makes much sense, but tell the old man to put the vice on that axle and straighten it out for me again. Please."

When the old man got it he nodded his head and said, "yes, yes, yes," several times.

"He'll do it," said Vinciguerra.

"I know. That's what I don't understand."

"I know you don't," said Vinciguerra.

"And you," I said to him, "can give me that drink."

"Gladly."

And I didn't understand that either. I needed to sit.

Chapter 8

But as the pain in my head eased I did understand that the axle thing, and most likely the accident with the goats, had been set up to delay me. For what? Because Pino had to be out of town for some reason and wanted me to be here when he came back. And why out of town? To bring his warriors, maybe, or spectators as if for a fiesta, or for unrelated reasons of business, or just to harass me—

I could make a big list but no decisions. But that didn't matter to me anymore. Because I wasn't going to wait for him.

I went back into Vinciguerra's room full of nighttime but now it was just a room with the shutters closed in bright daylight, and the lamp lit on the table. He put the cognac on the table again and the glass and I poured. Once, for a shot, and a second time because I wanted more.

Vinciguerra didn't actually watch me. It was more like waiting. I looked at the cognac in my glass and felt the warm action inside from the drinks I'd had. I thought about the old man, about hitting him, and that there had been nothing to hit.

"Listen," I said. "You going to help me get out of here?"

"I would like to."

"I don't know if that's an answer."

Vinciguerra shrugged.

"You're the one kept me here," I said and still looked at my glass, "kept me here with the cognac the first time, and you're the one who took me to that old man."

"I didn't delay you here so the old man could bend the axle."

"And if you're a *mafioso* you're lying, and if you're not, you're lying because you're afraid of them."

"All that could be true," he said and looked at his hands. "But I wasn't lying. They don't need me, if they want to delay you."

"Ah!" First I took a long sip. "*They*, you said."

"The suggestion comes partly from you."

"Who are they?"

"Whoever *they* are, they would always be the *mafiosi.*"

"Yuh," I said and got up. "I'll be right back."

I went out fairly fast and all the way to the shop, which took maybe two minutes. I saw nothing new. In the shop, the old man had the bench vise on the axle and was tapping around with a hammer wrapped in rags. I went back to Vinciguerra.

"Is he working on it?" said Vinciguerra.

"Of course."

I poured more cognac in order to feel less impatient.

"And while he makes progress," said Vinciguerra, "you expect them to either come back to the shop, for more damage, or to come here?"

"Right. Something like that."

"You don't sound very efficient. And I think you drink too much."

"I'm not getting drunk. And for the rest, they always wait with the next maneuver till I actually try to leave."

Vinciguerra cocked his head and thought about it.

"And when it comes to leaving, I don't actually need that Vespa."

He folded his hands and just nodded as though he did not believe it.

"And if they want to wreck it, they'll wreck it if I'm there in the shop or not. And I'm not interested in the wrecking crew. I want the animal who started all this."

"Are you saying something philosophical or is this your use of...."

"Philosophical, crap," I drank again and felt angry. "I'm not making conversation, I'm talking Mafia."

"How can you. You don't know it."

"Shit," I said and got up again.

This time I just went to the outside door and looked at the square to see what went on there. Nothing went on there. Back in the room I lit a cigarette.

"Of course," said Vinciguerra, "with their silence they leave so much blank that it is easy to read a great deal into it."

"What's it?"

"You said you were talking Mafia," said Vinciguerra.

"Yes. Those animals with motors inside."

"I can see your hate talking. Do you know what spawned the Mafia?"

"Love."

"In a way. I was going to say hate; though love for one thing gives you hate for another."

"And hate for one thing gives you love for another?"

"No. That I was *not* going to say."

"I'm glad," I said. "Or you'd end up explaining that becoming a *mafioso* out of hate then transforms you into a giver of love."

"Of course I was not going to say that. But you must understand how all this came about. Imagine one invasion after another, for centuries, one after the other, an invasion of your land, your lives, your loves, if you like. You have no rights, in the end, except the right and wrong which you create yourself."

"You make these crooks sound like the vigilantes. You know them?"

"Yes. And that is the way the Mafia started."

I took my handkerchief out and spat into it. Then I put it back into my pocket. I thought of rotten liver and my old friend Colony.

"But the vigilantes are gone," I told him, "and the Mafia is still here."

"The justification still exists," said Vinciguerra.

He was either being theoretical, enjoying a conversation, or he was a *mafioso*.

"Like what, Vinciguerra? Like my paying for Pino's bottle of wine?"

"I'm talking to you so you understand. Judge later. Look," he said. "If we were standing on the terrace which goes around the church I could point inland for you and show you land as far as the eye can see and all of it belongs to one man. That man lives in Paris in the winter, in New York in the spring, in Acapulco in the summer, and someplace else in the fall. I don't even know where Acapulco is."

"Mexico," I told him.

"He has left an overseer who has an absolute power the likes of which you could not understand. He tells the serf...."

"Serf?"

"Yes. The farmer who works there—the many farmers—they are just that. He tells this farmer: tomorrow at five work in the orange orchard and I'll give you twenty cents for the day. Next day he says: tomorrow at four in the morning work in the packing shed with the women and I'll pay you fifteen cents for the day. Wait, there is more," said Vinciguerra.

I said I didn't mean to interrupt and I'd be right back. There was a commotion outside and I went to the outside door.

Same sun, same square, and now a knot of people under the tree. It was nothing that interested me and I hardly watched. Someone had come all the way up from the sea in a donkey cart bringing raw fish. I say raw, and not fresh, because that trip must have taken all night or more and the fish were just lying there in the cart, in different boxes.

I then went up the alley to the shop and checked there. The old man was sitting down. He was wiping his forehead with a black rag and when he looked up and recognized me he tried a smile, shy almost, begging almost, but then he just sighed.

"Done?" I asked him.

He understood that much and then he shook his head, shrugged, moved his hands around in a certain way. I understood that much, that he was not done but was trying, and perhaps in a little while, with more work—

I saw that his right hand was trembling, the one with which he had used the hammer. I felt sick inside and left.

"And the next day," said Vinciguerra as if nothing had interrupted, "the overseer says: tonight bring your daughter to the horse barn. Not the one who works at the house, the other one, the one who is twelve."

"Lovely story," I said. "Lovely Mafia now rearing its lovely head."

"Not at all," said Vinciguerra, "because now the farmer refuses. That evening his daughter is not at the barn but in bed with the other five children. And the next day the farmer asks the overseer where he should work, but there is no work. After days of this the farmer steals potatoes. The overseer has a private police and they beat the farmer up. Now only his wife can work, but she gets no work.

"When the overseer visits the next time to see how the broken hand is and the hernia which the private police have kicked out of the farmer, the farmer says: the horse barn, did you say, or the cow barn?

"That night the twelve year old is used in bed by the overseer and after that by some others, perhaps, but, at any rate, she does not come home for a week. When she comes home she has eyes like a hag and she hardly talks."

"Gimme a light," I said. "I'm out."

He gave me a light.

"The day after this," said Vinciguerra, "the overseer is not to be found. He is found on the second day when one of the women who works with the chickens goes to the grindstone to grind her butcher knife. There by the grindstone lies the overseer. He has absolutely no face. And the water in the trough of the stone is red and the stone smells foul and is full of flies."

"And next comes the farmer."

"Well, he's in jail. But he is sick and his hand is broken and he, in his shape, could never have done what was done to the overseer, so they let the farmer go."

"So where's the Mafia?"

"Who knows. The killers are never found. Silence."

"I don't get the feeling that you explained one damn thing," I told Vinciguerra.

"But I have. In the extremities of his helplessness, this farmer found a strength."

"You don't tell me, Vinciguerra, that a humanitarian organization has come to his defense and has improved his lot."

"When you're as poor as poor," he said, "you don't think of improvement, but only of holding on. But I was not finished."

"Happy ending?"

Vinciguerra did not bother to answer. He said, "The police don't find anybody so they pick up the farmer again. They don't want him, they just want him to talk."

"And he doesn't talk, so then the murderer...."

"Please. He doesn't talk, which is part of the law. They go very far in trying to make him talk, they have their reputation to think about, their record of solving crimes, he won't talk, they get clever, and the next thing, all else failing, *he* is accused of the murder."

Now I did want to know what happened. "All this is true?" I said.

"Yes. Not just this once, but often. And of course, he will be hanged."

"Cops and Mafia, not much difference, the way you put it."

"Of course not," said Vinciguerra. "They are both protective organizations, but my point—" He folded his arms and looked vaguely up at the ceiling. "On the day of the execution the priest comes to the farmer and they have confession. This is serious business...."

"More law."

"Yes, perhaps several at cross purposes, but more law."

"And hang the contradictions by hanging the man."

"Yes. So the farmer gives his confession of all his sins. He says nothing about killing the overseer. The priest says: but why don't you tell me about the murder you committed? I did not commit it, Father, says the farmer, somebody else did. The priest says: What? What? Who? Do you know who? The farmer says yes, he knows who committed the murder."

"We call this honor among thieves," I said and the dark room, and the square outside unseen, was beginning to bother me.

"This is something entirely different, if you will listen."

I frowned, but then I listened to him.

"The priest gets now very excited, he quotes divine laws, criminal laws, ethical laws, any number of laws which fit his fervor at the moment, in order to cajole the farmer into telling who committed this murder. After all, that's only right."

"No dice?" I said in English.

"The farmer says: If the murderer is coward enough not to come forward, I will not sully my name by speaking of him. I die with my honor clean." Vinciguerra coughed lightly. "They hung him and he died."

"Christ—"

It was true, this was not honor among thieves but the hanging on to the last shred of something, though it wasn't concrete, the last shred of something the man could call his own, which is a way of dying well.

Vinciguerra and his room, and his voice, and his talk— I got up and blinked a few times and wished that the shutters were open. I had a hard time coming back from where Vinciguerra had taken me, back to myself here in the vice which they were building around me in broad daylight.

"You tell this story in here," I said to Vinciguerra, "and something else goes on out there in the Square. And your shutters aren't even open."

First Vinciguerra gave a soft little laugh. I was turned away, so I didn't know just how he meant it. By the time I turned around to face him he was getting up, he wasn't laughing anymore, but his small smile was still there.

"Please," he said, and he came closer, hands out and then dropped them in front where he folded them as if each hand alone were too shy but together like that they might survive. "Please, I wasn't telling an allegory," he said. "I was telling you this to show very concretely how far a man goes."

"You don't mean a man. You mean a *mafioso*."

"Very well. In fact, though you may not know it and only made your remark out of viciousness, you are right. I don't think they are altogether human beings."

"You warning me?"

He ignored that and said, "Not that everybody is always whole and a human being, but these," and he jerked his chin at the square on the other side of the shutters, "they wish to be what they are."

"I'd like to be an animal myself sometimes, but...."

"I didn't say animal. Look. This man, this farmer, he can go no further. He must give up. Give up what? He gives himself up and puts all that strength into the law and the system. You think the Mafia is a machine? It has some of the invulnerability, the repairability, yes. But its strength is the strength which each member gives to this machine. And so, as if by a magic, he now has the strength of this machine too."

"All the worst in him doubled."

"And the best. You forget the sense of honor, the devotion, his predictable loyalty."

"Vinciguerra," I said, "I can't listen to you anymore. This is talk. This is far, far away from my pains and my problems."

"Not really," and he shrugged. "I am describing to you what you are up against."

"For a bottle of wine, Vinciguerra! For a stinking, cheap, bottle of wine, and a misunderstood gesture!"

"Of course. If you would really listen. The farmer is not a human being anymore who is stupid, wise, becomes big, becomes small. He is now something else and I want you to know it."

"What? Animal with a motor inside?"

"Yes. That contradictory. You take one human attribute," said Vinciguerra, "any one, any good one, if you like. Take that one grand, human quality and exalt it and the rest of him withers away." He ran one hand over the side of his face, as if to feel if he were still whole. "And what's left," he said, "is no longer human."

He was through, I could tell, and I stood there and still listened to him. If he was a *mafioso* I wondered why he had told me all this. If he was not, I wondered how they had allowed him to live.

"Why did you tell me all this? This is Pino?"

"To show you that there is no way out."

"What?"

"For the *mafioso*. He has killed most of himself and so is a cripple and can only live now as a part of the grand union with the others."

"I thought you meant there was no way out for me." I slung my jacket over my shoulder and went to the door.

"That I don't know," he said. "Because I don't know you."

I did not answer him. All I said was, "Good bye."

"*Benedicide*," he said, and I saw by the way he lowered his eyes for a moment that there was no irony in the remark.

Chapter 9

The square was bright with cold sunlight and I will call it that, even though, by standing in the direct light, the dry heat would touch the skin. It was close to siesta now which always meant an imperceptible speeding up of the little movements, the little cries in the air and in the crowd, the crowd thicker now or perhaps more spread out with motion, the whole thing like a speeding of breath, up to a big sigh, and then rest, which is siesta.

They got their way of running a day, I got mine, and I was out of Vinciguerra's dark room now, and also out of the limp waiting or the tense waiting for something to happen. I had my own plans. Plan is hardly the word. This felt much more direct.

There were perhaps half a dozen Vespas by the tree now and I did this much planning, I walked over there and checked which ones had the keys in the steering column. You can start those motors without a key, but without the key the steering column is locked and if you insist on driving you can only go in a very tight circle. None of that for me anymore. Out of six machines, four were with key.

Then I went up the alley (sunshine immediately forgotten, damp rot on stones) and next the cave full of wheels and the old man.

My Vespa lay on the ground again and the old man stood by the bench, looking tired. He held the wheel with both hands, like a plate, and was talking to the three men who were there. I didn't know them, but obviously they knew me. I ignored the sudden silence, the sudden stares which were as different from the slow stare of a cow as warm sunshine is different from lightning. Except with these stares there was never a crash. This hate just held. I thought the hell with them too and felt itchy all over my skin, wishing to move.

"Done?"

"I think so," he said, which was the end of his Italian and then came a pebble stream of Sicilian.

One of the three men in the shop helped us out and said the old man wanted to tell me how sorry he was about everything.

"Does he have anything else to say?" I asked. "Such as, how that axle got bent?"

"No. Nothing else to say."

All those three men were standing with their hands in their pockets, deprived monkey faces shut to me, they all looked alike. If they had kept their faces in their pockets and worn a hard, wrinkled hand for a face, that wouldn't have startled me either and it would have been just the right, ghastly touch.

"Put the wheel on," I said. "I want to go."

He nodded and put the wheel on. It slipped over the axle well enough. Then he spun the wheel. The wheel spun well enough.

He had some awkward trouble with the nuts but then the nuts went on too.

"How much?" I said.

He said he would like two hundred lire and I put them on the work bench while he tightened the nuts. I lit a cigarette and smoked in the doorway. Of course nobody talked and there was just the bad sound of breathing from the old man. He worked, kneeling down. When he was done he got up slowly, clawing himself up by the bench. I threw the cigarette out. I pushed away from the door frame because now the old man bent down again to lift up the machine and maybe, I thought, this'll shatter his honor and I'll make another hereditary enemy but I'll help him, I'll lift it myself because it's faster that way and not so hard as watching.

"That's alright," said one of the three men. "He'll do it."

"He's too old," I said, and tried to get by.

"I meant *he* will do it," and he nodded at one of the two others who went to the Vespa and stood over it.

The one who had talked pulled his jacket off—it had been hanging, sleeves empty, on his shoulders—and got into my way while putting his arms into the sleeves.

The one by the Vespa bent down to lift it.

"Never mind," I said. "You're too kind."

He stood bent down that way, holding the handlebars, and then he stepped over with his foot and the heel hit the cock of gasoline which shows under the seat.

"Sorry," he said, and lifted the machine.

I was still slow and everything went on so quietly and I looked at the old man in the corner where he had moved back, and I felt like him. He had moved back and his hand was over his mouth and not knowing where to look he had closed his eyes.

Then I didn't feel like that poor, old fright in the corner anymore at all. I said, slow now, let there be strategy, or something like that to keep me from just busting loose, which I would have liked best and felt like doing.

The one who blocked me was still doing it. I grabbed him under the arms, meaning to throw him, and I mean just throw him away to one side, but he hung on. He didn't kick or swing or pant about anything, he just hung on to me like a monkey, arms and one leg around me like some thing made of hooks, and if I moved now I'd fall.

The gas cock kicker was holding the machine and the third grey-faced man took a metal saw off the bench.

I think his slowness made me feel helpless. Or this passive way in which the hooking man was hanging on me. Or the indolent blink on the face of the one who was holding the Vespa. And the silence.

To shake the spell—I thought the word, and the spell went. I'll be as quiet about this as you, I thought, and also as empty about it of emotion, and maybe better even. I couldn't move without falling, so I fell.

I don't think he expected it. I made a small heft which was not big enough to make him let go, fine with me, hang on, just enough of a heft for the proper imbalance. I'm heavy, of course, and he knew nothing ahead of time, so I had the whole play to myself. He had no time to unhook before it had happened and I saw to it that he fell flat on his back, me flat and heavy on top of him so that we made a fine, solid thud, and his breath a sudden burst as if he was going to throw up everything that was inside of him.

Then I got up fast and stepped on his solar plexus so I could forget about him. Next, he did throw up.

The one with the saw had cut right through the front tire. He was on the back tire now, sawing away, and I did lose my head for a moment there and walked right into the foot that came up. The one who was holding the Vespa just kicked up his foot and caught me on the thigh.

I fell long enough to hear the back tire start hissing. They dropped the machine and walked out.

I was half up when they turned in the door, checking damage, the one with the saw still holding the saw. If I got up we'd have a fight and what would be the difference who won that one.

I gave them a good groan to hear and a grimace like pain searing my innards and collapsed again. The one with the saw dropped the saw, they both turned and walked out.

I thought for a moment, how curious for them to leave their puking buddy behind, but that would be thinking like a human being. You think like an animal with a motor inside, then it's easy. You did your job, the other animal did his job. *Basta.* You think like a *mafioso* who knows very well that he's nothing but a half-man unless he sticks to the superbeing then you stick for your life to the work for which you've been built. And the two who walked out never had to worry about the one who was still on the floor.

I didn't worry about him either. He was too sick and could hardly breathe. And the other two, neither good machine nor good animal, I was hoping they would be easy too.

I got up and shook my leg for a moment and looked out of the door.

They had gone away from the square, up the alley, where the streets were small and tangled and you could never look very far unless you are tall and look over the people. Pre-siesta time. I'm tall and then I followed them, hunched down to Sicilian size.

I didn't know whether they had looked back and seen me lope along there but they got off the street soon and walked into a house. When I got there, I went in too.

These houses, because nobody has a stove, have no windows at all but just a door. In the daytime, for the light, the door is always open and you walk into a whitewashed cave with an uneven floor, furniture stands around as if for storage. An old looking Pope has his pink and white picture print hanging there on the wall, pink and white Madonna print on the other wall, pink and white Jesus baby standing up all by himself before gold rays jetting out and green clouds behind that, always this sort of picture and this kind of whitewashed cave, and if there are more rooms than one, you discover the other one behind a sheet hanging there and the space behind it is in most cases all filled with bed.

So they couldn't have disappeared. And they stood right there by the bed in the dark room, and Pino was lying there, receiving reports.

They all turned with a jump and with a squeak of the bed and then the next thing happened as if there had been orders or laws for everything ahead of time.

I don't mean this was planned. They were obviously very much surprised. But then, there was no hesitation or question in their minds about what to do next.

While Pino jumped off the bed, the two at the end of the bed turned in their narrow space so that I shouldn't get through. But unlike the time in the shop, this time there was also no hesitation or question in my mind about what I wanted. I wanted that son of a bitch who was now sprinting out through the curtain in back. So I jumped on the bed, which gave too much. It gave so much I felt I was walking in dough. But I was anxious as hell now to get at Pino.

The first one who got in my way also got my foot in the chest. He made a sound which reminded of the two tires blowing air through their cuts. The man whistled the way I have never heard anyone whistle before. I didn't care about the second one. He got tangled up with his whistling friend long enough for me to jump off the bed, through that curtain in back, and out the door into a yard full of garbage.

"Pino," I yelled.

I don't know what I expected. He turned by the wooden gate at the end of the yard and looked at me. There was no expression in his face. No dislike, no hate, no fear, and no sign of any real interest.

"You wait till...."

Then he turned and ran.

I think I felt mostly interrupted. I stood there with my sentence hanging in the air, bewildered, because the little sense I had found in any of this was now running away from me just like Pino disappearing through the gate.

I didn't care who fell on the street when I pushed them aside or what was said while I ran by, I kept my eyes on the red pig hair ahead of me and then—I was yelling at him part of the time—I moved very much faster because they stepped aside when I came.

When he got into the square I saw him head for the tree. It didn't look as if they were making room for him the way they had done for me, stepping back in the street when I was running, but he dipped into the crowd there moving as fast as ever and the only thing that suddenly changed in the square were the sounds.

There had at first been the disorganized noonday clatter of voices, but when I got into the square all that became one low mumble. When I got to the crowd, there was silence and they all stepped away.

Pino was on one of the Vespas and just kicked the starter arm down. But it didn't catch. He had time for one more try and then I had him.

It struck me that this was the very first time that I had touched him. But then he was gone again. He fell off to one side and unless I wanted to sprawl across the Vespa and fall with it I had to let go.

The incomprehensible part of all this made me awkward. Why was he running away? Why was I chasing him? Had I really become a prisoner of Forza D'Aguil?

He was up now, on the other side of the machine, and I think he had hurt his wrist. He was holding his wrist and moved back rather slowly, into the crowd. I went after him. A square full of people, in silence, and when I came near, they moved away.

I could see his head all the time. He moved like someone meandering through a forest, around trees, always half out of sight, and around me, where I ran or darted or reached out to push my way through, there was immediately nothing. I swear it felt like I was going blind. It felt like tapping around in nothing, with no sound to the touch, with no touch at all, an insane dance in a crowded square—but an insane dance in a crowd which was never where I was.

"Pino," I yelled, and I could hear an edge in my voice, an unpleasant edge which threatened me and nobody else. "Pino!" again, very hoarse now.

I saw him stop and I stopped.

"What do you want?" he said.

Maybe I'm going a little bit out of my mind, I thought, just enough to understand nothing at all while everything still looks as it always has.

I took a deep breath and rubbed my face and then I said, very quietly, I think, "I'm leaving," I said. "I'm now going to cut out of this town."

"Go." I could hardly see him, just his hair and a leg, I think, though it might have been somebody else's leg.

"I'm going to walk straight out of here," I said, "and if you got any business with me, or think you got any business with me, let's have it now."

I saw enough of him to see that he shrugged.

"I don't know what you're talking about."

I took a step, just for no reason, one step, and they moved back.

The only thing that's going to keep me from going a little bit out of my mind, I thought, I'll get angry. I'll get mad. Not go mad, get mad.

"Listen," I said, "I'm not imagining everything." I said that more to myself than to him. "Come on over here."

"I don't even know you," he said.

"Then why all this?"

"All what?"

Then I screamed, *"Bastarde!"*

I was suddenly violently angry, I yelled that terrible insult at him—it means much more in Italian than it does in English—and if anything was going to make him come over, make him real, that would be it.

He shrugged.

"Goddamn you!" I yelled and crouched to run at him, but then the thought, or the knowledge, of everyone moving aside, away, and avoiding me—I think of a piece of bread and I put that in my mouth and bite down. My teeth click into each other and there is nothing else. I think of clutching that arm over there, my fingers curl around, and then dig into my own palm and there is nothing else. This at high noon, full daylight, stone houses, wood trees, and nothing—

Alright, easy now. Easy, my foot. I'll go berserk and let that carry me.

I didn't run towards him but turned around, back to the tree and walked fast, with hard footsteps, jolts going up into my body, a harsh walk like that to the Vespa he had there, and when I got there I jumped on. I didn't say I'm leaving again, but I was screaming that all the time inside of me over the throbbing pain.

I kicked the starter and it caught for me, and maybe I'll run somebody over now, this thing is faster than all these shadow men in the shadowless square.

In fact, they all stepped aside and I shot right out of there and I had the feeling they were not even watching.

This switch, with the Vespa, had been the other of the two plans; one, not to wait for Pino to move but to find him myself; two, steal a Vespa and cut out of that place without telegraphing the plan ahead of time like my earlier try—I had now done both and felt smart and sane again.

In the mouth of the street going down there was suddenly the cop. He stepped right out into the middle of the narrow street, duty strong on his face, stronger than fear for life. And me, sane now. Stomp the brake down so I don't run him over.

"What are you doing?" he said and I could see most of his teeth.

"I'm leaving."

"Ah. Very Well. Is that your machine?"

"No. This isn't my machine but I borrowed it."

"You did? With permission?"

"Yeah, yeah, yeah, with permission."

"Whose machine is it?"

"Pig head back there. Pino pighead."

"Where?"

I looked around, back at the square, and there were all of those shadows moving again, listening, but Pino wasn't there.

"He let me borrow it. That's why he left."

"Very good. But since that's your word only, you'll please wait till we find him, and we'll ask, eh?"

I felt like giving up. I was giving up, feeling heavy and empty all at the same time, heavy because I wasn't moving, empty because there was no strength.

"Besides," the cop was saying, "I don't know anybody by that name in this town. I think you just made it up."

I won't pay any attention to this, I thought very fast. Don't pay any attention to this blatant insanity.

"You know who I am?" I said.

"No."

"Haven't you seen me around?"

"I think I might have. I'm not sure."

Better no more of this. The more he talks, the worse it gets. And if I hit him or run him down, what's the difference? What's the good of pushing one leg against a thing like fly-paper only very much bigger, push one leg to pull free the other to get stuck with the alternate leg—

I got off the Vespa, hitched it back on its stand, walked around and towards the cop, who immediately stepped out of my way.

I'll walk out. I'm going to walk out, here in broad daylight, just walk, and everything else is imagination. I walked.

Chapter 10

Just how far this had gone, just how far I had gone, was never clear to me until much later, until after the next thing they did to me.

I say this without qualification, that they did this to me, that they provoked me and that I could be provoked. Which shows just how very helpless I really was at that point.

I walked and there was still no real sound from anyone, just the humming now, and then the first bike went by me. I kept walking, and like an exodus all these bikes went by me, going down the road, the way out of town. I felt jumpy and frightened but with no time—with no courage more accurately—to do anything but walk. No more problems now, please, and no choices, just walk.

When I got to the gate I saw them. They were on the other side of the gate, on the highway, leaning against the retaining wall of the road, arms folded, legs crossed, just leaning there with their bikes.

Oh God no, Christ no, I kept mumbling, no, this isn't at all what I see, this is a twist inside my own unpredictable brain, all of which was idiot talk because I saw what was there clearly enough.

The small monster boy was there now, walking up the road, to the gate, and his mean little monkey face was there as before, and a new stick in his hand, with tip.

"Go ahead," said one of the men by the wall and nodded at the boy.

The boy needed no nodding at or anything else.

I don't know what he had intended to do but the sight of this wrinkled hate on his face made me blow. The force of that place, of being trapped in that place, tore me open. I grabbed the stone on the road there and threw it at the child wishing to kill him. Of course the stone merely caught him on one arm.

The men by the wall, I think they suddenly felt the same way as I had when I threw that stone. They just busted open. They waved that suddenly, that swiftly—and then they stopped!

They stopped close to me, they held still, they froze me there with their interrupted motion, just one of them walked up very slowly. This shows how far gone I was. He moved his arm, which I saw, and I stood there. He slapped me across the face, while I stood there.

I wanted to lower my head or cover my face with my hands. That's how far gone I was. And then—I'm sure that it had been the kid—I got a sharp rap on the back of the head with a stick.

I fell down but wasn't all the way out, black waves cut my vision apart and no pain yet, but enough vision to see this. Pino, coming from somewhere, was standing, arms folded, looking down at me. Maybe I did something that was very funny, but next he pointed at me and then he laughed. I think I passed out because I gave up. In broad daylight in the road there, not quite out of town, I passed out.

* * *

I didn't know who was talking and for a while I just lay there without caring to open my eyes. If I open my eyes, I thought, maybe they'll roll out of my head, or my head itself might roll away. When I did open my eyes I couldn't tell if it was daytime or nighttime, which made me think immediately that I might be in Vinciguerra's room.

I had a fierce headache. It expanded and contracted in an undulant way inside my skull, a jellyfish of pain.

It was Vinciguerra's room and I was on his bed. I did not care to move yet but could hear very well. They were by the door.

"I'll tell him," said Vinciguerra.

"Tell him everything we have against him. Tell him until all that is straightened out he'll have to stay here."

"That's alright with me," said Vinciguerra. "Is Pino still around?"

"Sure."

"This one," said Vinciguerra, and I could tell by the voice that he had turned and was looking at me, "isn't like one of us, around here." I could hear him sigh and turn away again. "There are a number of things he doesn't recognize, or doesn't care for at all. What...."

"I give a damn?"

"Let me finish. Pino keeps showing himself, and that'll only provoke him. I think, there's a point where he can get to be like a bull and...."

"Stupid animal."

"So are you and I," said Vinciguerra. "But perhaps not as persistent. Perhaps not as strong."

The other one said, *"Mu—"* and just left.

I hadn't seen him. I thought he had sounded like the cop.

After the door had shut and a little time had passed, I sat up very slowly, holding my head as if it was a bowl of water, full of water, and I mustn't spill any of it. The water was pain and I didn't want to slop it.

Vinciguerra was by his table, hands in lap. He had just about the same paraphernalia on top of the table as the other time when I had been here like an invalid. Whenever I was in this room, I was an invalid and Vinciguerra would sit there, enjoying it.

"Move slowly," he said.

"I can't do anything else." I went to the table and sat down in the easy chair.

"Here," said Vinciguerra, and he pushed a glass of water towards me and held out two pills on the flat of his hand. "For the pain."

"How's the back of my head?" I said.

"Swollen, with a bruise. I cleaned it all up."

"Thank you, Vinciguerra," I said and then swallowed the pills.

"They'll take fifteen minutes," he said, "and then the pain should get dull."

"And me too?" I drank the water.

"A little, maybe. It's codeine."

I finished the water which felt very cold in me and sat back in the chair. I didn't really want to be awake yet.

"Look," I said, "I heard some of the things you said."

"That was the policeman," said Vinciguerra. "He brought you."

"You're supposed to tell me all the things they have against me and so forth."

"Yes. They are: resisting arrest...."

"When in hell was that?"

"When you left the Vespa and walked away from him."

"Why, of course. When he said, 'You're under arrest,' and then I smashed him down. Gimme a drink, Vinciguerra."

"And," he said, "theft."

"The Vespa I didn't take."

"And assault, twice."

"Which twice?"

"The time in the bedroom and the time with the child."

"Ah. They left some out."

"And trespassing. Again the bedroom scene."

"Gimme a drink, Vinciguerra."

He went to get the cognac and I sat there in the chair, disappointed with what I had heard. It had sounded so much more important, overhearing the phrase, "tell him everything we have against him—"

So I sat with the cognac and the headache and the grey doubts.

Just a few things were certain. They didn't want me to go. Which meant I couldn't, unless I got very much smarter. I drank the cognac, feeling weak and sick in the head and the only strength I felt was something like stubbornness. And why didn't they want me to go?

"Vinciguerra."

"Yes."

He sat with his little hands out of sight but then put them on the table.

They lay there like two little trained mice, waiting to perform something or other.

"I don't think Pino is after me at all."

The little hands curled up as if disappointed and went back into the lap.

"Oh?" said Vinciguerra.

"I don't think paying for his goddamn bottle of wine can be behind all of this."

"Let me tell you something," he said, "and this is true. A few years ago an old man came back from America to his home town in Calabria."

"That's not Sicily. That's the bottom of the boot."

"Their ways are just as old."

"You don't mean old. You mean hard, and no give anywhere."

"That's how you get when you're old," he said. And then, "He came back after fifty years away in America to look at his hometown, his dreamtown, perhaps, where he had been born."

"Idiot," I said.

Vinciguerra ignored that, except that he looked at his cognac bottle and how much I had taken.

"That first evening, after explaining himself, smiling at everybody, and wandering around, he sits in the café and invites all these strangers to be his friends. He buys the bottle."

"Alright," I said, "alright." I don't know if the length of his story annoyed me or the air of uselessness which hung in everything he was saying. As if everything had been settled ahead of time.

"He drinks with these friends and when it comes time for a new bottle, one of the peasants says: I offer this one. Well, the American is very happy about the gesture but he is much too generous and much too anxious to accept. He insists, he pay for the bottle."

"They allowed him?"

"Oh yes. They allowed him. The peasant shrugged and they drank more. The next morning, the American was dead."

"What?"

"Dead. His throat was cut. Neat, simple cut, because he had offended the peasant."

"Jaysis—" I said.

"So you see," said Vinciguerra, "they are treating you very lightly, in a way."

I said more, mumbling mostly, and getting increasingly more unprintable. I took another glass of cognac and pulled back in the chair, to brood.

That's all I was good for, then. I would wait this out, the headache and so forth, drink some, sleep some, and recover. I no longer felt the weird fright that had come outside, that was over, I thought, and next, I'd get

smart. I wasn't so much of a bull—as Vinciguerra had used the word—
that I couldn't change my methods.

"Vince," I said, "there's a telephone in this place?"

"Of course."

"I'm going to make a phone call. Consulate, and so forth."

"I wouldn't stop you," he said, and what he also said with the same few
words was, I'm sorry for you, *Poverino,* terribly sorry, but neither the phone
call nor any other kind of call that you might send out is going to do any
good, because there's a whole set of rules and laws which say you are the
victim, and victims don't do things on their own.

"Vinciguerra," I said, "how can anyone with your name, Vinciguerra, feel
the way you do."

"I don't like the name," he said. "It's so meaningless."

But I was full of false feelings of meaning and significances by now, full
with the pills in my head and the cognac too, everything was of the clever-
est in my head and this jag, of course, was like a rest, not like a delay, a resting up of the fly which hung in the spider web. But right now Vinciguerra and his sad, significant sayings were not what I wanted—this nutty
nighttime room was getting on my nerves—I'm going to take a walk, I
thought. I had the feeling I was perfectly safe, that's the way everything
struck me now, as long as I did not try to leave. Rest time. Next real move
I make will be at night. Take a walk. Also good for a drunk to take a walk
now, though of course I'm not drunk. Take a walk and look right through
them with great alcohol courage and the hangover clairvoyance which
always comes later.

"Where are you going?" said Vinciguerra.

"I'm gonna have another drink."

"Please," he said, "listen for a moment. It isn't I grudge you my cognac...."

But I didn't want to listen to him anymore and said something in English, something short and ugly, I think, and I think also that he understood
just by the sound of it, and then I had one more glass, quick, standing up,
and walked to the door.

"Vince," I said. "You got a gun?"

"That's illegal in this country," he said.

"I didn't ask you that. What I'm talking about is, I wish to take a walk
during siesta, in the sunshine, you know, but feel undressed without a gun.
Old Western custom we have, and what did I just learn here in Mysterious Sicily but an Old Western custom no less. Of course, in our case, the
custom died out, sort of, one hundred years ago...."

I could hear myself talking like that, an asinine drunk. And I knew Vinciguerra was not going to give me a gun. I had just said that to feel like I
could hurt someone and in order to make noise.

He said, "If you could try and feel differently about all of this— If you could try and—"

"I don't want to be like you," I said and yanked the door open and walked out.

When I passed the door to the restaurant I looked through the glass and saw Sophia in the room, walking to the kitchen. I must have stood there like an idiot for quite some time because Sophia did several things while I looked at her. She put a broom into a corner, she took tablecloths off the tables, and once she stopped by the buffet where all the oil and vinegar bottles were kept. She looked at me most of that time, but I never did anything. I stared back and then left. I felt like hell.

The square was empty and the streets I could see were empty. Three or four people sat in front of the *osteria* but they didn't move my way and they didn't stop talking to each other. I put my hands in my pockets and walked, looking down where my feet were moving. I called one foot Glum and the other foot Gloom, and said glum-gloom-glum-gloom in a rhythm until I got totally rattled. I walked around the square like that once (nothing happened) and then up the first alley next to the hotel.

At the back of that building was the kitchen door and Sophia was looking out, as if she had been waiting. I stopped and leaned against the corner and looked at her in the door.

"You been waiting here?"

"Yes," she said.

"For whom? Pino?"

She said nothing at first and rubbed her hands together. Then she said, "No. For you."

"Hah!"

"You must feel terrible," she said, so that I could hardly hear it.

But I heard it. I heard it and said to myself, please stop talking like that, little one, or I'll melt. I'll really melt right here in front of you and you would even understand that, even though I might not—

Since I had not actually said anything to her she kept looking at me there in the silence and then lowered her eyes. But she didn't leave.

"Sophia," I said. "Get back in the kitchen and do your work."

She looked up and then away again. She was just going to move.

"Are you off or are you working?" I asked her.

"I'm working."

"Take a walk with me, Sophia. To hell with working."

"Alright," she said. "I'll come."

I liked that very much, the way she had said alright, the way there had been no hesitation, because she had wanted to come, and no cover-up for this wish at all.

She went inside to take off her apron and I lit a cigarette while I waited outside. I wished very much now that I were less drunk but was drunk enough to blame Vinciguerra for this. He always makes me drunk, one way or the other, and his touch causes confusion. And less time with Vinciguerra and more time with this girl—a hell of a reason for seeing this girl, as an antidote! It is better, in fact, to see her because I'm feeling weepy, because there's nobody in town who will allow me to come near, not Vinciguerra even, he just wishes that I were sick more often so he could take care of me and prime me with confusion, but to touch, there's been nobody here, and maybe she isn't either and this is the liquor weeping inside me—

She came back and I snapped on a smile.

"What were you thinking?" she said.

She ignored my smile completely and I dropped it. I didn't take her arm, as I wanted, but we walked side by side up the dank street with the sunshine like a very quick lick touching just the tops of the houses. The girl had on a sweater with pockets and she put her hands into these. I put my hands in my pockets too.

"What did you say?"

"What were you thinking?"

I had known what I had been thinking as soon as she had asked, not before.

"How you can walk with me," I said. "When nobody else would do more than spit at me."

"Have they?"

"No. I made that up. But it feels that way. Their eyes spit at me."

I looked at her to see how she took that but I needn't have looked because she said how she felt very clearly.

"I know what they did to you. It's ugly," she said. She drew up her shoulders and then dropped them so that it almost looked as if she were shaking herself.

"Sophia," I told her. "Don't walk with me because of that. I'll get out of here, but you *live* here."

She looked at me but said nothing. We walked.

"Inside their heads, Sophia, they have a thing like this street. It's thin and dark and they run back and forth in that alley all their lives and nothing else."

"I'm walking with you because I like you," she said. "I don't have an alley in my head."

I touched her arm and gave a small squeeze, nothing else, because the empty street felt suddenly like the most public place and I must be secretive. I had no idea why.

"Where are you taking me?" she said.

I knew where I was taking her as soon as she asked.

"I don't know," I said. "Just around. Is that the church up there?"

I knew damn well that was the church after the next bend and also that I wasn't going to the church with her, but beyond. I felt secretive about that too, for good reason, and in fact wondered why I should think of taking that part of the walk with the girl, instead of alone.

"That's the church," she said. "It's about as far as you can walk, and then comes nothing. Just a big drop."

"Proper place for a church," I said. "Like a last resort and then nothing."

"There's a graveyard behind that," she said.

I had to laugh because of the double talk, and if she had been Vinciguerra there might have come all kinds of clever back and forth now, especially with me still slop full of liquor. But she said nothing else and only smiled. I think she smiled because I was laughing, not because of anything we had said.

"Sophia," I said, "if you'll smile like that more often I'll laugh more."

She gave me a sideways look and then she laughed herself, which was beautiful. And it wasn't the liquor inside me either. She just laughed beautifully. Then she ran up the steps to the terrace which went all around the grey church. I wondered how old the girl was.

She stood at the balustrade, waiting for me, and because of the wind blowing she took her hands out of her pockets and hugged herself. Oh brother, I thought, would I now like to hug what she's hugging there and what a hell of a time for a feeling like this and what a hell of a place.

"From here you can see the Mediterranean," she said and nodded her head at it.

The water was a white blaze in the distance, as if there were a sun below us, though far away. I told her that and she nodded again.

"You know," she said, "when I saw this the first time I thought the same thing. I looked across and didn't see the ugly land in between at all."

I stood next to her and our sleeves just touched. I didn't move a muscle. I made small talk.

"You sound like you're not from here, Sophia."

"I'm not. I'm from Rome. I once told you."

"That's right. And I said what a change that must be for you."

"I don't remember much. I just know that I'm not from here."

"Most people move away from here, not *to* Forza d'Aguil."

"My parents were killed in Rome, when the Germans retreated, and the people who lived in the same apartment with us, they were from here. When I was four or five I was sent back. The man had a mother here, an old woman, and she raised me."

"Don't orphans always end with the nuns?"

"That was wartime, so everything was a little different."

"It's a way of putting it, yes."

I was sorry I had started the small talk and to have lost touch with the sleeves, and then the padre came around the side of the church, walking with his hands folded. He was a big, rough looking man, hatless, and I thought he looked like someone disguised as a priest. When he walked by, Sophia stepped over to him and reached for him. He held out his hand, which she kissed, while he kept on walking without saying a word. Maybe he didn't like having his hand kissed and I didn't like it either. She ran next to him for a little ways, because he wouldn't stop walking, and then she came back.

"Hey, listen you," I said. "Come here."

She came and hugged herself again the way she had done it before and I felt the same way about it as I had before.

"You're taking this walk with me," I said, "so come here."

Then she surprised me by laughing again.

"You're jealous," she said. "You know you sound jealous?"

"Yes, yes. Looped enough to be jealous of the padre. Come here."

This time I took her arm and walked her around the church. I worked my hand under her arm for a good hold on it while she kept hugging herself like before. That was alright with me and my hand. My hand was nice and warm in there with all that softness.

We came around the corner where the cemetery showed and for that one crazy moment I almost reached over for her with my other hand, to turn her around and to pull her up to me, but then I didn't. I had not known that the memory still sat at that corner and I did not want anything to get mixed up and to run into each other. But I had the very distinct feeling, like knowledge, that I could have pulled her around and she would have let it happen right then. This made me feel fairly good, but we kept walking.

"Why the cemetery?" she said. "Why do you want to walk there?"

"I thought there was nothing higher here than this town," I said. "But the rock goes up some more over there."

"Not far," she said. "Then it ends and there's nothing again."

"Let's go up to nothing, Sophia, huh?"

She looked up and smiled and said that sometimes I talked very funny and that she didn't think it was the cognac either.

"But you'll come."

"Oh yes," she said. "I'm taking this walk with you."

We crossed the cemetery and on the other side met the path which went up the rock. It would have been easier walking separately now but we didn't let go. I say "we" because she was holding on too. Every so often, moving at different speeds, she would squeeze her arm into herself, not to lose hold of my hand. She did that quite unconsciously now and then because she kept talking about other things.

"There's a shack up there," she said. "You can't see it from here, not till the last moment."

"Who lives there?"

"Nobody. The Germans built it up there during the war, for a watchpost of some kind."

She had that all wrong but I didn't want to say anything about the shack, or about me, and the other time I'd been here.

I didn't want to drag in that old business because once she knew, the town would know and what effect that might have on my situation here was a complication which I wanted to avoid. I felt sure it would make everyone just that much more hostile because—I've mentioned this once before—we had been the victors and we had come up there to use the town in one way or another, but had never been friendly with it or had lived with it in any real sense. Sooner or later there would be somebody who might recognize me, but I was going up the rock path now, to the radio shack, and the way I had it planned I wouldn't be here long enough for anyone to start remembering this late in the game.

"I'm out of breath," she said. "Stop a minute."

I stopped and left my hand there on her arm.

"Sophia."

She said, "Huh?" breathing hard. I could feel her breathing motion where my hand hugged against her.

"Anybody using that shack up there for anything?"

"No. They've used some of the lumber and the windows are out, but the shell is metal and nobody has taken that apart yet. Why do you ask?"

"Let's walk," I said.

"Why do you ask?"

We walked and I made up an answer.

"I want to be alone with you a little."

Actually I didn't have to make that up at all, but one didn't have anything to do with the other, with the shack and where it stood.

"Nobody goes there," she said. "And at night it's too windy."

I got that very well, and since we were on the subject I said, "And I want to give you a kiss."

She stopped and looked at me again, this time with real astonishment.

"You are a little strange, you know that?"

"I don't think...."

"To say so ahead of time," she said.

Now that we were discussing it we were actually off the subject, with kissing or such no more than a topic. We looked at each other and knew it and we had to laugh.

"Serves you right," she said, "for talking too much," and pulled her arm away.

I didn't mind, feeling very good about her and me, and just followed her through the last bend which went up to the shelf.

There was the shack, like a long time ago. The doors and windows were gone and the shack looked very lost. I remembered the last time I had left the place, that last very early morning, and how Rosanna and I had left without once looking back for it. And now, as if being back here because I had forgotten to give the last look, and I had to come back for it. Sophia was ahead of me and then disappeared around the shack.

The wind was as always up here. And please don't disappear, Sophia, not at this moment.

She was at the lee-side of the shack, leaning against the metal which was warm from the sun.

"You look strange," she said. "What happened?"

"Nothing."

I stood next to her and leaned too.

"I was looking for you," I said.

I pushed my hand through her hair and this tilted her face up and she closed her eyes.

"Not a word," I said, "not a word, Sophia," and leaned over to her for the kiss.

Chapter 11

We sat down by the wall which was away from the wind and in the sun. We didn't let go of each other.

"Open your sweater," I said. "There's enough sun."

"Open it," she said, "and don't lie. That's not why you want it open."

I unbuttoned the sweater while she pushed her face close into the side of my neck and I could feel her mouth.

"God," I said, "I'm trembling a little."

"I know. I feel you."

"I wish this were someplace else. Someplace else altogether."

"Yes."

"But then it doesn't matter. Just doesn't matter—"

I could feel her body and how she pushed herself into my hand and I thought, I've actually never seen her before and this is the first time. I was not seeing her now either, with my eyes, but that wasn't the point. She and I suddenly knew each other all over, this sudden knowledge of you and I, stone under us, metal in back, none of that mattered. I wanted her now without any delay, and she answered.

We laid down, or fell down, and I could feel the strength in her motion, or her wish, which came to the same thing.

"Ah—" she said, a sound like an animal, and there were too many clothes between us. But perhaps that was the thing up there on the rock, the strain to reach and the strength of wish—words. I know how it was. That is enough.

I didn't do anything else up there on the rock. I hadn't forgotten about the original business, but that could wait till later, or rather, that would have to wait until later because this wasn't the time.

We straightened our clothes, pulling things this way and that, which was the only time we felt sort of sheepish with each other. The clothes embarrassed us, not anything else. Then we walked back together. I watched her walk and thought she was the most beautiful thing walking.

"Are you staying at the hotel tonight?" she asked.

"Yes."

She nodded and said nothing else. It was settled.

"When are you done working?" I said.

"At ten, perhaps."

"I'll be in my room."

She nodded again and we walked the rest of the way to the hotel without talking.

I did have one moment of worry about this. I was leaving. I had to leave. And on one hand I don't like to make love to a woman when I know I must leave, when the thought is so predominant, and on the other, why mess around now while I had this practically life-and-death situation to handle.

But that was just a thought and the rest was pretty strong feeling. The thing with Sophia was not really casual, a catch-as-catch-can-type interlude. And I also think this: If there had not been the ugly pressure of the town, that strange, vague situation, if that hadn't been, I don't think I would have paid any attention to the girl. Because in a way, I think, I went to her because of the contrast.

The contrast stared me right in the face when we got back to town and the siesta was over. Their stares again, and the groups who stopped talking when we passed.

"You don't have to walk with me," I said to Sophia. "You go ahead alone."

"*Mbu*—" she said, and no more.

This was the first time that sound had ever been really alright with me and not just a dead end. I smiled at the girl and felt good with her. I took her to the kitchen door and Vinciguerra was there. He was moving there and when he saw us he stopped. I could see how suddenly he became still and I could hear what he said. "*Maledetto*—" he said, and stared at us.

I have explained how he looks most of the time, with a spectrum going from sad to resignation, with variations in-between here and there, but never upset. But this time he was.

And *maledetto* is a peculiar word. It's a swearword but nobody says it in anger. The sound is almost apprehensive because its meaning is the opposite of benediction. When you see something that is not blessed—I have seen an old woman sit in her shawl in a dim room, street door open to catch the last evening light, and while she sat there in her silence a large moth fluttered into the room, also in silence. When the woman caught the movement in the air and saw the animal flit about like a shadow alone and looking for its body, she shrunk back and said, *maledetto*.

I stared at Vinciguerra and saw how stern he was now.

"Where have you been?" he said to Sophia, and came out into the alley.

"We took a walk."

I thought of the rock shelf where we had been and the big sky there over everything. Sophia's lie, I felt, is almost palpable. And then I looked at Vinciguerra and saw that his face seemed to shrink for a moment, hearing the lie. Or because he looked at her and saw what was palpable. Because Sophia, as is true for some, stood there and showed in some way that is hard to describe, in some simple body way, that she had just made love.

It is the quiet face, eyes at rest, the soft curve of neck which carries the head, the whole body both stronger and softer.

"Get into the kitchen," said Vinciguerra.

He sounded almost vicious. He said nothing else while she went in and neither did I. Then she was gone and the alley felt empty. Vinciguerra stood before the green stain on the stone wall behind him and I could hardly remember for the moment what I had done and how I had felt with the girl, such a short time ago, before this time in the dank alley.

"Please listen to me," he said.

This was not vicious anymore, or stern, but Vinciguerra as always. Except there was almost a pleading intensity in his face which seemed to say most of the time, I wish everything would be different.

"What?" I said, meaning what more, what else in addition to everything else.

"I don't know what you think about your situation here," he said, and talked rather quickly, "except that I have seen you both confused and scared."

"You're not helping that any. What do you want?"

"I once offered help to you...."

I gave a guffaw which was quite involuntary and not just for effect.

"What help, huh?"

"If you think nothing else can happen to you here, nothing beyond this harassment...."

"And you've been very much interested in all that, Vinciguerra, and have explained everything in a haunting way. Now what?" and I took a step closer to him. "I've had just about all the vagueness I can take."

"Stay away from the girl," he said.

"What kind of help that?"

"Don't you think your position here is precarious enough, without—" and he hesitated, "without involving yourself in a new way?"

"What in hell is that supposed to mean?"

"My concern for you," he said, and I thought he now meant to touch me, but the incipient gesture, the unincisive talk which he favored, the unfinished thoughts he left, all that got me now and I interrupted him.

"Never mind your concern." Then I got fairly loud with him. "It's like watching a goldfish in a bowl, sitting there and watch the dumb animal go around in a circle and you make up theoretical worries about how that fish might get away. That's your concern. That's just a pastime, Vinciguerra. But let me hear one concrete answer to one concrete question. Are you listening?"

"Yes, I am."

"What's the demented town planning with me?"

"Keep you here."

"How long and for what?"

"I don't know how long."

"You didn't answer the other."

"I have tried to explain the other to you. About how they think, what they must do to feel that they are alive, how you must learn to understand...."

"A stinking, cheap, lousy bottle of wine!"

He shrugged and looked away.

"What else, Vinciguerra? *What else is there?*"

I waited a moment and then I was sick of waiting and I was also done being excited.

"The *mafioso* silence," I said, and felt quite neutral.

"Imagine that you are drowning," he said.

"I don't have to," I said.

"Yes. Imagine that you are drowning and not far from you on the shore lies a man with his legs wired together and a chain binding his arms...."

"Such as you?"

"So that I cannot help in any way but to call to you, tell you what I know...."

I took a deep breath, and perhaps he stopped because he thought I was going to interrupt him with some remark, but perhaps he just stopped because his many-angled and overlapping loyalties simply left him so weak, and his effectiveness such a tenuous thing, that just a breath stopped him.

"Please," he said. He knew I didn't want to listen to him.

"You got nothing to give me, Vinciguerra. Thank you."

"Please promise me, about the girl—"

This was a problem of his own, he and Sophia, I thought. I have enough many-angled problems of my own to worry about his. I just turned around and left him to stand there, in the alley.

Chapter 12

I was alone which felt fine, because I had my own plans now and no more of those useless hopes and wishes for Vinciguerra's help. I did not think about him, or about the town for that matter, but only about the way I myself could now manage to shake all this.

When I got back to the rock shelf I stopped for a moment and just stood up there.

I did not even wish this were my last look around because I was so sure of the last look being soon and certain. And I did not think of Sophia at all.

I walked around the shack and away from it. I walked all the way to the end of the shelf.

I stood there and looked at the sun turning a very slow, late color of day and to think of it now, it had all lasted, all of this, for less than twenty-four hours.

And on this day, this hour, the vise had grown very much. "Do you think there is nothing else they can do to you—"

I didn't think they could do anything else to me, if everything was still right up here, and Sophia had told me—not that she knew it—that everything must still be right.

The thing was this. Anybody who runs a war in any sort of a luxury fashion will see to it that the personnel always has some kind of way out. And we of course—except for some desperate moments where you just had to die—had run a fairly luxurious war, especially for that short time in Sicily where we had been without enemy to boot. But—sign of luxury—there always had to be a way out.

One way to and from the radio shack was the rock path. And what if that path was blocked or sealed off in some way? The personnel on the shelf would blow up the shack and equipment and leave the other way.

I stood on the shelf and took my bearings—straight eye line along one wall of the shack so that the far corner would constantly overlap—and walked backwards that way to the edge of the shelf. I did this slowly, checking back and forth, and when I could see the drop I quit walking. I got down on my hands and knees and crawled to the edge where absolutely nothing showed but one thousand feet of air going down, and then a broken rock slope like the left-overs of somebody's giant tantrum. At the end of the rock rubbish below showed a piece of the highway which wound up and into Forza d'Aguil. The same highway showed here and there in three places. Which was the reason why I wouldn't try leaving except in the night.

I lay down at the edge, like a seal sunning himself on a rock, and I dangled one arm over the drop, seal flipper dangling.

I couldn't see the crack under the overhang, but I felt it. The crack was not wide and it was full of rocks.

There was a donkey walking by on the road below, and then two more, all in a line. I could see them nodding themselves ahead and after the last donkey came the man. He held the last donkey's tail in his hand while the donkey pulled. The man and the donkeys didn't look up and they seemed like something that walks by, nod by nod, on the bottom of a very clear pool. And then disappeared.

I waited a while and then took out the rocks. This was an unpleasant business. The rocks jammed and I cut my fingers and something else unpleasant about this, the thing was boobied.

Anybody who runs a war in any sort of luxury fashion will leave a booby trap. I have no idea why. For example, all the stuff in the radio shack had been boobied, but we took the explosives away when we took the equipment.

But under the ledge in the crack, coiled up there and luxuriously as brand new as ever—I could feel it cold under my fingers—there was a rope ladder thing made out of nylon and aluminum.

Played out it would dangle for maybe one hundred feet and the rest of it would then lie on the slant of the rock which went down for a thousand feet of pure air. The ladder was not one thousand feet long. When it ended you could start climbing down. After five hundred feet of that, on a little shelf down below you then did two things. Number one, blow the booby, which tore the ladder out of the stone so that no one could follow. Number two, you pray that no rockslide would follow you either.

If you have survived so far, and the engineers had said that you could, then you did five hundred feet of sliding and crawling. Next came the rubble slope and then the road. But first, blow the booby, which was sort of a convention of war.

But the convention which worried me now was the booby trigger and its irritability.

The thing had been set up to be investigated and handled by two men assisting each other on the ledge or by a man with a rope, so that he could get far enough down and see what he was doing in the crack with the ladder curled up.

I got my hand out and sat up and sucked my knuckles. I took time out to take the old bandages off which Vinciguerra had loved onto me and also took a little stroll around the shack, just for a look. But I was alone.

Back in the belly position, most cautiously now, last rock out of the way, I tapped around for the coils of wire. I tapped, wishing to touch nothing but the wire spool, and above all not to touch the spring trigger. The detonation man had said you could tap the trigger and you would probably survive that because the thing needed a yank from the wire which you took down five hundred feet with you, but who knows.

Where the ladder was hooked into the bolts they had driven into the rock, there would be the explosives package. And on top of it, like a scarab guarding the hoard, sat the trigger.

I yanked my hand out of the way as if I had been bitten and took another few minutes to relax again.

"You don't mind the wind?"

I was not so relaxed that I didn't spin around on the self like a lizard, and there was the padre. I got up slowly and wiped my hands. And being angry and frightened and having to cover up both, I managed to say something stilted.

"I am looking at the distant freedom over there."

"Hum," he said and came closer. He looked at the rubble I had taken out of the crack and then at the distance.

"I often come up here to contemplate," he said.

"The same thing?"

"I beg your pardon?"

"To contemplate the same thing?"

"Oh, the distant freedom? No. I don't need it."

Yessir, I thought, spoken like a citizen of Forza d'Aguil or maybe like a citizen of the church and of course everybody is wrong and I'm right. I want out.

"Are you staying long?" he said.

I almost laughed. I watched him push his hands into his sleeves and watched how his cassock fluttered. I was reminded of a large crow pulling its wings together for a rest on a branch.

"I don't know," I said. "Maybe you do. You know about me?"

"I saw you with the girl Sophia before," he said. He stood against the light and I couldn't tell what his expression was.

"I didn't mean that. I meant, you know what's been going on here since I've hit this town?"

"It's not my office to...."

"Alright. Alright."

I distrusted him and turned away. I distrusted him enough to suspect the innocence of his presence now, especially when he said the next thing.

"Where did you find those rocks?" he nodded at the rubble at the edge of the shelf.

"Up here."

He looked around and shook his head.

"I'm up here often. As I said, I have used the shelf for a retreat. And there are no rocks here that I've ever seen."

"You look for rocks while you contemplate?"

"No."

He had moved now and I could see his face in the light. He looked indulgent. Big peasant face and grey shock of hair, a muleskinner disguised as a priest, and indulgent with me.

"I found them in the shack, where the wooden floor had been torn out," I told him. "And I took them out here to throw."

"Throw?"

"Throw. I used to be crazy about throwing rocks in a pond, I mean crazy about it. And this one here is the craziest yet, I can stand there by the drop and throw way out into nothing, the aim being the ocean over there, and never knowing whether I make it or not."

"You sound strange," he said.

That was alright with me. It was fine with me if he would accept an idiot explanation by regarding me as an idiot.

"I am strange," I told him. "For example, I come here and feel that being an idiot is the best way to...."

He raised his hand for a preachment and smiled.

"In the eyes of our Savior...."

"Oh no," I told him. "He could tell the difference between one and the other."

"Perhaps if you stay with us long enough...."

"Go away and contemplate. You're interrupting my secular preoccupations."

He shrugged and pushed his hands into the sleeves again.

It was my feeling that he would have much preferred to belt me one with those big hands.

I turned away and waited to hear him leave. He had come to worry me with his watching, he had made me apprehensive, by asking about the rocks, and he was nothing but a useless irritation to me with his prescribed kind of offer for help. And the wind up there was making me nervous. When I turned I saw him walking away, the black cassock tugging and flapping. Big, black birds, such as crows, doom messengers in all ages—

I followed him after a while, to a place where I could see him crossing the cemetery. Then I went back to the shelf, laid down there, to finish my secular preoccupation.

The little trigger mechanism which I could feel with my fingers but which I could not see, had two settings. One, to detonate with the wire from below, so that the ladder would rip out of the rock and could no longer be used. Two, it could be set as a regular booby trap, so that the next man using the ladder would get blown to shreds just like the rock. Luxury war arrangement, choice of deaths.

I picked up my nerve and I closed my eyes as if that would make a difference and felt all over the scarab on top of the explosive. It felt the way I had recalled, the whole mechanism was depressed, and so inactive.

Which is how I wanted it. All I wanted that coming night was a soft, quiet exit from there.

Then I reached the spool of wire which triggered everything from below. I left it lie. Maybe, I thought, I'll change my mind later, set the trigger on action, take the spool down with me. One tug would set the booby trap, second tug would blow the works right then and there. Maybe later, in case I felt really vicious. The choice pleased me and I got up.

Before I left I did one other thing, I moved all the rubble about five feet over. The contemplating padre would still find the stones, but they wouldn't be likely to guide him to the crevice below the overhang. Then I left.

I now felt so good about having that choice with the trigger setting and about leaving the rock down that ladder, I walked through town whistling a little, not too much but just a little, because too much whistling interferes with thought. I had rather happy thoughts, for the first time since coming here. And I experienced a most delicious indecision. What to do about my little scarab?

I could leave the trigger alone, leave it on inactive. Chances that anybody would see a thin nylon ladder one thousand feet up a rock were not very good. And then the escape—no! Not the escape, because that is *impossible*. Yes, then the *disappearance* of Mysterious Matheson from the fastness of Forza d'Aguil would become legend, would become folklore in time, would inspire young shepherds with pointed sticks, would shiver the certainties of old Mafia ways, would drive the weak to hysteria and the strong into depression. Proverbs to frighten children would be invented, proverbs to rule the masses and to guide them in humble ways would flower from the Myth of Mysterious Matheson.

I couldn't think of one damn proverb so I dropped the subject and went on to the next one, which is called *Sudden Surprise*.

In the dead of night when the Mighty Matheson *disappears* (as legend will have it) right over the lip of the rock he will take the wire spool with him. And then, on the shelf below, with wire in hand between gently nervous fingers, he will then send just the barest tickle of tension up that wire. What? Nothing happens? Why, of course! Got to set that trigger first, which means jerk. Those clever engineers of ours, biggest jerk-off outfit ever. But enough of this wit now. The little scarab is waiting. He has the bit in his mouth while Muscular Matheson is holding the reins. And there'll be no jerking now please, none of that jerking of the reins when the sensitive scarab holds the bit in his mouth because with the gentlest nudge the sensitive animal will rear straight up. Now, little Scarab my Arab shall we—whammo! I'll call that a kick!

And while the rock lip rises like a snarl and then bursts into a roar, the sodden citizens of the town will finally hear something that they have not said themselves. They will hear in the middle of the night, in the middle of their safe, rockbound night, that their rock can tremble. Might even make a better legend than the other. Mighty Matheson *disappeared* in a rock-rending roar of—I couldn't make up my mind whether to make it thunder, laughter, cloud of smoke, ball of lightning, or what. I said to hell with it, because I had one to go.

I was almost at the square now and could see it lie in the sun. I saw nothing out of the ordinary except that I realized that I had not noticed any people throughout the length of my fantasy. Given the absorption of a killer you can even forget that you are in Forza d'Aguil. I passed the first man I had really noticed since leaving the high place in a marvelous reverie and was right back in the clutch of this place. He looked me straight in the face and his black eyes gave me the old story. You are a stranger and should never have come, and now that you're here we won't let you go. No exit. You'll stay here and dance us a dance of death till you collapse.

I looked back at the man and felt myself smiling. I had one dream to go and I'll drag you, *mafioso,* right into it. I'll give you, I think, Mighty Matheson's departure present called the *Delayed Doom.* That's where I leave the wire to lie on top of the plateau, friend, and then sometime you'll find it and pick it up. *Delayed Doom.* It's a long-term Mafia type of amusement, which you will understand. My little scarab will tear you to pieces with machine-like indifference, with that Mafia indifference to everything except completion of built-in doom.

Suddenly my meanderings felt no longer amusing and I was back in the square. Somebody stepped out of my way, almost brushing me, which caused me to turn and to spit on the ground where this somebody had just been walking. He whirled to glare at me. I didn't smile at this one. I just laughed out loud, full of myself. Then I went to the hotel.

Chapter 13

I knocked on Vinciguerra's door and he opened it. He stood between the sunlight and the lamplight, waiting.

"May I have a room for the night?" I asked him.

"Of course."

"And I haven't paid you for the last one yet."

He let that go by, but he said, "I saw the padre a little while ago."

I held still and waited.

"He says that you seem to be getting childish."

"He envies my innocence, Vinciguerra."

"There is a matter of throwing stones down from the shelf. It might be dangerous."

"Ah yes. A whole avalanche of things could happen."

"During the war you Americans had a radio post up on that shelf, and some of the installations seemed to require blasting. At that time...."

"What was installed, Vinciguerra?" I had to cough at the end of the sentence in order to feel real hardness inside my throat and my guts, instead of jelly.

"A shack."

"Is that right."

"You saw the shack up there."

"Yes. I don't see what required blasting."

"Perhaps the foundation," said Vinciguerra.

And the little crack in the rock, and the little holes for the little bolts for the long ladder, maybe. And I stood there and started to sweat.

"So what do you want, Vinciguerra?"

"Nothing. Just to tell you that some of the blasting made rocks fly down from there, and this caused a rockslide which was a threat to the road below."

He stood in the door between the lamp light and the sunlight and I stood there feeling like nowhere and what am I reading into this and what is really there—

"You don't want me to go up there anymore?"

"I don't care."

"Who does?"

"No one, I think. I was just speaking about throwing rocks."

You, Vince, were just talking life and death, and as always, didn't know it— Or maybe he did, always, but just did not show it.

"Fuie," I said. "And now I'll have a cup of coffee."

"The kitchen is closed, at this hour."

I knew it was too early but I said, "I know the help. I think I'll get a cup of coffee," and I turned away with his look holding on to me, that look I was beginning to hate everytime there was a reference to the maid, Sophia. But, he said nothing else.

In fact, the kitchen was not closed and there was somebody else in the restaurant, eating soup. Sophia came out and I told her I wanted coffee.

I think this room was the sunniest in the town, with several windows looking out on the square and no house close enough to make that eternal shadow of Forza d'Aguil. I sat and hunched myself over my arms and felt warm now and did some more playful thinking about the little versatile trigger. That line of thought, though, did not turn out very warming anymore. I'm not really a ghoul at all but need a great deal of scratch by irritation to enjoy booby trap thoughts for any extended period of time. And I did not feel scratched or irritated right then but felt strangely free with my afternoon. Everything was now settled ahead of time, no more important unknown anywhere. I had my way out. The vise no longer mattered.

Sophia crossed the room with a plate for the other table and we looked at each other, a straight look going back and forth, without innuendoes or any questions at all. No important unknowns left there either.

On her way back she stopped at my table and held her arms in that hug she liked.

"You know," she said, "I don't know your name."

And what was my name? Perhaps this close to the end the name wouldn't matter, they could take my name and remember that I had been here once before and to hell with it. They could add it to all my other crimes that I had invaded them once before and—insult or insults—without even knowing what a fearful place this really was.

"Matty," I said to her. Which was true enough, though I don't think the natives had known it.

She repeated the name and smiled and said that it had felt just a little bit funny to her, not knowing my name, after what we had done together.

"And in view of what we will do together."

She smiled and must have been thinking about it, she looked that way, when she hugged herself more, and softened with a small sigh which moved her breasts and her belly. All this in a little moment of time and altogether between us.

"Witchery," I said. "Cut that out and bring me my coffee."

She laughed and went. I watched how she moved, walking, and thought, Christ, how to do this thing tonight, and how to wait till tonight. How to do everything in one night, I thought, and I truly meant everything, sitting there with my lively sensations.

She came back with the coffee. The lights and shadows moved over her as she crossed the room. It made me envy the light touching her here and there and all over. Then my eyes did the same thing.

"You," she said and put the coffee down. "You should talk about witchery."

I grunted and moved my hand to the cup.

"You just touched me," she said, "while I was walking."

When she let go of the cup she slid one finger over the back of my hand and left.

Now if she keeps moving around like that, I thought, and kept my eyes closed for a moment, then I won't know what will be.

I opened my eyes and saw her at the other end of the room, by the buffet with all the bottles on top, and looking at me. Of course. She knows exactly how I feel and likes it. I nodded my head at her and she came over immediately.

"When'd you say you're off?"

"Very late, Matty. Very late." She raised her eyebrows, shrugged and went away.

That vixen, she enjoys this even more than I, and I felt like springing clear across the room over all the tables. She leaned on the buffet and when I looked at her she cocked one hip.

"Hey," I said. "Come here."

The man at the other table looked up, then kept eating. She pushed away from the buffet, brushed her hair back with a most crazy-making gesture of arm and hand and back curving, and went into the kitchen.

Goddamn this peajacket, why should I sit here and sweat. I took the peajacket off and got up. And there was Vinciguerra in the door to the kitchen. He just looked.

I sat down again and cursed him for looking at me and cursed me for taking his look in this way, this guilt and pity and puzzlement mixture of feelings—

He stepped aside and let Sophia pass. She had a glass of water on a plate and brought it to me.

"What in hell," I mumbled, thinking of Vinciguerra. "Get away from me."

"Take the water and say thank you," she said, "or I can't stand here like this."

And when she said the word *this* she pushed her hip against my arm, slow and insistent, and then away again.

"Goddamn it, girl, goddamn it—"

"He can't see this side of me," she said, and then moved away again.

This vixen, this hoyden from way back before she was born was having one tremendous ball for herself while I shivered and while Vinciguerra was dying there with his eyes. Then he left and she grinned at me from across the room. I drank the water.

The man at the next table got up, scarfed himself, walked out bent. He yelled, *ciao,* in such a universal way of address that I felt sure he must be deaf, and perhaps somewhat blind too.

Then Vinciguerra was back.

I, in order to keep this up—and I could not leave now—I decided to order a meal. I would now have ordered a banquet just to get the extra time with her. Also, I wanted to ask her something.

Vinciguerra looked at Sophia who was clearing the table and went to stand by the buffet.

"I want to order a meal," I called across.

Vinciguerra came to my table and said he'd take the order. I gave him some kind of order, feeling all kinked inside and ill-tempered. Then Vinciguerra went into the kitchen and in a while Sophia came over, to set my table.

"Listen," I said. "Come over to this side."

"I'm setting the table."

"Come on this side. I want to touch you."

"Tonight. Late."

"Listen, goddamn it," and I watched Vinciguerra pass like a shy voyeur on the other side of the kitchen door. There is nothing as ludicrous as a shy voyeur. "Listen, girl. What's with him?"

"Vinciguerra?"

"What else, I mean, who else."

"Nothing," she said.

"You been sleeping with him?"

"Who, Vinciguerra?" She laughed and left the table.

I sat in a boil there at the table, waiting for a meal I did not want. I watched Vinciguerra pass again and I bent the teeth of my fork. Then Sophia came back.

"Yes, Vinciguerra," I said, as if I didn't feel interrupted at all. "You been sleeping with him?"

"Oh no. He doesn't want to," and she left again, leaving a wine glass for me.

And the next time she comes by I'll grab her by the leg, throw her down, sit on her, and ask in a quiet voice: what did you mean, dear, when you said *he* doesn't want to?

This time when she came back she brought the wine for my wine glass. She looked very demure, carrying the bottle.

"What did you mean, dear, when you said *he* doesn't want to?"

She burst out laughing and left.

Of course Vinciguerra had to look through the door, he did look in through the door and I grinned at him, to show how I too know how to enjoy an innocent joke between myself and the help.

They ate early in this town, it turned out, because now with the sun still showing, a few people came into the restaurant and sat down at tables. Sophia went back and forth and Vinciguerra went back and forth, and I gave up. It was sheer idiocy, of course, to sit there and plan a mad tryst, to occur instantly someplace in the back of the kitchen, but I sat there with my glass full of sour wine and thought about it just the same. In a while Vinciguerra went out and I could see him across the square, in front of the *osteria*, where he sat in the cold shade and had coffee at a small table. His love for his chambermaid, he seemed to feel, was secure.

Sophia brought a soup which was yellow with saffron.

"Listen to me."

"Yes," she said.

"And don't stand there and wiggle at me."

"I wasn't moving a muscle, Matty."

"Then how do you do it?"

"Just naturally, Matty, but I'll stop it."

Of course she left then. And I'll say there was no wiggle in her walk but just the most natural swing to everything moving. I bent over and ate saffron soup.

I will now turn yellow like saffron and maybe then she'll come over again and ask me what was the matter. Or more likely, she would put something else on the table, something red with pepper so I could turn red instead of yellow, since she prefers red.

She brought pasta with olive oil on it, all heated and garlicked.

"I'm sorry, Matty. I won't tease you anymore."

"I'll smell from garlic."

"I don't mind."

"I meant to ask you...."

"Around ten," she said, having forgotten to cut out the teasing. But she stayed at the table, looking busy.

"Why does Vinciguerra act this way? He your guardian?"

"No. Nothing. I just work for him."

"He's in love with you?"

"I don't know," she said. "It's very strange. He has a history."

"Please don't go away yet."

"I'll just clear these plates."

She did but was back right away.

"He wakes me up in the middle of the night and perhaps he just wants to see how ugly I look, waking up and feeling all swollen."

"That's why you don't like him?"

"I don't know. I don't like not understanding him. I don't even think he wants to see me look ugly. I just said that before."

"He wakes you up and then what?"

"Like the time when you came for a room. He woke me up, I don't know why. Because there was a room all fixed, I told you."

"I remember."

"Other times he wakes me up—you know he can't sleep and sits all night—and asks me to make him some tea."

"So would I."

"But you wouldn't do what comes afterwards."

"Some ghoul type thing?"

"No. He has me sit with him in his room. He drinks his tea and reads to me, any of those things he has there, and then he tries to talk to me about them."

"He's hungry for conversation, Sophia."

"But why with me? I don't answer him. Not well, anyway."

"Maybe he thinks he is being fatherly and he wants you to like him."

She frowned and said, "I don't dislike him. But his strangeness troubles me."

"I've heard him talk. I've seen how he weaves a thing into being."

"Yes," she said. "That's all."

She left again and I ate. I did not think that was all.

Chapter 14

When I was done at the table the sun was out of sight, behind the opposite houses and this caused an immediate darkness and dankness everywhere. All objects were still visible but as if reflecting darkness and not light. My own small mid-afternoon madness was gone now because the kind of madness that can survive here does not have any fun in it.

I think Sophia knew something of this sort too because she came to my table once more, looking the same as before but cool now, not drawing me to her, and said she would be busy now with the dishes.

I went outside and wandered around the square which lay under the first touch of the nightwind already. I put my hands into my pockets and felt the warmth in there and nowhere else. That was alright. I was not looking for warmth anywhere else. I felt alone and that was alright too because it meant that I did not need anything else. I met Vinciguerra on my second turn.

"You asked about a room for the night," he said. "I'll have the same room for you. The one you had once before."

"Without *riscaldamento?*"

"As you wish."

Neither he nor I were interested in the remark as a joke. I for one wasn't interested in anything he might have to say to me anymore. I was really leaving. But he, Vinciguerra, perhaps he never came truly alive until this hour of evening, and only showed a spark of some kind when the light was grey.

"Are you reasonably well?" he asked and he looked at me with real interest, or even concern.

This question, of course, and this manner, I knew very well. Next he would start to weave himself into everything that he touched in a most infectious manner. I wanted no part of that.

"I'm fine. Thank you. Had a lovely meal, too."

"You no longer look as if you were waiting for everything," he said without any transition.

It needed no transition. The fact was simply there, and he saw it.

"I'm not waiting because I don't know what I'm waiting for, Vinciguerra."

"That's a very blind thing for you to say. As if one only waits for something one already knows."

"You can cut that out, Vinciguerra. Just cut that kind of talk out. I've had it."

"Alright."

But of course, he had me. I had to ask the next thing.

"What am I waiting for?"

"Well," he said. "They won't let you go from here, obviously."

"What's the punishment in this, Vinciguerra, the not letting me go, or the vagueness of the situation?"

"Avoiding you, the way they do, is part of it, yes."

"And why don't you?"

He raised his hands by his sides and then dropped them again, making a small sound against cloth. I thought that he suddenly looked incredibly helpless.

"I have tried to help you. This is a way of helping you. Don't you see?"

I saw that, I saw that it was the most pathetic kind of help there was, help offered kindly and openly, but useless.

I shrugged and tried to think of something to say to him but he turned away at that point and did not see my shrug. At the same time he started to walk again, as if knowing that I would follow. I followed him and we walked slowly.

"Of course, you think again that I haven't said anything to you because you listen for only the simplest."

"All I need at the present. I'm that reduced."

"I understand that." And nothing else.

I now felt as alone as I had before, but it was an alone of missing something. I blamed this on Vinciguerra. I always missed something with him.

"I'm not going back in there," I said.

He was heading for the hotel and when I made my remark he stopped and looked at me. This made me hear my remark again and I immediately felt cautious.

"I'm staying out a while longer."

He nodded and seemed satisfied. Then it struck me why he was satisfied. I felt annoyed.

"Listen, Vinciguerra."

"Yes?"

"Why is it, Vinciguerra, every time I'm with your chambermaid you start to tremble?"

He looked at me and around all in the same motion, the same motion you see in a bird gliding down to sit and hold on and stay at rest when the glide suddenly becomes a continuous swoop and the bird raises up and goes on. Then he looked back at me and said, "I just tremble."

I felt that this was perhaps the most personal thing he had ever said to me. Perhaps there had been others, but this was the least complicated response, the most direct answer.

"I know," I said and had nothing else to say.

"I have known her for some time."

"Yuh," I said. "How well?"

"My needs are few."

"But complicated."

He shrugged and started to walk again so that he was now ahead of me. But he stopped almost immediately and turned to face me with a fluidity that surprised me.

"Have you slept with her?"

"No."

The ease of my lie came naturally because in that instant I saw a Vinciguerra with two faces, a younger one from my earlier time here and the worried one in front of me now. While he had asked the question, for one moment, the habitual reticence of his face split, the eyes seemed to gush with pleading and his mouth was slack as from an extension of pain. My prompt no restored all that. His face did not show satisfaction—I don't think Vinciguerra knew satisfaction—but it sunk into repose.

We were only a few steps from the hotel and he walked there, then stopped again.

"I must attend to things in the kitchen," he said, turned, and left me feeling dismissed.

I not only felt dismissed but completely interrupted. I don't know what direction more conversation would have taken but since he had brought up Sophia, an uneasiness about the girl had been stirring me. Naturally, I had wanted to talk about Sophia. And now the old bastard, having gotten what he wanted, just left.

First, I thought I would walk some more, then I decided against it. I stood smoking and decided to go over my night plans once more, but that did not hold my interest either. Sophia interfered.

The thing between Sophia and me had been a straight body wish, good and strong, and we had been able to finish it. That kind of meeting needs no good bye. I had not planned on saying good-bye to Sophia, we would not have needed it. See her at ten, come together with a wonderful appetite for each other, feast, rest and leave happier.

I started to walk and felt stiff, almost tired. I leaned against the front of the hotel, under one of the restaurant windows, but felt too twitchy to rest.

Behind that window was a table and perhaps Sophia was there at this moment, very close. I almost turned. Perhaps I would catch a glimpse—

I have known fun women and a few love women though perhaps they had been no different but instead it had been my mood. I have not introspected on this but instead, so it struck me now, had led a life which involved running from port to port. It's a convenience, though it has also its pains. Once I had stayed a longish time which had been wonderful, the great wonder of waking up in the morning, needing someone very strongly, knowing that this need for this one woman will always be satisfied. It is one form of love. In the end something went wrong, we went separate ways, and since then I never much dwelt on it because I could do nothing about it until now. It might be we were just naturally quite finished with each other because we had not parted enemies. But what I have often mused over was this unique ache of a longing with the bright sureness that its answer was always right there beside you.

This had been a matter of memory. With a shock I now realized that it was moving into the present.

Sophia.

I slapped my hands against the stone wall behind me with such violence that the gesture pushed me away from the wall. Then I walked fast.

The insanity! To nourish the seeds for an involvement like this—at a time like this—and in Forza d'Aguil!

And Sophia? Wonderful funtime animal who knew nothing of this, felt nothing of this herself though she would surely be sympathetic.

I don't know how long I walked with a growing rage of self-hate building up inside me, over my self-ignorance, muddleheadedness, and over the ill-chance that I should wake up to a wish which was not to be answered. But in a while I was done with the hairpulling and with spitting into my own eye—to hell with tearing me up like this because I may be an idiot, but my own enemy I really am not.

I felt very much better and took a deep breath. Head clear now and feeling solid with energy. I'm not waiting till ten of course. I'm getting out right now. And Sophia? A good lust had covered the small presence of the other wish I had discovered and good lust was going to finish it off. That was going to be the good finish between us. I laughed in the dark and headed back to the hotel. It was by no means ten o'clock yet.

I looked through the glass of the restaurant door but Sophia was not there. My breath made steam on the glass.

Behind the stairs was a door which led to a narrow corridor which leads out the back. One of the doors off that corridor had to be to the kitchen.

A yellow bulb showed a room where the staples stood on shelves and the fat bag of pasta on the floor. Sausages hung from the ceiling and a lot of braids with the garlic knolls showing a color like pearl. The room smelled like a meal. I walked on where I heard the kitchen clatter behind the next door. The door opened and Sophia came out. She had a broom in one hand and a slop bucket in the other. She sidled out of the door with these things, back turned to me, and headed for the door at the end where the yard showed all black.

"Sophia."

She first put the slop bucket down, wiped one hand, and then turned around. She was smiling.

"My bear looks heated," she said and I think she used the double meaning deliberately.

When she walked towards me, broom in one hand, I saw she was playing the game again, like in the afternoon.

"It'll be way, *way* after ten, with all these interruptions," she said. But she wasn't addressing me. She was resting the broom on the floor, upside down, with the ragged palmfrond head right next to her shoulder. "Tell him, *caro*," she said to the broom, "that you and I are going to spend just the longest time together, and we don't want anyone watching." Then she stroked her hair back with an unconcerned gesture and next, most affectionately, she did the same thing to the palmfronds of her broom.

"Come here," I said.

She came closer and stopped very near. She leaned the broom against the wall and looked up at me with a sudden stillness in her. Her eyes looked and her mouth was not smiling.

"*Cosa*," she whispered. "*Cosa—*"

She said it exactly in the same way I had heard it once before. I looked away for a moment and my mouth felt tight. Then I felt her hand on my arm.

"Matty. Do you have to say something to me?"

I didn't say anything. I just nodded my head and then she was tight up against me, face pressed into my chest.

"Matty," I heard her say and then I think she mumbled, "No—"

We did no thinking or explaining but we were suddenly walking into an arm of the corridor where it was very dark. I smelled root odor and felt an old wall. When she stopped in the dark she turned my way again. She said nothing but I could hear her breath. I reached for her and she moved under my hands.

"Matty— but there's no time—"

"I know that. I know."

"Matty," she said. "Can't you wait? I know there is nothing to talk about but...."

"You can't talk to me. I'm mad."

"I am mad too."

I heard myself breathe in the dark there and I felt that I was breathing all through her and into her.

"*Dio*," she said. "*Dio—*"

For an instant she trembled but that changed into a wavelike motion, her body pressing into me. She bumped into something in back of her which turned out to be a small table. I took Sophia under both arms and lifted her on the wooden top. It was very dark. I think that neither of us wanted to see. I was glad that she could not see my face and I was glad that I could not see her eyes.

She held on with her arms. She let go once to pull her skirt out of the way and then she moved close up to me and opened her thighs.

The heat, the unbearable heat, and then the melting. And after that it was darker there, a much deeper dark than I had ever known.

Chapter 15

She left first and when I left she was not in the hall. I ran out of there. I got out to the yard and the cold air had started to blow and there was no longer the deep, deep black from which I had come but the air was glassy and had a sheen. Perhaps there was a moon. I saw that the yard had a wall all around it and if I wanted to get out to the alley I had to use a wooden gate with a padlock on it.

I went back into the hall where the light in the bulb looked sick and offensive, and the tall walls reminding of the skin of old men. I walked through and when I passed the kitchen there was Vinciguerra in the door. He was just opening it.

Nothing passed between us, no words or anything else, but he looked at me with his own peculiar and very private horror, which I had seen only that one other time. I went out. It was fitting, I thought, that this should be my last sight of him.

I went out to the square and started to walk. I felt a small edge of haste in me but mostly the strength of having a purpose. I took a turn around the square past the *osteria*. I was seen and I was avoided. Perhaps I was followed too, though I doubt it. The people of Forza d'Aguil were like ants, all parts of one organic body. I'm sure no signals passed to announce that the intruder was out on the streets. They were all of one mind. They needed no instructions. I walked and no one paid any attention to me. When I came within sight of the gate everything changed, slowly, undramatically, and as expected. There was less stepping out of the way, there were also more people. A ring formed behind me and men drifted to the gate, looking idle. They looked black with the lack of light and the wind moved their pants and their coats with the very sudden tug of a whip.

If I would stand there all night they would stand there all night. Once I left, they would leave too.

I turned and the ring which had formed in back of me opened. The further I got away from the gate the more I was ignored. The total mass action which had come into play the closer I had moved to the gate disappeared and they moved in their own, huddled ways, or gesticulating and talking, ignoring me.

I wandered around. I wanted the ants to know that this was my evening walk, that I had resigned myself after the silent scene at the gate, and that I did not know what to do. I watched an argument on the street between two old women. Their gestures were sharp, even violent in an attempt to lend meaning but they looked more desperate to me than successful. I watched a man unload the sweet-smelling brush from a donkey in front of the baker's shop. I looked in at the cave with the wheels and the bicycles. My Vespa, both tires slashed, was still leaning there. The white haired old man sat by his bench sucking bread and warming one hand on a glass of coffee. All this looked gentle and small and as if slowly antiqued. But I didn't believe it. My demonstration walk was over right there and then. I could feel the haste sit high in my throat.

When I got to the terrace of the church I gave one look back but there was no one in sight. I walked around the dark church, into the wind which was erratic now and impatient. Through the graveyard, up the stone path, I knew all this by heart and was up on the shelf before actually having gotten there. And then I was there. The moon held still like death, the sky was endless with stars, and the slab under me looked like metal where the moonlight touched it. And always the wind. Up here it had a push like a fist and a sound like anger and all that was alright with me too.

I trembled a little when I groped down from the shelf. I felt down and around where I couldn't see, while one thousand feet of pure air looked up at me.

I got the coiled ladder first. The metal bit with cold. I hauled the coil apart, which was sweat labor and took time. I didn't want to pull myself straight down into one thousand feet of nothing. I got a loop of the ladder up my way and laid it on the shelf. The anchored end I pulled tight up and the long end I left loose, not wanting to pull all of the ladder away from its resting place. Once the long end was out of the crack it would fall all the way down, hanging straight, and then it would be hell to pay to get off the shelf on an invisible ladder. The set-up had been planned with a rope from the shack, the rope letting you down till you reached the ladder. Or two men helping each other. I had no rope and no help but my way would work, had to work, even though there would be an unpleasant moment: I would slide, feet first, off the shelf, holding on to the ladder loop lying under me. There would be that moment of falling free and then the jerk as the anchored end of the ladder fell taut with me. After that, simple. Haul the free end which lay coiled in the crack out from there, let it drop, climb down, and away.

I knew all this so well and with so much certainty, I got very impatient. But I got the ladder loop up on the shelf where I wanted it. I had tears in my eyes from the wind and the effort.

But the confidence, the free feeling of making it now. So that I forgot all about my little scarab, guarding this treasure. For a moment I just sat and trembled, and then loving the rock under me which had not yet exploded,

I was trembling about that too, but went over it all once more, how the trigger worked and that I was safe.

The thing was down on inactive. If I wanted to, I could click it up, with my hand, so that the thing would work. Then, one pull on the wire and the thing was a booby. You stepped on the ladder or maybe just looked at it, off it went. Two pulls on the wire, to be done from below—

I now almost screamed with fright, but too frightened to move or scream, because there was a mistake!

If one pull on the wire would booby the thing, then how could I use the ladder without blowing to pieces!

A mistake. Easy there. I just hadn't remembered. Slow, calm thoughts now, sit here a moment and no wind is beating my face, fingering me like a nervous snake inside my collar, up the leg of my pants— Wait now, this thing must be simple, built for emergencies to be run without blueprints, to be run by frightened morons, that's how we built them, that's what I was—

I got up in a while and had it. Of course, you don't set the trigger on the active by hand, you are safe until—

No wind has a foot fall!

Then I heard nothing again.

Ghosts. No. Or perhaps the padre contemplating in the still of the moon and the roar of the night. Like hell he would. He'd come up to check over lover's rock to make the lover's leap. In this weather? Alright, ghosts.

I wasn't far enough gone to believe any of that but was trying to wait out the nervous giggle that now sat in my throat, think around it a while till it went away, and then be reasonable again. Reasonable is fine at a time like this, the very best out here in the wind anger and the far sky fear and—

I jumped with pure panic because whatever there was and wherever it came from, so help me it could not come from that side, not from the side of the one thousand foot drop!

I was true jelly after that, but jelly doesn't flutter around or apart, so that in that jelly-still moment I felt small and safe, sunken into myself.

All was simple, not speaking for the moment of my insane reaction. I had stood on the ladder loop on the ground and had shifted. With my weight off the ladder loop, the ladder with a twang and a slither, had dropped back and down under the shelf.

Let it go for a minute. Smoke—no, too much wind. And if the damn ladder had pulled all the way out of the crack and was hanging now, there'd be hell to pay, real trouble now to get that thing back up. But there hadn't been enough sound for that and to hell with it, I'll need strength for this one way or the other. Slow stretch and a walk.

I walked around the shack and was fine in a moment and the wind anger was really becoming my own now. I went back to the shelf and laid down.

I could feel the ladder and the way it stuck out and looped back, I knew that the paying end of the ladder was still in the crack, as before, and to pull the loop back to me would now be even simpler.

And I wouldn't forget about the trigger this time, as I had done before—I didn't think there was any more panic coming, I knew everything ahead of time now—I felt around for the wire spool first, found it, played it out carefully and got the spool up to me. I got up and played out some wire so that I wouldn't set the trigger on active by chance. This was delicate going, but now no more ghosts. Far away was a shimmer of sea, moon white. And also a shimmer of warmth, like a friendly light in a cabin—ghosts!

But I turned around, reasonably enough, and saw the yellow light in the shack.

It was true what I had felt. There was no more panic left.

Chapter 16

I had a pulse in me, small at first and then more and more active, a thump of pure power that went around like the blood.

"Come on out," I said.

The light went out with a little snap and then a red eye winked at me—why say eye? That was a cigarette.

"Come out," I said again.

The wind has no foot fall, just men do. I listened and waited.

I didn't know the first one and I didn't know the second one and both stayed at either side of the shack, leaning there the way they always lean, at the gate, for example, at the wall by the highway, looking black with lack of light and very still with a moonlike calm. But that was their affliction and I felt entirely different. The third one had the cigarette, and the pig hair too stiff for the wind to move it, and that was Pino.

"She was right," he said. "You were leaving."

Oh my god, how I hated him.

"We never knew about that thing there," he said, and he nodded at the edge of the shelf and walked closer. He was so calm about this, it looked like a manner.

I felt entirely different and when he was close enough I kicked out my foot. I even hit him, but it was just a smack. He jumped and gave a short laugh.

At any rate, the calm was a manner, or else he couldn't have jumped that well.

He stood away now and sucked on his cigarette.

"Is that how you get it up?" and he nodded at the wire that went from the spool in my hand to the drop, and away.

"How come you're here?" I said and I wanted to know just one thing.

"Because I don't want you to leave."

"How come you know I was here?"

"We watch. We are everywhere."

"Crap you are."

He grinned and said, "She told us."

I don't need a good bye but I do want a final act, and I knew now that the time in the dark passage with her had not been it. Or else I would not have run out of there with such violence, with the haste held in. But this was the final act. This, and now I could leave.

"I don't want you to take another step to that ledge," I told him.

He even stopped. I think the tone of my voice stopped him for a moment. He looked at his cigarette and then he threw it away.

"Pull it up again," and he nodded at the wire.

I put the wire spool down on the ground and when I straightened up again I undid my jacket. Pino cocked his head and then he looked at his buddies. I didn't care.

"I'm leaving. I'll first lay out every one of you, but I'm leaving."

"We are all one," said Pino.

The other two had moved closer, hands in pockets, and their ally, they thought, was the myth of their being all one and much bigger than each taken alone, a myth that can make me cry. Or can make me very angry.

I gave all this to the one who was nearest, a swift swing which had all my interest in it, and I'm sure that I broke his jaw.

This was not for demonstration and this was not the end, so I went right away for the other one.

The other one, as if hit himself (he did think they were all one) hopped back, or he staggered back, with the idiotic expression of those whose total belief has been rattled—but at any rate, he got far out of reach and I saw him smack into the wall of the shack.

Right then I turned to see how the pig hair was doing. He had the same expression of the one whose jaw was broken, so I turned back to the shack.

The idiot stare was still on the face, the strange mixture of idiot-animal, or the moonlight confused my impression, except for the clear fact that he had worked a gun out of his pocket.

"*Guarda*," he said. "*Guarda, guarda*," very fast and insistent, and the word means several things. I should look what he has there, I should better watch out, pay attention, and consider this.

I did all he said because he had the gun. So he had time to scramble up again, using the wall, and I could hear Pino behind me.

"That's one more count against you."

"Why don't you take a flying...."

"Everything's going to be held against you."

I turned and watched him but he didn't move.

"Play God a little longer, pig rump, and you'll end up just as disembodied."

"Which?"

"Disemboweled, pig rump."

And then he took the thought right out of my head, not to say that he took the job right out of my hands, and went right over to that wire there on the ground and gave it a yank.

I don't know what he expected, maybe some American miracle, some technologic erection, some kind of Golden Gate Bridge arching with unmentionable speed right across the thousand foot drop and into a pot of gold over there, or into Mother Leone's, Manhattan, New York.

I thought I might hear a click, and I did. I thought, either the thing blows and I'm dead, or it doesn't, and I live.

Nothing blew. The trigger, sweet scarab, was now set to booby. My sweet scarab was now all awake after a very long sleep.

Pino, of course, was disappointed.

"What's the trick here?" he said. "What's the trick?"

"The trick is this," I said, and I picked up the spool and held the wire so that there was just the slightest sag in it from me to the edge of the drop. "The trick is this." I stopped a moment because I felt very serious. I felt serious and did not want to rush it away. "This wire doesn't bring up the thing that hangs down, out of sight. This wire here pulls a trigger."

"Huh?" he said, and I hated him for his stupidity.

I felt serious for one simple reason. He had triggered the booby for me and I couldn't use the ladder without getting blown to bits. I might pull the wire again, blow the explosive myself, and perhaps stay out of the shrapnel of rock that would follow, but I would again lose the ladder.

Which meant all I had now was the threat of a death for him, even to the point of a demonstration.

Unless of course I fumbled my hand back into the crack and pushed the trigger into inactive position. I didn't remember if this was possible.

"What trigger?" he said.

"Look at the wire."

He looked and waited.

"See the belly in the way it hangs?"

"Huh?"

"I pull this thing tight, and I pull the trigger, and you, pig-rump, like the God that you are, join Kingdom Come."

He said something in Sicilian and I could only guess at the obscenity of it.

"So don't move," I said. I felt very serious and that made my hate for him just the same as the hottest kind of determination.

In fact, he did not move a muscle.

"Now tell the one behind me to throw down his gun."

"Huh?"

"You say 'huh' once more and I'll blow you up just for spite."

"And you too," he said.

"No. You're closer."

"And the one with the gun is even further away."

"Why worry about him. Start worrying about you."

"You can't get away," he said, and he was very certain about it.

"Pino," I said. "Pino pig. I'm getting out if it takes your death or my death or a crack down the middle of this basement town so the two halves just open away from each other and crash into Sicily and next there's just this cloud of dust."

I could see him hunch and I could see the sheen on his forehead, which was sweet, but there was not enough moonlight for me to see what his eyes looked like, what his mouth felt like, so that the next thing he said was a surprise to me.

"To hell with this town," he said. "To hell with it."

Next, I could just hear him breathe.

"So let me go," I said. "What's it to you?"

And that turned out the wrong trigger all the way, it just helped him to get back on his track.

"There's things bigger than this town," he said, and the myth was on him again. "And don't talk to me about this town."

I got the one human glimpse of him that I would ever have, that he could object to something all on his own. That made him a little more real to me and I hated the bastard twice as much. Because he was still in my way.

"You're one big, clever brute and if I get you down, there's two more filling your place, right, Pino?"

"Exactly," he said, and moved towards the wire again.

"But when you get torn apart because I pull that wire, that's just you getting crippled, that's just you all alone with your own guts in your hands. Can you understand that?"

I think he understood that, for just that one moment, because he said, "You're bluffing."

I almost pulled the wire right then, but I wanted the ladder more than I wanted him ripped apart. I didn't know for how much longer I'd feel like this, but right then I did.

"Once more," I said. "Go away," and I felt so intent on this, I almost said please.

He stopped and said, "Would you say please?"

"Yes. Please. I'm saying please." There was a moment with just the wind. Then he talked to his friend with the gun, but it was in Sicilian and I could understand just a word here and there. I got very involved with trying to catch what they said, very involved with wishing that they would decide something for me—

"I'll give you all I have with me," I interrupted. "Keep the Vespa. And I have twenty thousand lire here in my pocket."

They stopped talking and looked at me and then they looked at each other.

Pino gave a slight nod and the one with the gun lowered the gun and walked up to me.

"Okay," he said in English.

"Put the gun down on the ground."

He just grinned and came a little bit closer. We were all very cautious up there.

"Put the gun down or I'll trigger the bomb," I said.

"I don't think you will," said Pino, and to show that he meant it he even stepped closer to the drop of the shelf.

I hauled up the wire a little bit more, and made a great show of it. I felt badly on edge.

"Here," said the one near the shack. "Look, I'm not even holding the gun in order to shoot."

He now held the gun by the barrel, butt my way, and came closer to show me about the friendly gun.

He showed me. He showed me that he was quick as a snake and that there's more than one way to make a gun a weapon.

The next second—I'm not so slow either—the butt rushed over my face and did, in fact, catch me on the nose. Not a good smack but a painful grazing. All this only because I still held the wire and if I was going to move anywhere I would move towards the slack of the wire which meant away from that gun. I had been intent on that, which was the only reason he didn't tear off my nose with that butt.

Not that he was done. He was fast and was all gathered for action, so that I don't remember the details of any of this, just the fight meaning everything to me, and the pain when he got me in the groin and a pleasure like lust when I cut the side of his neck and the panic when we rolled so that the wire got tighter, and other things.

I had one arm only because it didn't strike me as foolish at all to keep holding that wire spool. But the one arm had all of me in it for a moment and I got to smash the other man's head down on the rock—we were down as it was—a smash with a sound like a palm smacked on water—but then I got suddenly weak and had to wonder why it hadn't sounded like bone on rock— He had me by the neck, I noticed.

I felt slow enough to wonder where he had learned that pressure grip without pain, that grip which stopped the strength from moving in me and gave me a cloud instead of a brain.

Then came the panic and I loved that panic because it can truly mean the final strength, which is very big, and then everything drops away that can hamper you, all the rules, all the qualifications—

I saw Pino get up from the edge of the drop where he had been leaning over, looking for things, got up because of the sound his buddy was making, and then I saw the gun lying there, between us and Pino, and though I got his hand off my neck I still couldn't get up.

"No!" I yelled. Or I thought I yelled. "I'll kill you from here! Pino, I'll kill—"

He laughed and bent for the gun.

He can laugh because he has reset the trigger!

"No!"

He laughed and I pulled the wire.

I felt it cut into my hand. Burn, little scarab, *burn for me!*

And the blossom came up.

I say a blossom because of the way it opened up but I say a sun because of the way it got big and searing.

I know I ducked, you don't have to plan something like that. And I know I saw Pino over me, ten feet over me, and flying there without legs. He looked like something half-way out of a hole. Something smacked me in the head and that was one of his legs. I didn't see the other one.

Chapter 17

Vinciguerra had his most satisfying hour of salving in years. He had three of us (Pino was dead) and after the soft hands and the soft salves I was shown to that room I had again and I lay down on the bed with three pillows behind me. I felt cold in my clothes (the room felt dank) and put a blanket across my legs.

Then Sophia came in. She looked at me and then she ducked her head as if slapped. I hadn't moved a muscle. She was now somebody who set down a tray by the bed, poured tea from a pot into a cup, and added one spoon of sugar. I hate sugar in tea but she could have put ten spoons full in there and I wouldn't have said anything. Then she left.

I drank the tea and when Vinciguerra came in I was smoking.

He sat down on the chair that was there and folded his hands.

"How are you?"

"Let's have the post-mortem," I said.

"Pino is dead."

"I know. Let's talk about me."

"They haven't found all of him," and he had a contemplative look on his face, as if contemplating all the various ways within range of possibility in which Pino might be distributed.

"Let's talk about me."

"The other one, whom you were beating, he's unconscious."

"Hasn't talked?"

"No. There's a concussion. Perhaps a rock hit him. One side of his face is fairly mashed and crippled."

"I hit him."

"Ah, so," said Vinciguerra.

"And the one with the broken jaw cries all of the time."

He sat there wanting to know something and I was on the bed, wanting to know something. I wanted to know, when is he going to ask, how come you knew about a booby trap up there, and a secret ladder, and aren't you the one who was here during the war?

"What exploded up there?" he asked.

"I don't know."

"Pino is dead, of course, and the other two, they can't talk...."

"They will."

"Not likely," said Vinciguerra. "They are on their way to the hospital in Messina and the doctor explained that he'll be too swollen, and the jaw

wired up, and the other one—it might be days. I have read about such con-
cussions."

"I can't help you," I said. I felt now so relieved, I could have gone to sleep.
I said, "I thought Pino had something or other, a bomb, and that went off
before he could throw it at me."

"Hm," said Vinciguerra. And then, "The one with the jaw tried to say
something."

"*Minquia?*"

"Please. He was confused. He said you had a wire, a special wire—is that
what made the cut in your palm?"

I looked at my palm with the plaster across the cut and said yes, that's
what cut me.

"He said you had a special type of extremely strong wire and you were
going to let yourself down the cliff with it."

"I was desperate," I said.

"What kind of wire is that?"

"Well, you know us Americans. We got all these remarkable inventions
you can carry in your pocket and they get you out of places like Forza
d'Aguil."

"Are you making fun of me?"

I sat up a little more, which hurt, and felt fairly angry.

"Look, Vinciguerra. I was trying to get away. I didn't make it and one
man is dead. You think I'm interested in talking about wires and explo-
sions and so forth, with that other business on my mind?"

"Of course, I see that," and he looked into his lap. "It was just puzzling
to everyone why Pino should carry such a bomb device, going after you."

"Going after me he also carried one extremely stupid head, two apish
hands too useless to ever have done an honest day's work, and finally one
bizarre notion about being able to tell me what to do. I'm much more puz-
zled why he should have brought those devices along, going after me."

Vinciguerra sighed and said he could fully understand my attitude and
my state of mind. And with that he gave up asking about the explosion.

I now had until morning before they might find the real answer, a rock
hole with telltale explosion marks, parts of the ladder. Then they'd remember who I might be and they'd have another resentment to add to their list.

Which, in a way, hardly mattered. At this point, I hadn't just bought a
bottle of wine in violation of their secret codes, I hadn't just walloped a kid
of theirs, to interfere with his smooth growing process towards becoming
a monster, I had now killed a *mafioso*.

"Where's the police, Vinciguerra?"

"I don't know at the moment."

"A man got killed!"

"I know."

"And maybe I did it!"

"I know that."

"So? That's all?"

"Of course not," he said, and got up. "In the meantime, try and rest up. Would you like some more of those pills I once gave you?"

"I don't want the goddamn pills you once gave me, I want something to *happen* now!"

"In the meantime," he said from the door. "Please rest."

He closed the door and I lay back too beat to worry about him and his unctuousness and in a while I lit another cigarette and watched the smoke go up making quiet spirals.

Now the vise was sprung. It had taken the death of a man to do it and it might take a great deal more legal to-do until I was out of it, but the vise was sprung.

The official law would have to come into this now, and the town threat and the Mafia codes, all that was over.

Then I sat there and waited. It was a long wait because I was impatient, and impatient, of course, because I would really get out now. No more groping, no more trying, but I just had to wait for it.

I had a watch (crystal cracked now, after the last interference) and it hadn't been very late actually when they found us on the rock and had brought us back. I had sat down on the bed at nine thirty.

I now knew all the cracks in the ceiling, every itch and ache in my body, I had listened to the up and down scales of the wind outside and now the wind had gone away. This was twelve midnight. And the wind had died.

What ate me up was my suspicion.

I got off the bed and tried the joints here and there. They were fine. I felt rotten but the joints were fine.

The hall was empty and the stairs too. The dim light was depressing, and the walls again the color and sight of a wrinkled skin. I touched the banister for support and the wood creak from that was the only sound in the house.

I looked up and thought of that girl, sleeping somewhere. The dim light was like mist. I looked up and thought of a sodden sleep, a mindless sleep and I wished a nightmare into it. Then I walked downstairs.

I went slowly enough and heavily enough so that the crack of light under Vinciguerra's door split open when I was still on the steps. I was on the second last step when the door opened there and Vinciguerra looked out.

Face of concern, eyes of wonder, next, anxious solicitude.

"But you should be in bed. You should...."

"Don't should me no shoulds, Vinciguerra."

He had a book in one hand, index finger between the closed pages, the book like a long snout which was holding his finger.

He stepped away, into his room, and I came all the way down. A warm wave of air came from his room where I could see the red mouth of the gas heater which sat in one corner. On the big chair by the table sat Sophia.

Let her nightmares be waking ones.

She wore the big robe I had seen once before, a girl head coming out of a big pile of robe. Her face, a child awakened from that mindless sleep. On one side of her head the hair was standing up.

"I'm waiting for the cops and I'm sick and tired of it," I said to Vinciguerra.

"Come in," he said, "come in."

This girl in the chair there, her head sunk down, her eyes closed as if asleep, as if wishing to be asleep, and the robe on her looked bigger now. A pile of folds and she's wishing there were nothing inside.

I walked out. I went all the way outside and there was the empty square, still and bare because there was no wind. There was nothing in the square, just cold air holding still.

I was so sure I could walk out of this now, this ruin, a graveyard except for your own imaginings—

I felt cold and sickish and why should I walk now. The vise was sprung and I'd wait for the proper procedure. I went back inside.

Vinciguerra's door was half open and I could hear his reading aloud. He read beautiful Italian, a language made for singing, and he read well. Then he stopped.

"Won't you come in?"

I pushed the door open for a number of reasons. I was cold and would wait there. I also wanted another look at that girl. Maybe I'd learn how she did it.

I walked in and closed the door behind me and sort of leaned there. She, the pile of folds, was at one side of the table and Vinciguerra, with book, at the other.

"You may go now," he said to the girl.

Sophia got up and held the big robe around her.

"Don't send her out," I said. "Maybe she's just getting very keenly absorbed in the subject matter. What's the book?"

She stood by the chair in a rather terrible way. Her eyes were half shut and her mouth was half open, caring for nothing. She looked badly punished.

"The book is called, *Bybilis,* by a Frenchman by the name of...."

"Did you like it, Sophia?"

"We're not done yet," said Vinciguerra.

She stood there, and I had to think: she is standing alone inside that robe.

She stood there without motion and cried. She blinked her eyes now and then but did not lower her head or clutch herself, she just stood there and tears ran and fell.

"My dear—" said Vinciguerra.

"Shut up."

Then I opened the door for her and stepped back so that she could walk out.

She walked out and I almost touched her when she walked by, I almost had a million feelings—it doesn't matter what, because I did nothing. She walked out and I closed the door.

Then I sat down in the chair where she had been sitting.

"I'm going to wait here," I said.

"Would you like me to...."

"No, I wouldn't like you to read that book to me."

He shrugged and put it on the table.

"How are your wounds?" he said.

I didn't have any "wounds." I had some cuts and bruises and that's all.

"They are bleeding in a most symbolic way," I told him.

My angry levity seemed to pain him, since we were on his most sensitive subject. I felt like picking on his other most sensitive subject.

"Why don't you go up and inquire after your maid? She seems to be having a tough time of it."

"Yes, the poor thing."

"Do you know why she was crying?"

"She is probably still crying," he said, and I thought, whose most sensitive subject is this, the way I feel now.

"You didn't answer me."

"About you," he said, and he accused me with a great look of sorrow. "You have been very cruel to her."

"That's a laugh."

"To allow a child like that...."

"Child?"

"Yes," he said, and he got up, walked some, and turned away and talked to the closed shutters. "To allow her to find an attachment to you while you are here so impermanently."

He had it all wrong from beginning to end, but since he had his own queer involvements with her I wasn't interested in any more talk about the girl.

I sat a while and smoked and he stood part of that time with his back to me. There were no sounds at all from the outside and in the room there was just the low hiss from the gas heater.

"Vinciguerra."

He turned around and said, "Yes?"

"You know what time it is?"

He quickly reached for his watch which he carried in a vest pocket, but I told him never mind looking, I have a watch of my own and had only asked him for dramatic effect.

"It's almost one," I told him. "It's almost four hours since a man got killed."

He nodded and shook his head and nodded again and sat down.

"I know," he said. "And it must be a serious state to...."

"Never mind. *Where are the cops?*"

"I know you are worried. But let me describe to you, so that you may understand, let me describe the difference to you between your sense of speed, your sense of urgency, which comes from a life...."

"Vinciguerra."

He cocked his head and allowed himself to be interrupted.

"I don't want conversation. I want information."

He sighed and just nodded.

"Where are the police," I asked again.

"Have you seen our station?"

"I thought I just asked you a question of that selfsame type."

"Please don't be impatient with me. I...."

"Oh no. No, no. It would only add confusion to the dizzying speed of events, eh?"

"I mentioned our station, which you have obviously not seen, to answer your question about the police. Our station is one room of some files and a desk and a nail on the wall where the local *carabiniere* hangs his belt."

"And the nail came out and he can't find his belt."

But there was no rushing Vinciguerra, and no ruffling him either. This was his night time way, and his night time conversation, and he wasn't going to forgo the luxury.

"Therefore," he said, "you can see that we really have no police here."

"I know that. I know that from other evidence."

"The real police station, equipped and so on, is forty kilometers from here. So, it takes time."

"Ah," I said, and thought over whether this made any sense as an explanation.

"It has been sufficient in the past," he said.

"Because there's no crime in Forza d'Aguil."

He seemed to light up, and I knew him well enough by now to know why. Crime is a generalization, and Vinciguerra loved those.

"You are right, of course. In an important sense of the word, you are right."

He sighed at a distance which he had to imagine, there was no distance in this room anywhere, no clear depth and distance at all, and I looked at the little cabinet on the wall where he kept the medicines and the liquor.

"Because crime, in a basic sense, exists only to the degree that someone takes offense."

"And since nobody takes offense at an offense here in Forza d'Aguil—I mean, excepting such things as paying for a gift of a cheap bottle of wine...."

"You understand nothing, do you?" he said.

I took note of his remark and I took very much note of his manner. He was dead serious and it was true that he had probably not been making just conversation. And that, in a way, he was the only one here who could see more than one world. He could speak to me of mine, and he had tried to tell me of his, or rather, of the world here, in this town, because I did not think that he altogether belonged here. I didn't know where he belonged.

I acknowledged what he had said to me by making glib remarks. I said nothing else and he did not either. He asked me if I would mind if he continued to read and I just nodded at him. Then we just sat, he reading, I waiting.

I have waited for this or that, in a doctor's office, in a customs line, that kind of thing. But I have never sat like this, and knowing so little, waiting for a judgment. But I did then, and I think it may well have been the last time.

Chapter 18

When it came I had been half asleep.

"*Signore,*" he said from across the table.

I had never been unaware of his presence, of the room, of the waiting, but when he addressed me I gave a small jump. And I did not ask him, what do you want, or anything like that, because I knew. Then I heard what he had heard, that the silence outside had changed. Beyond the shutters I could hear murmuring.

I got up and stretched carefully and then, because this was good bye, I went upstairs to my room and picked up my peajacket.

When I was back on the landing the house was as quiet as ever and I could not hear the murmuring outside. The light made the same yellow indoor fog. I looked up and thought of the girl sleeping. I wished that she were sleeping. Then I went downstairs.

There was Vinciguerra and the cop with the long teeth. They stopped talking when I came down and watched me.

"Alright," I said. "I'm ready to go."

The policeman just nodded and then I saw that Vinciguerra had put on a coat.

"You coming too?"

"Yes," he said.

I had the distinct impression that he wanted to say something else.

The policeman stepped back to let me through and Vinciguerra buttoned his coat. I could hear the murmurs outside. Then the policeman opened the door for me.

There was no cold blast of air, there was just cold air now, very motionless. And they stood in the square, motionless, and the murmuring stopped. There were not many and they all looked the same. The men, the women, and the old ones who could have been either.

I could tell nothing else about them—they stood too far and held too still—nor did I sense any feeling from them, such as curiosity, anger, a hostile air. They just stood, waiting. They made the square seem emptier. And I saw no car.

"We're going to walk 40 kilometers?"

"We walk."

We walked. I did not know where the police station was and I could tell by the crooked route we took that I had never passed it before. Behind us came those dark ones.

Once I looked up at the sky alley above but it was so dark there, it said nothing either.

Once we walked along a narrow way with the wall of the town on one side, higher than the houses, and I thought of deep basements and prison. I have never been in prison but clearly I have felt it.

Once I said, "Vinciguerra," and he came up to walk next to me.

"Yes?"

"You coming along because you're curious, too, like the others?" The feet behind me were a dry rat shuffle and a soft moth touch of sound.

"No," he said. "Even though you resent it, I can only tell you again that I might be able to help."

"I speak Italian."

"I was not speaking of Italian."

"I know. I'm nervous."

"I know."

And then we came to a house which was totally drawn into itself with narrowness and lack of air, one window deep set and blind with crooked boards nailed this way and that over the opening and the sight of it like a scab. The doorway an arch, stone again, deep old stone and an ill-fitting door. We went in, it was dark inside, I went in there and felt as if entering into a hollow stone.

Further on was the door with the light behind it and coming closer I smelled a deep green smell, a vegetable smell of rain on leaves and of green rotting to brown.

The cop pushed the door open and there wasn't much in the room. It was like a cave again, as I've described their rooms, and all around stood the baskets with vegetables. And there sat a woman with a black shawl on her head.

I stood in the room and looked around, at the woman in the chair and the baskets and nothing else.

"What is this?"

"The law," said the cop and then went and stood by a wall.

They all came into the cave and stood around in a ring behind me and the woman in the black shawl never moved. I looked at Vinciguerra and was glad he was there. I would have liked it best right then to suddenly hit somebody, hit hard and with exasperation, but all I did was talk.

"Everybody nuts here?" I said to Vinciguerra.

"Please," and he looked around as if to apologize for my tone of voice. Then, while they still shuffled around and the black woman sat, he came closer and said, "I was trying to tell you about crime, in the room, remember? I was then going to try and explain to you about law. And how sometimes an old law makes a new law unnecessary."

"Are you trying to tell me...."

"Please, she is looking up...."

I turned and saw that she was now looking up. And the room became quiet and entirely hers.

Out of nowhere I remembered a fanciful tale, a children's tale but not quite a children's tale, about Kaa the rock python who would wind and unwind and stare at the wild monkeys and they would hold deathly still and then they were all Kaa's.

"That's him?" she said and looked at me, and then somebody said, "Yes, that's him."

Then she just looked.

Sophia had said that Pino's mother sells vegetables.

She was not large and sat with her legs wide. She put one hand on each thigh and I could see her large, pregnant belly. She was a black egg with legs, with old hands the color of roots, and with a square, white face, from which the cheeks had gone and the lips had gone, and there was a lot of sick color around her eyes but the eyes were alive.

"You killed my son," she said.

It is strange, but I did not feel accused. She and her way were too foreign.

"He's dead," I said, "and if he weren't, I would be."

"That doesn't matter to me."

"Woman," I said, "I don't care what matters to you. I can feel this for you or that for you, but what matters to you is something else. I don't even understand it. You don't even cry."

"I don't have to."

"I'm sorry."

"I don't care if you're sorry he's dead."

"I didn't mean that. I did not mean that at all."

There was a silence, and the kerosene lamp made the smallest flick which became a very large, very quick lash of shadow across the room. Then nothing again, just the smell of green in the white cave.

"Why did you kill him?" somebody said behind me.

But I did not even have to turn around.

"I don't care," said the woman. "He is dead and the question is stupid."

"I know one that isn't so stupid," I said. "How do you know I killed him? Or are you interested?"

"He's dead. I heard what you did to the others."

"Listen to me," I said, and for the moment I forgot how everything with these people is always settled ahead of time, there is then no need for change, no chance for a turn or a shift in anything, one wooden law over the other, over-lapping, like the layers of boards on that window outside, and the window is no longer a thing for looking out, but a hole that has been successfully barred. I said, "Listen to me, woman, if an animal leaps at you for the kill, what do you do?"

"You are stupid. Nobody killed you."

"That's because...."

"Don't shout," said the cop, and then the woman said, "Nobody wanted to kill you. Pino did not want to kill you."

"Were you there?"

"No need. It wasn't his place to kill you."

I think my mouth hung open and I remember that I heard the words and understood nothing. Only this, that she knew everything ahead of time and even a new thing coming her way would fall into a mold which was already there, take its shape, and so become old.

So I stood there and gave up, or rather, I stopped trying with her and just stood there to wait out the end of the court session and whatever I could do afterwards I did not yet know.

"Shall we wait for Guetano?" said the cop.

She turned her head and seemed to think about it—I had no idea who Guetano was, Lord High Executioner, probably, though I didn't care at the moment—and then she said, "He has something else to do." Next she looked at me, but not as a human but like something fixed to the wall or put under glass, it was that sure a look from her, and then she said, "If he lives, it won't be Guetano who will deal with him."

I say that the quality of sureness about this woman had an effect, a true fascination. To be with such centered strength—there is a mystique about it, an almost answered wish for that state in oneself, and so you stay and wait and perhaps that's what it means to become a vassal. And I say that while she gave no warmth—even the earth smell in the room was borrowed from leaves in baskets—she gave with her very absence of heat (perhaps I mean anger) a touch of completely mindless security to those she engaged. She did it to me. I wasn't the monkey, frozen by Kaa, and I wasn't the supplicant at this forever altar, but I had respect for her and so was open to her.

Which must have accounted for the effect she was able to throw into me.

"Who will revenge Pino?" from behind me. "Who is left?"

"I am feeding him now," said the woman.

She looked at me and her eyes were full of black life. She put one hand on her belly and said, *"He will kill you."*

Chapter 19

I remember the silence rising like a great mist after that, and hanging there in the room, but with no sense of suspense. To everyone there, the silence was one of acceptance.

In my case it was something else. This feeling, evolving from the blankness of mist, this was pure awe, pure wonder at something which did not yet have any meaning, and when I found meaning in this, it was pure, awestruck, horror.

What sat there on the chair by the white wall, and surrounded by baskets, that was no longer a woman who sat there, but a maker of laws.

She was pregnant and that has a mystique of its own, and she sat there with her rich belly resting. She breeds like an animal, I thought looking at her, and then she trains her brood to be nonhuman.

Because what she had said, what she was planning, had all the spontaneity drained out of it.

And now I recognized her, the great black bitch giving birth to death, the breeder of mindless things, of acts without feeling, a breeder of instruments. Because what hate (or what love) can last a lifetime without change, or for generations, unless the feeling is mummified out of it and what's left is an obligation which smacks of a curse—

And she was breeding that.

I took one step towards her to see this face better, the white face without mouth, the sick color around her eyes, and only the eyes showing the life she was hiding.

"You," I said. "You have a life in your belly."

"That life is for...."

"Be quiet, woman. That life is not for anything. That life is just life."

Somebody drew a breath behind me, but said nothing.

"But you'll use that life in there. You'll make a purpose out of it, no?"

"I'm the mother."

"You're the mother and already that life in you is no longer innocent!"

"We are born in sin," somebody said.

"You're going to soil that child with your hate?" I said like an afterthought. And then, "Wash yourself, woman. Wash yourself!" and I stepped back because I was really through with her. I could not reach her.

They got out of my way in back of me. That was good. I would not have wanted to touch them.

"You won't get away," she said. "I'm feeding him with my blood and he sees you with my eyes."

I shrugged and felt as distant from her and her struggles as if I were watching a mirror that had gone blank with age, and what I could see there—

"Your belly," I said, "your black egg," and I stopped by the door to say this to her face. "If I were to touch it, it would feel cold as a stone!"

And nobody moved. I think they, in the room, felt now as I had felt, when she had told me what she was breeding there inside that stone.

I went back to the hotel with the cop and Vinciguerra because the cop had said that's where I should wait.

"For twenty years?" I asked him, but he hadn't understood right away. "Or will the small monster be ready when he is ten?"

He understood me then, I could tell by the breath he took through his hooked teeth, but he said nothing and we just walked.

I was through talking to anyone.

But when I got back to the hotel where I meant to wait for the police I found out I wasn't quite ready yet for a rest and by no means finished.

"I'd like a cup of coffee while I wait," I said to Vinciguerra.

I opened the door to the restaurant, turned on the light in the cold room. I had no intention of going back into Vinciguerra's sanctum.

"The kitchen is closed," he said, and looked worried.

"Then wake up your crazy maid, promise her you'll read choice things from *Decline and Fall,* if only she'll brew me a cup of coffee."

"I'd rather...."

"Alright, show me the way, and I'll make one myself."

"I would like to explain...."

That's all I needed to hear. I was in the room by then, next to a table, and I picked up a chair and then I threw it at him. Immediately the cop stuck his head into the door and while the first chair made a leggy clatter down one wall and a ways across the floor before it stopped under a table, the second chair was off flying and broke the glass in the door.

I was off and didn't care. Or rather, I enjoyed it. I smashed all these chairs against walls and on table tops, a great senseless smashing and breaking, but how senseless could it have been, giving me so much pleasure. I wouldn't even call it an impotent rage just because the breaking of chairs wasn't my actual object. I was after exhaustion and only a muscle act could give me that and I broke, threw, tore this and that and when I was done I sat down on the floor.

I sat with my back to the wall, on the floor, and when I looked at the door I could see the three faces. They were all somewhat white. There was Vinciguerra, the cop, and the girl, Sophia. I looked at them and had to roar with laughter because I could not stop that either.

Chapter 20

I sat on the floor a while longer and smoked a cigarette, planning nothing. In the middle of that Sophia came in with a cup of coffee. She was again someone bringing something, coffee in this case, and I waved that she should put the cup down next to me on the floor. The cop was still in the door, looking at me, and I thought maybe this had been the cop's idea, he had heard that I wanted coffee, and let's give him the coffee, for God's sake, so this maniac will calm down.

I was quite calm as it was and drank the black stuff. Then the cop was gone and Vinciguerra walked around in the hall a few times, clicking doors, and the girl was gone too and next there was no sound of anything anymore. In the distance I could hear a car.

It was really a car motor and nothing else, and then, far off, it stopped. They would have to stop in the first square, right behind the gate.

I got up, brushed myself off, and took a breath. It was time now. I sat down on one of the tables. I dangled one leg and watched that for a while. Outside, I heard feet running.

So I went outside and stood in the door where I looked at the cold square, empty, no black watchers, but a man, perhaps two, and they were going very quickly away, up one of the alleys. Then I saw Vinciguerra come towards me, all alone across the square. I had no idea where he had come from. He came and stood below me where the steps started and looked up. He looked as always.

I said, "Well, it's time, isn't it?"

And he said, "Yes. It is, Mister Matheson."

He stepped forward to come up the stairs to the hotel and I moved back as if he were pushing me out of the way. I backed up like that and watched him open the door to his room and turn on the light inside. Then he looked at me over his shoulder and that meant, won't you come in now, and naturally, I would come in now or any other time he might mention.

I remembered the exhaustion I had felt, sitting on the floor of the restaurant after smashing all the chairs and tearing their legs off. That had been a fine exhaustion, leaving me relaxed. This now was a different thing. This exhaustion was a weight and it diminished me.

"Close the door, Mister Matheson."

He lit the gas fire and turned the lamp on by the table.

"Would you turn off the switch by the door?"

I turned off the switch by the door.

"I apologize for wrecking the room." I thought it was the last thing I had to give him.

"A drink?" he said, punctuated with that Vinciguerra look of sympathy. Why not. Why in hell not. I got the bottle from the cabinet and a glass. I put both on the table and poured for myself and took a sharp swallow. Then I put the glass down.

"How long have you known my name, Vinciguerra?"

"Since you came."

"Since the evening in the *osteria?*"

"I sat down at your table and recognized you."

"Why didn't you say anything?"

"Did you, Mister Matheson?"

"No," I said and took my glass again.

"I won't ask you why. Your answer, I think, would be the same as mine."

"I don't know," I said and put the glass back on the table. "I don't know." I felt too exhausted to think. "Who came before? I thought it would be the police."

"No," he said. "Not the police."

I thought he would tell me who it had been and I would just have to wait. I watched his face and there was no secretiveness, there was really no definable feeling at all. I thought that he too was exhausted.

"That was Guetano," he said.

"Did I see him run across the square?"

"Yes. To see his wife."

"Who?"

"The woman who lost Pino."

"Ah," I said. "Yes. And after he's seen her he'll come here."

Vinciguerra nodded and picked something off his sleeve. He turned around to look at the fire and then he stood by the fire, warming his hands.

"And I'm not waiting for the police at all, am I?"

"No," said Vinciguerra, without turning around. "You may be waiting," he said, "but they aren't coming."

We said nothing else after that and I drank the cognac. I thought about his knowing my name all this time, but I didn't care to think of anything very much at that point and just saw this, "yes, Mister Matheson." hang in front of me, in the black air out there where he had said it to me.

The outside door gave a rattle as if it were locked to the corner, or—since the door wasn't locked—as if the man out there was impatient.

Then the door banged shut, a few steps in the hall now, and the knock on Vinciguerra's door.

"Come in," he said, without turning around.

I felt the same way, why turn around anymore.

The man who came in was not impatient. He opened the door quite normally and closed it the same way, with just the common sound which a door makes when it is closed. He nodded at Vinciguerra and said, *ciao*, and then he looked at me from the door, and said nothing.

He did not look impatient to me. There was a stillness about him which reminded of his wife, though he can't be described as simply as she. His sureness was not as concentrated and stonelike as hers, but there seemed to be waves of life interrupting the calm now and then. I saw this in his eyes, which moved away when I looked at him, in his walk from the door to the chair (he moved fast at first, and then slowly), and when he sat down he ran his hand through his hair, a gesture of tiredness.

He had the same hair as his dead son. (Pino's hair had always looked dead, it struck me, dead the way straw is dead, or wood shavings.)

"I'm sorry about your son," I said.

I thought he looked surprised, and I myself was a little surprised to have made the remark, but there was an air of shock on him, an uncomprehending look.

But then it was gone. Perhaps I had even imagined his helplessness. He did not answer me, looked down at his vest, where he pulled a watch out of a pocket and seemed to study the time. I felt like an idiot for having made the remark because here was Guetano, grand executioner. My mood switched immediately.

"I thought I'd have more time," I said.

"*Cosa?*"

He said that like his son. He put his watch away and looked at Vinciguerra who left his place by the heater and came to the table.

"He means," said Vinciguerra, "what Anna told him. About her unborn."

"Oh," said Guetano. Nothing else. He ran his hand through his hair again and sighed a few times. "Haven't slept in two days," he said to Vinciguerra.

I got up and jarred the table, which was an accident, but the sudden sound and the jump it put into the air was alright with me.

"If you're not too tired," I said to Guetano, "try to understand this. While you were gone, your son made up a feud with me, something stupid about a bottle of wine. He kept me here for some twisted reason. There is a dead man now and that's police business, no matter what you think. And it's police business, no matter how long you delay it and no matter how much you crave to do all of this business yourself."

I leaned over the table and thought, maybe, seeing he's tired and worn out and the shock is on him, maybe I can sway him and crack this nightmare open. He doesn't look like an executioner type to me, he doesn't even look stubborn and bullish like his son, or demented, the way I recalled his wife.

"Guetano, you understand what I'm saying to you?"

His reaction was strange. He sat as before and then, for a moment, he seemed bewildered. Two days without sleep and his son dead and nothing made sense to him anymore. Then he looked at Vinciguerra and frowned.

"*Cosa?*" he said. "He knows nothing?"

"No. We were waiting for you."

"Waiting for him?" I said. "You mean to tell me I was held in this town to wait for him to come back? Make sense!"

"I will," said Guetano. "You don't know who I am, do you?"

"I've never seen you in my life."

"That doesn't matter. Sit down."

"I'll break your back in about one second. I want...."

"That doesn't matter either. There are always others."

"Tell him," said Vinciguerra. "He might well do what he says."

Guetano got up and his tiredness was he himself and his voice and his manner was somebody else's. He acted so clearly the instrument of an impersonal purpose that he reminded me of a strange, life-sized puppet.

"You remember Rosanna, I think," and he looked at me without any emotion.

Now I did sit down. I sat down slowly and looked at him.

"I am her uncle," said Guetano.

"Rosanna," I said. "Where is she?"

"She is dead."

"Dead—what is all this?"

"She died in childbirth, Matheson. The child was yours."

"My God—"

"So that you killed her."

I waved his words away with my hand. "And the child? Where's the child?"

"So I was waiting for you."

"*I said where is the child?*"

"That is no concern of yours. This has never concerned you."

"Is the child alive, man? *Answer me!*"

"I'll tell you nothing about the child, just as she knows nothing of you. The child does not even know me. That is the best way, since I have to kill you."

"*What?*"

"I am her uncle. There is no closer relative."

"You? Kill me?" and I lunged up from the chair, reached across the table, and grabbed Guetano by the front of his coat.

Perhaps he was surprised, or very slow with tiredness, but he gave like a rag doll when I yanked him up and then I threw him across the room so that he crashed into the door and slid down to the floor. The nightmare was no longer a nightmare at all but everything made a kind of demented sense.

Rosanna had died and the fault was mine.

Then came the Mafia logic. I would sometime come back, or be found, to be killed. When I came back to Forza d'Aguil my hangman was out of town. While he rushes back, taking two sleepless days and nights to fulfill his office, his son keeps me from leaving. That the son was dead now was so far incidental. First things first. The iron of law. First kill because of the dead Rosanna, and the death of a son was another matter. Maybe Matheson can be killed twice. Maybe Matheson makes it and kills his father. Even that is just so much delay, because the next in line for the death job on Matheson is already drinking the black blood of his calling, warm in his belly ignorance, asleep with the whisper of law in his veins, all prepared, all ordained, all fixed in iron.

I grabbed for Guetano again and kicked his legs out of the way. I got him good by the throat.

"No," said Vinciguerra. "Stop it!"

He, of course, could go to hell. This was my life and I had to match these men to take it back. I cracked Guetano's head against the wall.

"I have a gun," said Vinciguerra. "Stop it."

So I dropped Guetano and turned around and there was Vinciguerra with the gun in his hand. It was a big, old thing with a very long muzzle and when I turned Vinciguerra stepped back.

"I can't have you kill him," he said.

"Of course not, you son of a bitch. That wouldn't be right, would it?"

"I'm sorry."

"Screw you!"

There were a number of other things I had in mind for him but he stood too far away, he held the gun like before, and then Guetano got up. He moaned a little and moved very carefully and he too didn't come any closer.

"When's it going to be?" I said. "Now?"

Guetano held his head and didn't look at me.

"You didn't know it before," he said, "but you know it now, that you are a prisoner here, and why. And that there is no way out."

"I'll go *baah* like a lamb for you."

"I am not a criminal and, unlike you, I don't act from impulse. Everything will go the regular way."

"At the crack of dawn, with drums."

"You will stay here and I will come for you tomorrow."

"And I'll just wait for you here."

"Of course."

Then he left.

And I stood there and had dribbled myself out with stupid small talk, all the true concern and the seriousness crapped up and confused now, so that I stood there in the room and looked at the closed door as if there were something to see.

"Can I put the gun away?" said Vinciguerra.

I took a deep breath and sat down in the chair and told him, yes, he could put the gun away. He stayed by the heater and put the gun into his pocket. It looked big and wrong there. It had even looked wrong when he had been holding it, Vinciguerra, sad mouse, with gun.

"You were the first to recognize me, Vinciguerra?"

"Yes."

"And then you gave the word."

"Yes."

"And all this, everything here, is your doing."

"I told them that you were here. Yes."

I closed my eyes for a moment and rubbed my face.

"I don't understand it. I don't understand you."

I looked at him and he shrugged.

"Why?" I said.

He looked at his shoes and then at me.

"It took no thought, Matheson. It was simply the way."

"The law."

"That is true," and then he made a movement in my direction, something he did not finish but which looked like a wish to touch, and he said, "Painfully true, Matheson. Can you believe that?"

I didn't answer him because I didn't know. I sat at the table a little while longer, looking at him and hating his guts. There was not much else I could do. Then I got up and left.

Two men stood in the hall, by the door which led to the outside, and one of them leaned on a shotgun. I could do nothing about that either. I went upstairs, found my room, and sat on the bed a long time. I did not turn on the light but just sat in the dark for a long time.

Chapter 21

I cannot live alone, I know that, and it is the difference between myself and a Vinciguerra swimming in the rich yolk of his imagination. He is as alone as I, of course, but with the need for touching always padded by the cotton of speculations and theories. In that way, his starvation may be more chronic, but I get hungrier.

I think of this, remembering how I sat in the dark room on the bed and I think of this because perhaps it explains what happened next.

I got up from the bed and felt stiff as if having slept in a sitting position, though I had not slept at all. I had been holding too still. I went and opened the shutters on my window and saw the thin light on an opposite wall, and the wall and the sky the same color of stone.

Two stories down was the yard, also stone. And in the yard, rolled up in a blanket like a turtle drawn into its shell, sat a man. He did not see me at the window but his face, what showed of it, was turned to the downstairs door. Next to him, by the wall, leaned one of those sticks with an iron tip.

I sat down on the bed again and wanted to sit like he, but had nothing to look at. I felt as washed out as the thin light outside, as empty as the silence inside the house.

Then the steps, soft and slow. I didn't even move from the bed and just looked at the door.

It opened slowly and then I saw her black shock of hair and then, slowly, her eyes. In the half light her face seemed very white and the eyes so much blacker.

I had to think of a cat in an alley, met by surprise, and the animal holds stock still and just looks. Then the animal usually runs.

Sophia came into the room, each move a hesitation, or each move as easily a readiness to run away as to come forward. Then she stood on the inside of the door, but very close to the door which was her protection. She did not hold on to it but slowly put her arms around herself, for that hug. She was dressed, wearing the big sweater, and hugging herself.

"Go away," I said. I whispered.

"I will."

She whispered too and curiously enough this identical manner of speech, with its secrecy, felt intimate.

"But I want you to know this, both for you and for me," she said.

"Why you tipped them off. Why you used the thing between you and me for that."

"I have to tell you because I cannot bear to be hated by you, and don't want to think of you hating. Both of those."

"You told Vinciguerra that I was leaving."

"I told him because he asked. He asked where I had been so long. And I told him, with you."

"And doing what?"

"That is nobody's business. Only yours and mine. I told him I had been with you and had been so long because you were leaving." She held herself closely now and bit her lip. Then she said, "And I made love to you for the same reason. Because you would be gone."

It had been as innocent and as right as that. And in any other place but Forza d'Aguil I would have known this without her telling me.

"Please believe me," she said. "And then I go."

"Sophia—"

She looked at me and held still like the cat I have described.

"Sit here, Sophia."

She came slowly and when she was halfway across I got up and waited for her, standing. Then I took her arms, to make her stand close against me, no hug, no struggle, just the whole touch, and this touch too was like a whisper.

"I believe you. I'm sorry."

Her head was under my chin and she leaned her cheek against my chest and I could feel her take a deep breath. When she finished the breath I closed my eyes, and I think she must have closed hers, because it had been that kind of a breath. In a while she put her hands on my arms and looked up.

"Are you back now because you killed Pino?"

"We had a quarrel, on the shelf."

"I heard. Are you waiting for the police?"

"Come here," and I took her to the window. "You see him?"

She looked down at the man turtled up in his blanket.

"I think that's Ernesto, the butcher."

"Doesn't look like the police, does he?"

She looked at me and then down into the yard again and then she knew as much as I did.

"The *mafiosi*," she said. "And there won't be any police."

"No."

For a moment her fingers bit into my arm and then they relaxed. No. It was more as if they were giving up. She knew the same about all this as I was learning.

"Who will come for you?"

"Guetano."

"He is back?"

"Yes. A few hours ago." I then wanted to tell her the rest, why Guetano had really come back, but in a way that was detail and could wait.

And I didn't feel so full of wonder, and full of perplexity any more about all this, no longer so entirely surrounded with that cell-like isolation. At the point of survival comes bounce. Always, sooner or later.

"Is Vinciguerra asleep now?" I asked her.

"Usually. When I go to work he usually sleeps."

"He has a gun, Sophia. Do you know where he keeps it?"

"Gun—" she said. "Matty. There's a better way. I'll try and reach the police."

I thought about that and I thought that the idea was fine, but how would she do it. Run forty kilometers? I didn't think it would be possible for her to phone.

"How, Sophia?"

"I don't know yet. I know the man who runs the exchange, he's one of them, and if I said...."

"And as soon as you do, aside from not getting your party, they'd get you too."

She thought for a moment and I said, "Where does he keep the gun, Sophia?"

"I'll think about this thing with the police," she said. "Perhaps something will occur to me." And then, "I think he keeps the gun in the top drawer of the chest near his bed."

"I'll look," I said. I took her to the door and stopped her there. "Sophia."

"Yes?"

"From now on, Sophia, you say nothing. From now on, you are no longer one of them, or their friend, or someone safe from them. You understand that?"

"I understand that."

"You share this with me. No one else."

She closed her eyes and lifted her face. Like opening to me.

"One kiss, Matty," she said. "One kiss."

This was as quiet, and secret as darkness. And this dark touch became our terrible bond.

Chapter 22

I went to the landing after Sophia had gone down and soon she came back to say that Vinciguerra, behind his door, was breathing quietly, and that the two men who were watching the front had gone across the square to the *osteria*. They were standing in front, she said, watching the hotel while drinking their coffee.

I sent the girl away, not to be seen with me on the stairs, and went down. The bulb over the stairs was off and with the grey half light coming in from the front door it was now darker on the stairs than at any other time. The light was deceptive and so, I thought, was the safety it gave. I took very long going down the steps.

His door, it struck me, might be locked.

It was neither locked nor was it pulled shut to latch, and in the crack which I opened, I saw the lamp light.

He would sit with a book and the first thing I would see would be the head rising, the deceptive sorrow in those eyes looking at me, the gun next, touch of the real, touch of the jump in me now while thinking of it, and I opened the door.

Lamplight yellow and all alone, chair empty, table bare—he cleans up before going to bed, to be able to wake up to blankness—and then I saw him laid out in bed. I say laid out because the sight was like that of a corpse.

He slept on his back. His mouth hung open as if he had taken a gasp before falling away into sleep, a frozen gasp on his face as if he were still falling, eyes closed, feet making a pointed tent under the blanket at the end of the bed. I could not see his arms because they were under the covers but I was sure they must lie next to him, he and his two arms stretched out all side by side, an unnatural straightness in his sleep, and sleep no more than a therapeutic necessity.

I walked across the room and felt as unmoving as he so that I had to force every move, like a rusty gate. I might creak, I thought.

But then, what if he stirs, or wakes, what then? What would he see that he did not know, what could he do now which I couldn't stop him from doing there on the bed. Scream? Jump? Attack me? But the attack was all in me, not in the sleeping man on the bed, and then I was done with that moment's problem of fear and I went to the chest where he kept the gun.

I got the drawer open and there was the gun. I could hear him breathe very close by, but here was the gun. I put my hand on it and thought, he isn't breathing anymore. I turned my head and there was his face, looking at me. Eyes still and open.

But I had the gun in my hand which helped me, so to speak, take a leap and skip over the shock he gave me, which his eyes gave me, looking at me from wherever he had been, and perhaps he did not even see me—

"There is no point to it," he said.

I took up the gun.

"It isn't loaded, Matheson."

Everything here is loaded, I said to myself.

The gun was a revolver and while he lay as before and I held the muzzle his way, I checked the cylinder. I broke it out and turned it. There were six empty holes.

"Where is it? The ammunition."

"I don't have any."

"I'll twist it out of you, Vinciguerra. I can do it, you know that, Vinciguerra."

"I am not a brave man. But I could tell you nothing. I truly have no ammunition."

"Last night? Last night the gun was empty too?"

"I only had the empty gun."

"You're lying. Goddamn it, you're lying!"

"No. I have withheld things from you. But I have not told lies."

I put the gun down on the chest. The gun felt very heavy. He has only an empty weapon, I thought, and that's Vinciguerra all over.

"And now what?" I put my hands in my pockets. "You'll report this too, like a good soldier? And another count against me?"

"Not needed," he said. "Nothing else is needed. You should know that."

I stood there with my hands in my pocket, empty gun on a chest of drawers, two killers drinking coffee across the square in the dawn—crack of dawn, I thought, and next I'll hear drums rolling and that wouldn't surprise me either. Just as Vinciguerra no longer surprises me, lying still in bed with his eyes open.

"I think I'm dreaming," I said.

"No. I often do, but you don't, Matheson."

"Sounds like envy."

"It is. Believe me."

Anytime, I thought, anytime he wants to spin a web over me made of tender vagueness, anytime he wants to pull me into his dream, he can do it.

It took a kind of a wrench on my part—crack of dawn, I thought—and I'm not his dream.

"When it's just talk," I told him, "you've always been willing. Tell me something."

"Of course." He still hadn't moved, but he seemed awake.

"When the drums and the firing squad?"

"I don't know. I don't think they have planned that yet."

"Where is Guetano?"

"He must be asleep."

I had to remind myself how they did so much with so little heat and it was likely and true, perhaps, that Guetano was asleep.

"Then there will be a meeting," said Vinciguerra, "to decide the right way."

"And maybe I'll have twenty years to wait after all?"

"No. Guetano is here now."

"Vinciguerra," I said and felt oddly silly, "I can't stand the suspense anymore. How long?"

"I don't know. But not beyond tonight."

I kept in mind how it is possible to kill and plan kills just by cool prescription, how they did it that way, and I myself felt properly chilled then, with the real knowledge that tonight I would get killed.

This is not an easy thing to realize. It is perhaps never accepted, and death is a surprise. And I could realize this only in sudden jolts, in a temporal, sudden shock; like surprise. Here I was walking around in a hotel, talking to a man lying in bed, thinking of the light changing outside— Death was just conversation.

I had to get out of that room.

"If you want breakfast, I'll have something sent to your room."

I stopped in the door and watched him sit up in bed. "Who'll bring it up, the maid?"

"Why not?"

"Not worried anymore I'll spoil her innocence?"

"No," he said. "Not anymore. It is a sad thought, in a way, why I'm no longer concerned, but I've seen you turn into enemies, here in this room. And then, of course, there is the other matter."

"You are the coldest bastard I know, Vinciguerra."

"No. You are wrong. The law is."

He put his head down and with his thin little legs started hunting around for the slippers under his bed. Perhaps he put his head down because he did not want to look at me.

When I got back to my room I thought, goddamn it, I should have picked up that gun, at least the looks of it would be worth something, and as a matter of fact later, when Vinciguerra can no longer report the theft, then I'll steal that gun or send Sophia to do it while Vinciguerra is out.

I looked out of the window—the light was better now—and looked at the turtle sit there as before.

For the rest, I might have a whole day. To make a bedsheet rope in some fictional fashion, to convince Guetano he was about to commit a great sin, to discuss all manner of things with Vinciguerra, to send Sophia here and there, running vital errands.

My own idiotic levity appalled me and from my stir-crazy meanderings I fell abruptly into a depression. The empty room got me, the grey light from the window, the really unfathomable nature of this still-faced town, and then I felt the trembling inside me, felt it grow and shake me badly. Then it ran over. I stood in that ugly room and just cried.

Chapter 23

She brought me the food on a tray, under a napkin, and she looked very pale. When I looked up and she saw my face she bit her lip and there were tears in her eyes without any transition.

"Matty," she said. "Are you giving up?"

"No," I said. "I'm not giving up. I cried and now I'm not giving up."

She put the tray down on the table and came over and held my face. When she moved back she was smiling.

But then the smile went and she was pale as before and her movements were hasty.

"What?" I said. "So soon?"

"No," she said. She brought the tray over and put it on my lap. "But I didn't feel it so real before—all this, what they're doing to you. Look."

She took the napkin off the tray. "They are in the front, and in the back, and one was in the kitchen, watching me."

She had a cup of coffee on the tray, bread, and the fontina which she knew I liked. But there was no spoon, no fork, and no knife.

"He took them off the tray and said you would have to eat without. And why eat at all, he said."

"Now stop it," I said.

I smiled at her and gave her a small tap under the chin because she was blinking her eyes very hard and pressing her mouth together. She looked terribly young when she did this.

"You're alright?" she said.

"I'm hungry. And I've got all day and I won't need that much to figure something out."

"I haven't figured out anything yet," she said, and almost started to cry again.

"Cup of coffee?"

"Yes."

"Not all of it, you. Leave me some."

Then she smiled a little and took a sip.

"When does Vinciguerra get up?" I asked her.

"He's up now. Because you woke him, he said."

"Is he across the way, having his coffee yet?"

"I don't know. I have to look."

I couldn't tell by the light outside what time it was because the day was grey like the early morning. I looked at my watch and it was only eight.

"Do you clean up his room, Sophia? Can you go in there without any trouble?"

"Yes. When he goes across."

"Now listen. He's got the gun in that drawer, where you said it would be, it's there and it isn't loaded. Don't worry. Go into his room with your broom and the bucket and a rag in the bucket. Put the gun in that bucket and a rag on top of it. Then bring it here."

"It's not loaded?"

"Unfortunately, no. Can you do it?"

She nodded and then she said I should eat. When she was gone I started to eat everything with my hands and felt like a beast.

When I was done eating I heard the sound outside the window, the fast patter and then like a handful of sand thrown at the glass, and it was raining.

That would drive the bastards indoors and the house would be crawling with them, with their shot guns and steel tipped sticks. Though, what difference would that make. They were here, anyway. The rain drove this way and that and let up a little and picked up again. On and off the window would run with water and it made me think of my radio room on the ship, and how the rain would hit and let up, hit and let up, depending on the way the ship rolled. Then I felt tired. Two nights without sleep and then food in me, rain on the window— She will wake me when she comes with the gun, I thought, and what also is there to do now. I laid down, dressed, and went to sleep with a wonderful efficiency.

"Matty," she said. "Matty, quick!"

With moronic concentration I noticed first that it wasn't raining anymore but the next moment there was another gust of water flying at the window and it seemed immediately as if I had not slept at all.

"Matty, they're coming!"

"Oh Christ," I said, and swung my legs off the bed and stepped into the bucket.

"You got the...."

"Yes, quick," and she pulled the bucket off my foot, stuck her hand under the rag at the bottom and gave me the gun.

I jammed it under my belt and put my peajacket on very fast. It was good and bulky and showed nothing underneath.

"Guetano and Vinciguerra were coming across the square and I just got out of there before they came to the front door."

"Coming for me?"

"I don't know. But they were coming."

"Good girl," I said, feeling nervous suddenly.

I did have a plan, a very simple plan, actually, using their own lawfulness. But it was such a last resort, such a poor thing without any finality—

"Get out of this room, Sophia, in case they come."

"But what...."

"Beat it girl. Now. You stole the gun, you remember."

She picked up her bucket without any haste and when she was at the door she said, "I know that, Matty." Then she left.

I don't think pride is a virtue because it goes beyond straight regard for oneself, even beyond self esteem. It is borrowed esteem, and balloons you beyond your natural shape. But Sophia, when she had said, "I know that, Matty," had shown a very simple pride which came from knowing very clearly what she had done, what it meant to me, and to her. When she walked out with that bucket she looked sure and beautiful.

I had no idea if the visit downstairs was for me or just a thing between Guetano and Vinciguerra. I wouldn't put it past them that they were just having a kaffeeklatch. But at any rate, what with time and my meager resources, a little surprise might even help. I was working with all the slimmest margins.

It was raining, but nobody was in the hall downstairs. I went down fairly fast. It never occurred to me to run out of the door. I had tried that too often. I stopped at Vinciguerra's door, looked around once, saw my guards jump up in the restaurant. But I was in Vinciguerra's room before they had gotten as far as the door with the broken glass.

"I don't want to know," Vinciguerra was saying. "I really..." and then he looked up.

"Finish," I said, and leaned against the door.

Behind me they came bumping across the short hall and I stepped away from the door so I wouldn't get knocked to the floor. They burst in like Mack Sennett cops.

There was a great hassle with attack stance, shot gun in bayonet charge position, steel tipped stick held for some kind of a hottentot death rush, but of course nothing happened. I just stood to one side and they were saving me. This was not yet the ceremony.

"You don't need them," I said to Guetano. "I came to talk."

"Why?"

"I'm nervous."

"So talk."

"They make me even more nervous."

There was a hesitation while the two guardsmen remained at ready. They reminded of a daguerreotype, stiff and outdated, and ridiculous.

"And while they stand outside the door," I said, "what can I do to you?"

The two guardsmen stayed exactly the way they were, except that they started to move their heads around, waiting for the word. The way they moved their heads they might have been sniffing the air for a scent.

"Alright," said Guetano. He looked at me and said, "You stay over there," and then he told the two weapons carriers to get out.

I could hear the rain make a hissing sound in the square, and closer by, on the side of the house, there was the splash of water which must have been arching out of a spout on the roof. The two men sat in the lamp light and these two might have been two tired friends, sitting at the same table from habit.

"Finish, Vinciguerra," I said.

"I don't remember what...."

"You said, 'I don't want to know. I really....'"

"Oh." He ran one hand over his face. Then he nodded at Guetano and said, "He was going to tell me about you. About you, later this day."

"Just to ask if you could be kept here until then," said Guetano.

They really were both tired. And to top it, I thought Guetano felt defensive.

"Tell me," I said. "I'm interested."

"Why should you be interested. You know what you have to know."

"I'm a voyeur. I want to know what happens without having to participate."

"A what?"

"He means," Vinciguerra started, but I made an impatient gesture at him and he stopped talking. I felt left out by my own small talk, a disgusting feeling, and I started over. "I want to know," I said, "so I can prepare myself."

"Oh. Yes, I understand that."

But there was no real interest in his manner. Which I understood. Everything, after all, had long been settled. Except for the mess. I was interested in the mess.

"When, Guetano?"

He looked at the closed shutters and was listening to the rain. He didn't like the rain. The bizarreness of the situation struck me, urging my own executioner on. (Vinciguerra would have liked to hear about that. He would be full of words about that absurdity. Until it would be no longer absurd—)

"Siesta," said Guetano. "During siesta."

I didn't say anything simply because I knew I would have no voice. I have mentioned that the reality of all this struck me just now and then, like a very quick shock, and then no more for a while. This same thing happened to me now. I said nothing and closed my hands inside my pockets, for the warmth of the palms, I think.

"What else," I said in a while.

He made a movement again to look at the shuttered windows when I suddenly had to yell.

"What? The rain bother you? Call it off on account of the rain, you son of a bitch."

Somehow this pulled him together more than it did me and he fairly jerked around and his face looked much sharper now.

"No. During siesta. I will be up on the shelf and they will bring you there. Up on the shelf where you killed Rosanna."

"And your son?"

"I am talking about Rosanna!"

"I don't want to talk about her!"

"Aah..." said Vinciguerra. "He hurts." And he almost moaned.

He and his strangeness fixed me and for the moment I was again fairly calm.

"Alright," I said. "Let it be all about Rosanna. And let it be all about my never having forgotten her. And how we swore to never come apart."

"But you did."

"Yes, we managed. And let it be all about the child I have."

"You don't have a child."

"Where is it?"

"The child was not even born here and is not known here and is on that account no part of any of this. *Basta.*"

Basta can be a fairly final word when used with the right tone of voice but Guetano—I've mentioned this once before—showed little strength. He said the word almost with exhaustion.

"And when you kill me up there on the shelf, Guetano, what will you think of?"

He did not answer and his face seemed to become darker.

"I'll tell you what I'll think of, Guetano. About my mistakes and about your mistakes too."

"I make no mistake," he said. "There is no mistake."

"Then there is a lie, Guetano. There sits a lie in this room."

"I don't know what you mean. I don't want to know what you mean," and he started to get up.

"Wait. What difference can it make to you, to sit a while longer?"

"None."

"I know. You'll kill me and it has nothing to do with you. It has nothing to do with your feelings, your loves, and your hates, because all this is so old."

"That is true," and he sat down again.

"*Now* you lie."

This is a fairly strong thing to say to anyone, but particularly to a Sicilian. He looked at me and for the first time showed any real emotion. If I had said this to him in a café, as a stranger, or as a friend, he would have jumped me. But to him I was already dead.

"You lie because I know how you'll do it up there on the shelf. You'll kill me with a shot, and then you'll empty the rest of the bullets into me, kick what is left, stomp what is left—because you're not doing this because you are somebody's uncle, a girl dead for years, but *because you are a father.*"

"*Bastarde!*" he said and jumped up from his chair.

"That's the lie, Guetano. To pretend that you are a good *mafioso,* at the price of being a very bad father."

He trembled, but then he didn't move. He sat down again. I think it was because he felt weak.

"Why all this?" said Vinciguerra. "Why not stop?"

"Because I want to talk to the man! Because he wants a fight, not an execution. And I'm talking to tell him that I'll give him the fight!"

I could not fight their laws and their inhumanity. But I felt that I could fight a man. That was my simple purpose. Then I said one more thing.

"And after that, Guetano, after that, no matter how it comes out, then your son can be born and be just a baby. Not another thing full of the misery which you know right now, but just a baby."

The rain made a whip sound outside, and then a low rattle.

"Guetano! Did you hear me?"

He looked up. He didn't look tired. He had one hand on the table and it lay there like a crab. Then it began to move like a crab, it scrabbled there while it stayed in one place.

"You fight me?" he said.

"What else."

"I have to think," he said.

Vinciguerra coughed and by the motion I saw in his arms he seemed to be rubbing his hands in his lap. Or perhaps he was wringing his hands.

"There is one other way," he said. "Are you listening, Guetano?"

He had used almost the same phrase I had used with the man and Guetano looked up. His stiff, almost wooden hair stood up in various ways though I didn't remember that he had done anything to it with his hands.

"What?" he said.

"There is the police," said Vinciguerra.

I was so astonished, I think my mouth hung open.

"A man is dead," said Vinciguerra, "and the fact is, the real fact is that we don't really know how he died."

"You shut up," said Guetano, and he was suddenly hoarse. "You shut up."

Then he put both hands on the table and looked at me. The hands lay very still there.

"If I thought you would live," he said, "I would tell you not to say any-thing about this to anyone. Because to do this is a breach. It questions my honor."

"Then why mention it?"

"To show you how far I am going, how much I want this and how little the breach means to me now." Then he sat up straight, hands out of sight. "You still want to do this?"

"Yes. It's my chance."

He only shrugged at that. Then he got up.

"Now I don't talk anymore," and he walked out of the room.

The rain outside was the same.

Chapter 24

The way he handled it, I imagine, was the same way it had been arranged for the execution. Except that it was not yet siesta, and that seemed to cause some talk out in the corridor.

There was no talking between myself and Vinciguerra. Perhaps he wanted to talk—he probably did—but perhaps this silence of his was respect for my situation, or perhaps it could have been some anxiety that if we were to talk I would ask him about his switch here in the room, another one of his contradictions, when he had suggested to give all this over to the police.

I imagine his answer: "I don't know why I did it." And then, "There are so many loyalties, Matheson. Sometimes one of them wins, sometimes the other. I never win. They do. I am only confused."

I thought a moment and then did not want to ask him anything.

I sat and I waited for the fight, something finally that I could handle.

I don't mean that I sat knowing I could win the fight. I knew nothing about that. But I sat knowing that all of me could now go at this thing, no more shadows, no more shadow dances in a bright square, no more screaming and not even an echo.

He opened the door and let it swing back. He had a coat on and a hat and stood there waiting till I got up from the chair.

"You can walk ahead," he said. "You know where."

"I have the rope for his hands," said the one with the stick.

"He can walk so," said Guetano.

The two behind him looked at each other, but that was all. I walked ahead and thought, Guetano will give a good fight.

Because of the rain the square was almost empty. But there were some. There were some on the square and then we met some when we walked through the street. I looked back once and saw we were all walking in single file. I had buttoned my jacket and kept my hands in my pockets and then I put my big collar down because all it did was catch more of the rain. My hair was wet and itchy.

Guetano also walked with his hands in his pockets and the rain ran off the brim of his hat to one side so that I could only see a single eye. It was looking at me and then I turned front again.

The one with the stick and the one with the gun walked as if they disliked everything. They hunched and huddled and all their movements seemed to mutter and stutter.

I remembered Guetano looking at the closed shutters and disliking the rain.

I mentioned that here and there someone would be walking along on the street. When they saw us they looked—like they always look. Except, not quite the same. They would look away, step away into doors or go in another direction. And as if the town always knew everything simultaneously, in a while there was no one on the street anywhere. Once a wet cat came running.

The town had shut its eyes and was holding its breath. It let the rain wash down, let the rain make a great sound of water and wash out the clear view, wash out the clear view—

On the terrace around the church the rain came with a slap of almost horizontal fury. The wind was spitting.

Sogginess, crossing the churchyard.

Bad, hesitant going, on the rock path up. But the wind let up a little.

On the shelf the rain changed, it changed very strangely to a soft falling, a thin veiling, to a tiredness which I caught too for a brief moment.

I had been here before, I had been here so many times, but I remembered nothing about that now and turned around and watched Guetano.

Guetano had turned around to the others and made a sharp gesture at them.

"*Via,*" he said.

"But we have...."

"*Via!*"

There was a great deal of cut in his voice and the two left immediately.

He stood a while longer, with his back to me, just about as long as it would take them to get out of sight in the nearest bend. Then he turned.

"Come into the shack," he said.

We both walked into the shack and he had his hands in his pockets again. The rain on the metal roof made a sound like a mother shushing a child. But every so often it hissed.

He took his hands out of his pockets. He had a knife in each.

"Take one. Either one."

They were both the same. They were straight knives with wooden handles and the blades were very stiff and about as long as my hand.

I pointed at one of the knives—I forget which—and he held it out to me, grip my way. I took the knife and hefted it to see how it felt. He stood by, with his knife hand hanging down.

"First," he said, "I want to go outside."

I had a quick, rather inane notion about what he meant by that, but then he nodded at me that I should come too. At the door he put his knife on the floor and then he waited for me to do the same. I put my knife down and understood nothing but just went out with him.

The rain had started to race again and made running prattle marks on the shelf. They sometimes ran across from one end to the other and then flew into nothing. Sometimes they just prattled in one short explosion and then disappeared. The wind was nervous, like many interrupted breaths, one after the other.

He walked to the break in the shelf where the packet had gone up. There was a broken bone kind of jaggedness at the edge now and here and there on the shelf were chunks of rock.

He stood by the edge and there was nothing to see. The rain made a sheet. No sky, no ground, and there had never been a sea in the distance. Then he turned around and looked at me where I stood by the shack. We were not close together.

"Tell me how it was," he said.

"I wanted to leave. I was going to make it and wanted to leave."

"Alright."

"Since that time when we had an installation up here, there had been this ladder. We had...."

"I don't care about that."

"You just asked me."

"I am asking about my son, Matheson."

He was asking about his son, I knew this, but I hadn't known how to talk to him. He had said, "Now I don't talk anymore" and I had felt that would be the best and the easiest.

Fight or talk, but not both.

The rain made that splatter stream down one side of his hat again and I could only see one of his eyes. I don't think he even blinked once.

"I was going to make it, and then Pino came. He did not come alone, but with two others."

"He did not come alone?"

"No. With two others."

"I don't care about the two others. Go on."

I did think he cared about the two others, or rather, he cared that his son had not come alone. But I could not see Guetano very well. He had veils on him now. I don't mean just the water.

"They surprised me, of course. They had waited until I was almost done."

"Done with what?"

"Done preparing. There was the ladder, and then there was the wire which would pull the trigger. You didn't want to hear about that before."

"Then why do you tell it?"

"Because that's how Pino died."

"How?"

"Two were in back and Pino was there, in your place."

He drew up a little, or perhaps he meant to step away, I don't know which. But he did nothing else and seemed very tense.

"And I was there, holding this wire. And I said, 'I'm leaving if I have to kill you and me, I don't care, but I'm leaving.' And I showed him the wire and said when I pull it the rock would blow up."

"The explosive was here?" and he pointed to the jagged edge behind him.

"Yes."

"And you?"

I stepped closer to him and stood in the rubble which was now around me and told him this was the place where I had been.

"Why didn't you get killed?"

"I didn't have the blast close behind me, and the shelf had an overhang there, which went mostly up."

"I see the rocks where you stand."

"I was lying on the ground. Pino was standing."

"Are you lying?"

"About what?"

"About how close you were."

"No," I said, because I wasn't lying.

"You were lucky," he said. "And Pino wasn't."

"No. I wasn't lucky, Guetano, but I didn't care. And Pino wasn't unlucky, but stupid."

He didn't say anything to that. He waited, wanting me to go on.

"There was gunplay...."

"What?"

"One of the three had a gun."

He slapped at the brim of his hat. Something annoyed him.

"And the way it went," I said, "the gun slid that way, to Pino, and while I was down with one of the others, he, Pino, went for the gun."

"Three," he said. "Three—" And then he said, "Go on."

"That's when I yelled at him what I told you before. I'll pull the goddamn wire and blow him to kingdom come, no matter what else."

"Yes."

"Then he stooped for the gun...."

"What did he say?"

"Nothing. He laughed at me."

"*More!*"

"There is no more. Then I blew him up."

I had nothing else to say and Guetano said nothing but turned slowly. He turned looking at everything he could see, the shelf, what else was there, and the ghosts perhaps which I had told him about.

He stood very still. Sometimes the wind tugged at him and gave him a sham motion. He was turned half away and I could not see his face.

Chapter 25

I had been there on the stone shelf so many times and each time I had
not thought of the times before and when he turned around now I was
not even thinking of the reason for which we had come up. This is not to
say I had forgotten. But something new happened.

He turned around with purpose, with some strength, which seemed a lot
like the strength of stone. His motion had that quality.

He turned and took off his hat and wiped his face. His face was very wet.
The rain was running all over us but I thought he had been crying.

"Are you crying, Guetano?"

"Yes."

And he just stood like that.

I took my hands out of my pockets, I almost took one of them all the way,
but then pushed both of them back.

"Listen, Guetano." I talked loud, not straight loud but here and there up
and down, because I thought of the wind pulling my words away and I
wanted to reach him. "Guetano," I said.

"Yes."

"Listen. I once said to you, on an impulse I said to you, I'm sorry."

"Don't say it again."

"Guetano."

"Don't say it again."

Then he walked my way and stopped when he was close.

"Now we go inside. And fight." Then he walked right on.

In a short moment I followed him. I did not know what else to do anymore and the fight would now be the last thing.

He stood in the door and held his knife.

"Take yours," he said, and stepped back into the shack.

I got my knife off the floor.

"We fight in here," he said, "so that one of us will get killed. There is no
room for anything else."

He was at one end of the shack and I was at the other. He dropped his
hat into a corner and then he unbuttoned his coat. He shook it off and it
made a heavy, a fat sound almost, when it fell down full of water. Next, he
took off his jacket.

"You can keep yours on," he said.

"What?"

"It's thick. I am very good with the knife."

"I'm very good with the knife too, Guetano."

He only shrugged.

But the shrug was final and he really meant death now and I thought only of that.

I am not too fast anyway, so the jacket slowing me didn't make that much of a difference. I kept it on. I kept it on to keep my life longer and if he was so much better than I—I now didn't doubt it, the way he was weaving— I crouched too, the way I had learned it, and thought of my reach.

What I knew about knives I had learned from a book. A book and a thin, bookish man in the army who had jumped around with us on a rec hall stage, using matador grunts and banzai yells when he demonstrated, which had sounded funny to us coming out of such a thin, bookish man. And he had said, "Matheson, you'll never be any good at this because you use that knife to keep me away, which is misusing your reach. You're supposed to kill me, Matheson. Think of that."

Guetano came straight and steady and quick. I thought of the snakehead weave I had learned, throwing the knife back and forth from one hand to the other so that the other man wouldn't know which hand would do the thrust.

The maneuver made him halt for a moment and I thought, maybe he's never seen it before. I stopped worrying about dropping the knife with this maneuver, and then I dropped it.

"Pick it up," he said.

I hesitated for a small moment, but then I saw red. Pick it up, he had said. He had stood there and had waited for me to pick it up. I was in such a sudden rage, I almost threw the knife at him.

But then he wasn't there anymore. Like a snake he was close and low and ripped up through my coat.

I let out a yell, just from anger, and that yell freed me in a way. I didn't know at that time if he had cut more than the jacket, I just flung back, hit the wall, and—as fast as I could—kicked at him. And with that I let out another yell.

He got out of the way of my kick and gave me distance.

"Shut up," he said very quickly. "Shut up."

So the banzai yells and the sudden grunts did seem to mean something or other, and I got excited. I went after him.

No more snake weave now, but play for the straight reach.

He chopped my knife out of the way with his blade and for a moment I thought I would lose my grip on the handle. But my reach hadn't been so far out that he could have cut me higher. Just the blades went *ping* and I didn't let go.

But it was still book stuff to me, and I'm sure he knew it. Maybe he knew about the feint of leaving yourself open, legs wide, weapon arm almost to one side and, make a dart at me, close enough, and I'll spin so your head comes off. Or the throat opens up, or the eyes are gone with one sweep.

In truth, it must have been my reach he kept worrying about, and none of those other things. I don't know. But he stayed back.

I gathered up again, like a spring, and I saw him blink.

I screamed "Yaah" again and cut straight out, the idea being to catch him on the down-blink and to stiffen his eyes wide open with that yell I had learned.

I never even touched him. He was far and gone, smacked the wall, and while I was overextended he levered away from that wall and came like a pointed rock.

That time he got me in the sleeve and the best I could do was to tangle him. I did not pull away, I stayed as close as he had come, and whipped my arm to tangle his knife in the sleeve, and to hell with the cut it might give me.

I could hear him grunt and I think that gave me the fire back, and not just the speculation. I felt his grunt was his effort and his effort is one thing and nothing else, he wants to kill me.

I didn't cut him with my knife—that arm was tangled—but I cut him with the edge of my hand. I was pressing after him to give him no room and then cut him hard on the side of the head.

I hadn't meant the head, which hurt me more than him, but the hand as a knife is as handicapped with no distance as a close swing with a real knife, so the failure angered me and I gave him the fist on the top of the head.

I had made that up on the spur of the moment. I had never heard of such a whack. But when I jumped back I saw him gyrate his neck and maybe the vertebrae had all been mashed together.

My knife hand showed blood which ran out of the sleeve.

"Stop yelling!" he said again.

I had done one of those grunts at him.

And then, hoarse, "Now, now—" and in the middle of that he came at me with fast slashes.

I don't think everybody can gain from getting excited, and Guetano wasn't one of them. To me his slashes looked wild.

A maneuver then. It's a maneuver and next something cool and precise— But why doesn't he—

He kept slashing, slashing, coming closer and closer and the maniac look on him now, it could turn into hysterical laughter, into screaming tears, he's losing, the man has lost somewhere!

I screamed—this wasn't textbook stuff anymore but really me screaming—to gather me up and to fight this thing off, and on the next through swing he did I rushed him while feeling really like some kind of locomotive with steam belching, sparks spraying, big iron chest ramming in there and I pinned him that way with his weapon arm crippled up across his own body, and we fell down.

I fell right on top of him and my knife arm was free, my free hand fishing for him where he squirmed with the knife for something close and ugly through my coat, into my belly.

And my God his face now, his face so close I can see this face with the fight tearing wrinkles across, back and forth, and the fight going out of him with the skin falling, with the skin sagging there like wet washing, then the fight up again, purple bursting from the inside, and the eyes, a sick bird fluttering, a dead bird staring, a wild bird thrashing to get into the wind—

I know it was then, at that point, that I got an inkling why the fight had gone my way. And that it did not very much have to do with my skill—

I think that could have been the end of it, somehow, for him and me, but we didn't make it.

There was a clattering in the back, the curses they threw out, hoarse with anger, and then Guetano shrunk under me—he did not go limp or ball up but he shrunk—as if he could not stand to be there.

I rolled off fast and the gun butt made a rush sound past me, through the place where I might have been. I kept rolling and scrambling as far as I could go. I was a very fast crab on the ground there and then I crouched in the corner.

The one with the stick stood over me and he could have gone right through all of me and nailed me into the metal wall. Except, that wasn't the scheme.

He held me pinned without bothering to touch me and said, "Guetano?" the voice very urgent.

I was dead if Guetano made the wrong sound. If he said nothing. I don't remember ever such terror.

"Nothing," said Guetano.

He sat up and felt his arm.

"We waited down there and waited," said the one with the gun. "And then the screams. Then we didn't wait anymore." The one with the stick stepped away a little, wishing to see the other two.

And I knew now why Guetano had been so frantic about the screams I had made.

"Drop the knife," he said.

"The hell you say! I'm keeping that knife till it drops out of my hand and the way you and I made the agreement...."

"*Shut up! Shut up!*"

He was livid. He yelled right into my sentence and his eyes were torn so unnaturally there was no way of telling what they were saying. Hate, fear, desperation, stupidity, I don't know which. Besides, all these states overlap a little.

"What did he say?" said the one with the gun and nodded my way.

Guetano got up and put the knife in his pocket. Then he said it again. He was hoarse and his voice made no more effort than goes into breathing.

"Drop the knife."

I had heard everything he had screamed and I was aware of the particular moment when he had screamed at me.

"If I thought you would live," he had said in the room with Vinciguerra, "I would tell you not to say anything about this to anyone."

I dropped the knife and sat up.

The one with the stick picked up the knife and looked at it.

"How did he get it? And the gun, where is your gun, Guetano?"

"I forgot it."

"And the knife he had. It looks like one of ours."

"He had it. Move over. I want my coat."

The man moved over and Guetano picked up his coat which was heavy with rain in it.

Chapter 26

He walked ahead, not in back of me, and we walked down to town again. The rain was steady now.

The two others were walking behind me but I didn't think of them, or look at them, but only at the man walking in front of me.

He had forgotten his hat and the stiff hair on him was different now, darker in color, like earth, and many limp rope twists hanging down from wetness. He walked with a heaviness which did not go with his size. Once I saw him wipe at his face again.

The few who saw us in town looked at us from their deep windows. I could see a swift face now and then. The streets were empty. Not even a cat.

When we got into the hall of the hotel Guetano stopped and looked at the other two.

"Stay, like before, and nothing else. I'm not done."

I imagine what he actually said was, not a word about this, and I imagine that they understood him. At any rate, they stayed in the hall. They stood in their own puddles and one looked at the ceiling and the other one looked at the knife which he still held in his hand.

Guetano didn't knock, he just walked into Vinciguerra's room. The gas heater was on and Vinciguerra was eating a fish on a plate. He looked up and I thought he choked. He put his fingers into his mouth, the way you do when a fishbone is pricking you, and then he took his hand out and wiped it on his pants.

"You have anything to drink?" said Guetano.

Vinciguerra nodded at the cabinet on the wall and looked from one of us to the other. I went and stood by the heater.

"There's blood on your hand," said Vinciguerra, and got out of his chair.

"Forget it," I said, and folded my hands behind me. "Just forget it."

"But take off your wet jacket. You...."

"Forget it."

He very much wished to say more, he had his helpless look of wishing to help, but there was Guetano in the room, and I was alive, both of us living, and that meant here was actually more confusion than Vinciguerra could handle. He managed to say that I should have a drink too and when I said yes he poured a glass of his cognac and I took it. I used the hand without the line of blood on it, so that there shouldn't be any more distractions.

Guetano put down his empty glass and then he took off his coat. Vinciguerra made a move to pick it up and to put it somewhere with solicitude but Guetano would not let him touch it.

"I must say something now," he said, looking at nobody.

"Don't you think it's better to ask Vinciguerra to leave?"

"What, what?" said Vinciguerra.

I had never thought of him as a very inquisitive man, or a highly curious man, and the touch of anxiety in his voice even now didn't give the impression that he was just being nosey. But I think that he felt almost as if he were being evicted when I made my remark. Or he was like a hen who had caught a vague movement and suspects that one of its eggs will be stolen.

"You can stay," said Guetano. "It doesn't matter."

"What doesn't matter?" I said.

"Stay," he said again, and then he looked at Vinciguerra and said, "I'm beginning to feel like you."

I took a deep breath and felt the wetness on me like an unpleasant lick. I went over to the table and poured out another drink.

They said and did nothing while I took a swallow, and the same silence was there when I tried to light a damp cigarette. I gave up on the cigarette and went back to the heater.

"I don't know all your rules, and your ways," I said, "but something new happened here. Something different."

"Did you fight?" Vinciguerra looked back and forth.

"Yes and no," I said.

I looked at Guetano. Still nothing from him.

"Are you hurt?" Vinciguerra asked him.

And when Guetano did not answer right away I said, "Not that way. He got hurt so it'll never quite heal as before. He needs something entirely new. Or there's nothing for him."

Guetano looked up and it struck me how small his head was with all the hair soaked down.

"Americano," he said. "I don't need your riddles."

"I think what he means, what he might mean...."

"He doesn't need yours either, Vinciguerra."

I finished my cognac.

"I must think," said Guetano.

The gas heater made a song like a cricket and now the rain outside made no sound at all. The wind was mounting and it could not have been raining very much anymore. I tried to light the moist cigarette again while Guetano was thinking and in a while I got it lit. While Guetano thought.

"Look," I said. "You still want Vinciguerra to hear?"

"I said so before. It doesn't matter."

"I want something to matter," I said.

"So would I," said Vinciguerra, as if to himself.

"Guetano. Listen to me. When you stood up there in the rain you were crying."

"Yes. I said so."

"You stood there where your son had been and you cried."

"Over my son."

"Oh yes."

He looked at me exactly the same way he had done once before, his first charge with the knife.

"What did you cry about, Guetano?"

"Over my son," he said. A hacked voice, hacking the same thing over and over.

"Over his dying, Guetano? Or over the way he died?"

"Yes," said Vinciguerra, "you never said how he died."

"Say it Guetano."

But there was nothing. There was a hard man and a beaten man and you put the two together and it looks like splinters.

"He died a coward!" I said. "He died a silly, dumb coward!"

Guetano moved very slowly and when he had his hands on the table he held them, one on top of the other. And then again nothing.

"He came with three, and not alone. He came with a gun, and not alone. He went for the gun when I was strictly a target, and then laughed about it, *that's* how he died! And I think, that's why you cried, Guetano."

But even then he said nothing. He moved his shoulders under his coat and held his own hands.

"Not important?" I said to him.

He shrugged.

"It's not important to everyone," I said, "but I think it is to you."

He suddenly slapped one hand on the table. But when he talked it didn't match the crack sound he had made with his hand.

"You know nothing," he said.

"Alright. Then I'll ask you something."

"What?"

"How was the fight?"

"It was a rotten fight. *Mbu*—" he said.

"Let me tell you about the fight, Vinciguerra. You want to hear about this fight?"

"I'd rather not."

"Vinciguerra, I could repeat the whole thing to you, the whole fight. I could do it in words with as much skill as it was done in action. *That's* how rotten a fight it was."

"Ah?" said Vinciguerra. "That is a curious fight."

"With knives. Does Guetano know how to use a knife?"

"Guetano? Why he is...."

"You know I am good," said Guetano.

"How was I doing?" I asked him.

"You? Bah!"

"Then how in hell come you didn't kill me?"

This time he was silent again but it was not from stubbornness. I'm sure he felt helpless.

"You didn't win, Guetano, because the fight was out of you. There was no fight in you, over your son, because of what I had told you about him."

He yanked around in his chair to look at me now but before he talked I'm sure that he checked himself and said less.

"You lied the whole thing, Americano. How do I know that you didn't lie the whole thing?"

"You can ask the two in the hospital," said Vinciguerra, surprisingly simple now, and to the point.

"Did you believe me up there on the rock?"

"Yes. Then I did."

"How come you believed me up there?"

He started a sound like a groan, but only some of it. The roughness of it but not the melting.

"It was the place," he said, "where he had been."

"And in such a place, such a sorrowful place, you would stand there and listen to me blacken your son and you would cry over it? Answer me!"

"I stood there," he said, "and couldn't help it."

"Yes. You didn't jump me, you didn't kill me right then and there, but you cried because what I said was true. And you must have known it was true, or it would not have torn you like that. Torn you and destroyed you so much that you could not fight. Cursed you, and all that you had ever known about right and wrong. Because you had raised your son by all you had ever known, and he had turned out vicious filth!"

"Don't say that again. Never again, Matheson."

He had not called me *Americano* this time, which meant he had not used an insult. Calling me by my name was almost as much as saying, "please."

I did not repeat what I had said, but I wanted my point. Because my point, hope against hope, might save me.

I didn't hit him with my voice anymore, or use it like pounding on a door, but I talked to the man now, the man with the dampness across his back, with the damp doubt in his bones, and with his face full of the helpless wrinkles of his new confusion.

"And the only other time you listened to me," I said to him, "was a while ago in this room."

"What," he said, "when?"

"When I said something to you, when I said the only thing to you which made you become Guetano, and not just the *mafioso.*"

He looked anxious now, which seemed to be such a new thing to him that it was truly distressing to see.

"When you broke all the rules in you and then went up to the rock with me to fight me for something I had done to you, not went up there to execute me like you cross a 'T' because 'T's are crossed because that's what they say in school."

"What?" he said again. "What did you say?"

"When I said: and then your son can be born to be just a baby."

"*Dio,*" he said. "*Dio,*" into his hands.

"And then you wanted to fight, for your son to be born like that, instead of a doubtful thing, a hard, twisted thing, twisted with iron shoes that don't fit, twisted with a stone for a heart which can't beat, twisted by breathing dead air that has been used up and fouled up and thrown up by everything that is already dead."

I put my hand to the side of my face and looked at the wet in my palm. I thought, I have rarely talked so much. And I have rarely felt it all. I finished, and said, "Then, Guetano. When you knew all that, then you acted."

There was a quiet in the room now, with all of us quiet, though I don't know what all the different reasons were for the quietness. I walked once to the door, and then back to the table. This caused no alarm, and was no alarm. I sat down at the table and looked at Guetano for a while.

"Can you forget all that now, and look at me and still be the *mafioso?*"

He looked at me and then at Vinciguerra. I was frightened by the indecision I saw in his movement. Perhaps I was frightened because he was frightened.

I said, "Vinciguerra. Did you understand me?"

He nodded and said yes.

"Did he understand me?"

Vinciguerra looked at the man bent at the table and Guetano didn't look up right away though he must have known that Vinciguerra was waiting for him. His hand, a slow, old crab, moved on the table and one finger opened up out of the hand and touched the glass of the bottle that stood there and then touched the paper spine of the book that was lying there. He looked up and the two men looked at each other and I remembered when Guetano had said, "I'm beginning to feel like you."

"You understand him?" said Vinciguerra.

"Aah—" said Guetano, and he straightened a little, almost like a stretch, and he pulled his hand back, close to the edge of the table. He made the groan like once before and stared straight ahead. Through me, or past me, through the wall, or there was no wall. He stared. "I understand," he said, "understand what he said before. I feel destroyed."

I sat and somewhere I trembled. I didn't want to know where and paid no attention. For me he talked life and death now. If he would say something now, if he would say it—

"In pieces," he said. "Who can live that way."

"I know the same thing," said Vinciguerra.

"Who can live that way. Nothing. There's nothing."

He kept staring and his mouth got the same kind of fixity, it drew into itself, hard and close, and this hard ring of muscle pushed out a little, it pushed like a stare.

"Listen to me," said Vinciguerra. "We know each other. We are both from here."

Perhaps he should have said more or he should not have sounded so supplicant soft. Or I should not have sat there, just waiting.

Guetano cracked his hand on the table with a suddenness which made me jump. Then he glared at Vinciguerra—I felt that I was not even there for him—he glared with his eyes and he blared with his mouth.

"You and me? What makes you think I'm like you? I'm no more like you than that paper spine on that book is like my fist! *That* I know, and talk be damned for making a worm out of me, a worm cut in pieces, be damned to that, for making my strength go thin like paper. *Americano,*" he said to me, with a sound no louder than an arrow would make and with the same point and cut. "I know better, *Americano,* I'm born on a rock and I get my strength there. I got the strength and why give it up!"

He kicked his chair out behind him and stood. He had back what he had lost—lost from talk, he had called it—and then he did become like a rock, something sunk out of sight in him, and he could talk again without any passion.

"The way it was," he said, looking really at nothing. "During siesta."

Then he went to pick up his coat.

What he lost I gained, and if he was like stone I was like fine muscle.

I didn't want him to get to that coat and I don't think he heard me make a move when I got out of that chair.

"Guetano!"

As if I had hit him in the back of the neck. He jerked and turned. He did it with a stiffness, but fairly fast. He saw my face and the gun in my hand and the two together really froze him up.

"You can believe me, you dried up son of a bitch. I'm now ready to kill you."

Something in his throat made a sound like glue.

"Not a word," I said to him. "Put your hands so you hold onto your hair."

He put his fingers into his hair and held on.

"Hey," he said. "You've had— had the...."

"Shut up."

He did. I looked at Vinciguerra who stood by the wall. He was very pale. He looked at his gun in my hand and I moved a step so it would be a toss-up whose face I'd break first. Vinciguerra closed his eyes and I could see his mouth tremble.

I told Guetano to move slow like a bad dream, move to the other wall, the other side of the door. Then I told him to put his hands on the wall. Put the hands there like the wall was an animal in a bad dream, and to touch it without waking up. And then I told him to lean ever so gently, lean into his hands on the wall.

I had tried for all I was worth to get to him, around all the things which were in the way between him and me. A bust. A near thing, so painfully near, and then bust.

All I had left now was the simple plan, the poor thing without any finality, last resort without any finality, which sounds a little bit like a contradiction, but it really isn't.

I hadn't been able to get around their terrible lawfulness. Now I would use it.

"Pick up your head so you can hear this," I said.

He showed me the back of his head and I let him have it. If Vinciguerra's gun had been loaded, I don't know about this, but the way I felt I may well have used it. I hacked the back of his head so hard that the head snapped away between his arms sticking up as if there were no head any longer between those shoulders. But fast was all this was.

This had to do with their lawfulness.

I had no idea about how his skull was and how long he might be sick— a head snapping out of the way also means that there is a lot of give to the blow—so I made sure about their simple lawfulness.

I dropped the dead gun and picked up his right arm, both hands on the wrist, for strength, step back for some play, like throwing a loop into a rope on the ground, I did that selfsame thing fast to his arm, and the shoulder joint jumped out of kilter.

He had the blow on the head, but he screamed. How he screamed, one sharp scream like a sting flying out of him. Then he was still.

I scrambled for his coat on the chair, I got there and felt the gun in the pocket, I got that far and no further when the door flew open.

Perhaps if I hadn't turned to check distance I might have had the gun in my hand before it was all over. But I fouled that, I got hung up with my hand in the wet pocket while the two who came busting into the room saw immediately what was up.

The first one kicked me well enough so that I collapsed on one knee and was no good at all for the moment. The next kick was in the ribs and I had one business only now, which was to fight for my breath.

I sat on the floor and fought for my breath, and this was part of the lawfulness. You do nothing else to Matheson because he's got to get it from Guetano.

And the other part of the lawfulness, Guetano's gun arm or knife arm would be out of the running for a fairly long time.

It was a poor thing without any finality, gaining time.

Chapter 27

They weren't through with me. I mean, two kicks wasn't all I got before this part was over, because when they had it clear what I had done to the hangman they felt wild and loyal about that and went at me again while I crouched there on the floor trying to find my breath. I was a curled snail or an armadillo and at the center of the curl I found that small space like the inside of a hand, a little dark air there, and I tried to breathe it. I concentrated almost entirely upon that. The rest was just bitter life, always knocks and bumps, but the valuable thing and the thing I must have was this small, handful of air.

I think they might have done worse by me if Vinciguerra had not been in the room. I could not see him, but I knew he was sick. I could hear that, and afterwards his weak voice.

"Leave him," he said. "You must!"

"Must? Did you see— you saw what he did to him, you...."

"Leave him. That fight was part of the big thing, it was the fight he could put up before he had to go under...."

"Damn right he'll go under."

"But this is *not* part of the big thing! This is just you kicking and scratching!"

"The way I feel about him...."

"Means nothing! Remember that!"

He had a weak voice after being sick on the floor but he spaced his words with great emphasis and I was reminded of his reading to Sophia from a book. But he stopped them with what he said.

When they took me upstairs the going was slow and I might have looked at Vinciguerra without knowing it. There had been a kick in the head and my eyes had the flimmers as if I had facets on them, like a two hundred pound fly.

But now this had been the second time of new contradictions. First, when Vinciguerra had said nothing to Guetano about the empty gun, and now, the second time, when he stopped them from punishing me. And he was the one who had set them on me to start with, and he had held the gun on me that first time when I had gone after Guetano—

I didn't think about it anymore and the stairs seemed interminable. I could walk fairly well, just shock buckled me now and then, but I could hardly see. Though I realized they were not taking me to my room. And then we went past my floor, next flight up, and then a door so low, it could not lead to a room.

I hit my head and ducked down, black in front of me, though it might have been brown, or mauve, or simple shadow.

"Hold it."

I held it as best I could, I was a two hundred pound fly, and I leaned my head against the wall in front of me, the wall with the low door, a wall made of wood.

They crossed my wrist on my back and I was tired of everything. I had more tiredness than I had pain. They tied my wrists with a rope made of woven grass, which I recognized by the sweet smell and by the smoothness of fibre. They tied me up good, and right then a thread of pink wool would have done the trick just as conclusively.

I wasn't going to use my hands, or my head, or my eyes, or anything else that ached, though it wasn't the ache so much as I have mentioned, but the tiredness inside of me.

One of them pushed my head down so I would fit into the door and another one pushed my behind in with his foot and I rolled ahead trying to tuck my face.

I clicked my shins on something going cross-wise and I dug my head into something that gave. Then the door slammed shut and I thought, thank God I'm alone. By the time they were done rattling and scraping bolts or chains or who knows what else, I knew that I had fallen on top of a bed. I thought, thank God it wasn't a barrel with nails inside, though if it had been a barrel without nails inside, a small barrel even, I also would have been satisfied.

If they give me just a little bit of the time which Guetano will need to recover, I'll recover.

I humped around and squirmed around on this bed which had a straw sack for a mattress and then I sighed, blowing strawdust in front of me, and fell asleep.

Sleep is a deep mattress which is all around you, and even though you are inside, it does not interfere with the regular breathing. And it doesn't scratch, or lump up, or get sweaty on one side and touch cold on the other. It is all around so that you can sleep on your back, on your side, or your stomach, without having to turn around for any position. If you lie stomach up and want to sleep on your stomach you need to turn nothing at all but you simply sleep on your stomach while you lie on your back.

I sometimes have a good sleep like that, with all those conveniences possible, and I had one at that time, with hands roped together in the small of my back. I would float up out of this sleep mattress I am talking about, float up with more rapid breathing, and then I'd say, give up, Matheson, you can't escape it, this comfort, you can't get away from it no matter how you pant. I was right all of those times and would sink away again.

When I did wake up it was pretty terrible. Because now I wasn't tired anymore. Now I was wide awake, widely aware, but could do nothing and see nothing. I was aware of what had led up to this, and I was aware of what would follow, which caused sharp anxiety because all that would follow was so unreal.

I would hum and I would drum into me a thing like a lullaby, you got time, Matt, you got time, and to have time is divine—

In a while I got sick of my humor, and then I got sober about having to solve all my problems, and next, finding that I could do nothing, fright. And I finally reached a right state for me and for these so actually limiting circumstances, I lay there in great tranquil indifference about the great problems which I could not even touch. This was made possible by the fact that there were a few things which I could do, and I did those again and again, as the need arose. I moved this leg, curved that spine end, I rubbed my calves with my feet and my feet with the back of my knees. All those kinds of things.

It sounds like a joke but it wasn't. I worked at my comfort. Such as a good leg, for a kick. A clear head not cluttered with anything until anything happened.

This took concentration, and I think I was awake like that for about as long as I had been asleep.

I also found out about my black space. I could not stand up without hitting the ceiling except at one extreme end. There was a terrific slant to the top of my box. At the high end of the black space was a suitcase on the floor and a wood box beside that. The wood box, I discovered, had things laid out in it, square piles of cloth things and I felt disconcerted that I had them completely messed up by the time I had fingered some clarity out of what I was touching. I was clumsy with my hands on my back and a numbness was starting.

Then there was the bed and nothing else I could find. There was just room for the bed in this space and the two other things I have mentioned.

The bad part was the longest but is the simplest to describe. I got bored with everything and I got helpless with the only accessible problem that remained. My hands were in bad shape. This long stretch of time became compounded torture, because boredom and helplessness got to be pretty much the same.

When I heard the steps I had given up listening and then I went from fright at what came to joy over the change.

This went back and forth.

After the door had been opened and someone had come inside, I still didn't know anything.

I knew it was as dark outside as inside, and that something sat on the bed. I was standing at the tall end of the room, holding still.

I heard breathing and I heard hands sliding along the mattress. I thought of assassins, of revenge, of meanness in the night, and of Forza d'Aguil.

"Aren't you here? Matty, please, aren't you here?"

"Oh my God," I said. "Oh my God—" All this without reverence, but mainly as two articulate sighs.

Then she was where I was and I could smell the fine odor that lay warm in her hair.

"*Caro,*" she said, "darling, I couldn't come sooner. I've been lying awake and awake and dying with the most terrible thoughts, thinking of you."

"Sophia," I said, "very sweet Sophia. I'm fine. Almost fine."

"I heard about some of it. Are you badly hurt?" and her hands touched me like small wings touching the air.

"No. Really no. But my hands are tied together and they are dying off."

She left me for a moment and made sounds in the dark.

"Turn around," she said.

I turned around.

"*Mater dolorosa,*" she said, "they feel like balloons blown up tight with hot blood inside—"

I said nothing and held painfully still while she cut the grass ropes with something.

After that, the real pain started. It covered the scale. It felt like a pleasure itch sometimes, and then knives. It felt like ice burn sometimes, and then fire which brought on cold chills. It got better of course, and the hands more my own, but it took awhile.

"Sit on the bed," she said. "Here, I'll guide you."

"I know the way. Where am I, Sophia?"

"I sleep up here. It's under the stairs to the roof and I sleep here, except they told me to take out my things...."

"When?"

"This noon. While you were still in the room downstairs."

"You saw me?"

"No. Not till you went up the stairs. You didn't want to walk."

"I couldn't, little idiot."

"Oh," she said, "oh—" and touched me carefully.

"And Guetano?"

"Well. They *carried* him out."

"You said this noon. How long...."

"Yesterday noon, actually. How I waited and waited to...."

"What time is it, Sophia?"

"I came up and it was one in the morning."

I had slept a good long time. Except for my hands, I did feel like I had slept a good sleep and for the right length of time. I sat in the dark, feeling done with the incubating, and plans leaped up, or the new will leaped up which had grown inside the rest, and it had been no less the touch of Sophia who really was the one loving creature I knew now, her touch and the life in her voice did for me what sleep had started, which is, to come awake.

I had to reach for her and find her face and give her a kiss, just out of nowhere. Out of nowhere is a weaseling phrase, because what I mean is, out of thank you and love.

I held her face and kissed her twice or three times, like plunging at her, and in between I kept saying, "Thank you, thank you, *bella*, thank you."

She made a gasp when I let go and said, "For what? What came over you just then?"

"For nothing at all, *bella*. I mean, for no reason, just for you."

"Hm," she said. "I wish I could see your face."

"And for the love of you. I love you," and I kissed her again.

She held on for a moment after that and I said nothing else right away. The quick exuberance which had leaped out of all this darkness was gone now, and instead of a leap like sparks there was, I felt, a most seriously hot, banked fire burning. This was the life left in me, she had been there when it lit again, and I sat on the bed with her now, feeling quite serious, and even the pistol swing seriousness I had felt with Guetano, that was in there too.

"Sophia."

"Yes. I'm listening," she said, and put her hands on my knee.

"You say it was one when you came up, and I'm sure Vinciguerra is still awake. Is he at all regular about his habit of getting you up in the night?"

"I'm so late to see you, because I was with him till one. First I couldn't come up because the taxi man has his room by the stairs and he sat drinking there with his door wide open. And he would scramble up every time I tried to go by his door and would grab for me here, and would follow me up. So I didn't come up."

"Who is this bastard?"

"He's asleep now, Matty. Very drunk."

"Who is this bastard?"

"He brought Guetano and since he hasn't been paid for his long trip, he's staying until he collects."

"Alright," I said. "Okay."

"And a good thing, Matty, because then Vinciguerra came up the stairs, wanting me, and if I had been up here with you— You know how he's been acting whenever you looked at me. And what you said about never to let on in this town, after I had decided to help you."

I stroked her hair and then I said not to worry about Vinciguerra too much, and how even he had helped me.

"Little confusing about him, but he has helped, if only by not interfering. But just the same, a good thing that he found you in your room."

"I pretended to sleep."

"He want anything special? Was he alone?"

"He was alone. He wanted tea, just the usual. But he seemed badly upset, or depressed, I don't know which."

"Did he say anything, or did he just read to you?"

"No. I had to read to *him.*"

"Nothing about me? Plans?"

"No. He hasn't left his room since that noon time."

"Listen, is he likely to come for you again?"

"I don't think so. He's never come twice. And he went to bed when I left, something he has never done at that hour."

"He must have really felt all the double pulls, from both sides."

"He was sick, you know. He took something for his stomach tonight."

"I heard him."

"And pills to sleep. He has strong ones."

"Alright, to hell with him. Now something else. How's the town since what happened this noon?"

"How, did you say?"

"How, *bella,* how? Are they watching the same way they've always watched me? An eye here, legs walking there, men loitering at the gate, standing around?"

"Matty," she said. "Are you leaving?"

"If there's a time, *bella,* this is the time! I'm beat up, I'm tied into knots in a closet, and special guards in the house, front and rear. With all those safeties, Sophia, that's the safe time to slip them!"

"Yes," she said. "There are guards in the house. The same two who know you already."

"Fine, fine. We'll get to them later. Now about the town. Do you know anything about the town, like I asked you? If I were to walk out in the square at three in the morning, run down a street...."

"No," she said, "I don't think anybody would stop you. Except something by accident, maybe."

"I don't mean accident, I mean method."

"No," she said again. "It's like you said, they feel the way you described it."

I took a deep breath but stopped it half way. Double check first.

"How do you know, Sophia? What have you heard?"

"I've heard them talk the way you did, about why should they bother now. And I saw the policeman come out of the *osteria,* very drunk because he was going home. He hasn't slept much, you know, since you've come."

"I hope he dreams he's having insomnia."

"And the men they've had at the gate going out of town, they won't be there. Two of them were in the restaurant talking."

Now I took a deep sigh and I clamped my hands into each other, the way the prizefighters do, or the wrestlers, and if you hold that gesture in your lap, it looks very demure but if you hold the hands up high over your head, there is hardly a sight more exuberant. I did it about half way in between, because I was still sitting in a dark closet. And I noticed my hands took it and didn't hurt too much.

"Now one more, Watson," I said and squeezed her cheek the way Sherlock Homes would never have done it, be it to Watson or the Queen of Sheba. "Come here," I said, and where I put the squeeze I now put the kiss.

"Matty, I can't see you," she said, "but I feel nervous with you. Are you acting nervous?"

"Yes," I said. "As a matter of fact yes. Alright now, calm now." I swallowed and started over. "Transportation. What do we know about transportation?"

"I don't think your Vespa is any good."

"No. Forget that. Is anyone parked outside, that kind of thing."

"No. I didn't look, but there never is."

"Christ, I've seen...."

"In the daytime, Matty."

"Yes. You're right. Of course you're right."

"And if they do park outside, they don't leave the key. Pepe leaves his outside, because he's here from another town. But...."

"Who's Pepe?"

"You know the guard with the shotgun. Nobody has a shotgun here so they called him in."

I found her hands and held them very still and she read that as if she had been seeing my face. She said nothing and did nothing while I thought everything through. Then I said, "It may work, Sophia, and if it doesn't then there are other ways. Though this may be the fastest. And most important, you must say yes or no. Because the weight is on you."

"Yes."

"I haven't told you yet!"

"Yes, Matty. It's still yes."

That's how Sophia helped.

Chapter 28

The danger was suspicion, which in Forza d'Aguil was bad enough. But the real source of my anxiety while I sat in the black closet was the fact that she had to go it alone.

But I was greedy for speed and sent her alone while I sat in my blind closet and sweated fear. But that isn't paying for what you want, that's just doing penance.

I planned all I could, but then she went and did it.

She tied up my hands again and I lay down. She ran her finger through my palm and then touched with her hand.

"Don't sweat, Matty. And when I come back I'll tell you how everything went so well."

I didn't answer anything but was whispering a lullaby to myself, the most miserable way to make something come true, I kept saying, "I know best and she knows better, done already, *Donnerwetter!*" It was that kind of miserable thing to myself, until she shut the door and made the noise with the bolts and what-not, when I shut up and stopped muttering and lay there like a very small but a very heavy mouse.

On the third floor, where she had her closet, there were no roomers along the corridor and there was no light at all until she came to the wall. She walked down to the second floor, looking slow and sleepy, because anyone seeing her between those two landings would hear the following most credible tale.

"That door kept banging and banging till I thought I would go out of my mind. So much so I got out of my warm bed to creep all the way up there and along in the dark—I can't help it if I'm frightened— Well, it's closed. *Porco*, listen to that wind!" She had decided to be very vulgar. That always stops a man.

She didn't meet anyone and stopped on the second floor where she took a deep breath and put on her other face. She practiced it all the way to her room where she turned on the light and took off her sweater. She hung it over the chair in the room and then she stopped. And this new little wrinkle she thought up while she stood there in her bra, took no change of face and no change of theatrics.

She had a smile which was only slightly visible on one side of her face, but it was there like a teasing itch because the other side of the face looked so hard. Especially the corner of her mouth. It would only go up to open wide and then there would be clanking, unhumorous laughter.

She pushed her hair forward, and while she cocked her elbow she cocked one hip. Then she unhooked her bra and dropped it on the bed. For a moment she held her breasts in her hands and she almost changed her expression and closed her eyes.

But then she clucked her tongue and took a brisk breath and went to the curtain that covered the wardrobe. She didn't have much in there but she looked at her things awhile, humming, to make a great choice.

There was a black Sunday dress, a white blouse of satin, a starched blouse with no sleeves and the color was red, two work smocks which belonged to the hotel, and a skirt, which she didn't even consider. She had a skirt on.

"Hum," she said. "What's bare arms. And what's red when it's starched?"

She put the satin thing on, over her naked skin, and kept humming while she looked down at herself to do the buttons.

She kept cocking her hip in a rhythm, slight but sure, and wouldn't have cared if any number of eyes had been watching. If they were men.

Then she unbuttoned the blouse again to do it over, but this time wrong. So there would be a sloppy gap. And then she unbuttoned the top one (which was actually not near the top at all) and looked down at the deep, smooth dent showing between her breasts.

She picked up an old pair of stockings, turned off the light in her room and went to the door next to hers. She heard the snoring through the door. The hard side of the face she wore was most prominent, and she meant it. She opened the door, turned on the light, watched the man give a start and turn over. When he snored again she dropped the stockings by his bed and left without turning off his light. She also left his door open.

At the second landing she looked down into the tiny hall, at Vinciguerra's closed door, and at the restaurant door which showed light through the broken glass. The hall itself was empty. The two guards—of those two she was only interested in Pepe—they were in the restaurant, filching wine.

Then she walked slowly down the last flight and unconsciously held her breasts in her hands because they moved under the satin without much restraint. But then she let go again, fixed her face as before and shrugged. She said, *"Fa niente,"* half aloud, which is nothing obscene but can sound fairly cold-nosed and then it means something like, "What the hell." She walked down with a free, unconcerned bounce.

She stopped on the bottom step before she could be seen from the restaurant, she stopped there because now she had a problem. She wanted to see Vinciguerra, and then she wanted to see Pepe too. But the two jobs needed two different faces and the problem was that Vinciguerra and Pepe might come up to her at one and the same time.

"Pepe first is no good," she thought, "because first I need Vinciguerra.

And Vinciguerra first is a trick, because when I stand at his door, Pepe can see me."

"*Mbu*—" she said, and leaned forward enough to see Pepe and the other one sit at a table. "And if they could see what this leaning produces they wouldn't sit there so calmly bored."

The smile side of her face went up when she thought that and for the moment erased even the bitchy side. Her eyes slanted more like a cat enjoying a slow rub on her neck.

"*Mia*," she said, low like a purr. "*Mia*, the things I can do—"

But Pepe and the other one weren't looking her way, they looked at the bad cards in their hands and the lost ones on the table.

She stepped down, turned her back to the restaurant, and stood close to Vinciguerra's door. She could see the light through a crack and she could hear his breathing.

"I'll go in quickly, and I won't even knock."

Her face went dumb with sleep, sullen with annoyance, then she made a quick pluck at her blouse. One shoulder seam hung below her own shoulder and the sleeve on that side went too far down on her hand. Then she held the front of her blouse.

"Slut, maybe," she said, "but mostly asleep. And what a hasty dresser I am. *MIA*— the things I can do."

She put her hand on the door and Vinciguerra gave a long, wavering yowl.

She pulled her hand back, and held on to the front of her blouse for real. She was not, for example, afraid of the dark, but this dog quaver from a bed where a human was lying—

"*Dio*, how he dreams," she mumbled. "He can infect with those dreams—"

"Hey! Hoy."

She turned around very quickly and saw Pepe come across to the door.

"Quick," she thought, "the other face now—how was that— Huh, as if I didn't know."

She actually had very little to change in her appearance, just the face mostly, and a forward stroke to her hair. (When she cocked her elbow to do this, she also cocked one hip.)

"Ay, and the front, of course. This way it would mean nothing to Pepe." And she dropped the hand which had been holding the blouse, and then she took a deep, sleepy breath, which spread her front magnificently.

"Sophia—" said Pepe and he just stood there at the door. He looked at her and remembered the sweater, and how could I have overlooked, I mean, even a sack over such, not to mention the sweater—

"Did you hear him?" she said, and walked to the door where Pepe was standing.

"Yes. Uh—are you often—I mean, is he often like that?"

"Oh no. Not often, Pepe."

She walked into the room of the restaurant while Pepe turned as she passed.

"I saw you at his door," he said. He hardly thought of what he was saying but was watching her walk.

She turned around and sighed, so that Pepe could see the sigh, feel the sigh, almost as if touching the girl where she sighed so magnificently.

"I came down because I thought I heard him call me. You know how he calls me at night."

"Yes," said Pepe. "I know. I know. He calls you every night."

"Mostly."

"Angelo," said Pepe to the table, "would you imagine Vinciguerra calls her every night?"

"Never. If I hadn't seen her come down these nights, never—"

"He drinks tea," she said.

Pepe laughed with the slow wheeze of a donkey winding up. Except that he didn't wind up very high. He stopped the wheeze and only kept the leer on his face.

"*Poverina*," he said, and touched her here and there with his eyes. "How you must suffer—"

She hugged herself, which came naturally, and what it did to her was perfectly natural, except that it was rarely seen.

She thought, what a situation. One in front, one in the rear. I can feel both of them looking, and oh my, how they tickle. Any more of this tickle and I must— What is the matter with me tonight—

"Other times I've seen you walk in there...."

"May I sit for a moment, Pepe?"

"Oh yes. Oh yes!" And he pulled a chair out, pushed a chair under her, held it so that when she sat down he could feel her soft weight in the lean of the chair.

"Little wine?" he said over her shoulder.

"Certainly not," she said, smelling his breath.

"Other times," said Angelo with a sudden loudness which startled everyone, "as I was saying. The other times I've seen you walk in there to Vinciguerra you always wear that terrible robe."

"It's convenient," she said, and shrugged one shoulder. She shrugged just one, something slipped on the other, and there was a little bit more sweet sheen of skin visible now.

She watched the two men and the smile side of her face contained a great deal of pleasure.

Oh my, she thought, how such a little can cause such a lot and of course this isn't the real me— Ha!

"What are you grinning about, Sophia?"

"Some little pleasure."

"Last thing you said was, it's convenient."

"Isn't it, Pepe?"

"Maledetto," he said and he flexed his eyes as if flexing a muscle. "What was in that bottle? Where's that bottle now?"

"Never mind the bottle," said Angelo with a voice like once before and with the same purpose. "I said, 'why you wearing that terrible robe into his room,' and you said, 'It's convenient.' We're still on that."

"On what, dear Angelo?" She leaned her chin into her hand and she leaned a little bit over the table. She sort of shrugged herself onto the table. "You're on my convenience, did you say?"

"What was that? Uh, I said what? No. Mine. My convenience, is what I was saying."

"Sophia," said Pepe and put his fingers on her arm. "Your convenience and my convenience, little Sophia, would all come to the same thing."

His two fingers were in the crook of her arm and though she didn't look at him or say a word, she gave an elaborate answer. She closed her arm slowly, the move was hardly visible, and when her arm was fully bent she flexed her muscles, just very little. She held his fingers like that.

"Oh—" said Pepe.

"What? You said what?"

"I think he thought of convenience," Sophia told him.

"Yes. Back to that. It's a terrible robe. *Terrible* robe."

"And I'm thinking of convenience," Pepe said at the air, "and I'm thinking that the robe is just right for that, because or else this young thing here would be walking into that room stark naked."

"Young thing? How old are you, Sophia?"

"Right, Sophia?" and Pepe moved his fingers away.

"Of course, Pepe."

"So *why,* is my question, did you walk in there just now fully dressed?"

"Fully dressed?" said Sophia, and she slowly cupped herself. "Oh! You mean the second time."

"That's right," said Pepe. "Tonight she came twice."

"Fully dressed," said Sophia, and she breathed so that it filled her hand, "because the second time I only came down because I suddenly thought I heard him calling."

"For tea," said Pepe.

He watched her move her hand away now and he mumbled, "Oh God, tea—"

"What was that?"

Such a talker, thought Sophia, and for the moment paid only attention to herself. Ah, somebody should now rub my head. What a strange evening—

"Where's the bottle?" said Angelo.

"Empty," said Pepe.

"I mean the other one."

"Empty."

"Damn it, damn it," said Angelo. "When did that happen?"

"Who cares," said Pepe.

I don't either, thought Sophia, and for a moment, just to watch the effect, she decided to use the unpracticed, evil side of her face. I'll punish them, she thought.

But nothing happened because nobody was watching her face.

I'll punish them, she thought. Why should I be the one that suffers? After all, there are this kind and that kind of people, some like to smoke, which I don't, some like this and that, and there are some who just love to be touched. That can't be helped, just as I can't help having this nose.

"Do you like my nose, Pepe?"

"Huh?"

And then she did feel touched and by now the play and the real were so happily merged, she could not have answered why she did what she did next.

"Pepe," she said, without looking at him. She felt his hand on her breast.

"What? Why not? You yourself just touched it."

And whether she first moved into his hand because she was breathing that way or whether she moved out of his hand because she now had to stretch, she couldn't have said.

"Then don't stretch that way, if you want nothing," said Pepe.

That's reasonable, she thought. That's at least reasonable from where he is sitting, but then what does he know about what I want? I don't entirely know myself, and I'm not worried, so why should he? *Mia,* how I can confuse myself on this special evening.

"He said, 'then don't stretch....'"

"Angelo," she said, and for this once she was certain that she meant what she said, "I just don't like to be touched that way unless I'm naked."

Pepe wasn't saying anything for the moment, so Angelo talked again. "And you're dressed."

She shrugged and the collar moved back into place.

"Why, I want to know, are you dressed this time of night?"

"I wasn't sleeping, Angelo. I was wide awake."

"With what, a book?"

"With the chauffeur upstairs."

"Aah—and to top it all, that pig from another town drinks nothing but cognac. Didn't we see him buy two bottles of..."

"I know," said Sophia, and she leaned back in the chair so she could hug herself.

"Alright," said Angelo. "Now. And you just got through saying here, you said: 'I just don't like to be touched unless I'm naked.'" He stared at her and she knew for a fact that he could beat her down.

She didn't answer but sat with her arms around her and feeling the satin with all of her fingertips.

"So what are you doing dressed with the chauffeur?"

"But I told you, or you told me, I forget how it went, that he drinks all that cognac."

"Oh, oh, oh," said Pepe and hugged himself the way Sophia was doing it. He said, *"Poverina, poverina.* Tea and cognac. Tea and cognac."

"I know," she said. "It's terribly terrible."

And then she let go of herself so that the sight was a sudden delight. She spread her arms out quite spontaneously and without any design and she looked so generous, and such a delight.

"Pepe!" she said. "Listen to me!"

Pepe could not speak and Angelo had been looking away.

"Pepe," she said again, and this time she jumped up. "Pepe, are you listening to me? Open your eyes."

He did not open his eyes right away but he said, "Sophia, I don't open my eyes to listen to anything. I open my eyes...."

"Pepe, give me the key to your Vespa."

"Wha—?"

"To your Vespa. Give me the key to your Vespa."

"Sophia, I'm looking at you now and see everything and I don't understand a word."

"Look, Pepe," and with both her hands she took hold of his nearest hand and while she talked she moved it back and forth, toward him, toward her, toward him, toward her. "I'll get him up, Pepe, and I'll take him out and I'll give him a ride on your Vespa. All that cold air and he'll sober up. Think of the cold air and how it will sober him up!"

"I don't like to think of that cold air, Sophia. Don't push my hand."

"For me, Pepe? Would you do it for me?"

"Listen," he said, and leaned forward. "I've got a better idea. I'll tell you what I'll do for you."

"And another thing, Pepe. While we're gone, he and I, you go up to his room and get the other bottle of cognac. And that way, you'll get a bottle too!"

"Too?"

"Oh, Pepe," she said, "if you don't let me take him out, you can't possibly get the bottle."

She let go of his hand, moved behind him, and stood in back of his chair where he could not see her. She stood there so the short hairs on his neck stood on end. She moved her hands over his ears and said, "Wouldn't you rather have both, *mio* Pepe?"

"Wait a minute," he said. "Stop this with the ears."

"I haven't said anything, Pepe."

"You mean—and I'm no longer discussing the bottle...."

"You mean then you'll do it? You'll lend me the key?"

"Let go my ears, Sophia!"

She let go and stepped away from him. She came around and had both hands on her hips.

"You want to know when?" she said.

"Yes. Did you mean you got to go with him first?"

"Of course, Pepe. Does that worry you?"

Mia, she thought, what I can do makes me shiver. And perhaps just now it showed?

She looked down at herself and seemed to discover where she had buttoned up out of line— She first touched her hair and when she crooked her arm, she also cocked one hip. Then she moved one leg out, foot resting on heel, and on that long heel she waved the foot back and forth. All this time she looked down at herself and undid all the buttons, and because of the way she was tucking her chin down everything she said came out in a negligent mumble.

"I don't see why that should worry you, Pepe."

"Now, wait one moment. I've been sitting...."

"I don't know why that should worry you either, Angelo. Damn," she said, "I got it wrong again," and she again undid the buttons.

Pepe was suddenly hoarse and had to cough several times while he talked.

"Look. I like it better the other way. You and me go together first. After that, like a good girl might, you just might get that key."

She didn't look up once and just mumbled.

"Okay. Now I'll get them straight."

Then she looked up suddenly and with a real show of anger jammed her fists down on her hips. The narrow slit of her open blouse went down to her skirt and the slit played a terrible torture play with the two men who were watching her.

"No!" and she tapped her foot for effect. "I promised the chauffeur and I keep my promise."

"Sophia, hold still, don't get mad like that."

And her voice was like calm waters now, "And I promised you, Pepe, and I keep my promise," and then she nodded at Angelo with the right kind of smile. Just as suddenly she was again black with anger.

"And if you think you can tell whether you're the fifth or the first...."

"Sophia— please—"

Mia, are they ever afraid of vulgar women, and just what could be the matter with me? Maybe I'll button up the blouse—

"Sophia, wait!"

"No," and she kept on buttoning until she was all the way up to the neck.

Then she stepped over to Pepe, calm as water now, and the slow smile. She just held her hand out and then he gave her the key. She smiled like a queen.

"Just for that, Pepe, do you know what I'll do for you?"

"Yes?" he said and would now have given her the Vespa too.

"I won't let you wait for more than a minute. I'm going right up there and fetch you the bottle and you won't have to wait till I get the chauffeur out. And perhaps—I don't know yet—I'll just let him sleep."

And the way I'm walking out, she thought, the way I feel all over, how can they sit still and not leap at me—

Must be the backside which I'm showing. I'm positive I accept and appreciate my own backside even more than they appreciate my front side. And I really mean, in a mirror too! Even without any motion.

Look back? To hell with them, the way Matty says. To hell with them and let them starve. All the buttons up all the way up to the throat—anybody ever tell me a single thing about my lovely throat? All the buttons up and those one-minded ones, one-fingered ones and one-mouthed ones over there, over everywhere, could just starve!

I'm their mother? What mother would allow this kind of thing with herself the way I allow—wrong word, little one! The way I enjoy—

Mia, but how heavy now. Are my legs too heavy, what I mean is, up here? Nothing's too heavy on me. I could stand still in this blouse and except for the thin material showing this and this and a sheen of skin, if I were to stand still in this blouse now there wouldn't be anyone who could tell if I wore a thing underneath, yes or no. I might ask them about it, I just might.

Ever get anything without asking? Ever have the feel on me of getting everything, everything ripped right off? Oh no, I would have to ask them.

And why do the stairs make me feel so terribly heavy. And what do I ever get without asking. And what is so special.

I have a cold. I have to wipe my nose but my eyes are running—well, naturally. Standing there naked like that with those two and the chills— Those were chills, little one, those were chills, and no one really touched me.

And why doesn't anyone really touch me. And what do I ever get without asking. And what's so special—(blow your nose, little one)—and what without asking, and why ever be a whore for more than one day.

And *why* must he leave and never say when he's coming again—

Chapter 29

The first thing she said was, "Matty, I've got it. He gave me the key."

I let out a breath as if I hadn't breathed since she had left, which was true in a way. And after that breath, I rolled over so she could get at those ropes.

She got the last of the ropes off which was the first time I actually paid attention to her.

"You been running up those stairs?"

"Why, my breathing?"

"Yes. And blow your nose, *bella.*"

Then the ropes were off and I sat up, looking for her. Looking for her is hardly the word, since there was no light, but that's what I was doing.

"Blow your nose, *bella.*"

"I must have caught a cold, Matty."

I could hear her throw the rope into a corner and then she sat down on the bed.

"Are you cold?—Christ! No wonder!"

"Matty, everything went just the way I told you it would. The...."

"You haven't told me how. All you...."

"Listen. The chauffeur never woke up when I turned on the light and then I never needed the light because nobody came up to check if he was there on the bed with the bottle and what I had left on the floor."

"What? Wait a minute. What?"

"Later. I'll tell you later. And when I got the bottle out of the room and turned off the light again he just kept snoring."

"Did you lock his door?"

"Yes, when I came up here. If they come up to check on me and him they'll have to think that we're both drunk in there."

"Now wait a minute. I want you to explain something to me. All I said was, leave the door open and the light on, so it would look as if you might have been there."

"Well, this other stuff was just detail, Matty. *Will* you listen."

"Little one, you still sound like you're running."

"Well, right at present those two are down there in the kitchen, on the kitchen floor they are, and Pepe is going to sleep all the time and the other one keeps talking to somebody who's not there."

"To whom?"

"How do I know," she said. "The only thing that didn't work was Vinciguerra."

"Oh." I thought a moment and said, "The way you describe those two guards, we won't need the sleeping pills."

"And Vinciguerra never woke up."

"Good. Very good. Best that way, with his nocturnal habits. And I'm just as glad you didn't ask him for sleeping pills, knowing your nocturnal habits."

"What?"

"The way you sleep like a log."

"You've never seen me sleep," she said.

"Right now I wish I could see your face, Sophia. Come here." I felt something wrong between us.

"No."

"Hey— you're not wearing a goddamn thing under this."

"I don't always."

"Well, I mean, I appreciate that. But first touch, first of all there was no sweater. Now, second touch...."

"Matty. That hurt."

"I'm sorry. Please, Sophia—"

"Well, anyway, it's all set." And she got up.

The wrong thing between us became dense.

"Sophia, please answer me. I'm sitting still here, I'm not groping for you, just please answer me."

"Ask."

"I thought you were gone very long. Why so long?"

"Because I went back a while later to make sure they were drinking. To see if they were drunk."

"What happened with Vinciguerra? Why didn't you get into his room?"

"Well, it just worked out that way, Matty. You weren't there, were you?"

"And I'll never forget that—"

"And now everything's fine, isn't it?"

I said, "Yes." I sat and didn't know exactly where she was standing. "Will you tell me, Sophia, how you worked the thing with the drunken chauffeur? You said something...."

"But that was just a little invention I made. Right then on the spur of the moment. What *do* you want, Matty," and I thought she was stamping her foot.

So I got up. I first bumped my head but I didn't pay any attention to that. I did not hear her move and then I touched her on the arm. We stood in the high part of the closet. I left my hand on her arm and touched for her face with my other hand.

"*Bella*, I don't want to press you and I won't. I don't need that, Sophia, and you don't deserve it," and I dropped my hand from the side of her face. Then, further down, my hand caught in her blouse.

I would have moved my hand away simply enough, except at that moment she stiffened. I could feel it in her arm under my hand, and in the belly muscle I touched with my finger.

"Sophia—"

"Alright!"

"Not so loud."

"Alright," she said again and her voice was low and a little bit hoarse, the way some Italian women are all the time. And then her whisper was as wild as a shout.

"When I left down there the blouse was buttoned all the way up to the top. And then I went back to the kitchen to check on them with their liquor and that's when the blouse came open. The second time, the first time on the way down the stairs, like a whore in a house, the way she might make an entrance. And then in the restaurant with those two men, still playing a game, still not knowing anything, and you can ask me if you want to know whether I was enjoying it. Did they touch me? Ask!"

"I'm not...."

"Ask, did they touch me? Here!" and she took my hand and rubbed it over her nipple.

"And what when they weren't touching anything? I just showed them. I just sat there and moved there, and oh what I learned that I knew, just simply knew about everything. And while I made them look we did the rest just with talk. That I sleep with Vinciguerra every day, that I just came from the chauffeur, that I wanted Pepe after that and if Angelo were interested too, so what, he too. You hearing all this, Matty? Do you hear?"

"Yes. I'm right here."

"And then I walked out."

"Why do you tell me...." But she wasn't listening to me. She was doing all this to herself and went on without hearing me.

"Hah!" she said. "Feel this?" and she pushed up against me and snaked her body back and forth like a most unreal animal. "That's how I walked out." She dropped her voice and said, "And then I left and still thought that all this was a game, but how sad it was getting, how miserably sad— And sordid, very soon now. Sordid with everything just thought and not done, sick because nothing was tasted but only exaggerated, and I got so far up, so far, all buttoned up, and then I went down again. I said, unbutton me, and they were very happy. I said harder like that, so it hurts! They were happy. Then I said, where? Here in the kitchen? And they said, well, you work here in the daytime, it's your due to have pleasure here during the night."

"Did you?"

"It was very exciting, even though they never took off my clothes. They had me there half-way up on the sink— They had that and they were very happy. And I was singing, what the hell, what the hell, up there on the sink and I sang it out the way you always do it. And they were very happy."

"I was," I said.

"And that was my special day, with *so* many specials about it. *Don't* do that!" and she jumped like a spring, not like anything animate.

I did not touch the small of her back again. I took her arm and pulled her just so, closer. This had been Sophia with the pain talking out of her and I didn't want it to become any worse, not for her, not for me, no more pain in a tight black closet. Let it be over. I pulled her up and said, "Listen to me. The least you can do is put on something warmer."

"*Cosa—*" she said, the way I had heard it before.

"The night is cold as it is and on top of that riding a Vespa is extremely windy. The way we'll be going."

"No," she said. "Oh no—"

"Sophia, now what? Are you listening?"

"Matty, you said this? You just said all this?"

"Yes. And bring nothing you can't wear on your back."

"Say it over, say it over again."

"On your back."

It was hard to tell whether she laughed or cried, both were possible, I think she did both. And she said, "You have to explain...."

"Later. *Avanti!*"

"But I have to know, I must know what this has to do— I know this has something to do with it—"

"You're not making sense and I like you stupid. When you're dressed...."

"What it has to do with tonight."

I gave her a shake and said, "That I like you better than they do. That's all!"

I had to hold her now because she went limp. And suddenly she held on to me.

"Words," she said, "words. All they do is, they make questions. Give an answer, Matty. One answer—"

"I want you with me!"

"Those are words and perhaps they mean I'm just going to run."

"Sophia, you talk more than I. Get down there and take what you want, just what you can take on your back and...."

"You," she said. "I take you."

We both went silent at the same time, and I think we both started to laugh at the same time, low and close.

"On your back," I said.

"Words," she said.

And she was still talking when I pulled the blouse off her back. There had been one button which hadn't been open and that jumped off and something ripped. Then the rest, she and I, and since we couldn't see we had to feel that much more.

"This is the first time I'm naked with you," she said, and I said something which I forget, and a remark here and there, I'm sure. We made love with a great deal of excitement—some of it hurry pushing us because we would leave, some of it because we made this our beginning.

Then we lay quietly for a while, just sides touching, but not for very long. She said, "I'm now very beautiful, do you know that?"

"You feel very beautiful, yes."

And she said, "I can turn that around and say, I feel very beautiful, and then you can say, yes, because you are very beautiful."

"And then they are both the same."

We got up and now everything was very fast.

"I dress here while you run downstairs."

"I'm running."

"Wait, I got your skirt here under my foot."

"I don't care, I don't care, I'm not taking that one," and she pushed open the door and I could see light.

"You're stark naked!"

"So are you," she said. "But you've got to...."

"I don't care, I don't care anymore, nothing here matters anymore. Look. First time, no?"

"You are beautiful."

She stood outside the small door, stretched, and relaxed again. A dim yellow light lay on one side of her, molding her.

"And now I'll swat your plump rear, which I haven't seen yet," and then I was going to say the rest, about hightailing it downstairs without further delay, but I first crawled up to that ridiculous door.

She turned halfway, beautiful again, and then she was suddenly something else.

She was not ugly but she was not right. A crouch can't hold that long and be right.

When I got to the door hole she did stand straight again, very calm with herself, and looking at something. She was looking and didn't care what looked back.

"Sophia—" and then I came through the door hole when she said, "I never thought of the light. That there is no light up here."

I got out then and stood up next to her.

The lamp was on the ground where the stairs went down, yellow flame making a quiet lap.

I didn't see all of him but mostly his face. One hand on the corner where the stairs went down, the little mouse hand hanging there, not used for anything.

But Vinciguerra's face was something different now. He looked and he didn't see. This was the impression. And this in spite of the fact that his eyes were the wide open, startling feature which made you ignore all the rest of his face. His face was grey, I think. And nothing went on in his face, until he screwed his eyes shut as if in great pain.

Chapter 30

Then we tore out of there, like rats running, mice flitting, all this a very sharp and electric energy, I into that hole for the last time and Sophia downstairs. Vinciguerra had gone from my sight before then and disappeared down the stairs, I think, even before Sophia had gone down.

When I was dressed I broke the bed apart and took along one of the legs.

She came out of her door when I came to the landing. She had shoes on but no socks or stockings. And the big sweater again.

I didn't give one last look to anything. I knew this place well enough and we just ran. In one hand I had her hand, in the other the club. Glass broke in the door when I slammed it shut.

Into the square and just run now. Nothing but square, nothing but street, steps, a turn and the lower square.

I allowed no feeling yet. We just kept running. Though in a way this is incorrect. There was no feeling yet because there was no room. Just room for energy pumping into the run, pumping from where I don't know into this bursting and ending run.

In the square were two Vespas and a car.

"The blue one is his." (I don't know where she got the breath.)

The gate out of town had a lamp in it and nobody was by the gate either. We slowed and then she gave me the key.

"He said there's gas, lots of gas—"

"Stop talking. Breathe."

She stopped and so did I. Everything, without exception, stopped for this moment.

He, Vinciguerra, came out from behind the car, and his hands were in his pockets and this small man was exhaustion itself, whatever was left after that agony of looking at us from the stairs.

And the threat was there though I don't know where it sat, I can't say where the air sits either, but there is air. And there was nobody except Vinciguerra.

Sophia put the key into my hand. She pushed it. That was real. I could feel her hand.

"Please," said Vinciguerra, and with that first word his dry leaf calmness and his shy smallness, all that became unimportant and disappeared.

Because all the energy he had left was in that voice. Not a big roar of sound but a sharp darting out, hasty plucking of sleeve with nails holding on again and again and they won't let go. All this with his face worn out. His pathetic contrast of wishing and weakening was there, worse than ever.

"Run," he said. "Run immediately back to the hotel and get the keys to this car. Run!" he said to Sophia.

She stood still.

"But we don't need..." I started to say.

"Nothing, you have nothing! No gas, empty. Sophia, run. Please, child, run!"

I wanted to say thank you to him but it didn't fit. I felt no gratefulness. I said, "What happened now? What new..."

"I'll tell you everything, but she must run!"

His insistence was like a hypodermic and what he injected was his own panic. I felt it.

"Tell her to go!" he insisted. "I took the key from the chauffeur. In the red book on my table. Tell her to go!"

She waited for me and I turned and said, "Run, Sophia, go!"

He was too weak to fake and what at first only hung in the air was now entering me. It came from him. No threat now. Pluck of panic.

"My God," I said, and I knew why Vinciguerra had been loving me and hating me, helping me and hurting me, all at the same time.

"Not both of them," Vinciguerra said. "It cannot be."

"Bastard! Son of a bitch!" I shouted into the wind. "Guetano's wrong, I didn't kill her. Tell me where to find my child."

"I have never been told. You must be satisfied with all you have done." He dropped his chin to his heaving chest. "Now you go."

"Sophia...."

He dreamt a web with me in it, immobile, and I hung there in this congealing horror which can only be apprehended in immobility. (This is the brother of death. Sleep isn't, but this is.)

And if I were to stay, then he, Vinciguerra, would tell her and show her the same thing and would cause her to feel the same thing I was going through now, unless I did something, finally did something for her alone—

The roar of the motor wasn't enough and going fast through the gate wasn't enough to cover her scream reaching for me—

* * *

It is always reaching for me. I have left Forza d'Aguil but I am still there. I had gone back much too late and now they have won, after all, keeping me there. It is the doubt, the eternal doubt which eats into me, whether Vinciguerra had not been lying. How to find the strength to say to her, yes, I am leaving Forza d'Aguil but I'm coming for you—

THE END

Hard Case Redhead

By Peter Rabe

The alarm screamed and kept screaming as the two men leaped out of the dark, ran down the alley and into their car. When the screaming did not sound so loud any more it became like a bug in the ear, a bug that stung.

"Don't choke it, for God's sake, don't stall now—"

"Just shut up," said the younger one, "just shut up—"

He made the car roar. They shot down the alley with the back end skittering because the wheels spun so fast. The older one tossed the black bag to the rear so that it bounced on the back seat. His hands were free now to get at his gun. The alarm raced along with them.

"That was the money?" said the young one. "The way that bag bounced, Tolman, so help me if that was the wrong bag—"

"Drive. Shut up and drive—"

They were both crouched in the front seat as if both were driving or as if both were holding a gun, sitting there in the dark with the spring-like crouch which is a readiness to fly or jump or claw into any direction. The alarm stung at them. It came like a new shock when it suddenly dimmed as they passed the bend in the alley. Then Tolman, the older one, took a breath, not very deep, not done yet with the waiting, but easier now. He looked at the young one driving and said,

"Now slow for the end of the alley. You can slow some now. From the end of the alley it's only three minutes till we make the highway."

But the words didn't help the driver. He didn't want help, because he had his anger. It sat in him big and hot and he raced the car, which was like his shield.

"You shut up, Tolman. Once we get in the clear I'll...." but he didn't get any further.

He might well have made the turn fast with the outside tires squashed flat and squealing because he had the practice and liked driving that hard. But he didn't.

"Watch it!" yelled Tolman. "Manny, *watch her!*"

The redheaded girl at the mouth of the alley jumped back. She had leaned forward to look into the alley, to watch the car coming, but the car didn't have any lights and was on her too soon. The wind of it tore at her coat. The big car rushed past. The girl still stood there when the car bucked in the turn down the street—just like a mean horse, it crossed her mind—but the tail lights flared on and the illusion was gone. Then the gears clanked; the bulk of the car shot back at her, making a high whine. She again thought of a horse, but not long. She stood frozen all over and did not think either.

Tolman twisted in the seat and saw the mouth of the alley again, black and getting bigger and the girl standing there close to the wall.

"Manny, you gone out of your...."

"Get your hand off that wheel!"

Tolman pulled back his hand, afraid of making the car crash by a struggle. The car was shooting back fast now.

"I'm wheel man," Manny kept saying. "And I got enough outa you for a long time."

The car stopped very suddenly, with the girl next to it and flat by the wall. She was staring at the two men in the car, seeing the gun in the hand of the nearest, but all of it was meaningless. She was terrified.

"Grab her, Tolman! Don't sit there and...."

"You stupid bastard—" Tolman started but Manny, from the wheel, reached over and slammed open the door.

"She's staring at us, you son of a bitch. *Grab her!*"

Tolman got hold of the girl's coat in front and pulled her up close. When she was close enough he swung one arm around her and hauled her into the car, on top of himself, then got his leg out of the way fast because the car door was swinging shut from the sudden leap the car made when Manny went forward again.

They swung left. They made the highway three minutes later. They didn't hear the alarm any more. Everything had worked out as planned.

Except for the girl. Tolman could feel how stiff she was, sitting on top of him. Even when he moved his hands off her wrists she stayed as she was, not moving.

"Get in back," said Tolman.

He had to say it again and give her a tap before she moved. Then she moved quickly, because this way, in back, she was at least a little bit further away from the two men.

"You gonna have her sitting in back, at least turn around and keep that gun..."

"Manny," said Tolman. "Just drive."

The girl thought that the older one acted tired. Or perhaps he wasn't really much older than the one driving the car but acted older, without the edginess of the other one. Perhaps the older one was the worst, not showing himself very much in the way he behaved. The main impression she had of him was the lines in his face, but maybe they would not show as much if he were shaved. The young one, at the wheel, was blond. She had no other impression of him—except for his edginess—because his face was not memorable.

"That was a fool stunt," said Tolman. "I wish you hadn't done this."

"With her standing there and seeing it all?" Manny kept driving fast but was trying to see the girl's face in the mirror. "I don't make the kind of mistakes that...."

"Taking her was," said Tolman. "But now it's too late." He put a cigarette in his mouth and lit it.

The girl in back sat very still, trying to feel invisible. Neither of the two men looked at her nor talked to her. Small and dark in her corner, she began to feel alive again, in this small space.

Manny was checking mileage but when he was done it had not distracted him. He looked sideways at Tolman and said,

"You know damn well this was your fault, Tolman. Anything goes wrong from here on in, with her there," and he nodded back without turning, "it's your fault."

"Stop digging," said Tolman.

They both talked quietly now, the girl noticed. They both sat apart, sitting still or making only very small movements. The girl in back, in the dark, thought this was frightening.

"Your fault the alarm went off, wasn't it?" Manny was not asking it like a question.

Nor was there any good reason for him to ask it because they both knew that it had been Tolman's fault. He, Tolman, had not seen that type of burglar alarm before. Which was no excuse.

"I made a mistake," was all he said. He dragged on his cigarette and stared out at the road.

"Damn right. And I *don't* make mistakes," said Manny.

He had to wait a long time for Tolman to answer or show any signs. When Tolman did, it made Manny slow down because of the other man's tone.

"Keep this up, Manny, and I break something in you. I don't care how fast you're going."

They did not talk for a while after that. Manny drove, sitting behind the wheel as if it might get away from him, and Tolman kept smoking. He smoked several cigarettes one after the other. Once he looked back at the girl, then front again. He kept smoking and thought mostly about the girl, and what to do about her. It was now too late to let her go.

Manny took side roads and went much slower. There were thick, black-looking trees all around and most of the time the road went up.

"You been watching her?" said Manny.

"She's all right," said Tolman.

"You didn't tie her," said Manny.

Tolman took a deep breath and looked down at his hands.

It was like an itch in Manny.

It wasn't bravery or anything like that. It was like a vile itch in him. He said: "And you got that money lying back there, next to her?"

If Tolman had meant to answer, he was too slow.

"Or maybe you got the wrong bag? Maybe you picked up those gold plate tools of yours first and to hell with...."

"Give me that bag," said Tolman. He turned to the girl, who drew stiff into her corner and said again, "The bag, girl. Give it to me."

It would mean letting go her body, which she had been holding with her hands and arms, and to lean over, touch something else—

"Watch her," said Manny. "I don't trust—"

The girl suddenly started to cry. The small sound grew, ran away with her, shook her while she tried to smother herself with her hands on her mouth. It shook her and shook her and would not stop.

Tolman reached back past her and picked up the bag. He put it on the seat between himself and Manny and opened it up.

"The money," he said.

Manny saw the bills but got no satisfaction from the sight. He just nodded and kept driving along the road, which was getting bumpy. He now thought of the tools which Tolman had left behind and how much easier it would be for the police to go after them, chase them down, and all this the fault of Tolman, the three time loser, who ought to know better but didn't because why else had the bastard been caught three times before for the same thing? And now the old son of a bitch kept his mouth shut. That had to do with his time in stir, time in solitary most likely, that was the reason.

But it wasn't the reason for Manny's itch, for the feeling like a fine hair in his insides stirring at him. What? Admire that son of a bitch for his quietness? Hate him for it. Hate him for that whole damnable feel of assurance which hung on the bastard!

But Manny said nothing to Tolman then, because there was an easier way.

"You gonna stop that yammering pretty soon now?" he said over his shoulder.

The girl didn't stop. She tried. She breathed badly for a moment, but she didn't stop.

"Shut up! Shut up back there or I'll push it down your throat!"

"You drive and watch the road," said Tolman.

"You telling me—you telling me—" Manny had to think of a stronger way, a more cutting way which would come out more easily and did not choke him. "Ha?" he said. It almost was like a laugh, but there was no place for a laugh now. There was nothing but rage coming out now, which would once and for all kill off his nervousness.

"You got it layed out already, all layed out in your mind, Tolman? You and that dish back there got it suddenly all...."

"I want you to cut it out, Manny."

"All I'm telling...."

"Lay off," said Tolman. "The last time I'm telling you."

No matter how it sounded to the girl or to Manny, Tolman was not calm about this. He was not a strong talker but that did not mean he was a calm man when pushed. He thought the man had gone far enough. First, all right, the man was nervous and working it off. Now, no more. Now, the man was getting far out of hand and this might become bad. Bad for finishing this job the way they had planned it, worse now with the girl in the back, though at least she kept her fright to herself and did not hack with it into anyone else.

Manny first. She would come later. First Manny, if he didn't line up, because he would have to line up, would *have* to— Because Tolman knew this: he would not get caught ever again. He had no margin for error.

"You stir-crazy son of a bitch—" Manny was saying, and other things to which Tolman did not pay attention. Tolman was sitting now with his teeth tight, trying to breathe without effort. How could he? There was no margin of error for him. He did not think of love for life, hope for happiness, freedom from restraint, but like this: for the rest of his life, by whatever ways, he was going to breathe deep and with no effort. He was going to stay out of jail, out of the way, out of the tight corners. Just to breathe deep, in and out, till he died.

"...and close that lousy window, for chrissakes!"

Tolman grunted. He had not known that he was rolling the window down but felt the cold night air now, with the leaf-smells.

"Tolman! You hear me talking? I said close...."

"Stop the car," said Tolman and to make sure of this he reached over, turned the key in the ignition, pulled it out. "Brake it. All the way to a stop."

Manny did this because it was the only way he could get his hands free, off the wheel, without wrecking everything. He was not yet sure about Tolman and what he wanted but would be ready for him because he, Manny, knew a few tricks of his own, fast things, and Tolman had never been fast. The car was just rolling now and Manny needed one hand on the wheel only.

"Leave the gun there," said Tolman.

Manny pulled back his hand. He bit his lip and did not think he would need a gun to scare off Tolman.

The fist caught Manny flush in the mouth, a back hand, he remembered later, and then his head snapped back through the open window. Tolman's hands were in his hair, holding him, and Tolman's face was close.

"Till we're out of this," Tolman was saying, "you try holding yourself to the rules. We got three days yet, before we can figure out moving. You hold still those three days, Manny. You hold still for what I tell you."

Then Tolman let go of Manny's hair and let him sit up. "Now get out of the car, walk around the hood, and sit in my seat. I'm driving."

Manny did like Tolman wanted it. Manny had his own gun in his pocket but he never thought—in the car or once he was out—he never thought of using the gun in any way. He walked around the car and came back in to sit next to Tolman.

Tolman drove the rest of the way, which was not far, where a cabin sat in the black woods. Tolman drove into a shed and nodded at Manny to carry the bag. Then Tolman opened the door to the back.

"You too," he said to the girl. "Out."

She came out and walked to the cabin with the two men watching her. The two men, seemed the same to her now, with the darkness making them look so, with their quarrel over. She waited at the door to the cabin because one of them had to unlock it. There seemed to be no fright left in her now, after sitting alone in the back of the car, nothing left now but a thick tiredness.

They knew the inside of the shack because Manny went somewhere in the dark, stopped, made a few small sounds with something, and then the kerosene lamp went on. The girl saw that the shutters were closed on the windows. Tolman closed the door.

"Open some cans," said Tolman, and Manny went to a cupboard and took out some cans.

There were two bunks on top of each other and a large mattress lay in one corner. There was a cupboard with a sink and a pump over it and a fat bellied stove in the middle of the room. The girl pulled her overcoat close around her and stood by the stove.

"We don't make a fire," said Manny, looking at her.

For a moment she had thought about a warm fire built in the stove, but not seriously. It had just been a thought that comes with seeing a cast iron stove, the split wood next to it, and a chair standing close by.

They had two cans of sterno with a little stand over each and they heated a small pot of water and a pot with thick soup from a can. It took a while to heat these.

"What's your name?" said Manny.

Now, she thought, *now they will start on me. They've made a peace with each other and now they'll turn on me—*

"Answer him," said Tolman.

He sat on the low bunk and smoked. He watched the girl and watched Manny, wishing there would be no friction.

"Ellen," she said.

"You from that town we just left?" asked Tolman.

She shook her head. She had a notion that all this was preliminary, that there was no point in talking more, because she did not know of anything she could say which might reach the two men. Anything would be useless, because they were only talking to build up to the next.

"I'd like to know," said Tolman, "what you were doing at three in the morning at that alley."

"That's right," said Manny. He was stirring the soup. "Middle of the night like that and you not a native there, huh? What?"

Was he grinning at her? He looked down again, at the soup, and Tolman's face, Tolman who smoked all the time. His face told her nothing. She could not see a thing there, which was the worst, leaving her to read things into him. Tolman was the worst of the two, probably. The way he had hit the other one, so suddenly—

"Well?"

"I— The bus station is just one block from there, from the alley where—"

"Where what? What did you see?" said Manny.

Tolman looked over at him and said, "What's the difference what she saw? What's the difference now?" Then he nodded at the girl.

"I was just walking. A half hour lay-over with the bus, that's all—" and she started to cry again.

There was no pity any place around her, so she cried. Not with the sharp pain and hysteria which had shaken her that time in the car but with a soft, melting pity for herself, so that she felt as if flowing apart. She heard the men say a few things, to her maybe, but it did not matter to her what they said and so did not hear the words.

When she was through she wiped her face which was very wet and then sat down on the chair by the cold stove. She felt limp.

The two men were eating soup. They looked up when she sat down and then Tolman came over.

"Here," he said. "Eat this soup," and held out the bowl to her.

She couldn't eat. She could look at the thick brew in the bowl and not even recognize it for food.

Tolman shrugged and went back to the cupboard where Manny was still spooning their soup. They ate and did not look at her. After a while they put the bowls in the sink and then stirred powdered coffee into the hot water.

"Maybe she wants coffee," said Manny. He brought over a cup and said to the girl, "Here's coffee for you."

She took it. The strong smell went straight into her and she wanted the coffee badly. She held the cup with both hands to let the heat get into her skin.

They did not talk again while each sat with his cup, Tolman on the low bunk, Manny back on one elbow on the low mattress, and the girl still by the stove.

She wished that Tolman would give her a cigarette but he didn't. He sat with his cup and did not look up. She did not feel so cold any more. The hot coffee, perhaps, the three people in a small room, the yellow kerosene lamp. It felt warmer, if only a surface warmth. The girl opened her coat a little while she kept the cup close to her face.

"She's here now," Tolman said.

It sounded very sudden to the girl. Tolman still did not raise his head but kept looking into his cup. "You've got any idea what next?"

Manny moved on his mattress. The small sound was like a sting to the girl. Manny was back on one elbow but did not find it comfortable. He shifted and took a gun out of his pocket. He put it down next to himself, on the mattress.

"I'm not sure," he said, pushing the gun over a little.

"We got three days here," said Tolman, "before they let up on the road-blocks."

"If any," said Manny, but he mostly said this from habit of contradicting. The plans were all Tolman's, because he knew best about this sort of thing. The route out of here and the contacts later, to get rid of the money, the plans were all Tolman's. Without him, Manny did not know how to go on from here safely.

"We got these three days," Manny said and looked at the girl.

She tried to sit so her legs would not show and she wished she had not opened her coat.

"You were coming through that town?" Tolman said to her. "From where to where?"

She was tense again and now about something else, so she told them more than they had asked, just to be talking.

"I used to live in Detroit. I used to be married there, and I'm going— I was going back home."

"I asked where."

"Fresno. My parents have a ranch out of Fresno."

"They're expecting you when?"

"They don't—I mean, they know I'm coming, but they don't know the day," she finished. Her voice trailed off when she said this, knowing how much of a mistake she had made, but no way to correct it now.

"Fine," said Manny. "Because you might be a little bit late."

She put her cup down on the stove, looked up from one man to the other. She felt a shaking inside her, from what Manny had said, over the hope he had given her— She stood up, eager now, and, "I know there won't be any trouble over three days. They won't know by three days when I'm supposed to...."

"Three days," said Tolman. "I don't know yet." He got up and put his cup in the sink.

The girl did not start to cry again, because it felt as if that part were over. She continued to breathe as before, though it was like someone else breathing, and continued to stand by the stove, though it was a young woman there by the stove whom she did not want to know, whom Manny was looking at—the legs, the rest of her showing under the open coat—and she herself, Ellen, hiding away somewhere in some place of dark smallness.

"Used to be married?" said Manny. "He dead?"

"Divorce," Ellen heard her voice.

"Gee," said Manny. His teeth showed, so she thought he might well be laughing, or smiling. "You must be hell on wheels for a guy to divorce *you.*"

He came over and took off her coat, like a gentleman. She let this happen and he put it on the chair behind her and then looked her up and down.

"How long was you married?"

"Three years."

"Yeah?" said Manny and stepped back, looking. "Either he was a queer or you're hell on wheels." He came closer and said, "You hell on wheels, Elly?"

It was a meaningless question to her, except for what showed in Manny's face. She had been divorced because they had always been broke. They had always been broke because the state had made Richard, who had been her husband, sick and morose. He had been sick and morose so that it shut her out of his life, or perhaps she had never been in it, except the way Manny was getting into it now, and none of this mattered, really—

She saw Tolman come back from the sink and he looked at her too, at her face.

If only they would not hurt her— She was afraid of them again, two strangers who beat each other in silence, two strange, powerful men whom she did not understand. If only they would not hurt her. She hung on that wish because it was the only one about which there was still any question. She would not care about anything else—

"You take the first six hours," said Tolman and nodded at Manny. "You, Miss. You want to sleep?"

The question confused her and she did not answer.

"Take the low bunk," said Tolman. "You keep the mattress," he said to Manny.

"Fine, fine—"

"Check outside before you go to sleep, and douse the lamp before opening the door. The rest of the time keep it on."

"Sure. I mean to."

"You'll have to sleep under your coat," said Tolman to the girl. "There's only two blankets." Then he climbed to the upper bunk.

"I'm tired," he mumbled. "I'm tired—"

For a while the girl just stood there and watched Tolman lie down. He looked terribly tired. It made him seem human, less of a puzzle, but just for that moment when she looked at his face with the blanket up to his chin and the eyes closed already. No longer than that. For a moment there had been a feeling for him, when he had told her where she should sleep. But then, he had done nothing about Manny and what Manny wanted from her. For another moment there had been a feeling for him when she saw him lie down, but then, why hadn't he offered to give her his blanket—

Tolman only slept, thinking of nothing. Once he woke up, very briefly, but did not raise up to look around. The lamp was on, he could see the girl's shoes on the floor. One of them had fallen over. And he could hear Manny breathing.

Tolman woke six hours later without Manny telling him. He grunted and sat up in his bunk.

"You up?" said Manny.

"Yes, go to sleep."

Manny was on his mattress with a cold cup of coffee next to him and a saucer full of cigarette stubs. When he saw Tolman climb down from his bunk Manny lay down and turned to the wall.

"Catch the alarm before it rings," he said and then curled himself under the blanket.

Tolman went to the cupboard and re-set the alarm for six hours later. He pumped water into a pot and put it on top of the primus. He didn't look over at Ellen until he was done.

She was in the lower bunk, which Tolman knew because he had climbed past her legs. She was sitting there and looking at him.

Her hair was mussed in back and there was no more lipstick on her mouth. She looked tired, as if she would like to but could not sleep. She had a white blouse on, which was open, but nothing else underneath. Tolman could see her breasts, fine and full, and he saw that she made no effort to cover herself. Her other things were on the floor. She brushed her hair back from her face and sat on the bunk.

"I'm going to have coffee," said Tolman. "You want some?"

"Sure."

When the water boiled he made two cups of instant and gave one to the girl. She took it and only nodded.

Tolman opened the shutters outside, walked around, came back in. He drank his coffee on the way. Then he went to the bunk and said, "Done?" holding out his hand.

"Yes," she said, and gave him the cup. She took a deep breath and lay back on the bed. She put her arms up next to her and looked now all naked. Just one leg and part of her belly were covered with the coat she had brought. She lay like that and looked up at Tolman, tired and quiet.

Tolman frowned, then took the cups to the cupboard.

She did not turn her head to follow him with her eyes but looked up at him again when he came back.

"Get dressed," he said. "You'll be cold."

She kept looking at Tolman and then leaned up on one elbow.

"You don't want to?"

Tolman put his hands in his pockets and looked over at Manny. Manny was asleep. He looked at the girl, who now held the blouse together between her breasts and said to her:

"No. I wasn't thinking about that. You can get dressed."

Then he turned away, as if a woman dressing were more of a private thing than a woman sitting half naked on a rumpled bed.

He went outside and looked through the big trees to the clearing. From the clearing, with a glass, he could see the highway they would be taking, though he could not see if there might be a roadblock at the place which would be most logical, the place where a second road joined, just before the state line. The state line would be some kind of safety. It would be good once he did not see the far dip in the road anymore from the clearing, but from the dip itself, the dip getting eaten up by the car and then the state line, which would mean a little more safety—

"Could I have a cigarette?"

The girl Ellen was next to him, dressed now. She had combed her hair but had left off the lipstick. That way she looked soft and small to Tolman, an impression he had with some women when they did not wear any lipstick.

He gave her a cigarette and lighted it for her.

"Don't look at me, please," she said, "—like that."

Tolman saw she was embarrassed. Now, she was embarrassed.

"Don't let it bother you," he said. "Why should you have thought any different, back there?"

She looked up at him and it didn't bother her any more now that he was looking back.

"Rough night?"

"I don't know," she said. "I don't know— I've never done this before— like this."

"Don't let it throw you," said Tolman which was the closest he could get himself to a mood of consoling. He looked away and smoked.

He was a very hard man, thought the girl. He doesn't feel like having me now but when he will, he will. And what happened to me during the night means nothing to him.

"You wanted something?" he asked. "You came out here because you wanted something?"

"I—I wanted a cigarette."

"Yes." Tolman walked to the clearing, going slowly so that she would follow him. "And you came out here for the same reason you let Manny sleep with you last night. Scared."

In a moment she said, "Yes. Yes."

"I didn't want you along," said Tolman. "I'm sorry."

It shot out of her without any forethought. "Sorry? You're *sorry?*"

"Yes."

It was—she thought—as far as he could go with his feelings. He had no feelings beyond that, but was dead. Less than an animal, because he had brains—

"I can't let you go in three days," he said. "But later. Five days, maybe, and we'll disappear. Then you can go."

The cigarette burned her finger and she threw it away without looking at her hand. She was looking at Tolman and smiled, then laughed and might have cried next if she had not touched Tolman then, not thinking about it but taking his arms in her hands. He raised one hand and patted her lightly just by her elbow.

It was a small, half-way pat, and then he stepped back. For a moment she even thought he had started to smile at her but if he had smiled, it was too fast. There had just been the half-finished pat and then nothing more.

She let go of him and felt like before when she had lain on her back, naked, to let him have her, and he hadn't taken.

"And you'll forget this soon," he said.

He said nothing else to her. He went for the glass and spent time by the edge of the clearing, looking around. He walked past her a few times and later, when Manny woke up, he talked to Manny. All he talked about was the route they would try to take, the closer look they would take at the highway on the second day here, and dry things of that sort.

She thought she had never disliked a man as much as this Tolman. She would sooner have Manny. He was mean, self-centered. But he was not self- sufficient. He was evil and possibly cruel, in a wide open way. But he was not shut tight.

In the afternoon she went to sleep on the bunk. When she woke up she saw Manny and felt his hand and thought, this is part of it, because they are not going to hurt me. But then Manny got off the bed and left her alone because Tolman wanted him. Tolman wanted two for the look-out, because there were sounds, motor sounds. They were far away, but not too close for Tolman. They went away in a while and about twenty minutes later a police car raced over the far highway. Manny saw them through the glass and until dark both men kept watching, seeing police cars every so often.

Only Tolman ate that night, and the girl. Manny was tense and did not talk.

"That's why we're waiting three days," Tolman said to him. "So they clear."

"Yeah. They got your time table in mind and clear out in three days."

"Go to sleep," said Tolman. "Your nerves are going to eat up your insides."

"I want out," said Manny. "I got a better idea about...."

"Shut up."

"You think...."

"Shut up," said Tolman, much too quiet now.

Manny lay down on his mattress. He rolled around for a while, unable to sleep, but said nothing all of that time. He smoked and looked at Tolman and the girl who sat by the stove and did not know what to do. The small room seemed thick with the unfinished.

Then Manny, on his mattress, fell asleep. The girl lay down on her bunk, dressed and with the coat over her. It was cold this night and Tolman spent much of the time outdoors, watching and listening. When he came back in he stood by the stove and smoked for a long time. He had turned on the kerosene lamp and put it on the floor, close to all three of them. He hoped there would be some warmth. Manny slept and the girl slept, with one leg showing up to her thigh. The skirt had moved up on her and the overcoat was not covering her well.

She woke from the touch on her calf but did not move.

"You awake?" she heard Tolman.

She turned slowly on her back and looked up at him. The light from the kerosene lamp on the floor gave his face an expression which she could not judge. She moved her hips to get rid of the wrinkles under her and then lay still again, on her back.

"Yes," she said. "I'm awake." And then, "Is the other one sleeping?"

"Yes."

"Oh," she said.

She looked mean and slovenly, all of a sudden, and Tolman felt like saying something to her. At least, he thought, he should tell her that she woke when he was putting the coat back over her.

He said nothing though, just moved the coat, the way he had meant to do, and here and there touched her lightly so the coat would not slip again. Then he walked away from the bed and did not hear her. She lay curled now, with the coat over her, and said, "Thank you," but very low, very carefully. She was almost sure that he had come to cover her.

She did not wake again until much later, when Tolman was asleep on the bunk above, and Manny was standing next to her.

"Come on," he said. "Get up.

"What?"

"What. Waddaya mean *what*," and pulled the coat off her.

He made her lie down on the mattress but this time she did not have to take off her clothes. He was excited and very impatient and was done with her fast. It had meant less to her than the first time.

But then he did not let her leave. He sat on the mattress and smoked, talking to her. He told her, if she made a noise he'd kill her like nothing and not to worry about the clothes all wrinkled on her, he'd get her new ones, better ones. And she shouldn't worry herself, don't you worry, baby, I always take care of my own and you're my own now, so keep that in mind. They would just wait till the light was better so there would be no need for the headlights. And one move out of her, she'd regret that—

Tolman woke because of the draft. The walking had not made him wake up because he expected that, with Manny checking. But the draft woke him, because they had left the door open. It showed bluish light, with the night partly gone. He heard no breathing, nothing at all. He leaped out of the bed with the gun already in his right hand.

The girl was gone, Manny, and the black bag. Tolman did not feel the cold air or anything, did not even think of anything but this one thing: if they were gone he would have heard the motor, and the one thing that must not happen was the sound of the motor. A cold motor roaring in the still woods— He did not think of hate for Manny or greed for the lost bag but only that there should be no sound, for God's sake, no sound now in the woods to draw attention—

They were by the shed, just got there—

"Manny!"

Manny whirled, dropping the bag, reaching inside his pocket, but he stopped there because of the way Tolman came.

Tolman had his gun on him and came to the shed fast. He looked so wide awake that the sense of movement and life in the man seemed like a charge around him.

It frightened Manny and it made the girl stare. It was not the way she remembered Tolman.

"I won't let you," said Tolman, "because it's my life. It's a bag of money to you, but to me it's my life. Come here."

Manny took one step closer, his hands away from his sides. He understood nothing about Tolman and how he felt, except that Tolman was holding the gun.

"Listen," he said. "Listen to me, Tolman. Let me kick the bag over to you. I don't want...."

"The hell with the bag."

"What—what else?"

"You stay. You stay till it's safe."

It was exactly the point of fear with Manny, to stay in the woods which were strange to him, to stay in the place where he could not see, to listen to the sounds which were all unfamiliar, and because Tolman said so. He, Manny, was not built the same way. He had never been caught in his life and it made him think that bravado was courage. That's how he was built, not like Tolman who could live with fear.

What always happened to him and his fear happened now. It turned into hate.

"Not the bag?" he said. "This is like a joke. You mean the money. You don't mean the dame now, do you Tolman, you don't mean the dame?"

"Ellen," said Tolman. "Walk away from him, girl."

"I knew it! It's her makes you crazy in the head, huh?" Manny licked his lips once, then talked faster. "Crazy enough to sit here, sixty miles from the place of the heist, with the place crawling with cops and what's it they call it, posses, *huh? Posses* all over the place and him honeymooning with this, this one here in the woods while...."

"Shut up. You're yelling."

"I'm telling you, Tolman, I'm...."

"Stop yelling," Tolman said again.

Manny lowered his voice. His breath came with much pressure but he tried to talk low, to make Tolman understand.

"Take her. Keep her. I've had her. And the money. We split now. We split it and then I split out of here. I don't give a damn for anything else, Tolman, you or the dame or the car even. I'm gonna split out!"

It was a long talk and a lot of nonsense to Tolman. The idea was nonsense, though he took the intention dead seriously. But Manny was talking now, running fast from the mouth, and Tolman, wanting no noise, put the gun in his pocket. He put the gun there and walked up to Manny.

"Understand—" Tolman started but it was his mistake to think now of talking.

Manny laughed. He had his hand in his pocket with no time to clear the gun. He pointed the coat pocket at Tolman and laughed.

"You move and you die, Tolman."

When Tolman held still Manny took out the gun. He held it good and steady and said,

"Now toss out yours. Over that way."

"Manny. You fire that gun and it rings up and down this hollow like a cannon. They'll...."

"They'll think it's some hunter," said Manny. Then he waved at the girl. "Come back here. In the car, baby."

"It isn't the hunting season. They hear that report miles and miles...."

"So throw out your gun."

Tolman did, so that Manny would not shoot. So that he would not make a noise—

"Please, Manny," said Tolman.

But Manny understood nothing. He understood having the money and he understood having the girl. He knew nothing of Tolman and his kind of desperateness.

"Walk back to the cabin, Tolman. Stay outside."

Tolman said, "Please—" once more but it only made Manny laugh. He understood nothing. He bent for the bag with the money so that he caught the movement just as a flick. But he shot at it fast.

The bullet cut into Tolman's leg, staggered him, except much too late. He would not have stopped if the bullet had torn his gut.

He had to stay close now, because he could not walk. He did not feel the pain yet but knew about this. He stayed close and the first swing, like an ax, cracked the gun out of Manny's hand.

As a fighter Manny was good and fast, faster than Tolman, and with good legs. But he did not have the desperateness, not the life-and-death desperateness that comes from having lost—

Manny connected good a few times, but with no time to puzzle why nothing happened to Tolman, why he didn't drop. Tolman held on with one hand, clawed into the cloth and the first chop broke Manny's teeth. The next one made a ball of fire out of one of his eyes, and from then on Manny tried getting away.

He did not get away even when Tolman let go. Manny fell from the punch that burrowed into his belly and even then Tolman didn't stop. Ellen watched and did not think he could ever stop. She saw the slash of the hand into Manny's neck and heard how it made Tolman grunt. Then

Tolman did it again, to the chin this time, but much less now. It was his last swing and he sunk down on the ground.

The girl came closer, afraid to breathe. She came closer and touched Tolman on his back. She did this without knowing why, just because of the way he sat.

"Can—can you get up?" she said.

Tolman looked at her as if it was not important. Then he looked down at Manny again and touched the head, making it move.

"He's dead," said Tolman. "You know that?"

It horrified the girl, but she could not react to it. She knelt next to Tolman and tried seeing his face. Then he turned towards her, and his expression was old and worn, old and fearful— Only his voice was the same as always.

"I have never done this before—"

Now, she thought, *he will break. Now, and I can't stand to watch it.* She reached for his head and held it close, held it tight against herself with both her hands covering him. She held him like that while she felt how he stayed there, how he let her cover him and hold his head.

It was not a question of time—she did not know how long they stayed there—it was only a question of feeling. When his breathing changed she let go and her mood went too. She got up, stood there with legs wide, and helped him stand up. He had changed again, but not to the way he had been. He had no time now, no time to hold still and wait out the chase, but was much the same way he had been coming at Manny by the shed.

"We've got to break for it," he said. "I don't know if anyone heard. Like him now," and he nodded down, "I've got to run."

He stuck Manny's gun into his pocket. She helped him into the car. She carried the bag into the car and sat down next to him without either of them having said a word. It was light and he drove out of the woods fast. He drove down the jolting road that went towards the highway, the one he had been watching, the sweat running down his face from the pain and his teeth hard in his lip. He sat still in a way which showed how much he wanted to scream.

On the highway he drove faster. He held the car steady and did not look left or right. He did not even change when the black and white car showed in the rear view mirror, the car which had suddenly swung out of the sides and after them.

He started to mumble and the girl understood after a while what he said. He kept saying it several times. "They won't—they won't—"

She said, "You're going faster than he— Did you know?"

"He doesn't have to go faster," said Tolman. "We're expected. He's got a radio and we're expected."

There came a big stretch and they could see far both ways. There was the small looking black and white car in the rear and there were two more ahead, but not moving except for the rotating blink on the top of one of them, and both of those cars stood in the road.

"Listen," she said. "Tolman," she started again, because she had to say this to him.

"Shut up."

Like a steel trap. He swerved the car off the highway so that she thought they would roll on their side. He held, the car held, and they tore through bushes before the car made the gravel road again, racing up hill now with small stones chattering against the chassis.

He was just running now. He had nowhere to go but was just running. It was all that was left to him and it was what he held on to.

The girl, Ellen, was afraid to say anything to him. For a moment she tried to think of the brief time after Manny had died, but it didn't work.

And then they came to the end of the road. The road dipped into a gravel pit and there was no way out. Tolman skidded the car, not to hit at the opposite wall, but he only did it from habit. To stop without hitting would not make anything easier.

The car faced half back and Tolman just killed the motor. He made a movement as if to reach for a cigarette but then let it go. He did not look at the girl and said, "Stay here. Stay low, Ellen," and got out of the car.

He could barely move. He looked to the mouth of the gravel pit because he could hear the sounds. Then one car, then another. They stopped with a lot of dust and there was door slamming and fast movement.

Tolman could hardly move and held on to the door of the car. He held it as if he might open it, standing still that way. She could help him, he thought. She could say that the other one had been killed in self defense, which was easy. She could say that the other one had been the thief and he, Tolman, like the girl herself, had been pressed into this innocently. That was one way, and maybe it would work. And then, another way would work even surer. And then—

They were shouting at him out of the dust by the cars.

He leaned down a little to look into the car. She was there, looking back at him, as if she were waiting. She moved one hand, the way someone does before speaking, or the way someone does in confusion, and Tolman looked away. "I'm sorry," he said, and again, "I'm sorry—"

Then he walked to the mouth of the of the pit. They could see him limp but they did not trust any of that. Tolman could see the police and the guns looking at him.

Why would she say this for him? Had he helped her, comforted her? Had he been anything but a hard skin of ice?

He walked towards the cars, limping badly and then suddenly crouched. His hand shot to his pocket and then, with arm out, pointed to the mouth of the pit.

They cut him down with two riot guns and with one Magnum.

When they turned him over they noticed that he had not gotten the gun out of his pocket.

At the station they gave her coffee and had a doctor in but she said that she did not need a doctor, that she just wanted to leave. They let her go in a very short time, after she had told her story. "The other one was the thief," she told them, "and the one you shot, he had done this thing in self-defense. He was in this the way I was in this—the pressure—whatever he did was his self-defense—"

THE END

THE RETURN OF
MARVIN PALAVER
by Peter Rabe

Chapter 1
A Close Call, and Then Death

I died at the worst possible moment in life, just when I was coming out even. I'm not talking you come out ahead, let's be realistic, but to come out even with Sidney Minsk, may he live to be a poor man forever, that is worth a lifetime of troubles.

After all my suffering and humiliation from the likes of Mister Sidney *Fershtunkener* himself, suddenly everything comes up roses, and then what happens? The worst possible thing happens, I die from success.

Was I felled by age, by cholesterol, by a little too much of this and that? Forget it. Felled by happiness is the truth of what happened.

And why me, I ask? Did I make a couple of million by screwing everybody in sight, like Mister Sidney *Macher* has done it? Did I, like Mister Sidney *Potz*, rob my closest friend of everything? Never.

But if you're going to be such a terrible person, at least have the decency to show a little guilt. What does Sidney do? Business as usual, is what Sidney does, which means—what else—give the shaft to poor Marve all over again, if at all possible.

He sat there looking short and busy and with his stupid moon face turned my way, sweating from the effort to look smart.

"Marvin," he said to me from the other side of his crummy desk, "I don't know why I trust you, Marvin, but I think you got yourself a deal."

He didn't pick up the fountain pen right at that moment, but I was starting to die from joy already. At the time, of course, I was thinking figuratively. I started to tremble a little, which Sid could not see on account of my bulk, a little inside shiver from suffering joy unexpressed, but don't let the enemy know about it. Not yet. Instead, I looked at him grateful and maybe I'm willing to kiss his feet from devotion.

No easy job, all that, while I'm sitting there on this chair like from a doll house. Maybe one for each cheek would be nice, but no, not in a crummy office like one that belongs to Mister Sidney Considerate.

Meanwhile, at this delicate point in the maneuverings, I thought I would just let Sidney dangle a little. Not act eager. So I shifted myself around on the torture rack which was all this time screwing itself into me from below, and gazed out that crummy window with the dried up sticker on the glass from the time when they put the window in maybe twenty years ago.

On the other side of the window was Lot #1, he called it, piled to the Brooklyn sky with carcasses of cars squashed flat like *latkes*.

This used to be just Auto Wrecking, S. Minsk, Propr., but not now anymore. There is Lot #1 because now there is also Lot #2.

How come S. Minsk, Propr. has Lot #2 which used to be called Palaver's Heavy Salvage, plain and simple, a wonderful place right next to the Lot #1 wrecking dump? Because Sidney is a *ganef.* A bum what steals.

May I be forgiven a little nostalgia. This yard of heavy salvage was nothing tinny like squashed cars. This was serious, the big stuff from dismantled factories, old railroad gear, a bridge now and then. Ah well—

"Marvin, hey—"

"What, what?"

"I just said you got yourself a deal and you're falling asleep! Maybe you got a condition what's serious? Maybe I should worry about your health?"

"Fine, Sidney, fine," and I shifted around again on that terrible chair which was unmanning me from below.

"Don't kid me, Marvin. You're looking at Lot #2 and you're sick, right? That's it, am I right?"

He started to cackle but had the decency to turn it into a cough. Then he started to run a dry palm over the skin of his skull, a sign I knew about. It meant that he was enjoying himself.

"Look at it this way, Marve. You got rid of a headache and I took it off your hands. You're not sore, are you?"

"Who's talking sore? If I got sore everytime the business goes up and down, I wouldn't have time to do business. Like right now, Sidney."

"You're not sore. I'm glad, Marvin."

"Sure. Look at it this way, Sid. I undertook a change in my cash position and alleviated an inventory situation," which I threw in because I knew that Mister Sid Smartass didn't know the word alleviate. If he did, by some chance, he probably thought it meant to relieve yourself as in urinate.

"That's the way, Marve. Piss on the problem and relieve yourself. Improve the cash flow, I always say."

Instead of signing the contract, he was sitting there giving me his crummy philosophy. Then he just sat there resting himself from the heavy thinking, looked across his own yard to the one that used to be mine, and tugged the points of his shirt way over the lapels of his jacket so that I could look at his naked chest with the different lengths of gold chain hanging down.

When Mister T was done preening himself, he started up with the small talk again and I still didn't know what he was after.

"The new job, you like it?" and he tried to smile at me like an uncle, at me ten years older than him and fifty years smarter.

"It's not a job, Sidney. I'm an entrepreneur, like always, except without the headache of running a yard. I'm brokering, Sidney, like this special deal of equipment I'm offering you."

"None of the headaches, that's nice."

"So you going to worry about my job or you going to make yourself some money and sign?"

"Don't worry, I feel good about that, Marve. A fine deal, the best in years."

"What do you mean, the best in years? Maybe you didn't get a wonderful deal when you took over my yard? Maybe by you highway robbery isn't a wonderful deal?"

"Don't get excited, Marvin. It's good. I take the *tzurres* with the good. That's business and I don't complain."

Now I could smell it. It always started with all the troubles he had which nobody knew about because he never talked about *tzurres* or complained or was the kind who asked for sympathy or—may God strike him dead—for a favor. So I tried to head him off with a little more flattery.

"But I am excited, Sidney dear, and so happy for you to get such a wonderful deal, first the yard, and now this great bargain where you sign on the paper right there in front of you, such a deal I would only get for you and nobody else." Which was true.

"I'm happy too, Marvin. I never complain, you know that. I never said a word about the state of the inventory and records but just took the mess and all the rest off your back when you needed a hand."

"What's that about inventory? You got a problem with inventory?"

"Don't always get excited, Marvin. All I said...."

"Is that I gave you a problem. If you don't know how to read a stock list, ask Schlosser. You took him when you took my yard and Schlosser knows everything about where everything is."

"I didn't take your yard, Marvin. I bought it. To help you pay your debts."

"Do I have to sit here and listen to you telling me what a sweet person you are? If you're such a sweet person, Sidney, how come you're rich? Do I have to sit here and listen to nonsense or are you going to sign and buy the carbon steel, the very high carbon steel I struggled to find for you cheap?"

It was a long speech, not the best thing for a pitch at this point of the game, but I was very nervous now, very nervous with that inventory talk by Sidney, may he live to be a pauper. Then I knew he was finished pretending and playing around, because he was patting himself for a cigar. He always did that when he came around for the kill, even though he wasn't carrying those stinker things anymore on account of his crummy lungs, but he was patting himself where they used to be, and me hoping he'd find one so the killer thing could do its work. Not very nice, but true.

"I'll buy it," just like that.

Of course I knew better. Then he added,

"And maybe you could do me a little favor, on account of the spot I'm in. There's this great outlay on Lot #2, which has to do with the inventory...."

"Sidney, listen to me, sweetheart. I couldn't go any lower, even for old times' sake or because we're such friends. Already you're getting eight hundred thousand worth of prime scrap from a deal what costs you just two hundred thousand which on the Japanese market where they're making cars like rabbits day and night...."

"Stop talking, Marve. Am I trying to quibble? I never quibble, Marve, you know that."

When he starts lying like that it was time to go to the heart of it.

"What favor?"

"Nothing, Marve. With your experteeze, you could do it in your sleep."

Do anything in your sleep with Sidney, and you wake up a very poor man.

"What favor, Sidney?"

"The way you left the yard in a mess, run that inventory for me, Marve."

"No."

"Marvin. I got a crew coming in and they took one look at the records you left and the way you got things stored in the yard and this stock man tells me, this is such a private system, or what I call a mess, that no sane person can figure it out in less than one hundred years."

"No."

"Marvin, maybe I shouldn't take on this deal till I know what I've got over there?"

It wouldn't be good for business, if Sidney noticed how I was getting nervous. So I looked up at the ceiling, as if I were seriously thinking about all of this, and wiped with my handkerchief where I was wet on the back of my neck and under one of my chins near the collar. That was alright. Fat men are supposed to sweat.

"You don't need some outside crew to do inventory," I told him. "Ask Schlosser, he knows. I'm not in the inventory business, Sidney, I'm sitting here in the business of selling...."

"I know, I know. You want me to sign here where it says I'll take delivery of stock worth two hundred thousand, ten grand up front, but I gotta tell you, Marvin dearest, where am I going to get ten thousand up front now that I got to hire a team that's going to cost every day while they take forever just sorting out your mess? I ask you."

"Sidney, please. If I don't sell to you, on account of your haggling, I'm selling someplace else. Today. My time happens to be money."

"Who's haggling? Do I ever haggle? I'm not buying until after inventory, is all."

He said more, of course, Mister Sidney Motormouth always did, but I wasn't listening anymore. The fix was in, or the shaft, or that chair I was sitting on, who cares, I was dying again, still talking figuratively at that moment. Because if he didn't buy that two hundred grand of iron from me before inventory time, he for sure wouldn't buy it afterwards. Why would Mister Sidney Bargain Hunter buy it once he found that he already owned it?

"And the way they charge, stockmen, accountants and all, how can I afford ten grand cash money down? Are you listening, Marvin?"

I coughed first, to get some authority in the voice. "When's inventory, before or after you buy?"

"I can only let you have five thousand, Marve."

"Okay, okay, when?"

"When what, the money? Right away," and he picked up his fountain pen where he had left it on top of the contract.

"The question I asked you, Sidney, when does the crew come to do inventory?"

"In ten days, with or without you. What's the hurry?"

"I deliver now to you, or to Carlotto in Jersey, or to Hanks in Pittsburgh, I don't care. I got my obligations and cash flow to consider, that's that," and I snapped my fingers which did not work because they were wet.

He looked a little worried which I thought was a good sign, except I felt such a commotion and shooting pains from the stress of doing this deal on Sidney, I couldn't enjoy how he was looking worried.

"You don't look good, Marve," he said and leaned forward a little. "Like an egg plant in the face. You should lose some weight, you know that?"

"Now or what?" I should have coughed first, because what he got there was no authority in it, the way I wanted, but more of a wheeze.

"Three thousand down?" I heard that unspeakable *ganef* whisper from the distance between us.

"Three already, sign it!"

And then I held my breath watching him pick up his Eversharp fountain pen, the Presidential Model with the metal filigree like an antimacasser around the barrel, I hated that but I loved it enough right then to kiss it— Do it, Sidney, do it, *boobele* my dearest and sign already, sign me the life's ambition victory deal, to sell the thief what he already stole, I'll take that deal!

So I quivered with ecstasy hidden inside my bulk while I watched him change the ten thousand down to three thousand, may he shit gold pieces all his life so they should flush right away down the toilet, and then I watched him sign the whole thing.

Tears of joy made my eyes swim. I knew happiness supreme. Then something else happened.

There came a bump in my chest and the insides of my head turned black. I leaned to one side on that crummy chair and felt embarrassed because I could not help falling. But thanks for small favors, I was dead before I hit the floor.

Chapter 2
Heaven, the Big Deal

You have a question how is it possible I should keep talking like this? Take my word for it, it's possible.

You have a question what goes on here, what it's like when you're dead? You must have heard the phrase, The Mystery of Life. Well, now you know there is also such a thing as The Mystery of Death.

First of all, I didn't come here because I wanted to know all about the place. When I'm busy, I don't think about traveling, what it's like in Acapulco and should I bring a bathing suit. What's the point, I got no incentive. Which brings me to reason number two.

Incentive means to do a deal on Sidney, or—even more incentive—to have him almost by the *kishkas* but not yet. And that was my situation. So, dying meant only one thing. I was interrupted with a lot of incentive not used up, so much of it that I'm here to tell you there was no way I could stop going after Sidney now. Falling off a crummy chair may be a little awkward, but nothing big enough to forget about a masterful *schwindel* to be done to Sidney.

Meanwhile, what I noticed first off, I was lying on the floor in that crummy shack and the chair had rolled over. Then I saw Sidney at his desk, and his face so white like he was ready to join me. As for me in that regrettable state, it was strange to see a dead person lie on the floor. I was also a little shocked to see how fat I was. But then, I had never been much on appearances, like Mister Sidney Brummel with the gold chains on his little chest.

Then Sidney got out of his chair. He went over to me and stuttered a little, wanting to know if I needed a glass of water. Then he tried to turn me over, but Mister Sidney Atlas he's not.

He went back to the desk, shuffled papers around like a man who's not certain about the future, and then he picked the contract up and shoved it under the blotter. The strange thing was, just about at that moment I lost interest. I think that's when I knew I was dead, when I lost interest. And then other things started to happen.

Where was I? That's a little bit like walking down Ramsey Street and somebody says, what is this? What can I tell you, it's a street. Here's the asphalt, there's the houses, and some trash cans by the stoop.

Now, this place was the same, except no asphalt, no houses, no trash cans by the stoop. But there it was, a space like a street, what can I tell you. There was one surprise which was the light.

When Missus Capp had her kidney stones out and was lying there in the hospital getting well, she all of a sudden had a heart attack and everybody right away thought she was dying. Missus Capp all of a sudden looked like she was having one big *schreck* with her eyes real wide open from surprise, then her head flopped to one side, her teeth dropped out, and she sort of got flat. Then she was dead.

Except, this was in the hospital. So they came rushing in with an electric machine and shocked her back to life so hard, Missus Capp made the bed bounce. And what does she say after she recovers from coming alive? I saw the light, I saw the light!

For the next two years, after which she died again, Missus Capp told everybody about the white light waiting for her at the end of the tunnel. And her daughter who is a *meshuggene* married to a weird person who was teaching at City College, he and she both kept egging her on about the beautiful light which is the entry to the higher realm where you go, what used to be called the Pearly Gates, and everybody had to listen to that nonsense.

Of course there is a light, stands to reason. When it's dark over here, it's going to be light over there, and if it's a pretty good light, let's say maybe 250 watts but bigger than a bulb, then naturally the rest of it in the dark is going to look like a tunnel. But there isn't any tunnel any more than there is a street. You just think so, if you're impressionable plus getting egged on by a *meshuggene* daughter.

It's all nonsense. Besides, I had no interest in the place, as I said, because I had unfinished business. Even so, a few other things did catch my attention, nothing big or important, but there they were.

Other people were walking around, no big deal. When you're alive, you're never alone either. But I do have to admit, it wasn't one hundred percent normal all the time.

I could be wrong about this, on account of that 250 watts in the distance, but one person walking around looked a lot like a rabbit. He kept rushing around in a sports coat but no pants and kept shaking a pocket watch by his ear. That's how I got the impression that he might be a rabbit, on account of those ears. He kept shaking the watch and saying: Oh dear, oh dear, I shall be too late, a nutty way of talking, but then what's special about that, you find crazy people all over, that's been my experience.

Something else was not normal, like this person came up to me and started talking just like that. I never heard of such a thing in New York, unless it's a bum who wants a hand-out or a pervert wanting whatever. But this person coming up to me did not look like either one or the other.

"Hi," he said. "You're new and just got here, am I right?"

What was this, Hicksville, USA? I was polite, but cautious.

"What's it to you?"

"You mean you don't know me?" and he smiled a little.

The funny thing was, he did look almost familiar, the kind of familiar which niggles at you but you can't put your finger on it. I summed it up and said,

"Why should I?" I'm always careful with strangers.

"I don't know from should," he said, "but you could," and he ran a finger along his collar, left to right, jaw held up like a bulldog who is trying to look at his chin.

There was plenty of that. He was much too fat, if you came right down to it, and always smiling. He looked as if he thought that life was some kind of a joke. Correction. In this case, maybe dead was supposed to be funny. Anyway, such a sense of humor I can do without. He did that thing with his chin again and then he said,

"Well, you ready to go?"

"What are you, the tour guide?"

"Why? You plan on doing the sights and then good-bye, Charlie?"

"What is this? Maybe you think I'm here on some kind of vacation and this is Disneyland with a crazy rabbit running around checking time, but the fact is I got business elsewhere and the sooner I get back the better."

"Are you serious?" and he sounded like he had just heard the most ridiculous thing in his life. He made a little shrug, like I was the *meshuggener* but he forgave me. "Tell you what," he said, "there's some people here you might like to meet."

"Forget it. How do I get out of here?" and I turned in the direction away from the light.

"I don't really know," he said. "And besides, I understand there are certain problems about coming back, travel restrictions, you might call them—"

"If you don't know how to get out of here, who does?"

He came drifting around where I could see him again, but he didn't stand there in any way to keep me from going.

"Actually, you do," he said. He started to fade a little. "I guess what you do, you just let the gravity of the situation take over and it'll pull you right down."

It didn't make sense, but it worked. The light went and he became faint. Just before he was all gone he waved an arm.

"Try and be nice," he called across, "and come back soon."

Ridiculous. Right then, as if nothing had happened, I was back in Sid's crummy shack on Lot #1.

Chapter 3
The Real World, You're Welcome

I don't know what came over me, but for a second there I was glad to see him. Of course, it wouldn't do that he should recognize such a thing, so when he looked up I changed my expression to something he could handle.

"Not to worry, Sid darling," I said. "I had to step out for a minute, got a little faint or something, but it's all under control. Now, we were saying—"

I let it trail off, the cheer, the sentence, the humbleness, because of the way he raised his head and looked at me glassy eyed like some kind of a stuffed animal, real impolite. Then he let out this terrible fart. Right after that he smiled like a baby.

"*Gevalt,*" he sighed. "That spells relief."

He got up, grabbed a folder off his desk, came my way and went to the door. And walked right through me.

I was so shocked I didn't believe it. As if to make the point, in case I didn't believe it, he came back and did it again. After walking back through me he stopped by the desk and picked up the phone.

"Herbie," he snapped in that wonderful way he had, "did you hear from the crew?— Whaddaja mean *no!*"

He kept speaking like that for a while to his foreman Herbie—keeping the men in line, he called it—while I thought about my new situation.

Like everybody else, I have sometimes thought what a wonderful thing it would be to walk around invisible, though right then and there I couldn't think what was so wonderful about it. So people could walk right through you? So I could stand there and listen to Sidney on the telephone?

"I want that inventory outa the way two days early! I got a customer waiting. And another thing. Call Schlosser what used to run things for Marve— No. You call him, I'm busy, call him at the shack on Lot Two and tell him to meet me there in one hour sharp. Do it," and Mister Sidney Silvertongue smacked down the telephone. Walked through me again and out of his crummy shack.

Alright, I figured, enough surprises already, now let's see what was left. What was left was myself invisible and Sidney about to do inventory ahead of time.

It was always those bald-headed thin guys wearing loud shirts and gold chains who were in such a hurry about everything, as if getting away from wherever they were might solve all their problems. Fat chance. What it did, it made problems for me. But before taking care of the pain about this rush over inventory, there was this little matter of a contract which was hid right there under the blotter.

So that was an advantage about being invisible. I could steal my own contract in Sidney's shack and nobody could see me doing it. Such an advantage. Nobody was here anyway.

I walked around the desk. I looked at this really crummy blotter—and at the paper still sticking out on one side in plain sight.

To have so much luck, I must have done something right in my life, was my thinking, when I grabbed the contract, grabbed the contract again, and watched my hand go right through the thing. Through the blotter, the contract, and the desk.

A wonderful advantage to be invisible and so right away and into the bargain unable to steal my own contract back. And without the contract, who's to make Sidney pay for the steel plate he owned already?

But no sooner was I getting upset from shock number one, when I have shock number two.

On the desk is a calendar and in the middle of everything else, I'm looking at it. It said April fifth. That was the shock.

The time when Sidney was signing the contract and I died from joy, that was when I had ten days left to fanagle before inventory time. Ten days, meaning April tenth. And now I saw by the calendar that I had lost already five days by rolling around heaven all that time. But what's the big surprise? Since life is problems, why should dead be any different?

The philosophy of that thought helped me pull myself together. Back to work. Five days lost in heaven, two days lost on account of Sidney always in such a hurry, so I had three days left. Time to see Schlosser right away. So I went.

How did I do this, you wonder? I did it the way we do it when you're dead. That means, you point your mind to the place you call the destination and you go there in thought, except the rest of you comes along too. Since I had always been quite a thinker, this new way of getting from one place to the other came very easy to me. So I found at least one advantage to being dead, after all.

Swift as I went, it still was a lovely sight all around. I went through a flatbed parked outside the shack, I went through a pile of *latkes* made from cars, through the big press at the end of Sid's yard, and then along the very neat rows of sorted stock in the yard what used to be my own.

Such a pleasure to be back here with the packed dirt on the ground, packed so hard it never made mud in the rain, such a wonderful sight all the tall piles of heavy clunkers and rods and shapes of metal which came in rust red or in different greys which could tell you the grade and the composition. And all around that faint smell of black grease and that sour touch of wet metal coming up your nose. All this, I used to love it, neat, heavy, in order. Life could be like that, except then there were always people in it. Which brought my mind back to Schlosser.

He was in my shack, except I don't call it a shack. It is a mobile home without wheels and big enough to have everything in it. There is the desk and files, which I call the office, a toilet, a kitchen sink and refrigerator, and even a place with a couch and a short legged table in front of it for the feet and the magazines. I had always been quite a reader. Every day, no matter how busy, I used to take time and sit there on the couch. Now who sits there? Schlosser sits there.

But Schlosser with his heels on my magazines was not a reader. He was sitting practically on his shoulder blades and in the meantime on his belly he was holding a bottle of beer. There he sat and was watching the bottle go up and down.

Now I started to worry. This was a person to help me in my present condition?

This question was very important. As a dead person with a superior mind, I could not talk anymore face to face, voice to ear like I used to do in the past, I could talk only from one mind to the other.

The problem? Here was Schlosser, no *wunderkind,* watching a bottle go up and down, and I had to go and find his brains.

I entered the place where it was supposed to be. Such a mish-mash I had never seen. This was a brain? Gefilte fish maybe.

"Schlosser!" I said on the level of that mind.

I could see that the bottle was going up and down just like before.

"Schlosser! Are we talking money or what?"

The bottle jumped on the belly, the feet came down on the floor. Schlosser frowned. But then he always frowned when a thought came passing through.

"You listening, Schlosser? It's me, your boss."

"Oh dear Jeesis in heaven!" and the bottle with the beer in it rolled around on the floor, foaming at the neck.

"No, no. It's Marve. It's me talking."

He calmed himself. Quick like a lizard he grabbed for the bottle on the floor and poured beer down his throat before any more could spill out. Then he shook his head and said "Ah." He sighed, put the bottle on the coffee table, and stood up.

So now he stood there, an old man with muscles. I also used to have a lot of muscles, it stands to reason, because how else was I going to move my weight around like a regular person? But I did not make a display of my muscles, I could fool anybody and look like a fat man instead. Not Schlosser. Like a stuffed sausage, was his way, with everything bulging out.

But what good was it? All I had to work with was gefilte fish. He now started to crouch a little and to look all around. Before he got set to wrestle Jesus maybe or to go look for another beer, I had to get his attention without spooking this very limited person who was also my only link with success in this very important business venture I was doing on Sidney.

"Like all the brainiest people," I put it into his head, "my thoughts come sudden, like from nowhere."

He came out of his crouch and cocked his head a little, trying to get used to thinking.

"But I'm getting used to it," I put in there. "It's time to crank up and get going on that wonderful Marvin deal."

"Huh?"

It worked fine, talking to him, as if he was thinking all this himself, but maybe I was going a little too fast.

"Okay," I put into the brain, "let's go out to the truck," and I made it cheery, like a fun adventure.

"What the hell," he said to himself. "Why don't I go out to the truck? Uh— Why am I going out to the truck?"

"The wonderful Marvin deal, the money deal, out at the end of Line Three."

He thought that made sense and he went out to his pick-up in front of my trailer and drove down the line, to the end of it.

Line Three was the alley where we stacked mostly I-beams on one side and the railroad axles on the other. At the end of that alley was an open place which we called the square. Here were the piles of stock that had not yet been sorted.

Someone was working the crane in Line One where I used to keep cast iron mostly. Since that stuff was all sorted and because there were no trucks for loading near the crane, this must have been the inventory crew starting to do Sidney's suspicious work, just the way he had ordered.

Schlosser stopped in the square. Three lines came in here, and the chain link gate was to one side where the trucks came in from the road in back. When Schlosser got out of the cab, I started to do his thinking again.

"There's the stuff!"

"Huh?"

"The wonderful Marvin deal, *goyisher, kopp*. Now pay attention."

"The wonderful Marvin deal, oh boy."

"The carbon steel plate, right behind the crummy girders hiding the steel, get it?"

"Got it!"

"Delivery time coming up in three days. Not much time to do all the work. So, first you got to call Tony at Coogan's, the way it was set up."

He was getting a little confused by my speed but he looked at the girders and then out past the gate. Coogan's Transport and Warehousing was down on the left of the road, the big place with a hundred trucks all over, all kinds, and there the road went on past a few machine shops and storage yards all the way to the road that went on to the Triborough Bridge.

"When you call Tony at Coogan's place, you tell him to set it up with the trucks like we planned, except he's got to be ready tomorrow night, not a week from now, because...."

"Hold it! Just one damn minute."

He was thinking on his own, which was not good.

"Why the hell bother?" he said to himself in his head. "Why bother anymore?"

"Why? I tell you why. Because it's a brilliant plan, the Schlosser-Marvin plan to sell...."

"Marve's dead."

"So what. A deal's a deal!"

"What deal? Everything with Marve was a deal," and he started to get back into his cab.

"Wait a minute! It was not!"

"It was so. He even used to sit on the toilet and say: Another *shtickle*, another nickle. After half an hour of that he used to come outa there and pay himself from petty cash."

Schlosser had a rotten way of looking at an innocent game. So I was a little constipated once in a while, which is no wonder when a man is all business and no time for anything else.

"The deal," I poked it into his head, "is still on, if you want to make that big money. For half a night's work, all that money, think of all that big bucks money."

"Oh dear Jeesis in heaven," he mumbled along. "Ten thousand bucks for half a night's work, if that fat jerk hadn't dropped dead."

"Schlosser, sweetheart, don't throw dirt on the memory of the one person in your life who's ever offered you ten, just a minute, offered you three thousand dollars for half a night's...."

"Hold it, hold it just one damn minute there, I'm not stupid or anything like that. It's ten grand for the job to move the girders and load five flatbeds from Coogan's in the middle of the night with Tony driving, take five loads from Lot #2 around to Lot #1, and Tony gets one grand and I get ten for the risk I take."

Judging by the heat he was putting into it, he was still interested, which was good.

"Who needs Marve, the poor, dear person who's dead now, because the marvelous plan is all set up to go with Schlosser at the wheel!"

"Me?"

"Right. Call Tony, set it up for tomorrow...."

"Who's paying? Where's the money?"

"Wait. That comes later. Right now...."

"And who knows if Sid's interested? If I know Marve, and I do know Marve, that fat man could put a whole scam together with nothing but hot air and a few names thrown in."

"Don't be a *meshuggener* all your life!"

"And maybe Sid don't know from nothing about carbon steel and has enough already to sink Manhattan."

Then he stared out of the side window of his truck and said "Jeesis" again.

So what else is new, but what came was not good.

Chapter 4
A Hard Bargain, Like Steel

On the other side of the back gate, which nobody ever used, except trucks and cranes, there stood the Cadillac, white with red upholstery inside behind the dark tinted glass, and Sidney-Who-Else sitting at the wheel.

But what you really pay for with your money in a car like this is the sneaky way in which that hearse slides up to you without the decency to let a person know that it's coming.

"Open up the damn gate, Schlosser!"

Such a commanding voice from a *nebish,* maybe you get that for gratis when you buy a Cadillac with colors like from a circus tent? But Schlosser, he didn't know from *nebish,* or from having no class, he jumped out of his pick-up and ran over there to open the gate. Schlosser had no class either.

The Cadillac came slithering through, Schlosser closed the gate, and Sidney got out on the driver's side. After slamming the door he put one elbow on the roof of the car and looked around like Napoleon inspecting the troops from the top of a hill.

"Schlosser!"

From the top of the hill he was now yelling down at the drummer boy who kept maybe missing a beat, screwing up the battle.

"Yessir."

"Where's that carbon steel?"

Schlosser and me, we were both surprised but for different reasons. Schlosser was surprised to discover his wonderful Marvin deal was not dead, and I was getting excited because the Waterloo of Mister Sidney Napoleon was really not that far away. Then Schlosser recovered.

"Whassat? You say what?"

Not bad. For a dummy, that was a very good way to get information.

"I'm talking a consignment of plate, Schlosser, a load what I bought from that boss of yours before he fell over dead and left me nothing but an inventory mess and a shipment what's missing. You're the foreman and you don't know from this? What do you know from this, Schlosser?"

"You mean you bought that?"

Sidney heard that and cocked his head, as if he were missing something. A man with a conscience as bad as his, he naturally always wondered if there was an angle. "What do you mean, have I bought that?"

"What I said."

"Talk English like a normal person and answer the question, Schlosser."

"I'm asking," said Schlosser, "did you pay money for it?"

"Of course I paid money for it. I just told you it's a deal what I made with Marvin, or maybe you heard from a deal with Marvin and it don't cost you money?"

"In that case," said Schlosser who was getting very single minded, "you owe me, let's see, fifteen thousand dollars, Mister Minsk-sir."

For a minute there I thought Sidney was going to have a heart attack, which couldn't have happened at a worse time. To have success snatched away not by one death but by two, that was overdoing it.

But it turned out alright. It was just Sid's way of showing surprise. He always acted surprised when somebody asked him for money.

"What the hell do you mean by fifteen thousand dollars in all my life I never heard such a thing or you take me maybe for some kind of idiot?"

"Well," said Schlosser as if he were thinking about it, "I don't know anything about that, but I do know what Mister Palaver said and he doesn't lie."

This made Sid speechless. I myself felt a lot of respect and admiration for Schlosser. But then, would I pick a foreman what turns out a *klotz?*

"When I close the deal, is what Mister Palaver said, you get fifteen thousand dollars, dear Schlosser, for a finder's fee and for extras."

Sidney regained his senses.

"Are you outa your cotton pickin mind?"

Now Schlosser started to walk back and forth, back and forth, arms folded in front, with a look on his face like he was waiting on account of the train was late. He was walking back and forth right in front of that pile of girders and he knew very well what was behind all that.

I was getting very, very nervous. Schlosser stopped walking.

"What I want to know is this: Since Mister Palaver paid you, which is what you said, where's my money, Sid?"

It was wonderful to see how Schlosser turned out to be a person that measured up to my own, high standards. Sidney, who did not like to be called Sid right after Schlosser had called me Mister Palaver, he was turning purple.

"You holding me up?"

"You going to pay me fifteen thousand?"

"You want your job?"

"You want your iron?"

It was a wonder to see how two people could insult each other just by asking some questions.

"I got a document," Sidney yelled, "that says three thousand, not fifteen."

This amazed Schlosser, who had heard that figure before, the time I had put it into his head. But I didn't want him to get stuck on some argument about money again, so I interfered just enough to get my own thoughts in edgewise. I said it through his brain and pushed him to say it out loud. With a little amazement at the suddenness of his thoughts, he then said it.

"You show me that document, Sidney, the contract, and I'll believe such a thing like three thousand." Then he shook his head back and forth, the way that rabbit had been shaking that watch.

But now I had Sidney good. I got him when he made the mistake of making that document public. So with a little help from Schlosser's greed and Sidney's stupidity—or maybe it was the other way around—this fanagle was going to come off after all.

Meanwhile, Sidney the Mark and Schlosser the Genius were at it again.

"That contract," Sid was saying, "isn't worth a damn until I get to see that iron, you understand that, Schlosser?" Then he switched to crafty. "So who's the seller and who's holding the stuff?"

Schlosser just stood there with his back to the steel plate in question. He smiled. Maybe this was the first time in his life that he had the upper hand in anything. He looked ten years younger.

"I don't get the money, you don't get the stuff."

Sidney controlled himself and tried to get clever. He must have been thinking that maybe he could confuse the dummy.

"I can't do that," he said. "Since Marve is dead, all this stuff gets handled through the estate, which means I haven't got the right to pay you," which of course was crap from horses.

"Who can pay me?" Schlosser, right to the point. "I'll take it up with Abbie. He's the executor."

"He's Marve's accountant."

"And now he's executor, which means no money till you tell me where the stuff is, or you interfere with the legal business of the estate, which means breaking the law and you could go to jail."

Of course Sidney was underestimating the power of Schlosser's mind. Or let me put it this way. It is the advantage of a simple mind that it can only hold one thing at a time. In this case that was: Get the money. Get it first.

"Get the money first," said Schlosser. "I mean get fifteen thousand, not three."

"I'll show you the document, lame brain!"

"You do that," said Schlosser. "And then you get me the money."

"You wanna keep your job?" and then all that started again.

In a while, Sidney broke it off, defeated by the inferior mind. So in a while Sidney went back to the only thing left a defeated man, which is his pride and a little spite.

"So what's that crap over there, behind you?"

"What crap do you mean?" and Schlosser looked all around.

"Right behind you those girders. Haven't you got girders at the end of Line Four? How'm I going to do inventory when all the crap is mixed up with some other crap, is what I'm asking? You supposed to be managing around here or what?"

Only a man with no feelings or respect for his business could stand there and say crap about the merchandise as often as Sidney had said it. But that wasn't really what worried me. What worried me came next.

"So move it!" Sidney yelled across the top of his red and white Cadillac.

That's what he said, gold chains clanking and sounding like God handing down the thirteenth commandment.

Of course Sidney didn't know what was behind those girders, but the real question was, would Schlosser keep it in mind how dangerous this development was.

"Get in that crane and move it!" from Sid the Almighty. And what does Schlosser say?

"It's five o'clock," is what Schlosser said.

This meant that he was not going to lift a finger, out of the question, unless he was going to get overtime. Even more out of the question.

"You move that crap by eight o'clock in the morning, eight sharp, you got that clear in your mind, you should pardon the expression?"

Sid did not wait for an answer. The red seat made a squish when he dropped himself into the upholstery, and then he drove down Line One to the gate at the other end, where his own yard started.

So it was a reprieve. Instead of getting shot at five in the afternoon, it was going to be next day, shortly after dawn. Unless, unless—

I noticed that Schlosser was troubled about the same thing. If he moved the girders, Sid would find the steel plates. If Sid found the plates, why would he pay for them? And furthermore, if Schlosser did not move the girders, then at eight o'clock in the morning, good-bye job.

I knew exactly what Schlosser would do with that problem, and he did. He got into his pick-up and drove back to my office, a place he now seemed to consider his own. He went to my refrigerator which he now felt was a place for his beer, and then sat on my couch so he could put his feet on my coffee table. Having done all this, he drank beer and thought about his problem.

I stayed away from his head, on account of the fumes, and did my own thinking. I drifted out to the square and hovered there for a while, as if that would solve my problem.

Unless everything I had worked for even through death and all was now going to go straight down the toilet, I had to move five flatbeds of steel by eight o'clock in the morning.

There was no way I could move that much iron by eight o'clock in the morning.

It was not entirely dark yet, but it was now much more quiet. Only Coogan's down the road was still open, and his trucks would be coming in and out all night long. And Tony, who was the super on Coogan's docks four to twelve, he wasn't going to think much of the plan where he should leave work at a moment's notice, authorize a flatbed to himself at a moment's notice, and move a zillion tons of steel from one end of the yard to the other. This man Tony had a lousy Italian temper. Why the hell move it from one end of the yard to the other? A limited person like Tony would be thinking along those lines when pressed for work at a moment's notice.

Who needs him? I could figure that out myself. Only a regular *shlemiel* would move what was already on the lot from one end to the other!

Chapter 5
An Early Delivery

Having solved the problem of how to make thirteen hours do, I zipped right back to the trailer, my office, my foreman, and was too late. Schlosser was already on the phone.

"Lemme have Tony," he said into the instrument. He wiped his mouth with the same hand that was holding the bottle.

"Which Tony?" said the night girl at Coogan's switchboard. "Tony Gallo, Tony Sforza, Tony Angelo, Tony d'Angelo, or maybe you had in mind Tony Curtis?"

She didn't seem to like Schlosser making a phone call right then any more than I wanted him to make a phone call at that moment. So while she was being snotty like that, I was trying to get into Schlosser to stop him, except I was having trouble with the fumes, eyes watering and sneezing and so forth.

"I want Tony Sforza, honey. You take Tony Curtis and I take Sforza, okay? And shake a leg, honey."

Schlosser, by the sound of it, was at the beer stage where you get all this courage, especially when you're on the telephone.

"Who're you?" said the honey.

"Tell him it's Schlosser. I'm the one runs the Palaver yard and the Minsk yard too. That Schlosser."

"Oh, you're the bald gut what looks like a stuffed knish. Let me tell you something, Schlosser. I don't shake a leg or anything else, comes to that, for an old guy with no hair and looking like a *Wurst* who talks to me on the telephone dirty and no respect. You got all that?"

"Huh?"

"Good," and the honey at Coogan's hung up.

Also, she had solved my problem. She had stopped Schlosser from going ahead on his own, when my way was better. Of course, I now had to convince him of that.

I got into his head and almost gagged from the fumes. I moved to the speech center, away from the more heady parts where the beer had gathered, but that gave me a raw throat and an urge to spit all the time. So I got back to the headache center and got to work, in spite of everything.

"Who needs them," I started out, figuring that a note of defiance would put a little muscle into all that sog.

Schlosser cocked his head but he didn't do much else. He got out of the

couch, put the phone back on the desk, and turned towards the refrigerator. I fought off his headache and got busy again.

"Single-handed Schlosser is what they call me. I'm going to pull the
whole thing off myself."

He stopped by the refrigerator and stuck a finger in one ear. Then he jig-
gled the finger around until I thought I'd go crazy from all the squeeking
and grinding noises this made. I suffered this till he was done and next I
got very loud and insistent.

"The fact is, I'm going to deliver the whole shipment by myself and on
top of it I'm going to do it by eight o'clock in the morning."

This had a strong effect on him.

"I better stop drinking," he said.

I had not intended he should have such a shock, but the shock turned
out good. Schlosser went back to the couch and sat down quietly. I also
noticed that the fumes were getting much thinner. Back to work.

"Think big," I said in that empty cavern where the fog now hung high
by the ceiling. "Think this: Who gets the steel?"

"Sid."

"Where's the steel?"

"Lot Two."

"Whose lot is Lot Two?"

"Sid's."

"So the steel is already delivered!"

Schlosser got up from the couch and let out a deep breath.

"Jeesis," he said. "How do I think of these things?"

I let him marvel about that for a minute, but then I had to get him to
work.

"Only a genius," I let it echo along the corridors between the empty
chambers. "A genius with brains, with *chutzpa,* and with muscle. So now,
which one are we going to use first?"

"Muscle."

"Right! We go to work. Sid wants the girders moved, so let's move 'em!"

He hit himself in the head and said, "Of course!"

"So now get the crane from Lane Four and move all the girders where
Sid wants them put. Three hours work."

"Four."

"Four hours work. Move 'em by eight o'clock in the morning and show
that crap head what a worker you are."

"What a genius idea," he sighed.

"And when you tell him at eight o'clock in the morning, at the same time
you say: Sidney darling— Just a minute. You say, Mister Minsk, not only
did I move the girders like you said, but I also got the Palaver delivery

brought in last night."

"And now," Schlosser added, "pay up, Sid darling. Like it says on the contract."

"Just a minute. Now listen. For that you need the bill of lading."

"Jeesis, I forgot!"

"So at seven in the morning you be right here, in Marve's office. Abbie will be here. You ask him for the bill of lading, because Abbie has the key to the files, ask him to give you the Trans-State papers on the delivery you took last night. Abbie gives that to you, and you take it to Sid. And take Abbie with you to Sid's, because that way you'll get paid."

"Jeesis," he said again. "How do I think of these things?"

I let him play with that thought for maybe a half a second and then I hustled him out to the crane. Another problem solved for the night. The next one was Abbie.

Chapter 6
A Problem of High Visibility

Abbie and me, we never had problems. I'm the uncle and Abbie is the nephew, which is different from being the son. But that I don't want to hear about. The only problem with Abbie, he is an accountant which is almost like having a *nebish* for a friend.

Such a person has no vision, no daring, no *chutzpa* of any kind.

I have never understood why a business man, a creative person, has got to have an accountant around, a person who is no artist at all. Two people like that should not even meet, let alone work together.

You may think you hire an accountant so the man works for you? Not in a million years you could be more wrong. You say to an accountant: I want this line of figures to show how I spent more than I made, because that's business. What does my nephew the accountant say? He says: No, because that's against the laws of the civil code and it's against the laws of mathematics. Then I say: Are we going to talk business or are we going to discuss juris prudens? Then it goes on from there.

He's a blood relative of mine from my brother's side, so he knows how to talk. The trouble is, he talks like an accountant, a man who goes around telling me I shouldn't make money, if you can believe such a thing.

Speaking of that, how come my nephew the accountant can go and live in Brooklyn Heights with a door man, like a regular Brooklyn address isn't good enough for the younger generation?

I appeared in my new and sudden ways on the tenth floor of the address where Abbie had his apartment—you should pardon me, it's a condo— around seven o'clock in the evening, a decent hour for any person that's normal.

By that time you have had a nice little supper, a little glass of the concord along the way, a *mandel broid* with the coffee, and it's time to sit down with the feet up a little, the evening paper maybe, or the TV if you can't read. So where is my Abbie?

In the dinette by the kitchen the table was laid for supper. There was a candle, already lit, in the silver holder I'd given him after Sarah had died, there were two places laid out, plus the salt and pepper and the dish with the celery sticks to clean the stomach.

Two places meant to me that Ruthy was staying in. She lived there, I knew that, though I never could understand why these young people don't also get married, but then most evenings she either took classes or sat around in the law library reading books which kept her from cooking and washing and keeping a decent place.

But that's none of my business, even though I could smell already that the chicken they had in the oven was plenty done, and the vegetables on the stove the same thing.

I stood there, if what I'm doing in the shape I was in can be called standing, and had a little bit of a twinge going through me on account of the nice smell, the warm steam of the kitchen, the candle, when all of a sudden here comes Abbie running fast, he turns off the oven and the pots on the stove, and right away runs back to the living room.

I ask myself, why does a man come running into the kitchen, dressed in a shirt and a tie and stark naked from the waist down, comes running in like that with a hard-on, turns off the stove and runs out again? I mean, this was seven o'clock and supper ready to go on the table.

"Did you turn it off?"

"What?"

"Did you turn—easy. Abbie, that's my belly button."

"Yeah, right, oi—"

"Abbie, try it a little...."

"Yeah, I turned it off, turnitoff, turnyeeoff, trujeenoff—"

"Stop talking, Abbie, talking, talkingawking—"

I don't know how to spell the other noises.

You don't need to guess what's going on here, but maybe you should take a guess where this *shtupping* is going on.

Here we have a perfectly decent condo with kitchen, big dinette, bigger living room, decent bath, and a bedroom so large it would accommodate a king size and a queen size, you should pardon the expression. And these two people are down there on a little rug in front of the fireplace with two lions for end irons crouching down and looking straight out at the living room.

I figured, *mazel tov*, I'll go in there, they can't see me, and I'll try and connect with that accountant of mine, considering that my business was really urgent.

It was going to take some effort. Even if I had been visible, that Abbie couldn't see, hear, or pay attention to anything. If the truth were told, he was right then and there going to pieces, groaning and jerking around like somebody with problems of the nervous system, while Ruthy lay there with her legs up and wide, a regular V for victory, and poor Abbie scissored inbetween and jerking. She, on the other hand, smiled up at the ceiling, very happy about everything, when she sighed and moved her eyes.

She was now looking straight at me. She made a very noisy gasp (which made Abbie very happy) and then she screamed.

"Good God it's—big as—bigger than life size—"

"Yeah, yeah, yeah—"

"Shut up, Abbie, it's your fat old...."

I whisked away from there, more shocked than she was.

She could see me, which was just another example of how death doesn't solve anything.

I stayed at a distance while they got themselves together again, and when they finally went to eat, I stayed behind Ruthy and melded myself half-way into the wall. I figured, let them have a nice, peaceful meal, that should get them tired, and as soon as they were sleepy enough to leave each other alone, I'd get in there and move Abbie's thoughts in the right direction. That was the wish. The reality was something else.

They had the chicken on the table, the gravy, potatoes, and the spinach too. But they weren't eating much. Abbie sat there dressed casual, playing with his food. He still didn't have any pants on but he was wearing a robe, a very handsome blue robe on that body without any belly, a blue that went well with his sandy hair and a face like from an old coin. No wonder that Ruthy wouldn't leave him alone, even on a rug.

She didn't have a belly either, but I could tell she was built for babies. Except she wore glasses, black frames like her hair which was polished stone black, like my Sarah before she went grey.

Ruthy sat there at the table wearing sweats, the kind that turn everything in it into a sack of potatoes. But I'll give her this, she looked handsome even then, except for her mood which was terrible.

"I do not hallucinate. I am intelligent, accurate in my perceptions, and not given to idle fantasies about fat persons who are dead. Particularly not a louse like your uncle."

"Alright, alright. Here, you should take more gravy."

"There is enough evidence cited in the literature at the present time to make an apparition no great shakes when it comes to an open minded observer. Startling, yes. To be doubted, no. So I really don't care much for the implication that I was beside myself due to your ministrations, or that I had temporarily flipped out."

"Well, you were pretty gone there, on the rug, you'll grant that much, won't you? This gravy...."

"That was sex. I'm talking apparitions perceived by an unprejudiced eye."

"On that rug, Ruthy, the world of the imagination and the world of flesh and...."

"Why would I imagine anything as reprehensible as your uncle Marve whom I avoided even when he was trying to be nice?"

"He was a nice person. Some times."

"I don't dislike him. He is not important to me, but I do draw the line when he's standing there and watches me making love. This is a dirty old

man so obsessed that he has to come back from the dead to watch two people screw on a rug, for godsake. That's disgusting, Abbie. Would you hand
me that gravy, please?"

"I still think...."

"Don't. He's fat, dead, and he's a crook. I don't want to hear about him."

Abbie didn't say anything else and ate. But as soon as Abbie kept still,
like she wanted, she also wanted to know what he was thinking.

"You are thinking about him, aren't you?"

"Not really. Just the crook part. That's an exaggeration, in a way, but that
estate business is a real problem because of the way he kept his books."

And that was going to be my in. He was confused about the books? Well,
he was going to be so pleased when some very sudden ideas would come
to him which would help straighten everything out. Except, I was not able
to make my move just yet.

They were done with the chicken and everything else on the table but
then the next move was Ruthy's, which left me out.

"Leave the dishes," she said, and got up from the table.

I forgot to mention that she was wearing sweats on the top, but not on
the bottom.

"The few evenings I'm free to spend here at home, Abbie, I don't want
to spend in the kitchen with the soapy water," and a few more endearing
remarks like that while she marched Abbie to the bedroom this time, not
the rug.

The poor boy was just completely spineless with her and Ruthy, whom
I bear no ill will, had this thing about showing her power. She is crazy
about that boy, but more important, she is very unsure of herself, which is
on account of such things as the glasses and because she's still going to
school at her age instead of the normal things which are done by a grown
woman. So what it comes down to, she needs a lot of proof that she's
grown up and somebody, which she gets by pushing Abbie around. I
mean, what normal person goes to bed and it isn't even nine o'clock yet?

So I figured, let them and *sollst mir sein qesind*. Let them get it over with,
because they got to get exhausted sometime before morning.

Could I be wrong? I had no idea how long this could take. I hung
around, I drifted back and forth, and all this business seemed to me very
boring. In that state, and for no other reason, did I find myself drifting
along to that other place, the street without houses where there was a
light at the end.

It was surprising for me to discover, but this place was not boring, even
though there was nothing to see. The closest thing by comparison that
came to my mind was my easy chair after dinner. There was nothing to see
there either, and still I was never bored.

I think that feeling of very nice everything, I think it had to do with the light. So even though I had other things on my mind, I slowly let myself move there, just a little.

"How nice you're back!"

Him again. I stopped moving immediately.

"I'm not back. I'm killing time, is all. Then I have to get back."

"I see," he said.

Not so friendly this time. He took a deep breath, the way a fat man does it, chin way out to help the chest get some room and in the meantime all the double chins disappear for one critical moment. Damn if he didn't remind me of somebody again.

When he was done with that labor he looked at me with a half smile only and at the same time made the eyebrows tilt up in the middle. This was a look like from a doctor who is getting ready to tell you that you're going to die.

"I was going to talk to you about that."

"Don't bother. I'm dead already."

"What?"

"I mean, I haven't got time right now, for whatever."

"Marvin," he said and put a hand on my shoulder, which made me notice that we were exactly the same size. "You have got to understand something about this place, Marvin. It isn't a railroad station where you just come and then go. It's a place where you come to stay and then you notice it's wonderful."

"It ain't Club Med, I can tell you."

"You haven't seen all of it yet. For instance, if you'd just let yourself move to the level of the light, you see up there where that rabbit is going?"

There was that damn rabbit again, walking on two legs and shaking the pocket watch around.

"You telling me that a place what's right for a demented animal with a watch is the place for me? Get serious, *boychik*. I got business elsewhere."

"What I'm trying to tell you, Marve, you've got to start accepting the fact that you're here now. You can't keep going back and forth, because there comes a point where you can't get back in."

"For this I should worry?"

"Maybe you should, considering the alternative."

"The what?" which I said not because I wanted to know what the word meant but because I was angry.

No alternative always meant: Now you do it my way and no more questions which is no way to run a life, or whatever.

"Just because a man's dead," I told him, "is no reason to treat me like an idiot. I got business elsewhere, not here. I don't need streets with no houses, or a white light bulb in the distance, or a chat with a rabbit what's got a watch but can't read time. It's not a smart place and I'm going." I turned away.

"Marve," he said behind my back. "When you get there, if you can't be smart, at least try to be nice."

The man was a *meshuggener.* He's telling me, a business man, to be nice?

Chapter 7
The Sorrows of Sleeplessness

I don't know how much time had passed, but by the looks of it, enough. Abbie was flat on his back and staring at the ceiling, and Ruthy lay next to him, propped on one elbow, and talking to him.

"I am not one of those chicken brained groupies of the occult, dear. I'm an intelligent woman. That means, when I see something it's there, and that thing, all three hundred pounds of him, was there."

"Ruthy, I'm tired of talking."

He is tired and it's from talking? But she went right on.

"What I want to know is, what is he after? They only come back, because they're after something."

"A restless spirit seeking sleep, the balm of hurt minds, great nature's second remedy—"

"Are you listening to me?"

"Ruthy, I've got every excuse not to," and he turned on his left side, facing her. He always used to sleep on his left side. "Because I'm tired, I've got to get up early for that executor crap, and I've had a lot of activity here, not to mention a lot of things on my mind."

"What things on your mind?"

"What things. I'm a book keeper, things like that, and tomorrow early that executor's crap."

Ruthy said something else, a regular *yenta* all of a sudden, where she got the stamina I'll never know, but no difference, Abbie was asleep.

But even after he was under I had to wait before I could get in there and put the thoughts in the right direction, because the sleep was that heavy, like a door I couldn't budge.

Then he started to dream, very anxious, all about how he worried about that lousy Palaver estate. I could work with that.

"Seven a.m., seven a.m.," I started out easy.

That was a mistake. He woke up, thinking he had overslept. He jerked around to look at the clock which had the face lit up and right away jerked back to the pillow and was asleep, just like that. Meanwhile Ruthy, she didn't move. She looked very sweet sleeping there, like they all do.

Abbie, on his own pillow, was sliding away into sleep, except not so deep this time. I was there, catching him.

"To solve all the problems you got," I intoned into the dreamscape he had made there. It was a street without houses and a Good Humor man came driving along. He drove his white truck and the little bells were going plinkuplink.

"I wanna ice cream."

Was I going to have a problem here? Abbie, my accountant, my executor of the will, all of a sudden he was four years old.

"Abbie, darling, you can't stay a four year old *potz* all your life. Grow up already, because I got wonderful news for you."

"I wanna ice cream."

"So eat the *vershtunkene* ice cream already and listen to your nice Uncle Marve."

"Yehk!"

"What kind of talk is that from a nice boy to his dear uncle who loves him?"

"I don't wanna ice cream that tastes like spinach."

I was starting to have as much *tzurres* in dreamland as I was used to in real life. The same with Abbie, of course, except he handled that by changing the dream.

In 1951 I used to have a wall calendar with pictures of American scenery, which is how I happened to know that Abbie was now in the Grand Canyon. He was in a diner in the Grand Canyon, looking at a plate of spinach on the counter in front of him. He was thinking: Why in hell didn't I order the ice cream?

He was thirty years old, like right now, and the waitress came up, a woman so fat she ought to be ashamed of herself, and she wanted Abbie to pay. Except my Abbie didn't have any money.

I tried to get in there and make the fat lady say something helpful, like: Never mind, I'm going to solve all your problems, when Abbie just changed the dream again. He was now standing all alone in the big, rugged canyon.

"I'm going to solve all your problems," I started again, making the sound come rolling along the canyon and booming like out of the Burning Bush.

"I'll be damned. You mean that?"

"Sure. *A kleinigkeit.*"

"Wow! You talk Yiddish too!"

"Does the Pope wear a beanie?"

"I'm really impressed. This is terrific!"

"That's okay. Don't grovel. So here's the solution. Go to Marve's office and there in the locked file under Orders, Special, get the bill of lading for the carbon steel, and give that to Schlosser."

He stood there for a while in the big Grand Canyon and in the silence of nature and didn't say a thing. Then he recovered himself from the experience.

"That's it? You mean that's *it?!* The Great Solution from the Yiddishe bush? Come on, you've got to be kidding!"

"Don't talk smart. You want to balance the dear Uncle's books, you do like it says here."

"Oh *that*—"

Such disappointment I hadn't heard since the ice cream that came out like spinach, only this time he didn't move off into another dream, he just dropped out of it and went into a sleep with nothing else in it.

As for me, once you're dead you don't sleep, which is maybe some kind of advantage when you've got something to do, but all I could do was wait around till Abbie woke up in the morning. Right then I made the mistake of drifting around without watching.

I was moving towards that light again. Maybe I could even have enjoyed it a little, except right then that fat guy came sliding in.

"I was starting to worry about you," and he looked at me, as if I owed him for worrying.

But like always, it didn't take long and he started smiling again. Right away I got suspicious.

"What's to worry?" I said. "I don't overeat, because I don't eat. I don't oversleep, because I don't sleep. And when it comes to anything else, all I do is float." Then I gave it the Cup of Gracie, as we used to call it. I said, "Besides, I'm dead, in case you haven't noticed."

He sighed and folded his hands across his stomach. This looked so phony to me, I immediately unfolded my own and stuck them in my pockets. Wouldn't you know it, so did he. He was hoping, I guess, he'd come on like a fat guy looking devil-may-care. That's a laugh.

"Don't you think I know what's been going on?" not so devil-may-care. More like a Jewish mother. "You've not been a very nice person, Marvin."

"I deserve this?" and I took my hands out of my pockets. "I deserve a fat person should come around and tell me how to live now that I'm dead? Not any more, Mister Goody Two Shoes. Not when I got business."

"Marvin. You better listen to this."

"Why, there's worse things than being dead?"

"Please be serious, Marvin. I mean it."

He looked so worried, I was afraid he might start to cry, if I kept on talking. So I made it short.

"I'm serious too. So I'm leaving."

"Wait! Listen! If you're leaving and you're not back here— Wait a minute, I've got to translate that into time— Nine o'clock."

"Or else?"

"That's right. Nine in the morning or else," and this time, just like that and no smiles, he disappeared.

Chapter 8
In the Morning, Weak Coffee

I came back so careful you wouldn't believe, looking out for Ruthy, but at six in the morning she had the eagle eyes closed. Meanwhile Abbie, such a dear boy, he was up and worried.

A little time on the toilet, a shower, a shave, a brush and a spritz on the teeth, and what comes out of the bathroom is a new man who can do things and move things and change the world. In the case of Abbie, he also needed a cup of coffee.

I could tell why these two were not married. Ruthy didn't show up in the kitchen till the coffee was done in that electric machine. Abbie, no matter how busy with his tie and his fly and hopping around while he put on his shoes, he poured coffee into mugs on the breakfast table—pardon me, it's a counter these days like in a drugstore—and now Ruthy came *shlepping* in.

I have got to be fair. She looked better than a *shlepper*, even with the glasses and the hair standing up on the side where she slept.

She sat down, took her mug, took a sip, and put the mug back down.

"You in a hurry?" she said. No good morning, no how are you, dear, just something you could say with a grunt.

"Good God, yes," while Abbie tried to drink coffee and tried to get his collar to lie down in back all at the same time.

"Because, in your haste, you seem to have put two spoons of coffee into enough water for six cups."

"God—I must have lost count."

"How can anyone lose count up to the number two?"

"Jaysis—"

I don't know why he had to refer to that renegade Jew so early in the morning, except maybe he was a little too worried, even for my good. I stayed out of Ruthy's range but kept watching Abbie very carefully. Ruthy was now tying his tie for him, finally a person with a little sensitivity, while he was sighing at the ceiling.

"I've got to be at the junk yard at seven in the morning."

"Junk yard?" said Ruthy like somebody had maybe broken wind. "You didn't mention that yesterday."

"I know. It occurred to me, uh, just this morning."

"The affairs of the Fat Man again?"

"I'm his executor, Ruthy."

"Why you? Why not his son?"

"His son-the-doctor? They don't even live on the same planet, Ruthy. One's a doctor in Beverly Hills, the other's a junk dealer on the East River."

"So after you're done rushing around without shoes and missing the count when making coffee, then who gets the money?"

"There isn't any."

"What?"

"He wasn't such a hot business man."

I'm a patient man, a forgiving man, but to hear such a thing I got so excited, I almost couldn't control myself from indignation. Moses coming down from the mountain, he must have felt this way seeing those idiots dancing around and talking nonsense. In the face of that, to do nothing except to tear up a few documents, that's a pretty kindly way of handling indignation.

I thought I was controlling myself pretty good too when Ruthy all of a sudden she slaps at the air behind her and then whirls around so fast I barely had time to get behind the wall paper and into the plaster.

"What?" said Abbie.

"I don't know. Some kind of heavy sensation—" and then she kept staring at the wall paper at the far side of the kitchen. "Damn," she said. "Do you see some kind of a tremendous grease spot on the wall over there?"

"No," said Abbie. "What do you mean, something heavy?"

"Forget it," and she rubbed the back of her neck where I must have been getting too close in all the excitement. "About the estate," she went on like a lawyer. "Since there's no money, then who gets the debts?"

"I do. I'm his heir."

"Well, I'll be," and Ruthy started to bristle. "No wonder you're so nervous. Of course, from the legal standpoint, and I hope you won't make a move without consulting me or some licensed lawyer...."

"Not to worry, not to worry. I think it'll be alright, once I've figured out the irregularities."

"Abbie, are you now telling me that he wasn't just a lousy business man, but that he was a crooked business man?"

"Not really," (thank you, Abbie dear), "just book keeping holes. Money spent and I don't know on what, that sort of thing. I might just find the right records this morning. No more shop talk, okay?"

"I'll make us a fresh pot of coffee," said Ruthy, and by putting in that little domestic nicety, finally, she got Abbie a little calmer, and me too. Abbie was following the track laid down in the dream, so I got out of there, to start worrying about Schlosser.

Chapter 9
The Return of Marvin Palaver

At seven o'clock in the morning, this time of year, it looks like four o'clock in the afternoon, winter time. When this kind of light hangs over a junk yard where all the old iron smells wet from the morning dew, that is not a very pretty place to be, for most people. But it is to me. Or aside from the beauty, the sight of all that weight, all those giant possessions, it can give you a lot of excitement from greed. That's what Schlosser had, the greedy feeling.

He sat on the stoop outside my trailer. He had a key to my place, but he sat on the stoop, feet together like somebody cold, hands in the pockets of his lumber jacket, and he looked kind of sad.

Maybe that was because the red coat was the only color in sight, or maybe because there was nobody else in that view of black dirt, grey iron, and that high sky over everything. That's not the friendliest sky, over Brooklyn.

I got into his head just for a moment and found it was as clear as it ever got. The plan for the bill of lading and then for the talk with Sid, all of that was there, simple enough. Aside from that, the mood in there was the same as in the rest of the morning.

I put a thought in his head, something he should like, saying that everything will be alright and he should go and have a cup of coffee. He got up and let himself into the trailer. He went to the refrigerator. No, I said, a cup of coffee.

He ran water from the faucet into the electric pot, plugged it in, put instant coffee powder into a mug, and sat down to wait. He was methodical like a bachelor, which is what Schlosser was.

When Schlosser was at the end of his cup, Abbie's little compact came crunching down the lane and then stopped by the trailer. This was it.

Abbie came in and stamped his feet, like there was snow outside.

"Hi, Schlosser," he said, and slammed the door.

"Hi, Mister Palaver."

"Call me Abbie, is okay. So," and he put his briefcase on my desk, rubbed his hands, and looked around. "Let's see now, which is the drawer with the Special Orders?" (Alright, Schlosser, get it right. The fanagle starts now.)

"The what?"

I was dying, if that was possible, with all the complicated refinements of business hanging on the workings of a *potz* called Schlosser.

Abbie said, "I'm looking for a thing called—watchamacallit, filed under special orders, or orders special, the thing when you deliver."

So now my Abbie wasn't such a genius either, but at least he was fishing around in his pockets to find the key.

"The bill of lading," said Schlosser clear as a bell. "I'm here for the same thing."

"Of course, bill of lading," and Abbie unlocked the file. When he pulled the drawer open he suddenly stopped. "What did you say?"

"Bill of lading."

"No. The other thing."

"I'm waiting for it. I need it."

(Careful, Schlosser. Get it right, sweetheart.)

Abbie turned and leaned with one arm on the open file.

"Let me get this straight. I'm here to get a bill of lading so I can figure out a missing transaction on the books, and you're here to take that self-same document off my hands? Just to throw some light on this coincidence, how come?"

"What coincidence?"

"Uh, never mind. Let me ask you this. Why are you here?"

"To get the bill...."

"I know that, of course. My question is, why do you want it?"

"So I can collect from Sid Minsk for delivering what he's got on that bill of lading that's been on this yard, not Sid's, Marve's, because of that."

(Schlosser darling, enough already!)

"You mean you were finished?" said Abbie.

"What you asked."

And so, this incredible thing inside Schlosser's head was actually doing me some good. It was keeping Abbie in the dark.

"Right," said Abbie. He turned away to start scrabbling through the file, like a man in search of a lost mind.

Then he found it.

"Hah!" he yelled.

And how did he know this was the bill he needed? Not because of the items listed for delivery, which was carbon steel, nothing like it. Because Abbie was a bookkeeper. He was happy because the bill balanced up some kind of tilt on his green record sheets.

"Fifty thousand dollars," he said to the paper. "So that's where you went!" Abbie peered at the document. "It went for what?"

"Transportation," said Schlosser.

This time Abbie was doing the part of the dummy. He said what again.

"What it cost to bring it here," said Schlosser. He knew this because he was the foreman, but the way he stood there and waited, he looked like a schoolboy again. "Can I have the paper now, please?"

"Just a minute," and Abbie walked back and forth, looking at the papers. "Coogan Transportation was the carrier, and they picked it up from something— what's this?"

"Tri-State. They're in Newark. That's across the Hudson."

"I know where Newark is. I want to know who Tri-State is."

"Can I have my paper now, please?"

"What is this with you and the paper? You wanna go home and show it to your Mommie? I haven't even graded it yet!" and then Abbie shook his head and groaned. "What the hell am I talking about. I'm sorry, Schlosser."

"That's alright. What were you talking about?"

"Just a minute," and he started pacing again. "Eight thousand to Coogan, which leaves forty two thousand unaccounted for. You know what goes on here, Schlosser?"

"No sir."

"Who's Tri-State?"

"A broker. What they do is...."

"I know what a broker does. What I don't know— Wait a minute. Don't they buy salvage at auctions?"

(Schlosser dear, start acting dumb, just act natural, sweetheart, or I'll kill you.)

"Yessir."

"So maybe the missing forty two thousand went for the stuff that Marve got from Tri-State. Which was, let's see here, two hundred *tons* of steel plate?" He looked at Schlosser for help. "You know anything about this?"

"Yessir."

(You want me to kill you, Schlosser dear, or are you going to say No Sir?)

"No, Sir."

Abbie looked at the ceiling, which also was no help. "Please don't say anything for a minute, Schlosser, but just listen. I'm no expert in junk...."

"Yessir."

"...but it seems to me that forty two thousand dollars for two hundred *tons* of *anything* is too little, is so cheap it's practically illegal!"

"Could I have my paper now?"

"Carbon steel? He paid *that* for carbon steel? Schlosser, where is that precious stuff?"

"Right out there, on the line, delivered. And it goes to Sid at eight o'clock in the morning. So I've got to have the paper now."

"Hold it. There's got to be a contract of sale someplace. This bill makes no reference to who gets all this."

"Sid gets all this, and Sid's got the contract, the same day when dear Marve fell down dead, is what Sid told me. If you lean down a ways this way, you can see the shack on Lot 41 where all this happened, the way Sid...."

"Schlosser, please. Take the damn paper, and tell Sid I'll be over shortly."
He handed the bill of lading over and folded his hands in front of his face.
Behind that, he was smiling. "Lucky break," he was mumbling. "That'll
clear up my books, once I check out this Tri-State crap," and he pulled files
from the drawer.

Schlosser left the trailer with the bill of lading in his hand, with three
thousand dollars on his mind, and with my gratitude licking him all over
for being such a good boy and not too smart with the questions and
answers.

Any minute now, it would be over. Any minute now it would be worth
all the work, all the *tzurres,* plus the fact that I actually died for all this.

So before I went over to Sidney's shack to attend the last rites and happy
conclusions of this marvelous deal I was closing, I drifted around like a bal-
loon enjoying itself, because it wasn't quite eight o'clock yet. Abbie, with
papers all over my desk, was being an accountant. In the past that had
always worried me, but not now. It was late in the game, pretty late, except
for me. And then Abbie got on the phone.

"Ruthy? — Fine. I mean, sort of. Listen sweet, I'd like you to do me a
favor. — No, you stay right there, it's on my desk. — Yes. Sort of a new
development came up here, maybe even a problem. — You want to help
me or you want to talk about Uncle Marve? — Good. On my desk, on the
left, the estate folder called Odds — Yes. Inside that, under *Questionables*
— That's what I said. I got papers in there where he kept dailies, transac-
tions let's call them, things on the backs of envelopes, on the bottom of
bills, see if you can find any jottings of forty thousand or forty two thousand dollars for something or other. — I don't know, maybe together with
a name Mac. — That's all I found here, Mac, could be an abbreviation. —
Could be, I have my suspicions. He bought two hundred tons of steel and
I can't figure where he bought it, how much he paid for it, except it traces
through a shipper or trucker called Mac and he may have worked for Tri-
State Transport which either does transporting or is a broker. — Wait.
Now I have a question for you: Remember that profiteering thing you
were talking about before the Grand Jury? — Right. Wasn't Tri-State one
of the dozen or so indicted? — Do that. Ask one of your teachers who
might be involved as.... Right. There were government auctions. —
Thanks, Ruthy. Call me back."

I floated out of the window. Abbie was into old things, not important
anymore. It was eight o'clock, time for Sidney.

Sidney had a hundred ways in which he could give you a headache.

Today, where he sat in his crummy office, he had way one hundred and
one. He had a jacket on which changed color every time he moved, like a
pigeon breast it flowed and flimmered in the light, except on Mister Sidney Brummel it did not look so good. His crummy gold chains, even they
looked better.

Sidney sat like that, shimmering, when Schlosser came in very excited.
He stopped in front of Sidney's desk and had to control himself while he
waited.

Sidney is the kind of rotten person who does not look up when somebody steps close to his desk, no hello, please sit down, please wait a
minute, nothing. He pretended that he was very busy.

I thought, *mazel tov,* let him have his little games before the sky falls in
and comes such a *potch in punim* his head should fall off. But let him have
his games, I'm a very generous person when I'm winning.

"Mister Minsk?"

This from a man built like a giant stuffed sausage, from a man about to
bring the Cup of Gracie but not gloating at all. Well, who says you can
have everything?

"Didn't I say eight o'clock you should be here, Schlosser?" Sidney didn't
even look up, such rotten manners.

"When you hear what I got to tell you, Sid, you won't mind the ten minutes."

Now Sid looked up, trying very hard to make a face he didn't have, like
a captain of industry yet.

"You moved the girders like I said and you want overtime, is that it?"

"Forget the overtime," said Schlosser.

This was such a shock to Sidney, right away the captain of industry face
fell off and left a blank of surprise, or maybe the look by a chicken what's
never laid an egg before, but here it is, the eggs rolling along right there
between his feet. I myself was a little shocked also. No point going over-
board, was my thinking.

Next, it goes without saying, Sid got suspicious.

"You got any more surprises? Something else you should tell me?"

"That's right," and Schlosser grinned right past both ears.

"*Gevalt,* what is it?" but not mean anymore, just plain worried.

"I got you this," and Schlosser threw the bill of lading on the desk. "I
went way the hell and gone outa my way and got the drivers to deliver last
night, I mean, all night we worked those loads in four hours, and here it
is, take a look." Schlosser pointed out the window, down Lane One where
the steel plate was waiting.

For a minute there I didn't recognize Sidney at all, he looked happy! He
showed a kind of a sweet smile, I didn't know he had it in him. He also

jumped up and down a little and slapped his hands like he was doing a dance. He even slapped Schlosser on the shoulder. Not that any of this lasted very long.

Sid ran out of the shack, looked down to the end where the steel was piled up next to the gate, then ran to the bungalow where he had a girl do the books and the telephone and where the foreman kept records. He told the girl to call Coogan's for transportation, then to call the customer to expect the stuff in one day, and then he got the foreman to chase up a loading crew so they could get that stuff out in a hurry.

All through this excitement Schlosser showed a lot of constraint. He waited and waited, and not until Sid got back into his chair did Schlosser come to the point of his meeting.

"Could I have my money now, please?"

"What the hell you talking about? You said you didn't want overtime, so what is this? You working for me, you better not turn out a welcher."

"My three thousand," said Schlosser. "Finders fee and stuff, the way Marve promised."

"Marve was going to pay you three thousand? Then why ask me?" and Sid laughed once, very mean.

"Mister Minsk—" Schlosser didn't quite know how to go on, he was that confused. Maybe he was even hurt by the meanness.

"Maybe something else you want?" and Sid looked like he liked what he was doing. "Maybe a new hard hat painted gold, like these?" and he flipped his gold chains around with a finger.

"I want my money," said Schlosser. I could hear he was getting stubborn.

"Money? What money?"

"The way it says on the contract you got with Marve. You said so last night."

"I did? You got that in writing."

"You've got it in writing or you wouldn't have the steel out there."

From the far end of Lot #2, my own lot, the first Coogan truck could be heard.

"Go out there and help them load," said Sidney. "Tell Herbie I said you should take the number two crane. And shake a leg, Schlosser."

"I want my money." Just like that, getting ugly.

I was beginning to see that this contract business might just ruin everything, because nobody had any copies except Sidney himself. And for that matter, what had that *ganef* done with the copies he had slipped under the blotter?

I looked. I went very close, nose down to the blotter, and looked, and *mazel tov*, I could see them by the edge of the paper between the desk top and the blotter where Sidney had not bothered to take them away!

Naturally, right away my heart sunk away, or whatever was sinking there in my present condition, because in that very condition, how was I going to pull the contracts out from there?

At that moment of great pain, Abbie walked in.

Sid saw him first and did his smile.

"Hi. Abbie, you finished with the books? A mess, I betcha. Can I help you with something?"

"I'm doing fine, more or less," said Abbie who never lied. "Did you take delivery yet?"

"What's that?"

"He took delivery," said Schlosser who sounded strong in kind of a worrisome way. "He's shipping it out to the buyer right now."

"Oh that," said Sidney and shrugged, but Schlosser wasn't finished.

"And he won't pay me."

"Pay what?" Sidney started yelling. "This guy's the foreman and knows from nothing!"

But that tone had no effect on Abbie. He waited for silence and then he said, "There's a contract," he said. "I haven't found it, but there's always a payment schedule of some sort, and certainly one that starts before resale takes place. You must have the copies."

"I'm supposed to know what you're talking?"

"According to these notations," and Abbie flicked a finger against the folder under his arm, "you and Marve signed on the same day that Marve had his heart attack and died right here. So that probably means you got all the copies of the contract you were signing. I need at least one of those copies, Sid, if I'm ever going to close this estate."

Sid leaned his bony elbows on the top of the blotter and smiled his lizard smile. His jacket went off like a neon sign when he moved, but now it had stopped blinking and looked just ugly.

"You see a contract around here?" is all he said.

There was a little silence, little but heavy. And now Abbie was catching on. His brain was turning legal and going very fast, I could tell that much, but he didn't move because there was nothing for him to do.

Sid smiled. For me, everything was turning black. Outside, one of the Coogan flatbeds was rolling by. And then the door opened and Ruthy walked in.

"Found you!" and she sounded relieved. "I got some news for you," she said to Abbie.

"Good. Please hold that a minute," and then Abbie looked back at Sid.

Sidney stopped smiling, not because nobody was introducing him to Ruthy, but because Abbie had changed to the kind of tone which you don't answer with a smile.

"Listen to this with a legal perspective for a moment," he said to Ruthy, and then he turned back to Sid. "I have notes and jotted calculations here," he tapped the folder again, "which amounts to strong, circumstantial evidence that Marve and Sid here had signed an agreement involving delivery of goods and of payment in money. Now, delivery has been made," and he pointed at the work at the end of Line One, "but money has not been paid. Meanwhile, Minsk here claims that there is no such agreement."

"He's lying," said Schlosser.

"Allow me," said Ruthy and gave a proper set to her glasses. "Mister Minsk, is it?"

"Call me Sid." He smiled at Ruthy and folded his arms. "You a lawyer, Miss?"

"It's Miz. Miz Ruth Golding. No. I'm a third year student."

"Oh, how nice, Miz Third Year Student."

"I want to address what is so far conjecture on Abbie's part. Do you say, Mister Minsk, that there is no contract?"

"What contract?" and he put his hands right on top of the blotter.

Ruthy looked at Abbie.

"That makes it difficult to proceed."

If I hadn't died already, this would have been the time to do it.

They talked, all of them separately, all of them at the same time, none of it going anywhere, except Sid's way.

I could see the contract, I could see Sidney's lousy hands on the blotter, I could see by the clock that it was ten to nine. And the steel was getting loaded, the second flatbed going out of the yard right now.

"Under the circumstances," Ruthy was saying, "you'd really have to go the lengthier route of a court order, based on the evidence which cumulatively—"

I couldn't listen. Desperation was all.

So I did it.

She was still talking when I moved around and got behind Sid at the desk. She was looking at Abbie, so I had to wait. Then she turned to say something reasonable to Sidney, something about contracts misplaced, perhaps, rather than non-existent. And then she stopped talking because her jaw would not move. And her eyes got bigger than saucers.

"*Good— God!*"

"Ruthy?" which was Abbie, very concerned.

"It's the fat, the fat uncle!" Then she shut her eyes and shook her head and made a dog kind of sound in her throat. A deep breath and she opened her eyes again.

"Ruthy, if you're looking at something...."

"*Still there!* I'm telling you it's that dead uncle of yours...."

"Mister Minsk," said Abbie, "I assure you there is no cause for alarm...."

"Shut up, Abbie!" with a very strong voice now, "and he's damn well there— Damn well pointing! He is damn well trying to say something with that finger pointing!"

"Mister Minsk," Abbie again. "What are you *doing?*"

"I tell you what he's doing," yelled Ruthy. "He's scrabbling at the blotter where your uncle is pointing, so help me I'm not making this up, will you look at that!" and she lunged across the desk, frightening poor Sidney.

And now the contracts were out, plain to see. The rest was routine.

I then took care to get out of the way, not wanting to be a distraction. I hung back and was watching how Sidney shriveled and suffered the rewards of his rotten ways.

He did not take any of this with good humor, with good manners or anything like that, but he did have to take it, oh dear me, did he have to take it.

"We'll forget about making charges for attempted fraud and so forth," said Abbie, "but you damn well pay up now, and I mean it."

"I didn't know about the three thousand to my foreman," this was Sid whining away while he wrote a check for the money that went to my friend, dear Schlosser.

"One phone call to your customer who is now getting load number three coming his way," with a wave of the hand at the window, "and your legal culpability is going to be extreme," said dear Abbie.

"I didn't know...."

"The hell you didn't. Here it says: One hundred and ninety seven thousand dollars on delivery. See?"

"Oh. What that means...."

"It means make out your check to Palaver Salvage. That way it goes straight into the estate."

"And you'll forget about the rest of it?"

Sidney wrote and Abbie waited and then he said, "Thank you, Mister Minsk."

Now the silence was light and soft and had a smile in it. For the first time in my life—in a manner of speaking—I knew fulfillment. I did not know that it could feel any better than this.

"Now that you've got that settled," said Ruthy, "do you want to hear the news?"

"Sure," said Abbie. "But if it doesn't concern Sid maybe we should leave him with his thoughts at this very moment and you tell me after we leave."

"It concerns Mister Minsk."

She opened her attaché case and took out some notes.

"The name Mac, which you asked about, belongs to a man called Mackey. According to notations in the *Odds* file, he's the one who collected forty two thousand dollars from Marve. And he's the one who used to work for Tri-State, which is why Tri-State is in the indictment."

"And what's that got to do with our devastated Mister Minsk here?"

"I'll make a complicated story short," said Ruthy, and now she looked at Sidney. "Mackey forged auction receipts, for carbon steel from army ordnance to go as government surplus. What it means, Mister Minsk, those loads which are leaving out there in the direction of your buyer, that steel is stolen property."

Sid got up from his chair, eyes wide, seeing nothing.

"Mister Minsk, are you alright?"

A question! Was Mister Minsk, my Sidney, alright?

After having to pay Schlosser, would everything be alright with mine Sidney? After having to pay for a shipment he owned, how's that for a businessman called Sidney? And after he paid for that, he finds out he doesn't own the merchandise, how would that be for mine Sidney?

I can tell you this, he turned a very bad color.

He then weaved back and forth for a while, in the middle of my wonderful moment, and then, I don't know how to say this, it wasn't so wonderful anymore. Did I lose interest? Did I get distracted?

Anyway, I know that Sidney made a gasp and fell down on the floor. It was nine o'clock.

✳ ✳ ✳

At the hospital, what do they know, the doctors, they couldn't believe their eyes. A man with a heart attack should have nothing wrong with his heart?

Schlosser had come along to the hospital. When they didn't know why to hold me any longer, he brought me my clothes.

When he gave me my jacket, I couldn't believe such a thing could be mine, it was that ugly. Then Schlosser gave me the chains.

"You're looking better already," he said, "after such an ordeal. I'll drive you back now."

I thought, what a decent person, this Schlosser, to watch out like he did and to take me home. I held out the gold chains.

"Take 'em, Schlosser. They're yours."

He held them in his hand and looked like he'd been hit in the head with a hammer, a big one.

"I don't believe this," he said. "Thanks, Sidney. You're nice."

Nice, he said. What do I know from nice?

THE END

Stark Houℓe Preℓℓ

1-933586-01-X **Benjamin Appel** Brain Guy / Plunder $19.95
1-933586-26-5 **Benjamin Appel** Sweet Money Girl / Life and Death of a Tough Guy $19.95
0-9749438-7-8 **Algernon Blackwood** Julian LeVallon / The Bright Messenger $21.95
1-933586-03-6 **Malcolm Braly** Shake Him Till He Rattles / It's Cold Out There $19.95
1-933586-10-9 **Gil Brewer** Wild to Possess / A Taste for Sin $19.95
1-933586-20-6 **Gil Brewer** A Devil for O'Shaugnessy / The Three-Way Split $14.95
1-933586-24-9 **W. R. Burnett** It's Always Four O'Clock / Iron Man $19.95
1-933586-31-1 **Catherine Butzen** Thief of Midnight $15.95
0-9667848-0-4 **Storm Constantine** The Oracle Lips/hb $45
1-933586-12-5 **A. S. Fleischman** Look Behind You Lady / The Venetian Blonde $19.95
0-9667848-7-1 **Elisabeth Sanxay Holding** Lady Killer / Miasma $19.95
0-9667848-9-8 **Elisabeth Sanxay Holding** The Death Wish / Net of Cobwebs $19.95
0-9749438-5-1 **Elisabeth Sanxay Holding** Strange Crime in Bermuda / Too Many Bottles $19.95
1-933586-16-8 **Elisabeth Sanxay Holding** The Old Battle Ax / Dark Power $19.95
1-933586-17-6 **Russell James** Underground / Collected Stories $14.95
0-9749438-8-6 **Day Keene** Framed in Guilt / My Flesh is Sweet $19.95
1-933586-21-4 **Mercedes Lambert** Dogtown / Soultown $14.95
1-933586-14-1 **Dan Marlowe/Fletcher Flora/Charles Runyon** Trio of Gold Medals $15.95
1-933586-02-8 **Stephen Marlowe** Violence is My Business / Turn Left for Murder $19.95
1-933586-07-9 **Ed by McCarthy & Gorman** Invasion of the Body Snatchers: A Tribute $17.95
1-933586-09-5 **Margaret Millar** An Air That Kills / Do Evil in Return $19.95
1-933586-23-0 **Wade Miller** The Killer / Devil on Two Sticks $17.95
0-9749438-0-0 **E. Phillips Oppenheim** Secrets & Sovereigns: Uncollected Stories $19.95
1-933586-27-3 **E. Phillips Oppenheim** The Amazing Judgment / Mr. Laxworthy's Adventures $19.95
0-9749438-3-5 **Vin Packer** Something in the Shadows / Intimate Victims $19.95
0-9749438-6-x **Vin Packer** Damnation of Adam Blessing / Alone at Night $19.95
1-933586-05-2 **Vin Packer** Whisper His Sin / The Evil Friendship $19.95
1-933586-18-4 **Richard Powell** A Shot in the Dark / Shell Game $14.95
1-933586-19-2 **Bill Pronzini** Snowbound / Games $14.95
0-9667848-8-x **Peter Rabe** The Box / Journey Into Terror $19.95
0-9749438-4-3 **Peter Rabe** Murder Me for Nickels / Benny Muscles In $19.95
1-933586-00-1 **Peter Rabe** Blood on the Desert / A House in Naples $19.95
1-933586-11-7 **Peter Rabe** My Lovely Executioner / Agreement to Kill $19.95
1-933586-22-2 **Peter Rabe** Anatomy of a Killer / A Shroud for Jesso $14.95
0-9749438-9-4 **Robert J. Randisi** The Ham Reporter / Disappearance of Penny $19.95
0-9749438-2-7 **Douglas Sanderson** Pure Sweet Hell / Catch a Fallen Starlet $19.95
1-933586-06-0 **Douglas Sanderson** The Deadly Dames / A Dum-Dum for the President $19.95
1-933586-29-x **Charlie Stella** Johnny Porno $15.95
1-933586-08-7 **Harry Whittington** A Night for Screaming / Any Woman He Wanted $19.95
1-933586-25-7 **Harry Whittington** To Find Cora / Like Mink Like Murder / Body and Passion $19.95

If you are interested in purchasing any of the above books, please send the cover price plus $3.00 U.S. for the 1st book and $1.00 U.S. for each additional book to:

STARK HOUSE PRESS
STARK 22`
HOUSE 70`   **31901050293143**

                                     EⱭⱭ.com

Order 3 or more books and take a 10% discount. We accept PayPal payments.